Peter Jordan

had chosen the easier way once before. On November ninth, 1938. In Berlin. For one hour. A short walk years ago had destroyed two lives and almost his own.

He had succumbed once. He had wanted to run, to escape his responsibility.

Now he was about to do it again...

THE BERLIN CONNECTION

JOHANNES MARIO SIMMEL is one of the world's most widely read authors, a master of suspense whose international following rivals that of Le Carre, Deighton, Ludlum, or Trevanian. Born in Austria in 1924, he published his first book of short stories at age seventeen. Since his first big international bestseller, *The Monte Cristo Cover-Up* in 1963, he has produced instant European bestsellers and sales that total over 60 million copies. His novels have been translated into 26 languages, and many of them, including *The Berlin Connection*, have been made into films. One of his greatest achievements, *The Caesar Code*, is the second bestselling book in Germany since 1945, falling just behind Günter Grass's *The Tin Drum*.

Also by Johannes Mario Simmel

THE BERLIN CONNECTION

Johannes Mario Simmel

Translated by Rosemarie Mays
(Original Title: To the Bitter End)

WARNER BOOKS

A Warner Communications Company

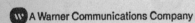

The First Tape

1

I can remember the moment even now when I died for the first time. I died several other times but the place and date of that first time will remain burnt into my memory to remain there as long as I live: Hamburg, the twenty-seventh of October, 1959.

On that morning a heavy storm raged over the city and, insistently, I still hear its roaring, its whistling, groaning, moaning in fireplaces, its rattling of rooftiles and metal, of signs, window shutters, gates and canopies. This storm found its way into my chaotic dreams and I heard and felt it before the ringing of the telephone disrupted my sleep.

The drapes were drawn and I switched on the lamp. My head ached, I had a sour taste. I felt sick as I sat up. Next to the telephone I saw cigarettes, an ashtray, a glass half-filled with Scotch, a vial containing sleeping tablets, the little cross of gold and my watch. It was three minutes past eight.

The door to the bathroom stood open. Through the frosted glass window above the tub, ugly early-morning light crept into my room blending with the yellow, weak light of the bedside lamp.

Picking up the receiver I smelled the whisky and nausea shook me.

"This is the operator. Good morning, Mr. Jordan. I'm afraid I woke you."

"Yes."

"I'm sorry. We have a transatlantic call for you from California, Pacific Palisades. Will you accept the charges?"

"Charges?" I was still too sleepy to form complete sentences.

"It's a collect call. The caller is Shirley Bromfield."

"My daughter?"

"No, Miss Shirley Bromfield."

"That's my daughter. My stepdaughter." What did that have to do with the operator? I had to wake up. "I'll take the call."

"You'll accept the charges?"

"Yes, yes!"

"Please, hold on."

I heard a click; it crackled and rattled in the open line and from both sides of the Atlantic I heard words, sentences, drifting, confused. A window was open behind the honey-colored drapes which covered one entire wall of the bedroom. I saw how the heavy fabric swelled and rose; I felt the icy air of the storm and heard its thundering, whistling and whining. It was draughty. The ventilators in the bathroom were open.

"Hello, New York relay . . ."

"Just a second, Hamburg, just a second . . ."

On the carpet by the bed were German and American newspapers, well-thumbed and read. The cover of a film magazine showed my face. I wore a blue open sportshirt. Joe Schwartz, the Hollywood photographer, had taken that picture. I looked at most thirty years old, seven years younger than I really was. In my black short hair were many white ones but they had dyed them, covered the wrinkles around the blue eyes with make-up. Only the healthy color was real. For weeks, before coming to Europe, I had let the sun tan me. Narrow head, high forehead, a strong jaw, beautiful teeth (all capped). The photo showed a laughing, dashing man, the embodiment of decision and confidence. All qualities I did not possess, much less ever had possessed.

AFTER TWENTY YEARS! PETER JORDAN, AMERICA'S UNFORGETTABLE CHILD STAR, IN FILMS AGAIN.

A draught seemed to give life to the paper mountain, made it shiver and breathe. The operator said: "Can you hear me, Hamburg? Here is Pacific Palisades now." One more click. Then I heard her voice, so loud, so near, so clear it startled me. "Peter?" It sounded as if she were in my room. Now I spoke English:

"Shirley! Did something happen?"

"Yes . . ." Her high childish voice shook as if suppressing a sob.

"To mommy?"

"No. Why mommy?"

"What do you mean, why mommy? Where are you, anyway?"

"At home." She was nineteen years old, but her voice sounded even younger, much younger. Across the Atlantic, across a continent, I could hear quick breathing, frantic, full of fear.

"Shirley!"

A moan.

"Tell me this minute what happened!"

And her high-pitched immature voice told me.

"Paddy, I'm going to have a child."

2

Paddy.

She had called me Paddy—the first time in years. She met me when she was four. Spontaneously she bore me the same hatred she felt for the devil who had been presented in apocalyptical figures to her by her priest. Only threats of punishment induced her to call me "Uncle Peter" which she did defiantly, through clenched teeth while averting her head. She told her mother again and again, "My dad is dead, but I'll always love him, only him. I'll never forgive you if you marry this Uncle Peter."

When we married she was six. After the ceremony, her voice harsh, she said, "You are not my father. I'll never call you dad no matter what you do to me. I won't call you daddy, either. To please mommy I'll call you Paddy, P from Peter." At thirteen her hate was smoldering instead of burning. That was when, shrugging her shoulders, she said, "Paddy sounds so childish." And from then on I was "Peter" —for six years, untill today.

The receiver had dropped from my sweat-slippery hand; it was lying on my knees; there was a quack, "Paddy . . . did you hear me?"

Now I held the receiver with both hands and smelled the whisky and the soaked cigarettes in the ashtray. The bed beneath me seemed to sway.

"Shirley . . . if someone should hear you!"

"No one can hear me."

"Where is mommy?"

"At the theater. With the Bakers. And I made it a collect call. So she won't find it on the bill." The bed rolled even more now. I could not get enough air.

"At the theater? What time is it there, then?"

"It's past eleven."

"Where are the servants?"

"I'm calling you from your bunaglow." My bungalow was a little way from the main house, it had its own telephone. "No one can listen in." What about the hotel here? The telephone operators? "Paddy, did you hear me? I am—"

"Don't say that word!" Almighty God. If my wife should return and look for her daughter. If someone should listen outside the bungalow. I stuttered: "It's impossible. It cannot be."

"I saw the doctor this afternoon."

"The doctor was wrong."

"I saw him twice. Today and two weeks ago."

"Two weeks ago I was still at home. Why didn't you say anything then?"

"I . . . I didn't want to upset you . . ." Her voice quavered. "I thought it was just late . . . you were so terribly nervous about your film."

"What kind of doctor is he?"

"I got his address from a girlfriend. He lives in Los Angeles. I was very cautious. I always took taxis. He doesn't know my real name."

"And?"

"He made two tests."

"And?"

"They are positive. He is sure. The second month." Suddenly she screamed, "I know what you are thinking. But I want to have it!"

"Don't scream!"

"You'll have to talk with mommy right away . . . you must or . . ."

"Shirley, stop it!"

"I'm not going to give it up! I'd rather kill myself! It's a part of—"

"Be quiet!"

She was silent. I heard her pant.

"Have you lost your mind? Do you want a catastrophe?" This conversation was pure suicide. Anyone on the switchboard with an ounce of intelligence who had heard only the last sentences could now blackmail me. Hoarsely I said, "I'm sorry I yelled at you."

She sobbed.

"Don't cry."

The sobbing increased.

"Stop crying. Please. You must stop. Shirley."

But she continued to sob.

I wanted to console her, whisper tender words, avow my love for her but I could not do that. I had to use cold and sober reasoning if I wanted to save us both from this sudden whirlpool. I had to force myself to seem angry and hard. "You are going to do what I say. Do you understand?"

"But mommy—"

"She must not know. If she finds out, we are lost."

"I can't stand it any more . . . Paddy, I can't look her in the face . . . can't talk to her any more."

I heard Shirley's voice, her beloved voice, clear and tremulous so well remembered from all those nights when, after our ecstasy, despair and guilt overwhelmed us. I was older. I was wiser. If I lost my composure now we would be lost. I had to speak harshly: "We cannot talk on the phone. It is too risky. Hang up. I'll write. Today. Airmail, Express. To the post office at Pacific Palisades. As always."

"And . . . and?"

"Everything will be in the letter. I have friends in Los Angeles. They will help you."

"I don't want any help!"

"You'll do what I'll write you. In our . . . in this situation you must. Don't you understand?"

Silence. Across the deserts, mountains and forests of the New World, across the dark depths of an ocean the whisper of a child reached my ear and rent my heart.

"I understand . . ."

12

"Good." Cold. I had to remain pitiless, to protect us from destruction from the meanest kind of dirt.

"May I . . . may I see Father Horace?" He was her priest. Shirley's mother had raised her a devout Catholic. Now she suffered because of it. Since it had happened I would not let her go to confession. She complied because she loved me. But I am certain that the dark prophecies and judgments which her religion reserves for sinners like us tormented her.

"You are not going to see him! Not under any circumstances!"

"But I have to! I must confess, Paddy!"

"No!"

"I am damned . . . I will never be forgiven if I don't—"

"I don't want to hear you mention that again! Not a word, you hear, not a word to anybody!"

Silence.

"Repeat that!"

"Not a word . . . not one word . . ."

"Not to Father Horace, not to your girlfriend, not to anybody."

Her voice was halting, choked with tears: "I'll do what you say . . . only what you tell me to do . . . forgive me for burdening you with this . . ."

My body was bathed in sweat. What had I done to her?

"My poor little one . . ." My poor little one—a father could say that to his daughter—right, operator?

"You'll have to be sensible now . . ." A father could demand that from his daughter—right, you ladies in the telephone exchanges of Hamburg and Pacific Palisades and relay board of New York?

"Paddy, I love you!"

I love you, she said. Could an upset daughter say that to her father? It sounded different in English, in English she could say that.

"We'll have to hang up."

"I love you. I have only you. I'm all alone here."

13

"Everything will be all right."

"Don't hang up yet! Tell me, please, tell me!"

The bed was swaying, up and down, down and up.

"Good night, Shirley."

"Tell me! Please! Then I won't be so terribly afraid!"

I told her: "I love you, Shirley. I love you with all my heart."

I love you, Shirley, I love you with all my heart, I said to my stepdaughter who was expecting my child.

3

I had been married thirteen years. My wife was ten years older than I; her youth was gone. I deceived her with her daughter who was trusted to my upbringing, education, custody and care. I wanted to leave my wife for this girl, her daughter, my stepdaughter.

A man doing that must provoke disgust and animosity in the moral world around him. If this were but a novel and not a clinical report written for two special people it would be a dangerous venture. The hero of a novel should be likable. Readers should be able to fall in love with him. No one could fall in love with a character like me. I would be the anti-hero.

It is to be expected that even the two specialists, for whom this confession is intended, will turn from the pages with horror. But I beg them to read on. I promise to lay bare the deep roots of this tragedy, to expose the hidden reasons of this drama in which I was a cursed actor. Perhaps then they will have more understanding for me. Understanding, I say, not pity.

After replacing the receiver, a spooky quiescence came over me, a kind of trance. Like a sleepwalker I got up, pulled my slippers out from under the newspapers, put on my robe and opened the heavy drapes.

The icy air of the storm hit me through the opened window. I saw the green-gray Binnenalster, the bare, black trees, streets still shiny from the rain of the past night, the old and the new Lombardsbricke. There were a few people who, bent forward, fought against the wind. A few ships were rolling on the storm-whipped water. Most of them were moored at the jetties. Under the wet boards of the deserted piers flocks of seagulls were huddling together.

Black-brown, green, dirty gray clouds were hurrying across the sky. Along the banks of the Alster the candelabra were lit; the white frosted bowls formed long ropes of lustrous pearls.

I knew that the California penal code provided a prison term for such a crime as I had committed. I don't want anyone to believe that I had not lived in continual horror since the night it had happened or that I was not aware of the seriousness of the offense I had committed—then and later on, again and again. But then, what force do ethics and morals and guilt have against the worst of diseases, the most horrible of plagues which we, presumptuous as we are, call love?

There had been a time when I had wanted to put an end to it all, when I had been ready to confess and to take my punishment. It had passed. Now I was determined to defend my love, the only love I had ever really known, which no one understandably could forgive or comprehend. To keep and cherish this love I had to become enmeshed in an adventure which, here in Hamburg, would have to be brought to a conclusion.

I love you Shirley, I love you with all my heart.

I closed the window. The dizziness was becoming stronger and stronger as I went to the drawing room of the suite. Here too, I opened the drapes. On the balcony beyond the large window I saw a dead seagull. As it had started its flight the storm must have thrown it against the wall of the hotel before it fell on the balcony. Broken feathers were lying around, the body had split open releasing bloody entrails, and only the head had survived the end without injury. The sharp, cunning eyes of the bird were open and seemed to be watching me maliciously as if it too knew that legal paragraph.

What was a paragraph? Who made the laws? Human beings, to protect human beings against other human beings. But what kind of human beings were they—who made the laws? Could they imagine all those situations that weak mortals could encounter? The worst ones, the most extreme ones? Could they too drink from that same cup I had drunk from?

The dead gull's eyes looked at me as if to say: blasphemer, liar, scoundrel.

I looked away quickly.

Passing the desk I walked to the fireplace. A photograph of Shirley stood on the mantel. The desk was heaped high with coins, paper money, bills, paper and a script.

JORKOS PRODUCTIONS
presents
PETER JORDAN IN
COME BACK

The drawing-room walls were decorated with faintly shimmering silk in cardinal red and gold stripes. The fragile baroque chairs were upholstered with the same honey-colored damask which had been used for the drapes. A single Chinese rug lay on the cardinal red carpeting. Old prints decorated the walls.

The color photograph in the silver frame was Shirley's portrait. Her skin a golden tan, flawless, so smooth, so young! The shining auburn hair, pulled back into a ponytail and forward over her right shoulder. The nose was narrow, the mouth generous. The green eyes below black brows. Her womanly appearance belied that little-girl voice.

Nineteen years old!

I was almost twice her age. What I had done, what I was still intending to do was not only a criminal offense in the eyes of the lawmakers, it was pure insanity. My wife's friends spoke of Shirley with admiration, mixed with envy.

"You have such a grown-up daughter—and still so innocent, so untouched."

"I have watched her. She never flirts. She doesn't take any interest in men."

"You are so lucky, Joan. My Ramona is only fifteen. I dare not even think what she does."

"Mary ran away from home when she was seventeen, you know. Youth today is spoiled rotten. Shirley seems like a miracle. You really are very fortunate, Joan."

And then my wife would say, "If only she would get along a little better with my husband. She still loves her father. She just can't forgive me for marrying again . . ."

I stood motionless before Shirley's picture. And silently I said to her, "You cannot have this child. It is the last sacrifice I ask you to make. Soon I will be free. Soon all the world can know that we love each other. Then we shall have a child, a child born of love, I promise. And we shall live in peace, you and I."

"No," I heard her say suddenly. Through the raging of the storm the high voice held a note of infinite sadness. In my growing confusion I heard the same words she had spoken on that hot summer day in my bungalow, in my arms, naked, drained of passion yet aware of guilt, "We will never be at peace because we do nothing to end this sin. God does not forgive that."

"God! God! Must you always talk about Him?"

"It's easy for you, you don't believe in Him."

That was correct. From what I could see it must be pretty awful to believe in Him. Poor Shirley. Incensed, I said, "You said if two people love each other He forgives them everything!"

"Not if they do not repent . . ."

"Shirley!"

"God won't forgive us because He doesn't love us, He can't love us any more . . ."

Now, how about Shirley's God? I heard her voice, "Paddy, I'm going to have a child . . ."

And this child was not permitted to live.

Dimly I heard Shirley say those words I had forbidden her to speak. "It is murder. If I do that I'm a murderess."

A murderess who believed in God and suffered—did she not live in the heart of Christianity? Who could know more about sin? Who could suffer greater pangs of conscience than a murderess who was a pious Christian? Didn't God have to forgive her before all others?

I could not stand to look at Shirley's picture any longer. Turning away I saw Joan's photograph, also on the mantel. Obviously it had been necessary to display a photo of my wife as well. The public relations department sold me to the news media as a happy family man.

Joan hardly showed her forty-seven years. First I loved my mother and then a woman so much older than I. Analysts make much of that.

Joan's figure was still that of a young girl. She had had her face lifted and the skin was smooth and without wrinkles—but only the skin of her face. The operation had been responsible for that. I always thought of it whenever I touched Shirley's skin.

Joan wears her brown hair close to her head, tips pulled forward over her temples, two soft waves rise from her forehead. One could still see that she had been very beautiful. She was apparently still desirable—I sometimes noticed at parties how other men looked at her. She smiled at me from the photograph. I stepped to one side. The brown eyes followed me. I had never noticed that before. I took another step and still my wife's eyes followed, smiling and guileless.

Smiling innocently?

Were these eyes unsuspecting? Was my wife without suspicion? What if she already knew and was just biding her time until she could revenge herself for the hurt I had caused her? Joan's eyes were ... Were they merely laughing or were they mocking me?

"If only she could get along a little better with my husband ..."

"So innocent, so untouched ..."

"God does not love us. How, then, could we be happy?"

My eyes were wandering aimlessly around the room. Shirley's eyes. Joan's eyes. The prints on the walls. Windows. Shirley. Joan. The evil eyes of the dead seagull. Suddenly everything was revolving around me, and then an invisible giant fist seemed to strike the pit of my stomach.

Without warning, from one breath to the next, burning hot and yet icy cold it struck with brutal force. So strong was the impact I folded like a pocketknife and collapsing, fell sideways into a chair standing near the fireplace. Now one overpowering thought was in my mind which made me panic, shook me as I collapsed. I thought, no, I knew: I was dying.

4

I died of a coronary. Now the end had come.

What I felt was my dying; this thing rising in my body was my death. The terrifying giant fist began to climb higher and higher, closer to the heart.

"Arr ... Arr ..." From far away I could hear myself groan, gasping for air, in vain. I pressed my two hands to my body to prevent the deadly effect of this fist.

But it rose.

The room was swimming, out of focus. My wife, Shirley, looked at me, disappeared, looked at me again.

The fist had reached the first pair of ribs. It continued rising, without haste, without pity. It had already left behind a partial corpse! Feet, thighs, hips, abdomen. Ahead of it, it forced the little life which remained in my body, breath, veins, blood: Blood which now began to throb violently in my fingers, in my temples, in my ears.

I was panting. Fighting for air, my body was horribly contorted. The heels were dug into the carpeting, the shoulder blades into the chair.

"I'm . . . dying . . ."

I heard myself babble. At that moment this terrible giant fist, which did not exist but nevertheless was killing me, reached my heart. Like a flood fear enveloped my brain and paralyzed it.

Fear!

I had never known such fear. Fear such as this had evaded my imagination.

I knew what it was to be afraid when a film studio went up in flames and I had been trapped by the grid and the flood and spotlights. I thought it was fear I felt when, at fifteen, I saw my poor mother suffocate in minutes from the tumor in her throat. Near Aachen one of our B-52's mistakenly bombed us when the wind shifted and blew away the demarcation smoke signals. A jet taking me to Mexico, through a malfunctioning of its automatic pilot, fell thirty thousand feet before the pilot could control it. In all those moments I was convinced no one in this world could have ever felt greater fear.

Fear?

I had not really known fear. Now I knew. Now true, real fear spread over me, paralyzed my limbs, robbed me of my ability to see and hear.

The fist opened. Its fingers closed around my heart and squeezed. I screamed in despair but surely no one could hear me; the storm raged and would drown out all screams.

Now. Now. Now.

Now came death.

But death did not come. Not yet.

The fist released my heart; I could feel it slowly sinking below the ribs and coming to rest in the pit of my stomach. There it stayed, insidious, certain of me.

I felt my heart beating furiously. I felt its beat in my back, my toes, my tongue.

When would the fist attack again? When would the fear return? Both of them were inside me, terrifying intruders. I was still alive. For how long? Who could bear waiting for death like this? No one. No one on this earth.

A doctor. I had to have a doctor.

I had hardly thought that when I heard myself groan, "No . . ."

Whatever happened, no doctor must see me in this condition. No doctor. Not now. Shirley's green eyes were looking at me, hypnotizing me, imploring me.

All would be finished if a doctor were to examine me now, our love damned and my opportunity lost: my last chance, here in Germany, here, in this storm-whipped city.

No, Shirley, no.

No doctor.

5

Whisky.

The word rekindled life in me. Choking greed for alcohol filled me. I needed whisky, good blessed Scotch, as my saviour. I could smell it, taste it, feel it flowing down my throat, smoky and wonderful, dissolving the giant fist, making it disappear.

Whisky!

My legs felt unsteady. I staggered to the bedroom.

Whisky, yes.

It was just Shirley's call. The scare. Too much alcohol the night before. The storm. The early morning. Everything else but not death. I didn't need a doctor. I would make that film. I could play my part. I would play my part.

The key!

I had already thrown open the door of the closet and grabbed the black leather travel bag when I remembered the key. The bag had a lock. The key was in my tuxedo.

I dragged myself, still terribly weak, to the chair where the evening before I had carelessly thrown my clothes. The trousers fell on the carpet, the jacket, too. I had to bend down. Blood shot to my head. The key, damn it, where was the key? My shaking hands emptied the pockets, coins, bills, cigarettes. There was the key. I staggered back to the bag.

There had been a time (fortunately it had passed), when it was said of me in Hollywood that I was a drunkard. What was said then was that I had been drinking for twenty years, since I could not get any work.

The talk had died down during the past two years. No one now could say I was drinking. No one had ever seen me drink, not even Joan, not even Shirley. I had been drinking more than ever these last two years—but secretly, only secretly. I hid the bottles so well no one could find them. I knew Joan and Shirley mistrusted me, had been searching for my whisky for years, simply because they could not believe my abstinence. They were not looking any more. Now they were proud of me for having broken this habit.

Whenever I traveled I carried my black bag. A store in Boston had made it for me according to my design. There were partitions on either side which could be locked. Whisky and soda bottles fitted into those partitions preventing the bottles from moving, rattling, breaking. The bag had as well a large thermos bottle which I filled with ice cubes. Even if I ordered only one single drink I could always get sufficient water and ice.

I was always well supplied: on trains and planes, cars, motor boats, hotels. This way I could drink more than ever.

The bag was an integral part of me, and it never left me. I always had to keep it locked, especially in hotels. The employees were always rummaging through everything. But not through my bag. No, Peter Jordan did not drink any more.

I opened the zipper. Two empty soda bottles, an empty thermos, an empty whisky bottle. During the night I had drunk everything.

6

Immediately I felt the fist again. If I didn't get any whisky—whamm!!!

I was freezing, my teeth were chattering. It seemed to me as if the storm was becoming louder, terribly loud. No one could bear this, this awful storm, the terrible fist, this empty bottle of Scotch.

There was still a half-filled glass on the bedside table.

I left the open bag and walked to the bed, yes, I could walk now, and gulped down the warm flat whisky. It stayed with me only a few seconds. I just reached the bathroom.

Gasping, I stood before the mirror, rinsed with mouthwash and, trying to splash Eau de Cologne on my face, dropped the bottle. It broke in the washbasin. I saw myself in the mirror. The black hair soaked with perspiration stuck to my head. The face was a dark purplish color; brownish rings circled the eyes. Breathing heavily, I suddenly turned deathly white and patchy. The lips remained black. Sweat ran into the eyes, the mouth gaped, the tongue was blue. No imagination could conceive of a worse face than this face, which belonged to me: me, once the Sunny Boy of the New World, the most celebrated and famous child star of all times.

PETER JORDAN, AMERICA'S UNFORGETTABLE CHILD STAR.

No, there was nothing now to link me with this laughing character on the magazine frontpage, with this handsome dashing man and his cheesecake smile, his playboy beauty. To think that the face in the mirror had made millions, untold millions a quarter of a century ago!

The fist rose. It stopped at the second pair of ribs.

I went back to the drawing room. I opened the door and pressed the bell for the floor waiter. Then I closed the drapes in the bedroom. He must not see how I looked. I switched off the lamps, too. The light in the drawing room and bathroom was sufficient. I pulled the covers up to my neck. There he was already.

"Come in."

He entered the drawing room, smiling and young, the best trained employee of a luxury hotel. He stayed by the door, didn't look at me, looking into space, spoke politely without emphasis, "Good morning, Mr. Jordan. Would you like to order breakfast now?"

Third pair of ribs. Second pair of ribs. Third pair of ribs. I could not talk. But I had to. "Breakfast . . . yes . . ."

"Tea or coffee?"

Second pair of ribs. Third. Second.

"Cof . . . coffee . . ."

"A five-minute egg?"

"Yes . . ." No one must know that I was ill. My secret. Or I would not get this film.

"Thank you, Mr. Jordan."

In my agitation, I reached for the little cross of gold on the bedside table. I pressed it and turned it in my hands.

Up to my departure from Los Angeles this cross, hanging from a thin chain, had been resting between Shirley's warm, firm breasts. After saying good-by (my wife stood aside crying) Shirley secretly pressed the amulet into my hand as I was already passing the gate. Since then I had been carrying it around with me, holding it in my hand at negotiations, production conferences, at the first screen test. This little cross had always inspired me with courage even though as a symbol it held no significance for me, since I did not believe in Shirley's God. But to me it seemed to be a part of her; she had worn it for a long time; it seemed as if I touched her velvety young skin, her young firm body, and every time I touched the cross it gave me courage, as it did now.

"Wait . . ." He stopped. I didn't care what this waiter would think.

"There are one hundred marks on the desk. Take the money and do me a favor . . ."

"Surely, Mr. Jordan."

This storm. This storm drove me crazy.

"In a minute my . . ." I stopped; the fist prodded my heart and the terrifying fear returned.

"Don't you feel well, sir?"

"Just . . . just swallowed some air . . ."

There he stood in the light and smiled patiently. There I was, writhing in the darkness, feeling death reach out for me, yes, death. And managed to squeeze out these words, "My production . . . manager will arrive any minute. I promised him . . . a bottle of whisky . . . and forgot to get it. Would you . . ."

"I'll send a busboy."

"But . . . right away . . ."

"Certainly."

"Before . . . breakfast . . ." Did not matter. Did not matter what he thought.

The fear. The fear.

"I'll take care of it right away. Would you like Canadian whisky or Scotch?"

"Scotch . . ." The fist. It reached my heart. It opened. Now it would close.

"A particular brand?"

"Any . . . Scotch."

"Would you like it gift-wrapped?"

"What?"

"I mean, it is a present."

"No . . . yes . . . I don't care . . . just . . . bring . . . it."

He bowed. Was his smile ironical? No matter. He left. The door closed. Simultaneously the giant fist closed. It had been too much.

I was violently pulled upright, felt my head hitting the wall and screamed for the second time. My brain still registered how I fell sideways out of bed, pulling the telephone, ashtray and the little lamp with me.

I plunged into flaming red fog. The tiny cross of gold was in my hand and I had a ridiculous, absurd feeling of triumph as I thought: No doctor came near me, Shirley.

And then I died.

I remember the moment precisely. Hamburg. October twenty-seventh, 1959.

7

I am a wicked, corrupted man. The story I am relating here will be bad and wicked.

I am telling this story to two people: my doctor and my judge. My doctor must know the truth to be able to help me. My judge must know the truth to judge me.

Today is Thursday, March third, 1960. My watch shows eleven minutes past eleven. It is already very warm in Rome. From my window I see a deep blue and cloudless sky. My room is very comfortable. In contrast to many other windows in this house mine has no bars and there is a door with a knob. Professor Pontevivo says he trusts me.

The Italian police have no such trust in me. It is not surprising if one considers all I have done since that storm-whipped October morning in Hamburg and this peaceful March morning in Rome.

Since the German authorities applied for my extradition the Italian police have been guarding me. Since I am very ill I will not be handed over—not yet. Professor Pontevivo has accomplished that. He is a famous physician and the authorities listened to him when he stated, "I refuse to be responsible if this man is removed from my care."

A carabinier is walking up and down the lovely park of the hospital. By and by I know all those changing shifts every eight hours. Day and night. They are young, they are curious; I'm sure they know what I have done. That is why they are often looking up to my window. And I begin to know their faces.

Magnolias, white, cream-colored and rose-red magnolias are flowering in the park. A sea of yellow forsythias is shining. Small, pink almond trees are bordering the drive. I can see a profusion of blue and salmon-colored crocuses, snowdrops and white and black pansies. There had been a gentle rain during the past night and now the new leaves of the olive trees, laurel stonepines, palms and eucalyptus bushes wear a bright fresh green full of new life. Full of life is this park with its high barbed-wire topped wall which encloses the park on all sides. Through the tops of old trees, behind the wall on the Viale Parco di Celio I can see the fourth and uppermost story of the Colosseum, its smooth outer wall, the flat Corinthian pilasters, and the rectangular windows through which the blue sky is visible.

Yesterday I began to tell my story into a small, gleaming microphone. The day before and the day before that I tried, too. As soon as the green light of the tape recorder

27

was switched on and the tapes began to whirr I broke out in a cold sweat. My heart beat furiously and I became so dizzy I had to lie down and close my eyes.

I panicked and thought, "I am not able to talk logically, I cannot form sentences. I am insane." Even if I forced myself to record my story it would be incomprehensible, because my brain is not able to think clearly and form sentences that would have meaning.

During the last two days I repeatedly told Professor Pontevivo, "Why don't you give up? I am incurable. My brain is damaged."

And he replied, "When you awoke from the deep narcosis you were eager to tell me all that had happened. You were not able to formulate your thoughts as quickly as the words left your mouth and that is why I could not understand you."

"That proves I'm crazy."

"You have received a great amount of medication. I can assure you that no patient has reacted any different than you following this treatment. Who suggested you tell your story to a tape recorder?"

"I did."

"And why?"

"Because I believed I could talk more easily to a machine than to another person."

"That was not the reason."

"What was, then?"

"You felt that your mind needed time to sort out your thoughts. It proves you are not insane. You said yourself another person made you irritable. So you chose a monologue. This tape recorder will be for you the ear of a silent priest at confession."

Swiftly this recalled Shirley, Father Horace, the evening of the catastrophe. Fiercely I said, "I don't intend this to be a confession to a priest."

"But something of a confession," he said. "And anyway, aren't we, physicians and judges, priests in a way?"

I thought, "Oh! God, won't you ever leave me alone, in peace?"

To the professor, I said, "I am afraid. Of the tape recorder too. What I have to say is too horrible."

"To alleviate your fear I could—provided you agree—give you a little medication, just enough to enable you to talk readily and easily. You will be under my supervision. You must never talk for more than two hours. Nothing can happen. But I need your permission anyway."

I gave it.

Today too, after breakfast, I received the injection. I feel relaxed, peaceful, without—

I was going to say without fear. But I interrupted myself when a formation of jets raced across the sky above our quiet park. The noise would have drowned out every word. So I halted.

Without fear.

It seemed appropriate that I should be so abruptly interrupted particularly by these swifter-than-sound riders of the modern apocalypse, symbolic of an unusual fear that daily haunts mankind. In fair weather, jets rattle the skies of Rome. In Hamburg and Pacific Palisades too, they rose with the sun, ceaselessly tormenting the skies until the last light faded.

I said it seemed appropriate to me, for what I am about to recount is a tale of fear and not only my fear. Those jets were a suitable overture.

The last few months had been an inferno for me.

Professor Pontevivo relieved me of that fear. He is a great man. Perhaps he will even be successful in restoring me to health.

To do that, he says he must know the truth. On the floor below me is the music room of the hospital. The Frenchman, addicted to drugs, is playing the piano. He is still very young and this is his fifth time here. A hopeless case. He will probably die soon or become insane.

When he was admitted, Professor Pontevivo told me,

he was halfway through a piano concerto. Without drugs he is unable to compose. The most noted musicians have implored Professor Pontevivo to help this sick man complete his concerto.

It is said that this hope and potential joy of the universal world of music receives just enough drugs to produce some immortal melody. Immortality from decay, almost insanity, almost death.

The young man works in the morning and afternoon as I do. When I listen to his melodies I happily hear again Gershwin's "Concerto in F." Though what he is originating is obviously his own composition. He is creating something beautiful and if he should die or lose his mind something beautiful will remain. I create something ugly. If I should go insane or die here something ugly will remain: the truth.

There is one thing we have in common: We both have to work diligently. We must not waste precious moments of the little time we have left. We must finish. The beautiful and the ugly, the good and the bad, unfinished, can be neither joy nor doom.

During the last few months I have transgressed all moral boundaries. A criminal could not have planned, thought, felt or done greater misdeeds than I. Nothing I did can be undone. The dead remain dead, the deeds settled. I can only tell the truth. I swear to do that in memory of Shirley, my love, my only love.

The little golden cross is warm and alive in my hand. This little cross of gold which has accompanied me on my journey through crime, darkness and disaster.

I think of Shirley and our lost love. And I swear by this love to tell the truth, the whole truth, not to add or conceal anything. And now I will continue in my report of the occurrences on the morning of the twenty-seventh of October, 1959, in Hamburg.

8

I drank whisky, wonderful cold whisky.

I could smell the zesty aroma. I could feel the tart, smoky taste. It burned my throat, oily and heavy it warmed my body.

I gulped the whisky as a drowning man does water instead of air. And, like a drowning man rising to the surface of the sea with his last strength, I returned to life from my unconsciousness.

Then I seemed to see whirling, fiery wheels and flaming stars, and heard a pitched hissing. The sea of flames turned gray and the hissing became the raging of the storm. I opened my eyes. The lids seemed weighted with lead.

I was back in bed. A woman I had never seen before sat before me and held a glass of whisky to my lips, pouring the liquid into my mouth. It spilt down my throat and on the pillow. I choked and fought to catch my breath.

"Well, now," said the strange woman.

I looked around quickly. The drapes had been pulled back again. I saw the dark sky and the black, hurrying clouds. The telephone, lamp and the ashtray were back on the bedside table. The ashtray was clean now. Next to it stood an almost full bottle of Scotch.

"Drink a little more," said the woman. Turning my head my teeth hit the glass. My robe hung on a hanger, my slippers underneath. The newspaper and magazines were folded. My glancing eyes took in headlines: US STANDS FIRM: ATTACK ON BERLIN MEANS WORLD WAR III, SAYS EISENHOWER. NEW SOVIET SATELLITE CIRCLES EARTH.

Who had put me to bed and cleared up the room? I

was sweating again. My heart was pounding. Something enormous, frightening was vibrating in me.

The fist!

I wanted to ask the woman who she was but only a hoarse whisper came from my throat. Then she spoke. Her voice was deep and melodious. She spoke very pure High German. "I am Dr. Natasha Petrovna."

"A doctor?"

"Yes, Mr. Jordan." She was dressed in a green, tight-fitting suit, green shoes with high heels. Her hair was blue-black, parted in the middle and pulled back into a bun. The little ears were visible.

She bent forward to feel my pulse. Her fingers were white and narrow and cool. Transparent nail polish covered her nails. I pulled back my hand. The sudden movement made me dizzy.

"Don't move." Her forehead was high and her features were typically Slavic, slanting eyes and prominent cheekbones. The wide mouth was dark red. The brows thick. Her pupils were black and luminous behind large glasses. "I gave the busboy who brought the whisky five marks."

"The . . . busboy . . ."

"A tip. I sent back the breakfast. I hope that was all right with you."

"Breakfast . . ." It took effort to pull myself together.

"I'm sure you only ordered it to have an opportunity to get the whisky."

The tone of her voice exasperated me. She was so sure of herself and strong, healthy and superior.

"How did you get in here?"

"I was asked to come. Luckily I happened to be in the hotel. A lady from Ceylon became ill and—"

"Who called you?"

"One of the managers. When you fell you pulled down the telephone too. When the operator did not get any reply a busboy was sent up."

"Who put me to bed?"

"The manager, the busboy and I."

"Go away."

"Excuse me?"

"I want you to go away. I don't want to be examined."

I was never to see Natasha Petrovna lose her composure. Not all the horror we lived through together made her lose her self-restraint. Only one gesture betrayed her effort at control. Her narrow white hands touched the broad sides of her modern black glasses and pushed them up slightly. That was all.

"Mr. Jordan, be sensible."

"Leave me alone."

She did not answer but opened her bag to take out a stethoscope. All her movements were deliberate and sedate. The wide cheekbones and the slightly slanted glasses gave her a feline look. There was intelligence in Natasha's face. It was a desiring, passionate face, passionately desiring knowledge and truth. The attractive long-lashed eyes looked at me without anger or impatience.

Today, here in Rome, after the catastrophe, I am able to describe Natasha, to confide in the silently moving tapes: I have never seen a more beautiful or compassionate face than Natasha's. On that morning in October I was blind to beauty, deaf to goodness.

"You cannot examine me against my will, can you?"

"No, but—"

"Then, go away!"

She looked at me silently. She was at most thirty-five years old.

"I am a guest in this hotel. Are you leaving now or do I have to have you thrown out?"

"Your behavior shows clearly how much you are in need of a doctor's help. I will call the manager." She reached for the telephone. I caught her hand. "Why?"

33

"I need a witness. You will kindly repeat to him that you refuse to be examined."

"Why?"

"I am responsible in case something should happen to you. I don't know what you might do when I leave." I saw her look at the whisky bottle, the empty bottles, the black bag and the empty thermos bottle. The manager and the floor waiter had seen that too: my dirty, well-kept secret. Now she wanted to call a witness. If I did not submit to an examination more people would come. Soon the entire hotel staff would know. Who would be the one to call the newspaper? The chatty columnists had their informants everywhere and they paid well for such news. PETER JORDAN COLLAPSES: WHISKEY! PETER JORDAN THROWN OUT OF HOTEL. I could see the headlines. Sweat trickled from my forehead and hands. I noticed I still had the little cross in my hands. Wrong. Wrong. Oh, Shirley, everything I did was wrong!

"Let me make the call, Mr. Jordan."

"No."

"Your behavior is childish. Then I'll just have to go downstairs."

She was so cool, so matter-of-fact, so very prudent. And yet, I remember distinctly, even at our first meeting I had the impression that this woman had had to exert all her strength to control herself so perfectly. We very rarely are aware that the people we meet have behavior patterns that influence their conduct. We expect them to react as we would were we in their place; we cannot, in most cases, understand or comprehend them. Today I know. Natasha was carrying a heavy burden. Suffering and misfortune had taught her to think always of others; had taught her to be calm and direct.

"Wait . . . wait . . ." I stammered.

"Yes, Mr. Jordan?"

"I . . . I have to explain . . . I am an actor. . . ." I could not continue. The fist hit my solar plexus. The fear re-

34

turned. The stoi .. raged. Somewhere in the hotel a window slammed. I heard glass break and hit the ground. Finished. Finished. Everything was finished.

"Paddy, I'm going to have a child . . ."

In retrospect this seems symptomatic of those hours: My emotions were ranging between rebellion and self-sacrifice, courage and hopelessness. "No one . . . must . . . know . . . I . . . am . . . ill . . ."

Natasha took her hand from the receiver. Her voice was friendly and calm, "No one will hear anything from me. A doctor is pledged to silence."

I had not thought of that.

Yes. Oh, certainly. Naturally.

Pledged to silence.

My spirits rose. I wanted to smile, say something. It turned out a grimace, a babble. She took the bottle and filled the glass once more as if it were perfectly normal to drink at nine in the morning. She held the glass to my lips and said, "Here, Mr. Jordan."

9

"If each person in the world would make only one other person happy, the whole world would be happy."

At this point in my report I remember this sentence. She said it to me after the worst had happened, when she understood what I had done. The look on her face told me that she did not condemn me, there was nothing she could not understand. The same look was on her face on this October morning, her voice was the same calm voice when she said, "Here, Mr. Jordan."

I held the glass with both hands and emptied it in one draught. She filled the glass again. I felt the whisky give new strength to my body. Suddenly I could see clearly, hear clearly. I did not feel the fist any more. Here I was, sitting before Natasha in my crumpled pajamas, very much relieved. Very quietly I said, "Thank you."

She went to the door and switched on the light. The chandelier sparkled.

"And now you are going to allow me to examine you?"

I nodded. That she had given me the whisky seemed to me the most important thing anyone had ever done for me. "When I was a little girl I saw all your movies, Mr. Jordan." A moment ago I had hated her. Now I thought her wonderful. I felt even better now. I took another little drink. "You are scheduled to make another movie here in Germany. You are afraid that the news of your collapse will become known. This is perfectly understandable."

How clever she was, and how likable!

"Are you Russian?"

"My parents were Russian. I was born in Germany. And you, Mr. Jordan? How is it you speak German so well?"

"My mother came from Berlin."

"Tell me what happened before you passed out."

"I had an attack."

"Can you describe it?"

I described it, drinking the whisky while talking. "The worst was the fear," I heard myself say; the whisky quickly went to my head. "Terrible fear. Horrible fear. I thought it was a coronary."

"Did you hear voices?"

"No." I had completely forgotten Shirley's voice.

"Did you see anything? Animals?"

"Do you think that I have the d.t.'s?"

"Please, answer me."

"No. Or rather, yes. I saw a dead seagull. But it is real. You can see it too."

"Where?"

"On the balcony." She went to the drawing room, switched on the light there and I could not see her. I called out, "Pretty awful sight, isn't it?"

"I see no gull," her voice replied. I jumped out of bed and ran to her. The light from the room shone into the darkness and the pouring rain outside. The flooded balcony was bare, the bird gone.

"But . . ." I was very shaken. I smiled crookedly. "Delirium tremens, after all?"

She looked at me without speaking. The fist. For seconds I felt it again.

"I swear to you, the gull was there. The rain must have washed it away."

"Probably."

My hands closed tightly around Shirley's cross. The little cross suddenly seemed to be all the protection and support I had left in the world.

10

Dr. Petrovna's finger described a circle in front of my eyes and she told me to follow it. I sat on my bed again. "Watch the tip of my finger, please, Mr. Jordan."

Her finger had moved sideways and I was hard put to see it. My pupils felt as if they were impaled on rough little sticks. My spirits rose again after having a few more gulps of whisky. Natasha permitted me to drink. The rain flooded the windowpanes, the storm rattled them. I was happy to be examined by such an understanding human being.

"Do you take stimulants, Mr. Jordan?"

"No."

"Drugs?"

"No."

"Never?"

"No. Only whisky." The finger circled.

"Watch the tip of my finger, Mr. Jordan."

"That has something to do with my head, hasn't it? Am I crazy?"

The finger circled.

"Doctor!"

"Yes, Mr. Jordan."

"I asked you something."

"Your nerves seem to be on edge. I'm sure you are very excited about your movie." This woman was terrific! How she calmed me down! How she questioned me to distract me!

"When was the last time you stood in front of a camera?"

"Twenty years ago. Nineteen thirty-nine. Can you imagine? I had to wait twenty years. And now . . ."

She took a little flashlight and shone it in my eyes. Her face was very close. Natasha's breath was as pure and clean as fresh milk.

"You drink a lot, don't you?"

"No one has ever seen me drink."

"That is something else again. How long have you been drinking?"

"For quite a long time."

"How long?"

"Well . . ."

"You must tell me the truth if I am to make a diagnosis."

"For twenty years."

"And how much daily?"

"That depends. Just lately . . ."

"More than one bottle?"

"No."

"Much less than one bottle?"

"Not . . . much less." Rather more would have been true. I said proudly: "But I never had any problems. I could work and sleep and I could always eat."

"Do you drink in the morning too?"

"You know . . ."

"I'm asking you as your doctor."

"Yes. I guess all day, a little. But secretly, no one has any idea."

"You must have a drink, mustn't you?"

"Yes. Well, you see if I don't I am very nervous. Jumpy. Unsure. I'm always afraid——"

"What are you afraid of?"

"Well, it probably sounds ridiculous . . . but I am talking to a doctor. Anyway, I just can't seem to take care of my business unless I have had a drink. It just gets too much for me; do you understand me? And just lately I have had more worries and excitement. Why are you looking at me like that? Don't you believe me?"

"I believe every word. But perhaps it is the other way around."

"The other way around?"

"You say you can't take care of your business unless you have a drink. Today you are nervous and agitated without whisky."

"Yes."

"Perhaps that is not the result of years of drinking but the cause. Perhaps you were always an overly sensitive and nervous man and that is why you began to drink twenty years ago. It happens. Especially among artists. Possibly you would never have become an actor without this instability." This impressed me very much and I looked at her admiringly. Natasha pushed her glasses into place. "When were you born?"

"January eleventh, 1922." She was so sympathetic. I respected her knowledge. A sudden urge for communication overcame me. Naturally, it was also the whisky. "My parents were actors, you know. They traveled all over the country. They played everything. Shakespeare and slapstick comedy. Operettas and schmaltz and *Abie's Irish Rose* . . ."

"Please lie back. Relax." She felt my glands, looked at my throat, my arms, and I babbled on.

"Apropos acting . . . they never gave me a chance to show what I could do! This last movie I played in 1939 stank to high heaven! Stupid Western. Actually my career was finished three years before that. You know when?"

"Turn over, please. When?"

"When I was five feet four. When I was only five feet three I was still Prince Charming, America's Little Sunshine Boy. Even another half-inch. After that, finished. All over."

"Hold out your hands, please."

"Do you understand? I was too tall for a child star. The studio canceled the contract." Natasha placed a sheet of paper on my stretched-out hands. It wobbled and fell off. She wound the blood-pressure cuff around my arm and inflated it. "I remember even now the studio doctor adjusting the little piece of wood on the height scale and shaking his head. Five feet four inches. That was that. That was the twentieth of December, 1935. My poor mother had a nervous breakdown. I was not even fourteen years old. I had various businesses and oil wells and stocks and bonds. But I was five feet four and finished. Isn't that comical? Now I have to be quiet, right?"

"Yes. Breathe deeply, please." She hooked the stethoscope into her ears and listened to my heart. "Don't breathe. Breathe." The flat disc of the instrument slid across my naked chest. I heard the rain outside. "Sit up, please." She examined my back. "How tanned you are!"

"Two weeks ago I was still lying in the sun in California. Tell me that you would never have thought I was drinking!"

"Breathe deeply."

After a little while I started again. "I am really in good condition. There is not an ounce of fat on my body. You can't imagine how I prepared myself for my work! Riding. Boxing. Tennis. Could I have another drink?"

This time she only poured a little into the glass.

"I hope you'll forgive me for behaving the way I did. I

simply lost my head. There is so much at stake. My first film in twenty years! Isn't that crazy? Isn't that alone sufficient to drive a man to drink? At six years old, still a baby, I made my first film, then fourteen more films, one after the other, and then no more. Ouch!" She had dug her fingers into my right side below my ribs and piercing pain went through me.

"Did that hurt very much?"

"Well, yes."

"Your liver." Now she took a little patella hammer and tapped my knee for reflex action.

"Are your parents still alive?"

"No."

"What did they die of?"

"My father of uremia. My mother of cancer of the larynx." I became sentimental. "She had a hard life. . . . My father left us when I was two years old. He just went off with someone on the chorus line."

Natasha tapped my right knee; my leg jerked up. "Good reflexes, right? I tell you, organically I'm perfectly healthy . . . Yes, he just left us . . . without a penny. . . . Mother then developed a facial paralysis. It was too much for her, you understand. And she could not act any more. . . . Now I was her only hope. We moved to Los Angeles. . . . Mother worked as a cleaning woman, as an usherette in movie theaters, and delivering newspapers. For a time she washed corpses for a funeral parlor."

"You loved your mother very much, didn't you?"

"Yes. She did everything for me. I learned to dance and sing, tap dance and ride. Many times there was nothing to eat—but she always scraped the money together for instructions. She took in washing, sewed at night and even begged."

"Begged?"

"Outside of nightclubs. I caught her twice doing it. When I was four years old there was not a studio in Hollywood where I was not known. Three years she dragged me from studio to studio. . . . If there were three hundred children waiting for one to be chosen for a two-day part . . . I was among them. . . . My compulsive talking is pathological, isn't it? Do you know that I have not talked about all this in years?"

"I am very interested, Mr. Jordan. After I saw your film *The Little Lord* I ran a temperature of 104°. And I wanted to marry you. Does that hurt?" I was sitting up now and with the edge of her hand she had examined the area around my kidneys. "No . . . not at all. . . . *The Little Lord!* I was eleven then and already famous. . . . But the awful time before that! Every morning the same hope when we took the bus to the studios . . . every night the same despair. . . . My mother often cried when we returned home, tired and dusty, to our dirty street. . . . Exhausted, she would pull me along, tears staining the cheap powder on her harried face always hidden behind a black veil . . . I will never be able to forget that . . ."

A vision of my mother rose. There in the dark, damp kitchen of our apartment in the slums of Kingston Road: the peeling wallpaper, the wash hanging above the stove, the bleak yard outside, the room across the hall filled to overflowing with shoes. There a single lightbulb burned for the hunchbacked Polish shoemaker who hammered without ever looking up. I heard everything again: the blaring jazz from many radios, quarrelsome children and adults who beat each other, insulted each other in Polish, English, Czech and German. I could smell everything, the dirt, the grease, the burnt cabbage.

Sighing, my mother dropped into the old rattan chair and I thought I heard her weak and yet indignant voice: "You should have gotten that part, Peter. You were the best-looking and most talented boy there. But that little fresh kid's mother was making eyes at the producer . . . whispered something to him, the pretty, common tramp . . . I can't do that with my horrible face . . ."

Natasha said, "Get up, please."

I got up, lost in thought of the past. In the storm outside the reflecting window I thought I saw my pale mother, her back bent, her hair dull. I massaged her swollen feet and seemed to hear her: "And still, one day they will discover you . . . and we'll be rich . . . and we'll be happy . . . and I'll never have to clean floors any more . . ." —"Yes, mother," I had answered, then, in that damp kitchen, "and we'll find the best doctor, and your face will be again as beautiful as it was."

Natasha stood before me now. "Put one foot close to the other. Closer. Toe next to toe, heel to heel. Close your eyes." I hesitated. "Don't be afraid, I'll catch you if you should become dizzy. That's good. I'll count to ten now. One . . . two . . . three . . ."

There I stood with tightly closed eyes. I had the sensation of weightlessness as if I were floating, flying, weightless. And again I heard my mother's voice and saw her standing in the burning hot sand, in the burning sun of the studio grounds. "Nothing again! And nothing again! And tomorrow we have to get out of our apartment!" She sighed deeply. "It's your fault! Only yours! You were sullen at the studio! You glared at Mr. Stevens."

"That is not true!"

"And you talk back to me?" She had slapped my face then in 1930, right, left, right, and today, in 1960 I sensed again the burning sting of those thirty-year-old slaps. "There . . . and there . . . and there . . . !" Only seconds later to press me sobbing close to her thin body, covered by her sweat-dampened dress. "Oh, God, what did I do? Forgive me, Peter, please forgive me, I am so despondent!"

Now I became dizzy. I swayed. And once more I saw my mother. The best surgeons in America had treated her. Now the skin of her face was smooth and natural— as long as she did not laugh. She had not laughed in a long time. Her body seemed to have shrunk, her head seemed tiny on the large, white hospital pillow. And once more I heard the terrible, almost unintelligible whisper which came from the cancer-ridden throat. "Those crooks, they have made millions from your films . . . now you are too tall for them . . . too adult . . . but wait . . . just wait, they'll come for you again . . . you'll be famous again . . . I know it . . . I've always known . . ."

". . . seven . . . eight . . . nine . . ."

I did not sway any more; now I fell into Natasha's arms. I clung to her and cried out, "Hold me! I'm falling."

Natasha held me. I could smell the fragrance of her hair, her perfume, I was conscious of her body. We were like lovers, the way we clung to one another, I with my naked chest, she in her green, tightly fitted suit.

I opened my eyes.

"You are very ill. You cannot make your film, Mr. Jordan."

I closed my eyes again.

11

Have you had the same experiences, dear Professor Pontevivo: You hear the noise of a car driving away; you see a plane ready for take-off, a young girl descending some old stairs; you make a certain gesture . . . and since your senses register these facts, impressions, feelings, since your consciousness is now aware and recognizes them, your memory is being awakened by a sound, a smell, a fragrance, a gesture. You close your eyes for a moment—you find yourself back in a different time, a different country, among people. Your past, suddenly present, has displayed the present. In the opening and closing of your eyelids, in a second so much of yesterday rises up in you. . . .

I held Natasha in my arms, she held me. I closed my eyes. Suddenly I was not in Hamburg any more, but in

Pacific Palisades where I held another woman in my arms.

We clung to one another, lovers in reality, passionate, heedless and desperate.

"Your mother . . . She might be back any moment . . ."

Shirley's body was slim but feminine. She had a slim waist and smooth hips. Her legs were long and well-shaped. Her skin, firm and young. The thick ponytail of her brown-red hair, which she always wore forward over one shoulder, had come untied and I felt the flood of hair warm and exciting on my chest. She held my head with both hands, her teeth dug into my lips and she moaned. I could not stand it any longer. Fourteen days we couldn't embrace, not touch each other . . . We did not see each other for fourteen days.

I had stood by the window in my bungalow, looking down at the ocean before she came. The bungalow, built on a steep hill thickly overgrown with gorse and prickly hibiscus, stood far apart from the main house. Only one path, bordered by orange trees, palms, and yucca trees with fan-shaped fronds hanging limply in the burning heat of this calm day in July, led up to the bungalow.

At the foot of the hill were grounds where sprinklers were forever watering the lawns, creating rainbows, with flowerbeds, gravel paths and the swimming pool at the end of the property. Immediately behind a rose-studded hedge, a thirty-yard cliff dropped so steeply that the beach below was not visible, only the deep blue Pacific.

The bungalow had been built in 1954. When my wife and I began to draw apart, a year and a half ago, I had had some of my books and records transferred to the bungalow. Then, when Joan was not well, or when we quarreled, I slept there. This is where Shirley came to see me.

It had happened here, in this bungalow, for the first time, half a year ago. And since then again and again, in the bedroom, here on the carpet, on the oversized couch by the fireplace. We would embrace fiercely whenever there had been an opportunity: at night, early mornings, afternoon, whenever Joan went into town, when the servants were away, during violent thunderstorms, at high or low tide.

From the windows of the bungalow the path leading to it was plainly visible. No one could have reached the bungalow through the surrounding thorny thicket. It would have ripped clothing, lacerated skin. It had become my habit to stare at the narrow path between that undergrowth when lit by the sun or by the floodlights, and always when Shirley was in my arms.

"Your mother . . . she might be back any moment . . ." I said it but still my hands were caressing her warm suntanned body covered only by a ridiculously tiny bikini. I wore shorts and sandals. It was inhumanly hot on this day but cool inside the bungalow.

"We have to wait . . . wait until it is night . . ."

"I can't wait, I've been away for such a long time. . . ." Shirley was then learning to be a film cutter. She had spent the last two weeks in studios in Culver City. There had been too much work for her to return home each night. "I didn't sleep one wink in those fourteen days. . . ."

"Nor did I, Shirley, nor did I . . ,"

Our lips met. Her green eyes closed. But I, from habit, looked through the window down to where my wife Joan was, by the side of the pool. She was lying there motionless in a black bathing suit, while I was caressing her daughter, whose tongue slid through my teeth, while—

Unsuspecting?

I felt hot and then cold. I released Shirley's lips.

"Where does she believe you are? With me?"

Her nostrils trembled whenever she was excited. "She sent me here. I am to keep you company while you are waiting for this telephone call." Without mockery but with increasing animosity she imitated my wife's voice, "I will not have you living here unless you are going to be a little more pleasant to Paddy! I mean it! I am not going to have my marriage destroyed just because my daughter doesn't happen to like my husband! She thinks we hate each other! She still thinks that . . . she thinks that is why her marriage is breaking up . . ." She grabbed my arms. "Those men down there on the patio . . . she says they are going to sign the contract?"

I looked down to the patio where, beneath palm trees, the Wilson brothers and the muscular Herbert Kostasch were arguing. "Everything depends on the telephone call I'm expecting."

"When the contract is signed—then will you tell her?"

"No."

"You promised! You swore—"

"First comes the film. Then I'll tell your mother."

"Don't always call her my mother! She was never a mother to me! All her life she only thought of herself! My father was hardly dead; then the men came! Always new men! All her life she only did what she wanted to do, nothing else! And I? Governesses! Nurses! Maids!"

"Stop it."

But she did not stop. "I was in a home when I was only four years old! That's nice for a child, isn't it? A luxurious home for millionaires' children! And then boarding schools! Always more beautiful boarding schools! Naturally I could only go home for the holidays. You were already irritable after the first week!"

"That is not true!"

"I know it is! I eavesdropped! You sent me away, because I was in your way! I grew up with strangers! Mother? That's supposed to be my mother?" Her voice broke, she almost cried. "It's her fault, it's all her fault!" She touched her forehead. "No, it's my fault. She is still my mother, in spite of it all!"

"Shirley!"

"I'm just a wreck! I can't eat, can't drive, can't talk any more. I can only think of you . . . you . . . and of . . ."

"Shirley!"

"I blush! I stutter! I drop things!"

"Pull yourself together!"

"It's easy for you! You are adult! You can tell more convincing lies! But I . . . I become dizzy if she just looks at me . . . Do I talk in my sleep? Can she tell by my face?"

"Now stop that, damn it! You are hysterical!"

"You forbade me to go to confession! Father Horace says—"

"I don't want to know what Father Horace says!"

"You are a louse! You lied to me . . ."

"That's not true!"

"You swore you would talk to her as soon as you had the contract!"

"I swore that when the film was finished I would! First I have to make that film!"

"Why?" Now she was screaming. Up here she could scream. No one could hear us.

"This film is my last chance. I have not waited twenty years for nothing!"

"I! I! I! Do you always think only of yourself?"

"Of me and you! We need money if I'm going to get a divorce!

"Money!"

"That's right, money!" My fist slapped into the open palm of the other hand. "If I may remind you, we are living on her money here! We have lived on her money for the past twenty years!" My wife, a ravishing Ziegfeld girl, had married an immensely rich Los Angeles realtor. Upon his death she became his sole heir.

"And your money? What happened to your money? You had millions!"

"Twenty years ago! You had not even been born then!"

48

"Just the same! Where are they?"

The truth was: gambled away, squandered, lost in bad business deals. Stupidly and senselessly wasted. A drunk among drinkers. Always drunk. But that I did not tell Shirley. No, I lied to Shirley, "I lost my money in the depression . . . the terrible time you know nothing of . . ."

"I don't need money! We can both work! I'll live with you in poverty! Just let's get away from here! Let's tell Joan the truth and leave, as quickly as possible."

I pulled her towards me by her long red hair. I must have hurt her because she stifled an angry cry. I spoke very softly, "I am not going to live in poverty, do you understand me?"

"Let me go!"

"Never again . . . never . . ."

"Let go of me!"

"Poverty and want . . . those are just empty words to you, meaningless . . . You have always lived in affluence . . . I didn't . . . when I was a child I had nothing to eat . . . cold and hungry . . . You have no conception of that! I'll never live like that again! That's why I have to make this film . . . only then will I be my own man . . . independent of your mother . . . and that is why you are going to pull yourself together . . . and wait . . . and let me work . . . so that we will be able to live in peace, you and I."

Her words then were to linger long in my memory.

"We'll never live in peace because we do nothing to end this sin. God does not forgive that."

"God! God! Do you always have to talk about Him?"

"It's easy for you, you don't believe in Him."

"You said if two people love each other He forgives them everything."

"Not if they don't repent . . ."

"Shirley!"

"God won't forgive us because He doesn't love us, He cannot love us . . ."

She had fought me, tried to pull away from me. The

contact of our bodies excited me, excited her. Her green eyes grew dark, smoky. She tried to fend me off but she also moaned.

"No . . ."

I unfastened the bra of her bathing suit; it fell to the floor.

"Don't!"

But there was desire in her eyes, her breasts were quivering, the tips hard and pointed.

"I don't want to . . . no . . ."

But she did not resist any longer. Her legs gave way and she fell forward into my arms.

A formation of jets raced above us toward the Pacific. Their roar shook the sky and the ground. We sank on the couch. Now Shirley was clinging wildly to me, her body writhed, her mouth dug into mine. I remember the crazy idea which occurred to me while our hands were already moving in unison, while Shirley dropped her bikini and I slid from the couch to the carpet. Now I was kneeling before her, now she was completely nude. Then I thought: Horwein is going to call me in twenty minutes from Frankfurt. If he says yes, I can make this film. If he says no, everything is finished. Now we are going to love each other. God, whom Shirley loves, whom Shirley fears. Now show me if You are going to agree to our love. Show me now if You are going to forgive us. We are going to make love. So let Horwein say "no" now that I am mocking You, provoking You.

"God won't forgive us because he doesn't love us, he cannot love us . . ."

Another twenty minutes, then we will see. Show me, Shirley's God, what You think of us, of what we are doing here, that which happened so many times before and which always carries us close to oblivion.

Shirley moans while my lips are caressing her. If you exist, God, then You know why I love Shirley. If You exist, then it is You who formed her so that each year she becomes more the image of another girl I shall never be able to forget. If You are, You are just as guilty of what is happening here as I am.

"Yes . . ." sighs Shirley. "Yes . . . oh, yes . . ." Her auburn hair has spread wildly in a great silken covering over her body and mine. Her eyes, not almost black, close. But I keep mine open and through increasingly denser, purple veils I see the path, the ocean, surfers, ships, my wife by the poolside.

Now show me, God.

12

Before going up to the bungalow to wait for the telephone call I had talked with Herbert Kostasch and the Wilson Brothers on the patio of the main house. Kostasch was my German producer. George and Jerome Wilson, twins and bachelors, were the source of our money.

They were sitting side by side, in swimtrunks, on a swinging settee, in their mid-forties, short, tough, each with a wide face, sly eyes, leathery skins. Their ears spread from their heads as those of bats do, with the round, black eyes and heavy lids of those flying mammals.

During the war they had invested their money in a company which built bombers. Several of those had crashed—not by enemy action. There was a scandal. Talk of faulty materials and fraud involving millions. Finally, a special committee of Congress verified that the Wilson Brothers were men of honor. They retired from the war business a few millions richer. Shortly after that they owned one of the largest slot machine businesses. Now they were financing movies.

In their swimtrunks they looked even smaller than usual. George forever giggling, apparently completely uninterested in business, stared at Shirley with delight every time she went down to the pool in her high-heeled sandals or to the house, her auburn ponytail over one shoulder. "Damn it all, Mr. Jordan, damn it all! Should I ever call you and a cop answers and says your wife shot you I'll know what happened, hahaha!"

"Hahaha."

"George!"

"Yes, Jerome?"

"I asked you if that's agreeable to you."

"I'll agree to anything if it's agreeable to you."

George simply refused to bother with business. His hobby was beautiful women. He was rich; their availability had been no problem for him despite his dwarfish stature.

Brother Jerome on the other hand loved to wheel and deal. He had found the ideal partner in Herbert Kostasch. Though both were usually shouting at each other their mutual esteem was high. Jerome was yelling, "Anyone would believe you already had the Cosmos million in your pocket, Kostasch!"

"I have, too."

"I thought Jordan was still waiting for a telephone call."

"That's pure formality. My old friend Horwein and I were agreed from the very beginning."

This was a bluff. I felt sick when I thought of the conversation I had with Kostasch after he had arrived in Los Angeles. It went like this.

"Everything went splendidly in Frankfurt, dear friend. Horwein is delighted with the script!" Horwein was the chief of Cosmo-Distributors.

"Then he signed?"

"No, not yet. Terrible heat you have here."

"He didn't sign the contract?"

"No, I just told you. He has to talk to his people about it again. He'll call tomorrow at twelve, your time here."

"But we'll have to talk to the Wilsons before that!"

"Do the Wilsons have to know everything?"

"What if he calls and says no?"

"He won't, you can rely on that. Money sticks to me and he knows it."

"And if he says no, then what?"

"You'll talk to him in any case. Should something go wrong you tell me—not the Wilsons, just as likely they'll have second thoughts."

"But—"

"Good God! By tomorrow night I have the twins ready to give us two and a half million! Then Horwein can kiss our ass. Then we can get any distributor in Germany! All I need now is time. Why are you looking at me? Don't you know how a film is financed?"

No. I had been too young to understand the subtleties of our industry when I had made my movies. There was Kostasch now talking to the Wilson Brothers about this old friend Horwein. I am sure he also told Horwein of his old friends, the Wilson Brothers.

Kostasch was fifty-four years old, came from Hamburg and had once been a German middleweight boxing champion. His nose had been broken and flattened, he looked brutal but was good-hearted. He was not afraid—never, of anything or anybody. He had suddenly appeared here the end of April. "You don't have to tell me, Mr. Jordan. You are finished. I know all that. Not even a dog will take a biscuit from you. But now comes Herbert Kostasch." He liked to talk about himself in the third person. "I have a story just written for you. Now, what do you say? After twenty years Kostasch is going to make a movie with you!"

As far as the German film industry was concerned Kostasch's reputation was legendary. Naturally I had made a few inquiries about him. In April of 1945 Kostasch had been a corporal in the German Wehrmacht, defending Berlin against Stalin's Red Army—a hopeless venture. Kostasch knew. In a lull of the fighting he and others, civilians and soldiers, were hurrying along Friedrichstrasse past a bombed branch of the Deutsche Bank. The vaults had been destroyed and millions of Reichsmark bills were lying among the rubble. In deathly fear, in expectation of the next Soviet offensive people hurrying by no one picked up a single bill. "Leave that junk!" a man yelled. "Next week it won't be worth the paper it's printed on!"

Corporal Kostasch did not share the man's opinion. He found two suitcases, a knapsack, filled them with bills and hid them with care. He found an empty apartment, clothes that fitted him, and finished the war in his own way.

The Reichsmark retained its value—for another three years. With his treasure Kostasch bought cameras, films, an entire studio. Now he was a producer. During the so-called 're-education' period he produced comedies and operettas. He had just finished three movies, financed with Reichsmarks, when the monetary reform came. He delayed their release for a time and then showed them when people began paying for their tickets with Deutsche marks.

Now Kostasch was rich. He became ambitious, produced pretentious movies in foreign countries with foreign actors, in co-productions which brought him honors, sometimes even money. He moved to Hamburg, overcommitted himself and was almost ruined. Banks helped him. Each time he took on too much; someone always helped him through a crisis. Invariably he landed on his feet—mostly through projects whose mere mention would scare other producers.

"Brainstorms," Kostasch called his sudden inspirations. He would track these down with an animal-like tenacity until writers, actors, financiers and distributors were brought together and another one of his extraordinary films was ready for shooting.

I, too, had been a "brainstorm." Kostasch had formed a new company, Jorkos Productions, Inc. and had registered in the principality of Liechtenstein for tax reasons. "The internal revenue is going to take the shirt off my back. Or do you, by any chance, want to finance the new Army? So there."

Kostasch and I were equal partners; we shared profits and risks. The movie was to be made in Germany since it was cheaper to produce there. The film's estimated cost was four million Deutsche marks or one million dollars.

The Wilson Brothers were to invest two and a half million Deutsche marks provided the German Cosmos-Distributors was to invest one million two hundred thousand Deutsche marks, which Kostasch, carefree, insisted they must. That would be decided at twelve o'clock through a phone call from Frankfurt. Once they had agreed, they would issue a guarantee for that amount. For the guarantee we could get cash from German banks. Kostasch and I had to raise the remaining three hundred thousand. For me it was thirty-eight thousand dollars. I had just about that much left, I could risk that—it was my last chance to obtain a divorce, to begin a new career, a life with Shirley . . .

"Now look here, Kostasch, you are only going to receive money from us on the condition that you start shooting at the latest on the tenth of November and deliver to us an English copy no later than the twentieth of March."

"Okay. Okay. Don't get excited, Jerome, my boy, you'll have your copy on the first of March. Herbert Kostasch promises!"

"We'll sue you if you . . ."

Jerome was puffing a cigar, by far too large for him. "We have obligations too." Kostasch was grinning. "Why are you grinning?"

"I can imagine what those obligations are. Obligations to avoid paying the Internal Revenue! Right?" Jerome laughed. They smiled at each other. Sharks in love. Then, shouting, they argued about percentages. Swinging back and forth in the sky-blue settee little George's eyes seemed to pop from his head. Shriley at the pool was pushing her auburn ponytail under a swimcap, stretched her body and dived into the water.

"Now, George, goddam, listen!"

"I completely agree . . ." George smiled apologetically. His eyes had become moist. Almost immediately he again stared at Shirley, who had turned over on her back. Thighs and breasts, her arms, the face was glistening tan and wet in the bright sunlight. I was staring at her too. I had been longing for her for the last fourteen days, fourteen nights. I forced myself to listen to Jerome. This was important, deciding my future, everything.

"Here in paragraph fourteen it says, 'In the event that the movie *Come Back* cannot be produced all obligations of the Wilson Brothers will automatically cease, etc., etc.' That, of course, is completely wrong. It should read: 'Should the movie *Come Back* not be produced within the time limit specified, etc., etc.' If you want to cheat us you'll have to get up earlier, Kostasch!"

I looked at my watch. Eleven-fifteen. Kostasch would have had a splendid career right here in Hollywood. I had never seen such coldness, self-control and effrontery. "This is the international formulation. If you don't like that, Mr. Wilson—with the 1.2 million German guarantee I can have a half dozen other partners by tonight!"

And we did not even have that guarantee! Supposing Horwein were to say "No" at twelve o'clock . . .

They were drinking orange juice. I filled their glasses again. George giggled, "Guess you'd rather have a drink of whisky, eh, Jordan?"

"Whisky?" I looked at him, devoid of understanding. After all, I was an actor. Lack of comprehension was easy to feign.

"Well, you used to drink quite a bit."

"That's all finished. Has been for a long time. You can ask anybody. Never touch it." My hand was shaking and

I spilled a little juice. Kostasch saw it, grinned as if to say, keep your cool, boy. I lived like this for fifteen years.

"If the paragraph is altered I demand a larger share."

"Why?"

"My risk increases."

"That's what insurances are for."

Thirty-five minutes to twelve.

Shirley got out of the pool, stretched and shook herself. George seemed to lick his lips. I tried to drink some juice and nearly gagged. I needed something different. I didn't have Kostasch's strong nerves. Another thirty-five minutes. Supposing Horwein said "No" . . .

"What's the matter, Jordan?"

"I'm . . . I think I'll go up to the bungalow."

Kostasch looked at me, irritated. He did not like me to show how nervous I was. "Already?"

"Perhaps the call will come through earlier."

Kostasch shrugged his shoulders, Jerome grinned, as if he had won a victory, and George continued to stare with ecstatic eyes at Shirley by the pool.

As I stepped from the shade of the palm trees to the terrace the glare of the sun hurt my eyes. I walked alongside the main house which had been built in the Spanish style. It was huge. Now it seemed old-fashioned, almost ridiculous, reminiscent of Valentino, Buster Keaton and Garbo . . . yes, and me, the famous, much adored child star, Peter Jordan. A lost, dead world of illusion.

My mother had bought this house in 1935 because it seemed to her the epitome of beauty and refinement. I was still living in this ghostly castle a quarter of a century later, as though time and life had stood still for me since I had reached thirteen.

I had to have a drink. Quickly.

I climbed the steep path to the bungalow, ran the last few yards. It was cool in the living room. I kneeled before the bookshelf. With a pocketknife I lifted out one of the thick floor boards. In the hollow space beneath it was a bottle of whisky. There were many bottles hidden around the bungalow; well hidden, no one had ever found a single one. I would drive thirty miles before I would throw the empties into the ocean.

With a soda from the refrigerator I fixed myself a large drink, drank it hurriedly, fixed another, drank it more slowly.

Never touch it.

Another thirty minutes . . .

I just could not take it without having a drink. I felt better. The whisky helped, it always helped. Many times I felt that whisky was my only friend, my only reliable friend.

I hid the bottle again, gargled, splashed my face with Eau de Cologne. I did this frequently because I drank frequently. During the last few months I had been drinking steadily. How else could I have stood the situation which I had created? I had been very careful, very clever.

The blessed tranquility which alcohol always gave me held me again. I stepped to the large window and looked at Shirley. She seemed to be disagreeing with her mother who wanted her to do something she was refusing. She shook her head and threw back her hair. Finally she rose, shrugging her shoulders. Then my heart began to beat wildly, she was coming up to me, up the steep path, closer and closer. Minutes later our lips were pressed together, we fell on the couch, wild with desire.

Then it was over.

She was in my arms, crying soundlessly. She often cried afterwards. I felt her tears on my chest, I looked down to the terrace, the arguing men, my wife by the pool, lying perfectly still, seemingly dead.

The telephone rang. I sat up. Twelve o'clock exactly. I heard the bells ring from Santa Monica. I was very calm and very relaxed.

Now, God, let me hear Your judgment.

"I have a call for you from Frankfurt, Germany."

"Hello . . ." I held the receiver with one hand, with the other I was caressing Shirley's body, her thighs, hips, arms, her breasts.

"Hello . . ."

"This is Cosmos-Distributors . . ."

A divine judgment. Now let me know Your will, God. Let Horwein say "No," if You won't forgive us.

". . . one moment, I'll connect you with Mr. Horwein . . ."

"Hello . . . hello . . . is that you, Kostasch?"

"This is Jordan."

"Oh, Mr. Jordan, how are you? I . . . I . . ."

"I speak German, Mr. Horwein."

Shirley sat up hurriedly. She clung to me, shaking again. I caressed her body. I was calmer now than I had been in months.

"That's nice, Mr. Jordan. Well . . . now . . . I have talked it over with my people . . . it is three o'clock in the morning here . . . you should see the cigar smoke . . ." I heard Horwein laugh. "Still, a lot of money remains a lot of money, right, even for us children of the wonder economy . . ."

I have blasphemed You, God, I have provoked You. Now, take Your revenge if You exist—or leave us in peace from now on.

". . . but at last we were agreed. We'll guarantee the 1.2 million. I'll tell you quite honestly, the fact that the Wilson Brothers are willing to invest their money has had a lot to do with it."

Herbert Kostasch. Money sticks to him. So he had been lying in Frankfurt, too. Eh, Jordan, didn't you know how a movie is financed?

"What is it . . . what happened?" Shirley whispered.

"Everything okay."

"Excuse me?"

"Oh, nothing, Mr. Horwein." Shirley began to cry again, she was completely beside herself.

"We have sent you a telegram to that effect. Letters and contracts will be sent tomorrow."

Now You have judged us, God. Then You are not angry with us. Or You don't exist. Now nothing and no one can change my plan.

"I'm looking forward to working with you, Mr. Jordan. My regards to Kostasch and the Wilson Brothers. I'll be seeing you soon in Germany. We wish you good luck. You can make your movie."

13

"You cannot make your movie, Mr. Jordan," said Natasha Petrovna. The rain was beating furiously against the windows of my hotel suite. Slowly I sat down on the side of my bed.

"You are very ill. You cannot make your movie, Mr. Jordan." I was staring at her and she pushed her glasses into place. "You have suffered a serious collapse. Your body and your nervous system have been damaged."

"By alcohol?"

"By alcohol. I can imagine how you must feel . . ."

"Really?"

". . . but as your doctor I must warn you emphatically. Your heart has suffered. Your liver is damaged."

"Then what ought I to do, Doctor?"

"You must stop drinking. Immediately. That is the most important thing."

"I don't think I can."

"You will with some help."

"You mean . . . in an institution?"

"In a clinic."

"No. I won't go."

"If you don't stop drinking the alcohol will kill you or—"

"Or?"

"—or destroy your brain," she said.

I thought of the dead seagull which had disappeared, of the terrible fear I had experienced. I was silent.

"Naturally you need specialists now. You have to get x-rays, cardiograms, blood and liver tests and so on." She touched her glasses, I could see she felt sorry for me. "One thing I can tell you with absolute certainty based on my own examination: If you are not going to change your life right away you will have only a short time to live. And during that time you will be utterly miserable."

The telephone rang. The desk told me a Mrs. Gottesdiener was waiting to see me.

"I don't know anyone by that name."

"The lady says she has an appointment."

"Oh, yes." Now I remembered. A lady of that name had sent me letters since I had arrived in Hamburg. She insisted she had something to tell me, to show me. I had not answered the letters at first. Then I had referred her to Jorkos Productions. But she did not give up. Last night, the worse for drink, I had told her when she telephoned again I would see her after breakfast.

"Please tell her I'm sorry but I am too busy to see her. Refer her to Jorkos Productions. They will help her there."

I replaced the receiver and looked at Natasha. The whisky I had drunk had slowed down my reactions. Slowly I realized the position I was in.

"But that's impossible. I have never had the slightest problems."

"Of all poisons alcohol is the most insidious. Your body has withstood it for twenty years. Now it has deteriorated."

"But I feel fine again."

"You have been drinking, too. You are very ill and in acute danger, please believe me."

"But I must make this movie!" I cried

"Mr. Jordan, did you have any exceptional excitement last night or this morning?"

I stared at her and nodded.

"Well, it caused this attack. If you are going to make this movie there will be excitement without letup. You told me you were very frightened of a heart attack. This was no heart attack. Not yet. But the next attack will be a heart attack. Most probably you will recover. Most people survive the first infarction. Not many survive the second."

"And . . . and if I go to a clinic . . . how long will it be before I am healthy again?"

"You want to hear the truth?"

"Naturally."

"Nine months."

"You could be wrong."

"Unfortunately, no. Any third-year medical student would make the same diagnosis."

The telephone rang.

"This is the desk again, Mr. Jordan. Mrs. Gottesdiener asks if you could not see her for even ten minutes. She says everything depends on her talking with you."

"Tell her to go away! Do you understand me? Tell her to leave me alone. And don't call me again!"

14

Any third-year medical student.

That was the death sentence. Only Natasha Petrovna did not know that. She had examined me today. Tomorrow I was to be examined by the doctor employed by the movie insurance company. If every medical student could see what was wrong with me he would see it too. And would advise his insurance company not to insure me. My life was ruined.

Staring at Natasha Petrovna my thoughts were running rampant. Today was the twenty-seventh of October. The appointment for the examination was for the twenty-ninth at nine o'clock. The insurance would then have been in effect—according to Kostasch's planning—for me, for the American actress Belinda King, for Henry Wallace and our director Thornton Seaton from midnight, the first of November. The fourth was to be the first day of shooting. We would have been covered by insurance against illness or death of one of the main actors or our director.

We would have been.

I suddenly seemed to hear little Jerome Wilson's voice, "Paragraph fourteen should read, 'In the event the movie *Come Back* cannot be produced within the specified limits all obligations of the Wilson Brothers will automatically cease. All payments, compensations or indemnities will be to the debit of Jorkos Productions . . .' "

It was one week before we were to start shooting. We had rented a studio, equipment, hired actors and actresses, musicians and studio and technical staff. We had to compensate . . .

I reached for my glass and emptied it. Jorkos Productions belonged to Kostasch and me. Even if we could make advantageous arrangements, the uninsured film would cost us a million German marks. I did not know if Kostasch had five hundred thousand marks cash. I did not. And there was only one person in the world who had and who was probably willing to give it to me, my wife Joan. My wife Joan, whom I wanted to leave in order finally, completely to possess her daughter.

"Mr. Jordan . . ."

I jumped. Natasha had spoken. "Excuse me?"

"I said, is it not possible to postpone this film?"

"We'd lose the people who are financing the movie."

"And if—I'm sorry—and if someone else were to play your part?"

"That's not possible either. The movie is the story of

my life. A forty-year-old American, once a famous child star, making a movie in Germany, is given the chance of a comeback. Naturally, the contract is in my name ..." I looked at her quiet, composed face. My words came hurriedly. "My position is desperate ... if I cannot make the movie we'll have to compensate all concerned ... as soon as anything becomes known of my illness people will make outrageous demands ..."

"No one will hear anything from me."

"That is important ... that is very important. I shall have to talk to my partner now ..."

"Is he here in Hamburg?"

"No, unfortunately not. He won't be back until tonight from Düsseldorf—he is looking for movie locations—that is if he does get back tonight ... he intended to stay until tomorrow ..." Herbert Kostasch! Desperately I was wishing him back, my imagination credited him with marvelous abilities. Cunning, wisdom, craftiness. He would find a way out with one single great idea. Oh! Herbert Kostasch!

"I won't have to go to a clinic today or tomorrow, will I?"

"No, but—"

"What I mean is, there is no immediate danger, is there?"

"Not if you rest. Your heart has to rest. You must sleep. You must not drink any more."

"All right. Well, no. You can still look after me for a day or two?"

"Only until tomorrow night. I'm just filling in for a colleague. Saturday I am leaving for the Congo."

"You are going to Africa?"

"Yes. I've signed a contract for five years with the city hospital in Leopoldville," she said and behind the thick lenses of her glasses her eyes were shining with contentment and happiness. I thought, it is true then, there are people, not only like me, with dirty secrets and desperate passions. No, there are others with true purity of soul. People, who set out to help their brothers, black, sick, poor, despised . . .

"You must sleep."

"But I have to reach my partner . . . I have to telephone . . ."

"Not now. If your partner is expected back tonight you have until five o'clock." She took a box of ampoules from her little bag. "I'm giving you just enough medication so you will be awake then. You cannot have any sedative containing barbiturates. It would put too much strain on your liver. I'll leave word you are not to be disturbed." She filled the ampoule. "I'll come by at eight tonight to give you an injection for the night. I'm doing this providing you are going to stay in bed. Will you promise me that?"

"Yes."

"You give me your word?"

I did.

Suddenly I felt tears running down my face. I wiped them away. I did not want to cry but the tears kept coming. Natasha was sitting next to me while she filled a syringe with the contents of the ampoule.

"I know how desperate you must feel now. You know there is a proverb in the Congo: The sun sets and rises, but our misery remains."

"Nice proverb. Thanks a lot."

"A false proverb, Mr. Jordan. Those people are not miserable any more. They have freed themselves. Soon they will be independent." Natasha reached for a tissue and dried my eyes. Indeed the tears stopped after the gentle, no, strangely tender touch. "Your misery will disappear when you free yourself of your need to drink."

I looked at her.

"You think you cannot manage your life. That is why you drink. But if you change your way of living you will be able to live normally. Then you will make movies again, have confidence and be happy. And remember what I said. Please, turn over on your side . . ."

She gave me the injection, shook my hand, smiled reassuringly and left. I felt myself growing tired. The storm continued to howl, the rain to beat down. And slipping into this chemically induced sleep I had only one thought.

And if I have to commit a crime to get that insurance coverage, and if they have to take me to the studio every morning on a stretcher, and if I die before the cameras—I am going to make this movie. I, no one else. Now and not later. Addicted to alcohol, yes, and ill, yes—now, not when I may be cured—yes, I'm going to make this movie. My movie. *Now*.

You, Professor Pontevivo, can probably easily imagine what a man, his existence threatened by destruction, is capable of. Your beautiful young assistant could probably understand the worst deed a woman would do if another one took her love. But neither of you, dear Professor Pontevivo, can imagine (not in the least and not in your wildest dreams!) what an actor, whose last chance of acting, after waiting half a lifetime for it, is likely to do.

Actors are not ordinary people. Their profession alone (surely that of writers too) is a continual provocation to any psychiatrist. Does an ordinary person take on a thousand different faces, does a normal person feel a thousand curious pains and desires, impulses and thoughts, speak convincingly the words another wrote, is a thousand different people in one but never himself?

The actor's profession demands that he be schizoid. And what of him who is prevented from acting?

I have seen, in Hollywood and elsewhere, what happens when those players, those actors are kept away from the studio, from the stage. I am my best example. I began to drink. Others became criminal, addicted to drugs, insane. Some killed themselves. A beautiful woman— celebrated star of the Roaring Twenties, finished with the advent of sound movies—undressed at large parties and gave herself to anyone who reached out for her, and everybody had to watch, everybody. She was not given any part to play. She then created her own role. Appear in public! To have an audience! Being seen! The most shameless whore does not possess one thousandth the urge of exhibition which even the most insignificant actor has.

I was an actor. And my existence was nullified if I did not make this movie. And my love was destroyed. Did I make myself quite clear, Professor Pontevivo? Can you measure the degree of determination to make this movie, even if it would mean my death, or if I had to commit a crime to secure insurance coverage for our production? I was determined. All I did not know was: Determined to do what? Twelve hours later I knew—thanks to a white-haired old lady by the name of Gottesdiener.

The Second Tape

1

The moment I stepped through the open plate-glass doors of the hotel, floodlights were switched on; a camera attached to the roof of a car swung toward me and about a hundred people, many of them women and teenagers, began to scream, wave and applaud. They were held back by police forming a barrier òn the other side of the street. Surprised, I stood motionless.

It was six o'clock in the evening. The rain had stopped but it was still stormy. The sky, a few stars already visible, was sea-green and cloudless in the twilight. I was blinded by the floodlights. The crowd broke through the police barrier ànd stormed across the street. Tires screamed on the rain-soaked asphalt; the traffic came to a halt. I saw many people waving autograph books and photographs. Two men came running toward me. One held a microphone, the other the cable. The people in the crowd were yelling joyfully. The picture was a familiar one. As did Dr. Pavlov's dog, my reflexes reacted too, the way I had been taught a long time ago. I opened my arms wide, nodded and waved, smiled, to show I loved them all.

I heard boos, derisive laughter. Then the reporter had reached me.

"Stop it, man," one of them yelled. The other pushed me and cried, "Get out of the way! You are blocking the cameraman's picture!"

Stumbling, I reached the other side of the street. Now I was in the midst of the crowd of screaming women. They were all staring at the hotel entrance. There I now saw Sophia Loren and Vittorio de Sica.

His white hair shone in the bright lights. Sophia Loren wore a mink coat over a skin-tight, gold lamé dress. She was throwing kisses, De Sica opened his arms wide, just as I had done a moment ago. The crowd was in a frenzy, the police powerless. I was pushed towards the entrance of the hotel bar, and I heard De Sica exclaim, "Amici, siamo felici d'essere in Germania!"

And Sophia Loren, "Questa bella città d'Amburgo!"

The crowd roared.

I heard whistles, patrol cars arrived. Policemen were trying to control the crowd and move the stopped traffic. I watched the beautiful Sophia Loren and De Sica, whom I admired as an actor and director, smilingly sign autographs. I recalled the time, the crowds, the commotion, now long ago and forgotten, when I, a little boy in a pageboy haircut, had appeared. The chaos at the Waldorf-Astoria, the hysteria at the Colonial House in Tokyo, where fans had torn my clothes to get hold of souvenirs, hotels in Vienna, Quebec and Rome.

Suddenly I felt sick and fearful again. I had felt well when I awakened an hour ago. I had showered, eaten and written two letters which I was now taking to the nearby post office. Those letters had to go quickly and I did not trust the bellboys. Since my attack I distrusted everybody. The waiter serving dinner seemed to be smiling ironically. Walking through the foyer I had the feeling that the desk-clerks were exchanging meaningful looks . . .

I had noticed a new symptom: agoraphobia. It had been extremely difficult for me to walk through the foyer. This was not a new symptom, once before, as I left my apartment, I found myself unable to enter the elevator. I was certain I could never descend in this narrow, hot cell with its mirrored sides without—

Without what?

Without doing something which would attract attention, something alarming, something I could not control. The realization gave me a fright; I ran back to my apartment where I felt safer as soon as I had shut the door. I was supposed to stay in bed. I had given Natasha my promise.

But the letters had to be mailed. Shirley and I were at stake.

I had to have a drink. There was enough left in the bottle. Then I tried again. This time I could not leave the elevator on the main floor but quickly pressed the sixth-floor button and went back upstairs. My heart was beating furiously. Another Scotch. I dropped into a chair. It was growing dark. I stared at the fog shrouding the Alster River.

Now I knew self-pity. I was alone in Hamburg, very ill. The symptoms terrified me. A long way from home. Which was my home? The Spanish-style ghostly house? A double bed alongside an unloved wife? The bungalow with Shirley, who was expecting my child?

I could not stand these thoughts and drank again. Then, with great concentration I tried the descent into the foyer once more. This time with success. I was somewhat confused but not drunk. I was standing away from the crowd, looking at the radiant Sophia Loren, the distinguished De Sica.

It's just as well no one knows me, I thought. In my condition I would hardly be able to smile, shake hands, sign autographs.

"Now I've found you," said a trembling voice and very strong, ice-cold fingers encircled my wrist.

Startled I turned around.

The woman holding my wrist was surely seventy years

old—a most dismal character, clad in a tattered Persian lamb coat. Distressingly thin, white hair straying from her old-fashioned fur hat, worn out high-button boots. Waxen face, hollow-cheeked. Dull sunken eyes, bloodless lips. In her agitation she could hardly speak. "It's almost six o'clock. I've been waiting since nine-thirty."

"Who are you?" Was this reality? Was this old lady flesh and blood? Or was she as real as the seagull?

"I'm Hermine Gottesdiener," she said with extreme dignity.

"You have been waiting that long for me?"

"At first I was waiting in the foyer. At three, when the clerks changed shifts, I was told to leave. No one has dared to speak to me in that manner, never! To think that my husband, may he rest in peace, and I celebrated our wedding right here in this hotel!"

"When was that?"

"Nineteen thirteen. And today I'm told to leave . . ."

She was carrying an old handbag slung over one arm and a flat, heavy package under the other.

"I said to myself you have to come down sometime. I would have waited another eight hours. I would have waited until I dropped."

"But why?"

Her fingers were still holding my wrist. "Because you are my last hope, Mr. Jordan. If you don't help me now I'm going to end it all."

She wept genuine tears and let them fall without a dab of a handkerchief. Her hands were otherwise busy holding her package, her handbag and my wrist.

I have never forgotten the poverty we endured when I was a child. I have never forgotten cold, hunger or shame.

"You must be hungry, Mrs. Gottesdiener."

"Yes. No. Yes."

"We'll go to a restaurant and you'll tell me everything. But I must go to the post office first."

Her nails dug into my arm. "You want to get rid of me. You'll go back to the hotel where I'll be thrown out."

"I won't go back to the hotel."

"I've waited too long. I'll come to the post office with you."

Now two shiny black cars pulled up in front of the hotel. Sophia Loren, Vittorio De Sica and their entourage got in. The people crowded around the cars. They yelled and laughed. Mrs. Gottesdiener was walking with short unsteady little steps. She was still holding on to my wrist.

2

The first letter was addressed to Mr. Gregory Bates, 1132 Horthbury Avenue, Los Angeles, California, USA.

The second letter was addressed to Miss Shirley Bromfield, care of Post Office, Pacific Palisades, California, USA. To my stepdaughter I wrote:

Dearest Heart,

I know exactly how you must feel when you read this letter. Let me say right now, before anything else: I love you. I have never loved anyone as much as I love you; I shall never ever want anyone as much as I want you.

Years ago a woman told me I could not love, did not know love. I don't know if that is true. All I know is: All I feel, tenderness, longing, courage, patience, selflessness, trust, loving care and admiration, is directed toward you. As great, or whatever love may be in me, is all yours and will be yours until I die.

Shirley, my All, you must now be brave and reasonable. Reasonable—what a horrible word. And yet, now we must use good judgment. It is impossible for you to have this child. The scandal would surely ruin our future. I detest myself for forcing you to do this dreadful deed but I swear I shall make it up to you, soon. I will take care of you, protect you, love you. We shall have a child, Shirley—but not this one.

I am also writing to Gregory Bates. You know him, he is my best friend, and you can trust him. Gregory knows many doctors. He will know who will be able to help you quickly and safely.

I am telling him that you came to me for help because you were afraid of your mother, and that the father of your child is a young man from the studio. Gregory will not question you. Since he is still producing movies I shall suggest that he ostensibly engage you as a cutter and send you to a different movie location for a few days. This way Joan will not become suspicious.

These letters will be on the jet leaving Hamburg tonight on a direct flight to Los Angeles. They should be in your post office by tomorrow morning. Please arrange to see Gregory at night. I shall telephone him at his apartment at eleven o'clock.

Shirley, dearest Heart, you know I'm making this movie here in Hamburg for both of us. I must, I will be as good an actor as I can possibly be. Don't despair. Be as brave as I know you can be and believe me when I say this is for both of us.

In my thoughts I am always with you—united with you on the beach, on our boat, in the bungalow and the dunes; everywhere where we were happy together. Soon we will be again. Forever.

Peter

P.S. As always, destroy this letter at once.

3

"In his speech before the First Soviet in Moscow, Prime Minister Khrushchev again threated Berlin . . ." The voice of the newscaster came softly through the dark little restaurant.

Mrs. Gottesdiener and I were sitting at one of the scrubbed tables. She was having sandwiches and a beer. I had ordered whisky.

The contents of Mrs. Gottesdiener's package, a heavy scrapbook, was before me. "Surely there isn't another collection like this anywhere," she said, her mouth stuffed with food. "Take your time. There are pictures from all your movies and travels."

Old magazine stills, postcards, pictures cut from newspaper had been carefully sorted and pasted in, bordered with colored pencils, decorated with little stars and flowers. There I was, sitting on Mayor La Guardia's lap. There was the tickertape parade on Broadway. There was my mother, her smile distorted after her face operation. There were the premieres of *Huckleberry Finn, Oliver Twist* and *Treasure Island.* These yellowed pages were my youth. This old book, emitting the smell of mothballs, evanescence and poverty reflected the years of my fame.

"Algeria. A new wave of terror hit several towns. Bombs killed 17 people, injured 65 . . ."

"This is only the first of three scrapbooks," said Mrs. Gottesdiener.

She spoke between quick, hungry bites, while eyeing other sandwiches stacked on the bar. Food had not eased her unhappiness; she ate greedily, without enjoyment, her knife and fork in staccato movements.

"Where did you get those scrapbooks?"

"Good God! My husband owned the largest newspaper

77

clipping service in North Germany!" She used a finger to capture an elusive bit of ham. "A very successful business with branches overseas . . ." Now her face was flushed.

"Wouldn't you like to take off your coat and hat?"

"I have very little hair. And I have pawned all my dresses. I'm wearing a duster. Oh, I'm so ashamed . . ." A piece of cucumber. "We were rich once, Mr. Jordan. We had a villa in Cuxhaven. And now . . . now . . . no, I must not think about it. We started the scrapbooks for Victoria . . ."

"Your daughter?"

"Yes. She admired you greatly! She treasured her scrapbooks, even when she was grown." Another sandwich on her plate, yet she kept her eyes on those on the bar.

"Would you like—"

"You must think me brazen . . ."

"Waiter!"

"Perhaps I could also have another beer?"

More sandwiches, another beer, and whisky for me. Another drink then I would feel better. I was uneasy and restless. I was sympathetic to this old woman. But did I not have my own problems? I was just wasting my time here. That's what I thought. A few minutes later I had changed my mind.

Mrs. Gottesdiener attacked her last sandwich. "I have a lot of debts, Mr. Jordan. The grocer won't give me credit any more. The electricity has been cut off. If I don't pay my rent I will be sent to an institution. Charity! For me! and we once had the largest clipping service . . ." The waiter came. She pushed the empty plate away, took the full one from his hands and ate and talked with little pause. "Victoria's death used up the last of my savings. You just don't know how much a reasonably decent funeral costs!"

"When did your daughter die?"

"On the twenty-fifth of April. Why shouldn't I tell you

the truth? She was a morphine addict." Another bite. "Out of the hospital. Back in the hospital." A bite of bread. "At the end she loathed herself." A bite of ham. "In one of her lucid moments she drowned herself in the Elbe." A drink of beer. "He is responsible, that man!"

"Who?"

"Schauberg."

"Her husband?"

"Yes, her husband, God help us! This criminal, this scoundrel. He was addicted first! Then he made an addict of her. Many doctors who are addicted do that, I've read a book about that. They want the people close to them to sink as low as they themselves."

"Your son-in-law is a doctor?"

"He was. He is not allowed to practice now."

"Why not?"

"Well, because of this addiction. And something happened in his office. He was an internist. He gave a wrong injection. The man died. His wife demanded an investigation. Mr. Jordan, please buy those scrapbooks from me. Help a poor old woman. Do a good deed for a woman who is the last member of a once respected family . . ." She continued to talk. That I could see. But I could not hear her any more.

4

Mrs. Gottesdiener's son-in-law is a doctor. He has violated his oath and the law. He is probably willing to transgress again.

Shirley now needs a person like that. On the other side of the world, in California, Gregory will find such a person for her. Here in Hamburg I have almost found such a man for myself. How curious that Shirley and I should simultaneously be in need of illegal services by unscrupulous people.

If Shirley were here now Schauberg could probably help both of us. As it is I alone can hope for his help. A million is at stake. My movie is at stake. Shirley's and my future is at stake.

The day after tomorrow is my examination by the insurance company. "Every student in his third year of medical school could make the same diagnosis." Natasha said. What if this Schauberg were to treat me first? A doctor without scruples has so many possibilities. And this Schauberg obviously has no conscience. I hope. This is my only chance.

And here sits Mrs. Gottesdiener, of all those people in Hamburg, eating and talking. Were I to read this in a script I would think it unbelievable and improbable.

Chance?

Whatever occurs outside our believable concepts is surely chance. But I think I recognize a law in all that is happening to me! I have provoked and blasphemed God. So He—assuming He exists—first dealt me a victory and then these blows. Now He lets this woman cross my path. And perhaps He is showing me a way out of my need, my darkness. I am convinced He is directing me to a definite goal.

But if He does not exist I am just another individual.

Among millions of destinies only my fate is unique; it is mine alone, different from all others—by an incalculable difference, the nuance of a moment, different because I want it to be, because I, aware and of my own volition, am going toward my goal.

Whether or not I am a toy in God's hand, there is the hand indicating the path I am to travel. I am still alive and I can still think, do, choose. Or God acts, chooses and thinks for me and pushes me toward the next break in my journey.

Its name is Dr. Schauberg.

5

"That man made her life miserable. He gambled, deceived her. And when he came back wounded from Russia she had to nurse him for two years." Mrs. Gottesdiener's voice brought me back to reality.

"And she could have married a general!"

"Who?"

"My poor Victoria. He admired her greatly. And is there something better for a woman than a general? No. Not in war or in peace. Even if he loses the war! Friend and enemy show him respect. He always receives h money, his wife, his pension. No one would ever him." Mrs. Gottesdiener sighed. "But she wouldn't to me. She practically threw herself at Schauberg . . ."

"How much do you want for the scrapbooks?"

"Five hundred marks." She said it too quickly and coughed, holding both hands to her mouth. After calming down she said weakly, "Well, all right, three hundred. But I need three hundred. My rent alone . . ."

"I'll give you five hundred."

She clutched my hand and kissed it. "I knew it! I didn't pray in vain!"

"When did you see your son-in-law the last time?" I had to be careful now. Luckily the money had diverted her attention.

"See him. Whom? Oh. Before the funeral. I went to see him to become reconciled."

"Where did you go?"

"To an old house near the harbor. There it stinks of fish and dirt and sin. He lives there with a blonde. I'm sure she is a whore. You know what he did? He threw me out!" Her voice rose. "Get out of here! I don't want to ever see you again!" Her voice broke. "That's how it ended. And she could have had a general."

She had drunk a lot of beer. I had to find out. "And he still lives at Mottenburger Street?"

"Mottengurger Street, why?"

"Number thirty-four; you just said so."

"I never said that!"

"But—"

"Why should I say that? He lives near the slaughter-house. Number four. Right near the fish market. With this painted whore. Gehzuweit is her name."

It had worked at the first try.

6

"Mrs. Gehzuweit?"

"Are you from the police?" Her voice was husky as if she had a cold.

"No."

"Then what is it?" She was big and indeed heavily made up. Violet eyeshadow, a black beauty mark, mascara and darkly penciled eyebrows. Her mouth was a slash of red.

"I would like to speak to Dr. Schauberg," I said.

"He doesn't live here any more." Mrs. Gottesdiener's description of the house had been accurate: stinking of dirt and sin. The green-gray paint was peeling off the wooden hall and stairs. Bare lightbulbs hung from the damp ceiling. Waterpipes were exposed in the hallways. Bathrooms were there too.

"Could you give me his new address?"

"No." And hurriedly she wanted to slam the dirty door with the chipped enamel sign:

But I already had my foot inside.

"Are you crazy? Get lost!"

Behind me water was flushed and an old, emaciated man shuffled closer, stopped, stared. Very loudly I said, "I guess then I'll have to go to the police!"

The dreaded word did the trick. Mrs. Gehzuweit shrank visibly. On my right and left, behind me doors were opened. People looked out, curious and greedy.

"Is he from the cops?"

"Now what happened?"

I pressed a fifty-mark bill in Mrs. Gehzuweit's hand. She sneezed thunderously. "Come in." At the curious in the hall she yelled "Why don't you mind your own business!" and slammed her door. Outside they began to whisper.

The apartment was small. Everywhere were suitcases and trunks, boxes and rolled-up carpets. A single bulb in a pink glass shade was giving a weak light.

Mrs. Gehzuweit stood there, breathless. She seemed close to tears and despair. Her dark red robe had opened and I could see youthful breasts and smooth white skin. She wore trousers, the suspenders hanging, and a pair of man's shoes.

"Where did you get my address?"

"From Dr. Schauberg's mother-in-law. She spoke of a Mrs. Gehzuweit."

"The old woman was me in costume."

"You are—"

"Eric Gehzuweit, female impersonator," he introduced himself with a short, military bow. He even clicked his heels. With a feminine gesture he pushed his blond wig into place. A door to my left opened and I saw a very pretty girl in a pale blue silk dress. She looked at me with curiosity and said affectedly, "Can I help you, Erika?"

83

"The gentleman only wants some information."

"Oh, what a pity!" Giggling, she disappeared.

"My partner," said Gehzuweit. He first looked at the fifty marks in his hand, then at me and sighed. "Not a cop. Then you surely need—"

"No."

"No what?"

"No drugs."

"Sh . . ." Frightened he pointed to the door. "Miserable bums," he yelled. Someone ran away outside. "Everybody here thinks us very peculiar."

"I must find the doctor. That's all."

"But I told you—"

"Tell me about him." I pulled another fifty marks. "Who were his friends? What did he look like? Perhaps then I can find him . . ."

"I really don't know much more . . ." He walked ahead of me into a bedroom with twin beds. "Excuse me, I have to get dressed." He threw off his robe. Again I saw the firm breasts of a young woman, a wide back, narrow hips, soft white skin. "Our first show is at seven-thirty."

"That early?"

"Special performance. A British destroyer is in the harbor. Those boys are just crazy about Raoul and me." He sneezed loudly and sat in front of a dressing table. "Imagine. We have to do our show six times." He said it with pride. He began to shave his underarms with a small electric shaver. And sorrowfully he said, "It's awful. The more one shaves the faster the hairs grow. And it shows in evening dresses."

"When did Schauberg leave here?"

"He didn't leave. I threw him out."

"Why?"

"I don't want anything unlawful in my house." He spat into a box of mascara and stirred with a small brush. "I swear, I didn't know about it at first."

"About his drugs?"

"Yes. As soon as I found out I threw him out. My partner, Raoul, and I earn our living as decent artistes. We didn't have anything to do with Schauberg's dirty business."

"I'm sure you didn't."

But he would not stop; he continued to lament, while he applied mascara to his lashes. "We have our license. We pay our taxes . . ."

"All right."

". . . We are being examined at regular intervals."

A small stove gave off heat. It smelled of powder, make-up, cheap perfume. Stuffed dolls, boxes of chocolate and silken cushions were strewn around. Photographs of the female impersonator and different partners hung on the walls. On the bed were silk stockings, ladies' undergarments, a décolleté black cocktail dress.

"Of course I thought it strange when so many people came. But he said they were his friends and I believed him. That's my trouble, I believe anybody. That's why I'm never a success."

"How did you find out about the doctor's business?"

"One of his customers had an attack here. You know, complete with screaming, frothing at the mouth, and all that. Very pleasant, something like that, right?" Plaintively he called out, "Where is my bra then?"

Raoul's droll voice answered from the adjacent room. "Just another moment, Erika."

I began to feel ill. The fist. No. No. Not here. Not now. I opened the window a little.

"What are you doing? My cold—"

"Just for a second. I don't feel very well." The cold air I inhaled smelled of the close-by harbor.

Gehzuweit paled. "Good God, then you are one of those!"

"No . . ."

"Just don't have an attack here!"

The fist rose. I held on to the window. Suppose I were to have an attack. I was inhaling deeply.

"You want a cognac?"

"Yes . . ."

I gulped the cognac. I felt better. From the window I could see the now deserted fish market. There, every Sunday morning at five, stalls and booths were erected. At the Hamburg Fischmarkt one can buy not only fish but groceries, housewares, toys, dresses—cheaper than anywhere else. Until ten o'clock. Then a siren wails and the booths have to close.

Every Sunday, at daybreak, the Fischmarkt looks like the set of a surrealistic film. The poorest and saddest humanity appears in rags, unshaven, drunk; whores, stragglers from the Reeperbahn, foreign sailors, ordinary people, busy housewives trying to stretch a penny; beautiful women in evening dresses and mink coats, jewelry-laden, excitedly laughing, escorted by gentlemen in tuxedos.

Then the bars are crowded. Now they are empty. Empty the 'Eierkorb' where I had eaten fried fish and drunk beer with Kostasch one Saturday night when jazz blared from loudspeakers, churchbells summoned believers to Mass, and the two girls we had picked up argued.

"Eh, you!"

Gehzuweit looked at me. "Please go. I don't want any trouble here." He was half-naked, made-up, powdered, and looked troubled.

"I'm all right now." I gave him the second fifty marks. He hesitated, torn between his greed and fear that I might have another attack.

"You never saw Schauberg again?"

"Never. I'm going crazy with the telephone ringing. It rings day and night. At three in the morning. And they are always dying . . . threatening to kill themselves . . . to kill me if I don't tell them where the doctor is . . . And they all have code names!" He took off his pants and shoes. "Blue page! Dwarf! Strict teacher! It's a regular nuthouse! I wish I'd never met the guy!" The door opened. His partner, swishing his silken skirt over many petticoats, came in and handed Gehzuweit a black bra.

"Well, it's about time."

"I sewed on both straps, Erika. Now the boys can go wild again." Raoul wore a black wig with braids. Coquettishly he pressed his index finger to his cheek and came close to me. "You like me, sweety?"

"Stop your nonsense and help me," said Gehzuweit. Reaching for the black panties on the bed, he became embarrassed and asked me to turn around.

"This damn bra," he groaned behind me. "You can't imagine. I can't breathe freely."

"You have such beautiful breasts," I said. "You don't need a bra."

"But I do. It's part of the act. We do a striptease. Good God, and now the girdle! After I threw him out I told the cops."

"Well, and?"

"They looked into it but they can't prove anything. Ouch, why don't you watch what you're doing, Raoul!"

"Don't feel so sorry for yourself," said the little fellow gruffly.

"Did he have a girlfriend?"

"Yes, he did. A blonde. Her name was Käthe."

"Käthe what?"

"I don't know. She was just known as Käthe."

"Did she walk the streets?"

"Yes, but she never brought a man up here. I wouldn't have allowed that. You can turn around again."

He stood there in silk stockings, high heels, and underclothes. He sprayed himself with perfume, put on large earrings and a pearl necklace.

"Käthe disappeared with him. Without a trace. I looked for her myself because I couldn't stand all those phone calls. I thought she might know where to find

Schauberg. But I had no luck." I took out another fifty marks. "Leave the money; you already paid me." He stepped into the dress Raoul held for him. Pulling up the zipper, the little fellow said, "Give me the money. I know where she is."

Unbelieving, Gehzuweit stuttered, "But . . . but, Raoul!"

"Where is she?"

"First the fifty," said Raoul.

I gave him the money.

"Do you know the Herbertstrasse?"

"No."

"It's near here. Everybody can tell you. That's where she is now. In a brothel."

Gehzuweit's voice was shrill. "How do you know that?"

"Because I was there."

"You were . . ."

"Ah, shut your mouth," said the little guy with the braids and gave the tall one a shove. Gehzuweit fell on the bed. Tearfully he cried, "Why are you so mean to me?"

"You'll have to ask around," said Raoul to me. "There are several houses. The entire street is nothing but brothels."

"Thank you." I walked to the door. I heard Raoul say, "She talks a Saxon dialect!"

Leaving the apartment I heard Gehzuweit's unhappy voice. "You're deceiving me!"

"Shut up!"

"I found you in the gutter . . . I've given you everything . . . and now . . . now you go to the Herbertstrasse, you lousy bum!"

"What did you call me?" And I heard a resounding slap. Gehzuweit squealed. Sobbing, he stuttered, "Oh, how mean you are to me. You've broken my pretty necklace . . ."

I opened the door. Outside stood a rachitic child, one

leg in an iron bar. He moved away from me slowly, looking at me, his eyes knowing and cunniing as those of the dead seagull.

7

My hands shook when I opened the black bag, took out the bottles and thermos, and fixed a large drink. The bag was on the seat next to me. I had parked the black Mercedes Jorkos Productions had put at my disposal at the lower end of the Reeperbahn. Neon lights, advertisements, pictures, and billboards tempted and extolled.

Genuine Paris nightlife, extravagant costuming. Eva, Paradise of the night. Continuous striptease. South American sex movies. Eat all you can for two marks. I had had the car brought from the hotel garage after Mrs. Gottesdiener had left. I had ordered whisky, soda and ice. I had taken my money from the hotel safe. I was certain that I would need a lot of money. Now I was here drinking while the storm raged around the Mercedes.

The weather had not kept the people away. The streets were crowded; men and women were pushing and shoving. Barkers stood in front of the bars, giving out leaflets, yelling and pulling undecided ones by their coatsleeves.

Lady Wrestlers in Mud. Lingerie Show. Taxi Girls. The Seven Deadly Sins. Pigalle. Nights in the Harem. The Bath in the Champagne Glass. Beauty Dances. Lola Montez.

I could hear the percussive force of riveting in the shipyards; the sounds of busy cranes, the bustle of the nightshift working as they did in industrial plants throughout this country, which lived in a fever, labored in a frenzy, enjoyed, earned and wasted.

Today! Today! What would tomorrow bring?

"Attack on Berlin means World War III, says Eisenhower . . ."

I saw sailors in the street, noisy, drunk; Chinese, Americans, Indians, Italian, Negroes. Girls laughed shrilly. Whores smiled lewdly. The wind wafted loud music from open entrance doors. Here they were greedy for the excitements of life. Today! Who knows what might happen tomorrow in Algeria, China, Mexico and India? What new disasters, dictators, wars could be expected?

Whistling, then howling and dying down to a high-pitched whine, a formation of jets raced across the harbor. And music flooded through the doors of the dance-halls.

Watching the flood of people pass by, I drank and grew calmer. I had to be very calm, very sure before going to the Herbertstrasse.

Better have another whisky.

8

Juveniles were standing outside the metal walls, trying to catch a glimpse of the bawdy-house street. They were prevented by the solicitors, all of a pattern, turned up collars, cigarettes dangling from lips, leaning against the enclosed entrances. My blue flannel overcoat, cuffless trousers, and short cropped hair was evidence that I was a foreigner. Half a dozen rushed toward me.

"Come with me, sir. First class yum-yum girls . . ."

"You want two girls?"

"Lesbians? Private show, just for you?"

I pulled one of the men into the street. The others remained. No one here interfered with another's business.

"You want the two girls?"

"No. There is supposed to be a blonde from Saxony. Her name is Käthe."

"What about her?"

"I want her."

"Why especially her?"

"Because I like her dialect."

He looked at me, then grinned. All kinds of gentlemen come here. "Give me ten marks and I'll take you to her."

The street was short, without sidewalks, paved with ancient cobblestones. The low paneled framework houses with little gables looked idyllic. At street level, each had large brightly lit windows at which sat half-naked women. Suitors knocked on the windows, called out laughing. Some girls signaled. Others were knitting. A redhead, dressed only in panties, sat in a velvet chair reading.

"Over here." My guide stopped at the entrance to a brothel. "Would you tell your mother I found you on the Reeperbahn? It doesn't matter to you. And I get a percentage."

Only after entering could one see how old the house really was. Low-beamed ceilings, creaking stairs, small upstairs windows. Worn furniture. Much velvet. Stained silken drapes, pornographic drawings. Photographs on buckling wallpaper.

The bar was crowded with singing, drinking men. A record player supplied music. Girls sat on men's laps. Couples walked up stairs to the second floor. Others were coming down.

I had hardly taken three steps when the Madam in a high-necked black dress embroidered with pearls welcomed me. She was stout but graceful and effusively polite.

"Bonsoir, Monsieur."

I indicated the pimp with my chin. "We had a beer. He says you have a girl here who talks with a Saxon dialect."

"Käthe, that's right. But you'll have to wait for just a little while."

"Good luck," said the pimp to me. And to Madam, "Don't forget me, mother."

"I have never forgotten even one single percent,

George," she said with dignity. Then she helped me out of my coat. "You have chosen a bad time, sir. Why didn't you come earlier? After lunch? Or after breakfast?"

"You are open that early?"

"We are always open," she said gravely. "Many gentlemen come regularly. Many before they go to their offices. A good husband has no time at night, isn't that so? Would you like to order some champagne while you are waiting?"

"If you would have a glass with me . . ."

She led me into another room with better furniture, many mirrors, and a heavy carpet. A huge waiter served. Mrs. Misere—Madam's name—drank, her little finger extended, smoked a cigar, and talked about her business.

"This is where we have our champagne breakfasts. We work in two shifts, you know. So some of the girls are always rested. Of course I always accept telephone reservations." The business was doing well; she could not complain. "Mainly tourists and sailors. But more and more gentlemen were coming now with their wives."

"The wives watch?"

"What do you mean? The gentlemen watch."

Madam Misere acquired this house in 1933. "My parents owned the Silver Ball. I'm sure you've heard of it."

"Unfortunately, no."

"That's strange, we were world-famous. The Danish King, Frederick the Eighth, died there."

"No!"

"But, yes! He was the king's grandfather. Heart attack. When he was with Edeltraut. That was the girl's name. Incidentally, she was from Saxony too. On May fourteenth, 1912. I was seven years old and lived with my grandparents. My parents came at night and talked about it. You just can't imagine the excitement. They closed off the house. Diplomatic couriers. I tell you, my parents were glad when they were rid of Frederick the Eighth.

And he had been a respected regular guest. Came every time he was in Hamburg. Naturally at that time no one knew he was his majesty." She laughed. "On the other hand, it was great advertising. Edeltraut was busy for months."

There was a knock. A voluptuous blonde entered. She was dressed to look like a little girl in a short skirt with suspenders. Her large breasts were visible through the open blouse. Her voice was affectedly high. "I was supposed to see you as soon as I could, Madam Misere." She curtsied to me. Madam emptied her glass, suggested we finish the champagne before going upstairs and excused herself.

"You like me, uncle?" Käthe played her part as an actress would after her hundredth performance. She was at most twenty-five years old, a pretty face, plump cheeks, pouting lips, a look of continual surprise in her wide eyes. She gave the impression of a generous nature and of naïveté.

"Yes, I like you."

"Cheers, uncle." Her dialect was indescribable. She wore flat shoes, ankle socks, a bow in her hair.

"I hope you are a good uncle. You know, I'm afraid. Because I'm still a little girl, I have never before—" She broke off and stared at the roll of money I pulled from my pocket. I gave her a hundred marks.

"This is for you. You can have more."

"Eh! But what do I have to do for that?" She pressed closer to me; now her breasts were outside her blouse. "Is it very bad what I have to do?"

"No."

"Whisper it into your little baby's ear . . ."

"You must tell me where Dr. Schauberg is."

The reaction was startling. She seemed so trusting and defenseless in her naïveté. At the mention of the name she paled and dropped her glass. It rolled across the carpet.

"Schauberg?" She had forgotten about her high-pitched voice, her childish manner. Now she was a ridiculously dressed up frightened woman. "I don't know any Dr. Schauberg!"

"Don't tell lies. Gehzuweit told me about both of you." She began to cry. "Don't be afraid, I'm not a cop." I gave her my passport. Only truth would help me now. Slowly she read, "Peter Jordan . . . you're an American?"

"Yes."

Haltingly she read, "Profession: Actor."

"Yes." Even twenty years later it said so in my passport. I had insisted on that every time my passport had been renewed.

"What . . . what do you want from him?"

"Then you do know him."

"Yes . . . no . . . please, leave me alone!"

"Don't cry. You know him: You love him, I know all that," I showed her the money. "He can make a lot of money. Look."

"I don't know where he is! You can lock me up! You can beat me! I don't know!"

"Here. Another hundred for you." I stroked her hair. She cowered. She had probably never known gentleness. Still fearful but already half-trusting, she looked up to me. "He is not in Hamburg . . ."

"But you do see him. He comes to see you."

"Yes . . ." Choked, she said, "We are engaged . . . we're going to get married. Walter gave me his word of honor. As soon as he gets ahead a little. Then I don't have to . . ."

I stroked her face with the money. "This would help him."

"I . . . I could call some of his friends, if it is really important."

"It is very important."

"Perhaps they would know where he is."

"Well, find out. Where is the telephone?"

"In Madam's office. But you must not come unless I call you."

"Okay. Tell his friends I have money. A lot of money." I drank a glass of champagne. Just in case. My car with my black bag was at the lower end of the Reeperbahn. For a man in my condition, even short distances became trying.

"Come, make the call," I said to Käthe. Champagne ran down my chin. I had drunk too fast.

9

Madam's office was next to the stairs. Through the glass in the upper part of the door, I saw Käthe make her call. When she put down the receiver and came to the door, her cheeks glowed with excitement.

"Come in. He'll call in a few minutes."

"Schauberg?"

"Yes."

The office was small. A typewriter and many binders in shelves gave evidence of a well-run business. We sat on an old couch. Käthe's blouse was still open. She looked at me, her hands folded. We could hear the noise and music from the bar.

"I hope it is true . . . that Walter can really earn some money . . . honestly, I mean . . ."

"Naturally, honestly."

"He doesn't do anything dishonest, you know."

"I know."

"I love him so. And I would love to get married." She sighed. "Naturally, something will go wrong."

"Why should it?"

"I'm just unlucky. He . . . he is well-educated, such a good man . . . a doctor . . . and I . . ."

Sadly, she chewed her lower lips. "I'm sure you've noticed what's the matter with me."

"What is the matter with you."

"I'm stupid. Clumsy. Every time I open my mouth, I talk nonsense. And I believe everybody. When I came to the West—"

"When did you escape?"

"Two years ago. I was a tram conductress in Leipzig. As soon as I arrived in the West, I fell for the greatest scoundrel."

"You did?"

"He was good-looking, had a big car. He promised me my own apartment and fifteen hundred marks a month. I was only supposed to perform as a dancer. After three weeks, he made me sleep with the guests who came to his joint. And beat me black and blue if I said no. I'm just too stupid, too stupid!" Sadly, she touched her hand to her forehead. "If I hadn't met Dr. Schauberg, who knows what else would have happened to me . . . Don't laugh!"

"I didn't laugh."

"I know what you're thinking. But I'm not like the others here. I have a future. I have his promise of marriage. The others don't have that."

Noise from above, and a woman screamed; I heard slaps.

"That's Nelly. Her fat guy is there today. He beats her."

"That's nice."

"It's only half as bad as it sounds. She puts on an act. If you knew what comes here . . . You should talk with the Mousetrap."

"Mousetrap?"

"That's what we call Olga. She has a very rich guy from Düsseldorf. He comes every month. Gives her anything she wants. He always brings some mice."

"What kind of mice?"

"Cute little white mice with red eyes. She has to put

them into the tips of her shoes and walk around until they are all dead. Olga is always sick for two days after he's been here. It upsets her stomach, you know. She feels so sorry for the poor little animals. Besides, she is always going to the doctor because of her toes."

The telephone rang.

Käthe jumped for the receiver.

"Hello!" She practically cowered when she heard his voice. "Yes, yes it's me, Walter . . . yes . . . I hope I did the right thing . . . here he is . . ." She held out the receiver to me. It was wet with perspiration.

"This is Peter Jordan."

"Good evening, Mr. Jordan." The voice was deep and somewhat mocking. I knew this voice. From where? "Were you in the movies when you were a child? Are you the famous child star?"

"Yes."

"You wanted to speak to me?"

"Yes." This voice. Why did it sound so familiar?

"Have you a car?"

"Yes."

"Käthe will explain how to go. I'm in Reinbeck. It is southeast of Hamburg. Just before you reach the village, you will see an old cemetery. Wait there for me."

"All right."

"Just one word of warning. Unless you are alone, you won't see me. You can be here in forty-five minutes."

I replaced the receiver. I asked Käthe to explain how to get there.

"Have you a piece of paper?"

I looked for some in my wallet. Shirley's photograph fell out. Käthe picked it up. "Is that your love?"

"Here is paper."

"I hope you are going to be happy with your love, if you'll really help Walter and me," said Käthe.

10

I drove toward Lübeck and Travemünde.

Houses now were lower, streetlights rarer. I saw few people. The waning moon shed its unreal light where no shadows seemed to exist. I drove along a canal, along railroad tracks. Roads were poorer now and had large potholes.

Then I passed the last houses. Tree trunks were close to the sides of the road, crippled, black, and fearsome. Locomotives whistled. Dogs barked. I drove through a few small villages. In the yellow light of my car beams, I read signs: ROTHENBURGSORT, TIEFSTACK, MOORFLETH. Out here, I heard the storm again, pushing and pressing against the car. The time on my dashboard showed eight-fifty.

I opened a window. It smelled of brackish water and peat. Then I saw the low white wall and beyond it stone crosses. The old wrought iron door was hanging crookedly in its hinges. I saw withered flowers, dead grass, and wreaths.

I stopped the car. I switched off my headlights and used the parking lights. Somewhere behind those tree trunks, behind that wall, was Dr. Schauberg who surely had good reason to be so cautious of his guests.

The storm chased leaves, branches, flowers across the cemetery. It brought to mind the cemetery scene when I, as a little boy, played Oliver Twist. That other cemetery had been built in the studio in California. Black earth had been brought. Machines made the storm, special-effects men, the fog. Lights with complicated lenses produced the eerie light. Only to the eye of the camera was that other cemetery deserted, for behind the lights, behind the machines, were about eighty people: electricians, prop men, script girls, cutters, my mother, my director, sound trucks, generators, mobile wardrobes.

And yet, at every new take that night, I had to fight fear and ice-cold terror which no one tried to calm. They were all delighted at how real my terror came across.

I did not only think of this while I was waiting here for Dr. Schauberg, but also of two hours last May. Of an afternoon when I replayed my Oliver Twist.

In Pacific Palisades, in the large house where I lived with Joan and Shirley, I had sixteen-millimeter copies of all my films, which I often watched in the viewing room.

On that hot afternoon in May, I watched my past, my Oliver Twist. Heavy drapes kept out the daylight, the life of 1959.

Inside, in the cool darkness, it was 1934. I, thirty-seven years old, on a couch next to the whirring projector, watched the silver screen where I, then twelve years old, a lonely, frightened Oliver Twist evading criminals, stumbled across that storm-whipped cemetery.

The door opened and closed.

I smelled Joan's perfume. She sat down on the couch with me. She often watched my old movies with me; Shirley, never.

"Shall I stop?"

"No. This is my favorite film." She felt for my hand and held it in her cool narrow hand. She moved closer and leaned against me; this woman I had once loved so much, whom I loved no longer.

"You're sure I'm not disturbing you, Peter?" She was especially considerate, especially loving, since she sadly watched our marriage deteriorate.

"Positive, Joan." I was considerate too.

"My plane does not leave for another three hours." I did not like the yellow dress she was wearing; it made her look older than she really was, simply because it was too youthful for her. Shirley could have worn it. But who could say that to a woman?

"I'll take you to the airport," I said. Joan had to go to New York for her aunt's funeral. An aunt who had left her a lot of money. Joan was forever inheriting. I could not accompany her. Herbert Kostasch, the producer from Hamburg, had sent a telegram which said, ". . . have sensational offer. *Come Back* practically certain." I was expecting him the following day.

Joan and I were sitting there, hand in hand. She probably thought how, since she loved me, she could save our marriage. I thought about how much I loved Shirley and that I could get a divorce if I made this film. And we both watched the twelve-year-old Peter Jordan, once the darling of the world.

There I escaped my frightening pursuers. There I starved in the orphanage. There I was with the mean Fagin who, with the help of a coat hung with little bells, taught me how to steal expertly.

Joan said gently, "Do you know you've never changed?" I turned down the sound. We both knew the dialogue by heart anyway. "You still have the humor, joy, thoughts of that boy up there on the screen. Those qualities distinguish you from all those other stupid, ruthless men."

Joan was beautifully groomed. Every hair in place; her make-up perfect. Everything was always perfect, I thought, exasperated. She was always right, now too. I had probably never grown up. Had I matured since making those movies? Not at all. Why did I always watch these old movies? Probably because I knew my best time had been when I was twelve years old.

"That is your charm, Peter, the little-boy appeal. That's what made me fall in love with you. My God, that was thirteen years ago; that's how long we have been living together . . ."

Thirteen years of doing nothing. Thirteen years of waiting. Thirteen years of whisky. Why did she have to bring all that up now?

"I don't know why I feel so sentimental. Maybe the plane is going to crash . . ."

"Nonsense."

"No one knows when one's hour will come. We . . . we were both so irritable lately. I wanted to apologize . . ."

"I should do that."

Oliver Twist took part in a burglary. Oliver Twist was caught. Maybe I had then been more grown-up than today?

Joan murmured, "I'm so much older than you. I ought to be smarter and realize that even a great love cannot remain constant. I don't mind, really . . . if only we stay together and grow old together . . ."

Grow old?

Why old? I had not even been young yet! What was I, after all? A child? A man in his waning years?

"I had warned you then; I reminded you of how much older I was . . ." Old. Older. Old. What is she getting at? "You were so wonderful! When I said, 'now it's all right but in fifteen years, when I have wrinkles . . .' do you remember what you replied?"

"What?"

"Then, we'll get you a face-lift!" She looked at me, her eyes moist. "That's what you said. All my friends were envious of me . . ."

I had said that. Now she had had a face-lift. And even though the operation had made her face smooth once more, to me she had seemed more youthful before. I had loved her laughter. Now she could not laugh as before because of that damn operation. It always reminded me of my mother. It is not good if a woman reminds a man of his mother. What an s.o.b. I was.

"You were wonderful . . . and we'll be happy again . . . an old married couple . . ." Old. Old. Old. Was she trying to hypnotize me using this word? "We have enough money . . ."

"You have!"

"But, Peter! Whatever is mine is yours too."

I could not stand this any more. She had succeeded. I lost my temper. "My life is not finished! It can't be! If I thought so, I'd kill myself!"

"But why?"

"Because I have produced nothing, because I have wasted all those years! Because I detest myself, so much so I can't look in a mirror!"

She was startled. Haltingly, she said, "You have produced nothing? Millions of people have been stirred by your talented performances. Talent is a gift which only few people possess and which cannot last forever. You have done enough, enough for your life to be fulfilled."

"No! No! No!"

"Why are you shouting?"

"Because it isn't true. Look at the screen! That is not acting. I was a handsome boy, nothing else! Today I could act! But no one gives me the chance. That is the cause of my irritability; the reason why our marriage is not as it was, nothing else." Shouting that, I actually believed it. "And that's why I'm waiting for Kostasch, that's why I'm going to accept whatever offer he makes. I'd accept anything if only I could act again!"

She averted her head.

"What's the matter?"

"I'm afraid of this Kostasch. Don't be angry but I'm hoping the movie will never be made."

"Joan!" Excitedly I jumped up.

"I'm frightened. I'm afraid I'll lose you when you make movies again . . ."

"So that's what it is! I was yours alone for all those thirteen years, confined in this goddamn house!"

"Good God, Peter!" In the dark, the beam of the projector separated and insulated us. We would never be together again. "I did not mean it that way!"

"Yes, you did."

"No, truthfully. I know who is destroying my marriage!"

"Who?"

"But I'm going to do something about it! She is not going to make me unhappy!"

"Who isn't?"

"Shirley!"

11

"Shirley?" Surprised I sat down. Was this a trap? Was I caught in it? What did Joan know? How much? Since when?

"Shirley is going to leave this house."

"But—"

"She'll be a cutter by Christmas. She will have to find herself a small apartment in Los Angeles."

"I don't understand . . ."

"You know perfectly well!"

Did the trap close?

"I do?"

"You are too good, too indulgent. I know what you put up with from Shirley." I was lucky it was dark. "For years you've put up with her outrageous behavior. You've ignored her hate."

"Well, you know, hate . . ."

How quickly one can recover!

"Yes, hate. She hates you. And you were always good to her; you've always hoped she would change . . ."

"Well, yes."

"And because you loved me you've never mentioned it. I know. And you know too. She is the actual reason for our problems. She drove you out of the house. Into the bungalow. I can thank my daughter that we do not sleep together any more!"

"Joan, really——"

"You had to listen to every fight. All our arguments. And after she had gone to bed we argued. You couldn't stand it any longer. She is going to leave the house by Christmas! I am not going to sit by and watch a hysterical teenager destroy my marriage just because she could not forgive my marrying again."

I took Joan to the airport in Los Angeles. I parked the car. It was very hot. The setting sun colored the sky blood-red. We ordered a whisky in the Horizon Bar; then her flight was announced. She kissed me good-by.

"We'll be alone again by Christmas, darling. I promise."

"Shirley is not the reason. It's the movie, my work, I told you!"

"I don't believe you. It is Shirley." She kissed me again. Softly, so as not to be overheard by the bartender, she said, "I know you are never going to leave me. But you are only thirty-seven. Perhaps . . . maybe you want to have a few affairs with . . . with younger women."

I could not answer.

"Go ahead, Peter, get it out of your system! I swear I really don't mind! Find yourself a few pretty young things. I know you'll always come back to me." She stroked my hand. "You'll tell me everything, I know; and you'll breakfast with me; we'll listen to music, go on trips and to the theater. And together with me you'll grow old . . ."

Then I watched her walk to the waiting plane. Again and again she turned and waved. I drank three whiskies one after the other. I was alone in the bar. The bartender did not know me. I could drink.

The Super Constellation began its take-off. I paid and went back to the parked car. It was now dusk. Sliding behind the wheel, warm naked arms encircled my neck; and full young lips found mine. Shirley's.

Shirley was sitting next to me, without make-up, breathless in skin-tight blue jeans and a sleeveless blouse.

She caressed my face, reached inside my shirt and caressed my chest. "I followed you in a taxi. I couldn't wait for you to return. I want to be with you every minute of these three days. Peter . . ." Her green eyes were dark and veiled. "We'll go straight home, okay?"

"Yes."

"I've dreamt of this. I've thought of nothing else for days . . ."

"I did too."

"Did it scare you very much when she suddenly spoke of me?"

"When?"

"This afternoon, when you were watching the movie."

"You were listening?"

"Yes."

"What did you hear?"

"Everything." Her voice was only a whisper. "Don't believe her, she says that just to rattle you . . . so you'll stay with her . . ." I could feel her young firm body through the blouse, through the tight pants as if she wore no clothes. "You are not a little big boy. For me you are the only man in the world. You know that there were others . . . boys and so-called men . . . men! It meant nothing with any of them! You . . . you made me a woman . . . only with you was it wonderful . . . so heavenly, I will never be able to love any other man . . . do you love me too? Tell me! Tell me!"

"I love you."

"She is always talking about getting old. You are not old! You are still young! She is afraid of Kostasch. I tell you, with Kostasch your life will begin! A new movie, a new career . . ."

"Yes."

"She hopes nothing will come of it. I pray you'll be working in a studio this year. Then let her send me away! We'll both go. Send me away!" Her voice shook. "That's all she could ever think of! That holds no threat for me any more! All my life she has sent me away, away from her!"

Shirley spoke the truth. She had been sent from one boarding school to another. Joan had always wanted to be free, especially after we were married.

"It sounds strange but I'm grateful that she never loved me, that she always pushed me from one place to another. Now my conscience does not torment me . . ."

But she was tormented: by her sin, her faith, her God, I knew. She was the most tormented of the three of us; she was the youngest and the most vulnerable. She was—

"Good evening." A deep, somewhat mocking voice broke into my thoughts. For a moment, my mind was blank but then I found myself in the present.

The storm was howling. My car was parked at the entrance of the little cemetery of Reinbeck. It was a cold night for October. A man looked at me through the open window of the car.

It was my father.

12

Naturally it could not have been my father.

My father died in 1941 in New York of uremia. So it could not have been my father.

But it was a man who bore a very strong resemblance to him. When my father went off with a chorus girl and left my mother and me, I was four years old and he, thirty-eight. He was a very handsome, dashing man with sparkling black eyes, a flashing smile, beautiful teeth and a little mustache. He liked to dress as a Frenchman and often wore a black beret. My father was always polite, flirted with the ladies and evaded any responsibility. It was my mother who had to take care of the three of us. How I admired my father then! He often brought candies and cakes which my mother could not afford to buy. I remember my mother once saying, "You love him more than me because he brings you candy. I can only give you bread."

It was after my father left us that I tried to hate him. But in my innermost thoughts I adored him until he died. He did whatever he wanted to do. He was very charming. Even a few months before he died, he was still pursued by women. He could have had almost anyone he wanted—at fifty-six. He did not try to contact us when I became famous and mother and I were rich. We knew he was living poorly and yet he did not come to us. No, he was very proud.

He was at mother's funeral and stood to one side. Now I should have hated him even more, now that mother was dead. Hate him? On the contrary. Now that mother was dead I did not see any reason at all to hate him. I tried to talk with him but at that moment he showed more character than I; he turned abruptly and left.

I had no pride about him at all in the following years. Repeatedly, I invited him to live with me in the large house in Pacific Palisades. He refused. "I need my freedom, you know, Peter." I would have liked to impress him more than anyone else, with my money, possessions, and fame.

"My son is very lucky," he told people. And when one of them admired my talent, he answered smilingly, "A child is only a child, not an actor." I was told this story and have never forgotten it.

He must have thought of himself as a talented actor but he never talked about that. Whenever he came to visit me, he was always friendly, always charming, and always aloof. He never stayed long. I transferred money to his account in New York where he lived. He was now working for a radio station. We corresponded, we telephoned and we saw each other from time to time. Then he was always accompanied by a different girl. Each seemed to adore him. He smiled; he took nothing and no one seriously. He called me "My dear boy," just as he would say "My poor wife." A young girl was with him when he died, not I who had long forgotten what he had done to my mother. From year to year my memory of him, a dark-haired man in shabby or expensive clothes but always looking like a gentleman, became more and more idealized.

With his casual elegance, his beret, reminding me of my father, this man looked at me through the car window and said, "Good evening."

His voice was soft and deep. Now I could understand why the voice had seemed so familiar on the telephone. I answered, "Good evening, Dr. Schauberg."

"May I see your passport?"

I gave it to him and he read it in the light of the dipped headlights. It was uncanny how much he resembled my father! He wore an old coat, the collar turned up.

"Fine. Now, what is it you want?"

"I can't tell you that out here on the street."

"You'll have to tell me here or not at all, my dear Mr. Jordan." ("My dear boy." My father again.)

"I'm ill. The day after tomorrow I am going to be examined by the doctor of an insurance company. Could you fix me up so I'll get through the examination?"

"What's wrong with you?"

"Heart. Liver. Circulation."

"Are you a drinker, my dear Mr. Jordan?"

"Yes."

"Have you been examined by a doctor in Germany?"

"No," I said. "Only in the U.S."

"You're lying."

"It's the truth," I lied.

He hesitated.

"Do you think I'm that crazy? To attempt an insurance fraud if a doctor had examined me here in Germany?"

That did it.

"The moment I have the slightest suspicion, I'll stop treating you."

"All right." Natasha Petrovna was leaving for Africa in two days. Or I would not have risked it.

"Do you have money?"

"Yes." I showed him a roll of bills. He walked around the car, his coat flying in the wind, his old trousers baggy, his shoes dirty. He opened the car door and got in.

"Drive through the village. Then make a right. What's in the bag?"

"Whisky."

"How convenient. You don't mind if I help myself."

13

The high barbed wire fences had toppled. The barracks were without windows, doors, or roofs. The paths, overgrown with weeds. Against the moonlit sky, I saw a watchtower, broken flagpoles, a parade ground with cracked cement surfacing.

"This is where you live?"

"This is where I work, dear Mr. Jordan."

We had left the road at Reinbeck and had driven into the open country. For a while, we followed the rain-swollen, fast-flowing Elbe. I saw two roadsigns. CURSLACK 6 KILOMETERS, said one, NEUENGAMME 17 KILOMETERS, the other.

Now we had reached the broken entrance doors of a deserted camp.

"I have a room in the Goldenen Anker in Reinbeck," said Schauberg getting out of the car. "But I work here. I'm sure Mr. Gehzuweit told you what happens if one does not keep those things separate. We'll have to walk a little now; I'll carry the bag."

Schauberg walked fast. I saw more and more barracks, groups of trees, a little lake, a dynamited air-raid shelter.

"And you're not afraid someone might surprise you at your . . . work?"

"No one even comes here. The few farmers around fall silent went the camp is mentioned. They wouldn't come even if there were buried treasures."

"Why not?"

"They are superstitious. They say the dead walk here. Have you any idea how many are buried over there, near the woods? Thousands and thousands!" The barge whistle came to us from the nearby river. "There were camps outside almost every large German city. Another seventeen kilometers and you'll be at the concentration camp Neuengamme. But no one in our beautiful country knew of those camps. Even the Führer himself did not know. Right outside our cities . . . And we? Concentration camp? Never heard of it. First we heard of them was in 1945. Everybody only did his duty . . ."

We passed a second shelter and more and more paths and trees.

"The farmers here had a parish priest who upset them. He told them, unless the living did not honestly repent, the dead would not rest."

"And?"

"So today, fifteen years later, they are still afraid. This camp is twenty-three years old! The Nazis built it in 1936. The location is good. Near Hamburg and yet isolated. So in 1936, they sent Communists, socialists, Jehovah's Witnesses. Watch out, there is a bomb crater. Can you walk a little farther?"

"I guess so."

"We're almost there. Then, when the war started, the political prisoners were removed and it became a POW camp. Poles and Czechs, Belgians, Dutch, French, English. Then in 1943, these people were moved to Flensburg and the camp here was used as a stockade for the Luftwaffe. Subverting the military potential—you remember? Oh, I forgot, you're an American. Your comrades-in-arms, incidentally, the British, were just as impressed by the ideal location and used the camp for big shots. At that time, it was crowded with Gauleiter and SS."

"Not for very long, I expect."

"Only until the change in our monetary system, naturally. Then the gentlemen had to return to politics and economy. Just a moment." He stopped at a heap of stones and hurriedly removed stones, pieces of cement and bricks. In a little while, he had cleared the entrance to a little cavern and pulled out a green metal box with the inscription *United States Army*—Rainbow Division. It had a heavy padlock. "Help me carry it."

"What is it?"

"My tools. I can't leave anything in the barrack." Between us, we dragged the box along. The air vibrated with the noise of jets zooming across us.

"Night exercises. Happens often. It's not far to the East Zone." We had reached a barrack with shutters. It also had a roof and a door which Schauberg opened now. He entered; I followed. "Shut the door." For a moment it was dark. Then an oil lamp shed its light on an army bed, a table, three chairs, an oilstove. Long-legged spiders ran along the beam from which the lamp was hanging.

Schauberg took off his old coat. With a sweeping gesture he said, "It's going to be warm in a moment. You can get undressed."

I looked at my watch.

It was nine-fifty-five.

14

I was sitting on the bed. Schauberg had just examined me and was now fixing two large drinks from my black bag. The green box, filled with instruments, syringes, medications, bandages, and a few books, was now open. There was even a microscope. Schauberg offered me the drink.

"Well, cheers."

"Prosit. Well?"

"Fifty thousand."

"You're crazy."

In his frayed trousers and worn shoes, he was leaning against a beam in the manner of a lord leaning against a fireplace. "The drink is good. Naturally, the fifty thousand will cover the entire treatment. Just fixing you up for the insurance company will not be enough. You'll need my help to finish your movie too."

"And you think you can do it?"

"For fifty thousand, I can."

He was still wearing his beret.

"I'm not going to pay that much."

"Is there enough ice in your drink? Tell me, dear Mr. Jordan, how much would your company lose if you couldn't make the movie?"

"I'll give you twenty thousand marks."

"Fifty."

"Twenty-five."

"Fifty."

"Thirty."

"Get dressed. We'll drive back to Reinbeck," he said with my father's tired, ironical voice. I suddenly felt my father really had been a miserable character!

"Okay," I said. "Okay. I'm not going to be blackmailed." I got up and reached for my shirt. The room spun around me and ridiculously close, I saw the long-legged spider near the oil lamp.

The fist.

I broke out in sweat and dropped my shirt. My mouth stood open. Breathing hard, I stared at Schauberg.

"What's the matter, dear Mr. Jordan?"

"This fear . . . I'm . . ."

He sipped his whisky. "Fear is a subjective concept, you know. You don't actually feel this fear now. You are at most afraid of this fear."

My legs buckled. I fell on the bed. The fist rose. I stammered. "You're a doctor . . . help me . . ."

"You really must pull yourself together!"

"Fear . . . this fear . . ."

"Fear of what?"

"I don't know . . . to die . . ."

"We all die. But not just yet. You're not going to die right now, I promise."

I reached for my drink; it slipped from my hand. Whisky spilled on the dirty floor. Schauberg said, "I hope you'll make it home all right. You don't honestly believe you can shoot even one single scene in your condition. Not to mention the insurance examination."

I closed my eyes. I thought of having to walk to my car and driving back to Hamburg. I knew I could never make it. Here, here in this dirty room, I would suffer another attack soon. Now. I knew I could not go through it again. Slowly I opened my eyes. Schauberg stood there, a little sympathetic, a little arrogant, just like my father when he had seen my Spanish-style house. I whispered, "Thirty-five . . ."

"Dear Mr. Jordan, don't think I want to torture you. As soon as we come to an agreement, I'll help you. Immediately. But I need fifty thousand. You know my circumstances. I must leave Germany. For you, everything is at stake—well, for me too." A moment ago I had seen a spider. Now I could not see any. I groaned. Had there never been spiders? Had there really been a dead seagull at the hotel?

"I know you are going to be reasonable," said Schauberg. He kneeled before the metal box, searched for a certain box and readied an injection. "You don't have to pay fifty thousand now. Listen. Right now, you give me three thousand. Two after I get you through the insurance examination. That's worth the money, isn't it? And the forty-five thousand, we'll divide by the weeks you have to make the movie." He expelled the air from the syringe. My breathing was quick, shallow. "You'll pay me the end of each week you've successfully completed with my help. If you collapse, the agreement is void. I can't be any fairer than that. Consider that I risk prison helping you." He came to the bed, the syringe ready. "Well?"

"And . . . you . . . can . . . really . . . help . . . me?"

"Would I suggest this if I didn't think I could?"

Damn, what was fifty thousand if he could help me? If he did not, I would need half a million. This character was clever and cunning. He would surely help me. Then I would have my chance to make the movie. To get my divorce. To have Shirley. Damn, what was fifty thousand?

"Then, you agree?"

"Okay . . ." My head lolled to one side. .

He really did not want to torture me, he just needed the money. His position was as bad as mine. He injected my arm. "Now," he said smiling, "if in five minutes you don't feel as well as if you were perfectly healthy, you don't have to have any trust in me."

Five minutes later, I felt better than ever before.

15

I know it sounds incredible.

But it was true. Five minutes later I felt no more fear, no pain, no depression. I felt great. With this doctor to help me, I could do anything!

"What did you give me?"

"You don't have to know everything." He smiled. He looked for some instruments in his box. He was working methodically now. It was hard to believe this man was a drug addict and his wife had killed herself.

The oilstove was humming; the storm rattled the shutters of the barrack. Schauberg used a large syringe and took blood from the vein in my other arm. He removed the needle and divided the blood into three test tubes. He put patches over the needle marks on my arms. Then he took blood from the tip of my thumb. He set the test tubes aside. "Now, for some urine."

I got up.

I felt like singing, embracing a woman, fighting against the storm. With every breath, I felt better, more optimistic, stronger. Fear? I had been afraid? Laughable. Surprised, I said, "You've really helped me."

"That was not difficult. How long before your film is finished?"

"Forty-three shooting days are estimated."

"That's going to be more difficult. Early tomorrow morning, you will go to the Hamburg Polyclinic to get an electrocardiogram. I must know how much your heart can take."

"But my name—"

"Social Welfare. Anyone can go there. They won't ask for identification. You don't mind if I help myself to another drink? Thank you. They will give you the cardiogram. Country doctors don't always have the necessary equipment, you know. Would you like another drink too?"

"Please."

"As soon as you have the cardiogram, you come right out here. Leave your car in Reinbeck and walk the rest of the way. I need you for injections and all that."

"You start tomorrow?"

"We start tonight. Every hour counts. Now we must concentrate on the insurance examination. Everything else will come later." Feeling good now, I could look at him more objectively. I almost felt the effort his intensely active mind was making to avoid any possible mistake. Apparently it sapped his energy. His vitality alternated with short periods of fatigue. He sometimes looked like a person in neon lighting. Had he used morphine? Probably. How long would the effect last?

"First we have your edema, which is retention of fluid in the tissues. Drink does that. You have it mostly in your legs. Thank God we have some excellent diuretics which will get rid of the fluid. Take two tablets now and another two every three hours until the examination. Drink it down with whisky."

"You think the edema will be gone in two days?"

"At any rate it will be much less noticeable. Now, every six hours, you'll also take two nitroglycerine tablets." He raised his hands. "I'm a poor man, I was not prepared for your treatment. I do not have all the medication I need."

"Yes?"

"I'll have them tomorrow, don't worry. Diphenylamine derivatives and other wonderful, expensive things. Before the examination, I'll give you a large dose of strophantin. In a week or two, your heart will be much better. Unfortunately, there is not much one can do in a day. It is very difficult to substitute an EKG. But we have to risk it.

116

Your heart is not bad. The insurance won't reject you for that. Your liver is in worse shape."

"Can you do anything about that?"

"Nothing at all."

"Then, what?"

"So the doctor will order tests. Which means they will take blood the way I just did."

"And?"

"Mostly, this is done by a nurse. I'll explain how; possibly it can be substituted. I'm going to give you healthy blood when you go for your examination. As soon as I know your blood group, I'll look for a suitable donor."

"Where?"

"At Madam Misere's in the Herbertstrasse. The girls there are all healthy. I will give you suitable urine too."

"If the blood groups match, no one can prove anything?"

"No one." His red face now paled. He drank. Now he was red again. "I'll have to calm you down and speed you up at the same time for the examination. I'll give you those pills for the moment."

"What are they?"

He smiled. "You'll find out. Two every three hours. Take two now." I swallowed them. "Don't ever take more. Don't be surprised if suddenly you should feel the urge to set the world on fire."

"I felt like that after your injection."

"Go ahead and go to the Herbertstrasse. But don't think it is going to last six weeks. There will be other periods. Now. Your blood pressure. It is much too high. I'll have to get some more medicines to bring it down. Where, by the way, is the money?"

I counted out thirty hundred-mark bills and placed them on the table. The last two slipped from my hand and fell to the floor. He bent down to pick them up and his beret fell off. From his forehead to the back of his head, through the gray short hair, ran a deep red shiny scar. It was so deep I could see the blood pulsating.

Schauberg picked up his beret and the bills. He looked strange now: up to the hairline he was a ladies' man and playboy; above the hairline, a devastated, horrible victim of the war. "Russia," said the charming monster. "Doesn't hurt any more, but at first it brought me to morphine." He put away the bills and put on his beret. Now I could see my father in him again, darling of the ladies, the man without worries or troubles. "To each his own," said Dr. Schauberg.

16

Jets again roared above the barracks. The glasses on the table tinkled. Schauberg raised his glass and looked up to the ceiling. "To a third time, then, gentlemen!"

"Listen, will your treatment be very harmful to me?"

"Did you expect to become healthier?"

"And if I die?"

"You can still stand a lot."

"All right. Okay. And if I do die?"

"Then we both lost." He pulled at his mustache. "Dear Mr. Jordan, you know I'm not a qualified doctor now. I'll tell you exactly what's wrong. I'm not concerned with ethics or morals. I hope you appreciate that."

"Naturally."

"So. You came to me; I did not come to you. Don't be dramatic. I'm not Satan tempting you. I'm merely an experienced mechanic—excuse the comparison—who is fixing up a car, a very damaged car, so no one detects the fraud when it is sold. Of course, in six weeks you will feel worse than today. Naturally, then you'll have to go to a hospital."

"And you really believe I will regain my health then?"

118

"Organically, you will be healthy."

"Does that mean—"

"I don't think you can be cured of your alcoholism. In ninety percent of those cases, it is hopeless. I, myself, have gone through several cures."

"Then, I will die of my illness?"

"Not necessarily. Morphine is not going to kill me either."

"Most people die as a result of their addiction."

"Because most people are stupid," he said. "Because most people have no structure. Take my poor wife."

"My poor wife." Just like my father! "She had no structure at all. Unfortunately." His face changed color again; every word seemed to be an effort. "But you have structure. Why? You are intelligent. You are strong enough to be realistic. You will understand that there is no cure. And you will learn what I've learned."

"Which is?"

"To live with the addiction. To control it, to limit it, to be as strong as it. It's a kind of marriage."

With a feeling of relief, I was suddenly aware that this man was crazy. As long as I could not detect any signs of anomaly, I had felt ill at ease. How reassuring that Dr. Schauberg was no superman. Though probably his theory of humans with structure was only one step removed from a religion of drug-addicted supermen.

I thought: The last war has destroyed more brains than buildings.

He was leaning against the beam, brilliant in his diseased intellectuality. Solicitously he said, "So, for God's sake, don't try to stop drinking while I'm treating you."

"I'm supposed to carry on drinking?"

"You must, dear friend. Within limits, if you can. You would just waste your energy—which you'll need for other things."

I finished my drink.

"During the next few weeks, we'll talk more. That will be the most important part of the treatment."

"What will?"

"My—I don't want to sound cynical, but I can't think of a more suitable word—my care of your soul, dear Mr. Jordan." He placed one hand on my shoulder and smiled. "You must not have any secrets from me. We're in the same boat. You'll have to trust me as one brother another. Or better: as a son, his father?"

As a son, his father?

17

Music came from the car radio when, at ten-twenty, I passed the dilapidated cemetery again. I heard Louis Armstrong's trumpet, his hoarse voice. I whistled the song which had now been on the American Hit Parade for three years. Schauberg's injections were working. I drove too fast, I could tell by the potholes.

So what. Who cared?

"I feel like a million." That had been the title of one of my movies. I felt like a million. Like a million which had been saved, thanks to Dr. Schauberg. I had left him in his barrack working with his instruments and equipment. A clever man. An anomalous man. I did not need a normal man now. As long as he was clever. And that he was.

I did not know Hamburg. Still I found the right roads through the dark suburbs which, fifteen years later, were still destroyed and in ruins. The incessant jets of a new German Luftwaffe roared above them.

By the time I arrived at the hotel the storm had calmed down. I found a parking space right away. Humming, I got out of the car, the black bag in my hand. The reflection of thousands of lights glittered on the Alster.

Humming, I crossed the street and entered the hotel.

A bellboy took my bag.

The foyer was crowded with people from all nations. "Ladies and gentlemen, the bus to the airport is about to leave." I stood, humming, and let them pass.

"Mr. Jordan."

I turned and saw Dr. Natasha Petrovna.

I had completely forgotten her.

"I have been waiting for you since eight o'clock." Natasha wore a dark red, easy-fitting dress. A beige flannel coat was thrown across her chair. She looked pale and angry. "It is almost eleven now. I would have notified the hotel manager at eleven that you were dangerously ill and missing."

Everything had gone so well. And now—

"You are very ill. You promised you would stay in bed." Her blue-black hair glistened in the light of the chandelier above her.

"Yes, but I had to—"

"You broke your promise." Why was she so incensed? Why was she so excited? She was capable of going to the manager. Or to Kostasch. In two days she was leaving Germany. But even in only two days she could destroy everything. I remembered Schauberg: "The moment I become suspicious, I'll discontinue treatment."

Then what?

Smiling, I said, "I'm fine again, Doctor."

"I don't believe that."

"Really."

"I would like to examine you once more," she said, looking steadily at me with half-closed shining black eyes.

I don't want to appear better than I am, but truthfully, it gave me a jolt seeing those veiled prompting eyes. I thought: So I really have to continue my path from one meanness to another?

I had seen eyes like that. I knew the meaning of such looks.

18

At sixteen I fell in love with an older married woman. Her husband, once a director, hoped to find new work through me. He encouraged me to enjoy his hospitality, though, without a doubt, he knew I admired his wife. I had arranged to drive him to the studios. When I reached his house, his wife came to the door in a dressing gown. Her husband had left unexpectedly; he would be away for a few days. I felt hot and cold when her black eyes, veiled and half-closed, looked at me. I had kissed girls before, petted in parked cars, but I had never possessed a woman up to then.

Her long silk robe partly revealed her breasts. She did not smile. She merely looked at me. I took one step forward. She was still warm with sleep. I kissed her awkwardly. She took my hand and silently led me to the bedroom. Her moist, half-closed eyes said: Come.

A few more times, woman's eyes met mine in that manner—at parties, once in a club in Las Vegas, once on board ship. The look was always identical. And now, on this night of the twenty-seventh of October, Natasha Petrovna looked at me the same way.

We only met this morning. Natasha had seemed cool and reserved. She ought to have been revolted by me. And still. She had waited almost three hours for me. Could a doctor have that much professional interest in a new patient? Was not this more the deep interest of a woman attracted to a man? It did not make sense; it was improbable. But what was—or is—probable, what absurd, between a woman and a man?

Natasha had the same look as that first woman had had. And I was certain; certain and shocked, as far gone as I was. I thought: Then must I continue on my path from one meanness to another?

19

I am not a writer. I am not the hero in a novel. Free of ambition and fear, I can report the truth. The truth you demand of me, Professor Pontevivo. The truth shows me to be repugnant and without conscience.

Yet, what does that mean; without conscience?

I loved Shirley. I was determined to do anything to be able to marry her. There was nothing I would not have done. Natasha Petrovna was a threat to our love. I had to remove that threat. I thought to avert the danger when I saw her eyes. Whatever medication Schauberg had given me, now it gave me strength and arrogance, courage and cynical desperation. I did not like doing what I was about to do—but I did it.

Natasha meant nothing to me, a strange, beautiful woman. Shirley meant everything to me. I did it for her—for our love. Not only the purest and noblest deeds are done in the name of love, but also the basest and most infamous.

20

I switched the lights on in my apartment. I took Natasha's coat. Intentionally, I brushed against her arm and she started as if she had received an electric shock. I was so sure, so completely certain . . .

My glance caught sight of my stepdaughter's portrait and silently I said: You know that I love only you. Since we found each other I do not look at another woman. I am not deceiving you. What I'm about to do, I do to safeguard us.

Shirley's eyes seemed to say: Yes, I know.

It was warm in the apartment. After the dirty house near the Fischmarkt, the brothel, the weird camp, this luxurious apartment reinforced my self-confidence.

While I hung Natasha's coat on a velvet-covered coathanger, she took instruments from her black bag. Her back was turned when she began to speak. "I'm sure you are surprised that I waited three hours for you and that I became so upset over your irresponsible behavior." She turned and again I saw the eyes of that first woman in my life. "For years I lived with a man who was very much like you, Mr. Jordan." She was a decent woman. First she had to explain. This first woman had given her explanation afterward. "I've never done anything like this before, darling. But my husband neglects me . . ."

I asked Natasha, "Shall I get undressed?"

"Just take off the shirt, please. Shall we go into the bedroom?"

Yes, let's go to the bedroom.

"This man was a painter, Mr. Jordan. An artist like you . . ."

An artist like me, I thought, opening my shirt. What incredible luck I had! Probably I did remind Natasha of this man.

". . . and he was an alcoholic like you."

An alcoholic like me. I switched on the radio on the bedside table. Melancholy, sentimental jazz.

"I tried everything to rid him of his need for alcohol." It was probably true. She did not seem like a woman who did something like this frequently. I could see she was upset and troubled. This beautiful, self-controlled Russian woman was troubled by her memories, her love. That is why she had waited. That is why she was here now.

I took off my shirt.

124

"I was not able to save him. He died of delirium tremens. He was thirty-nine years old."

"You must have loved him very much."

She merely nodded. And continued to look at me with damp veiled eyes. From the radio came music, played only by violins.

I had to do it. She was leaving Saturday. Two nights and two days with her. She would think of the dead man; I, of Shirley. No matter who would be in our thoughts. She would not give me away. She would leave for Africa. Perhaps there she would sometimes remember our affair. Nonsense. She would remember the man I resembled.

Natasha stood close to me. I put my arms around her.

"What are you doing? Let me go!"

I kissed her. My body strained against hers. I heard her moan and thought I had not been wrong. She squirmed in my arms, tried to push me away. Naturally, I thought, being decent, she had to try.

"Have you gone crazy?"

I held her tight. My lips kissed her cheeks, her neck, her lips.

"I'll scream! If you don't let go, I'll scream!"

She would never scream. Never. Another few seconds and she would dispense with her feigned resistance and sink down on the bed with me, return my kisses, give in to the longing her body craved as much as her memory.

Suddenly, I felt a sharp pain. She had kicked my shin bone. I jumped. She was able to free one arm and pulled it back sharply, hitting my nose with her elbow. The pain was paralyzing. Since she had not intended to hit me, the force was all the stronger. Blood poured from my nose. I reeled.

21

"I'm sorry. It was your own fault. Please lie down. Your head a little lower, please," Natasha Petrovna was calm, completely in control. She pushed her glasses into place.

"Natasha, please——" I blushed with shame. I must be insane. What had I done? But there also was fear. What would she do now?

She went to the bathroom and returned with a wet towel. She placed it on my face. She inserted a piece of cotton wool into my bleeding nostril. Her slanted eyes were large, clear, serious and without anger. A moment ago they had looked very differently at me. I could not understand it.

"You don't understand it, Mr. Jordan." Natasha cleaned off the blood from my face, neck, chest. "Everything seemed simple to you. You make love to me. I will not give you away. You will go ahead with what you intend to do."

"What do I intend to do?"

"You intend to finish your movie with the help of an unscrupulous doctor not afraid to drug and dope you." The cotton wool plug in my nose impeded my breathing. I was lying there with my mouth open. "Downstairs in the foyer I became suspicious. I just came up to be certain. Now I am convinced." Her eyes left my face and I followed her glance by raising myself a little.

I saw what she saw: those two adhesive patches Schauberg had put over the punctures the syringes had made.

I had not remembered to remove them. What an idiot I was. I sank back on the pillow.

22

Natasha said, "The man with whom I lived also found such a doctor. And died the most horrible death. He could not be saved. And neither can you, Mr. Jordan. I realize that now."

I remained silent. I admired her. She was everything I had never been, never would be, and always wished I could have been.

"You thought me to be an uninhibited woman ready to indulge herself. I'll do that by not paying any more notice to you." With that, she went into the drawing room.

I threw the towel into the bathroom and jumped up. Five steps and I had reached her. I grabbed her shoulder. "My movie . . . I must finish it . . . If you're not going to keep quiet—"

"I won't say anything."

"Not to anyone? Ever?"

"Ever. I have no interest in you any more. You have chosen another doctor. Listen to him. Make your movie. And perish."

"Doctor, I—"

"Take your hand off me. Right now."

"Please, forgive me."

"There is nothing to forgive."

"You must hate me now."

"I don't hate you, Mr. Jordan. I feel sorry for you." She took her bag and walked to the door. Taking her coat from the hanger, she turned once more. "The alcohol has done more damage to you than you realize."

"That's not true."

"Yes, it is, Mr. Jordan. Your heart cannot feel. Your mind is corrupt. You expect all people to be primitive and egotistical which you yourself are. It's a pity. Good night."

The door closed behind her. Only the scent of her perfume lingered.

I looked at Shirley's photograph and felt very much relieved. I had avoided one meanness. Whatever Natasha's opinion of me, I had not relished the thought of committing it. Now the mean deed remained undone and still I had achieved my goal. Silently I said to Shirley: Your God protects us both in strange ways. If He exists.

I went to the bathroom and carefully removed the plug from my nose. The bleeding had stopped. I washed, put on my robe, and from the black bag fixed a strong drink.

I took out the pills Schauberg had given me. I swallowed the ones I was supposed to take every two hours and set an alarm clock for the three-hour pills. I took my drink to the drawing room and sat looking at Shirley's portrait. The radio played softly.

I love you Shirley; I love you with all my heart.

I only intended to finish my drink and then go to bed. I had to be up early. But the music was lovely and I had another drink and, because I had escaped a misdeed, another. I felt very satisfied with this day, with Dr. Schauberg, with me, my whisky, and Natasha Petrovna's promise.

The thought that I had not been wrong about her would not leave me. Her eyes had been inviting and ready to surrender.

Ah, well, I would never see her again. Our relationship had ended before it began.

I was to see her again. Soon. A curious togetherness was awaiting us. And one night in my arms she was to whisper, "You had not been wrong. I had been willing . . ."

The Third Tape

1

Rome, March seventeenth, 1960.

It is so hot; one could well believe it to be the middle of summer. Pink and white roses wind themselves around the trunks of the old palm trees in the park surrounding the hospital. Gardeners with straw hats and green aprons tend the grounds. They talk with the carabinier guarding me. I know them all now and they know me. They smile and wave when they look up to my window and see me. I have requested that there always be Chianti and cigarettes for them in the kitchen. The policemen wear tropical helmets and white uniforms.

Now the guard opens the high wrought-iron gate to admit a small slender lady. I know her. She is the wife of the composer-addict. She always dresses in black, her face hidden by a veil hanging from a black hat. She walks slowly, sedately through the park as if following a hearse. She always brings a basket filled with oranges which, in contrast to so much black, seems even brighter.

She visits him often. The nurses say she is a good influence. Always after she has been to see him, he composes for hours. Suora Superiora Maria Magdalena often listens outside his door. Blushingly she declared, "It is love, Signor Jordan. He never plays better than after she has been to see him."

Only two weeks ago I began to entrust the story of my crime to the tape recorder. It will take many more weeks to complete it. "Take your time," says Professor Pontevivo. "You have all the time in the world." I share his opinion. I like being here. I am in no hurry to go to jail.

For the present the professor and his staff are working mainly to rebuild my body. Though talking to the tape recorder is a small part of my therapy. I receive many injections and treatment. Since I came here, almost eleven weeks ago, I have not had alcohol in any form. I do not miss it. I am just very weak and cannot sleep without medication. But I am not afraid any more. Not for the last five weeks have I been afraid.

I give the tapes to the hunch-backed Suora Superiora. They are transcribed as soon as possible. Since Professor Pontevivo has not mentioned the steadily growing manuscript I asked him yesterday, "Do you find my confession instructive?"

He is small, olive-complexioned, white-haired, rosy-cheeked, with a gentle voice. He wears gold-trimmed glasses. He had once worked in the United States and his English was fluent. "Every confession is informative, Mr. Jordan."

"Perhaps I ought to be more specific in certain matters?"

"I can understand your impatience," he answered. "You want to help us cure you. That is essential, too. I have noticed three things. One: you are always running yourself down."

"I am bad."

"You fell victim to alcohol. Someone inexperienced would only see the typical symptoms of degeneration of the addict: immorality, antisociality, apathy, egocentricity, inability to communicate."

"There you are!"

132

"Only someone inexperienced would say that, Mr. Jordan. Though drinkers hold themselves in low esteem and tend to self-accusation, they also find excuses. Not you. It is my impression that you, by continually excusing and humiliating yourself, are trying to relieve yourself of some pressure. It seems to be another way of repentance."

"Second?"

"You seem loath to escape from the past which is still so close to you, one could almost call it present. You very rarely speak of your real past, of ten or twenty years ago. You touch on it, that's all."

"But I talk about everything!"

"Not at all. You mention that you once loved your wife very much. Fine. But in the one hundred and eighty pages I have read, you had not one good word for her; you only spoke of her with ennui, irritation and aversion."

"I told you I was bad."

"No one is bad. Why did you love your wife? When did you stop loving her? You said your stepdaughter hated you. What changed this hate into love? Why did you fall in love with Shirley?"

"I thought I was quite explicit."

"But I don't believe you. For a complicated man such as you, the physical attraction is not always the most important." He wagged his finger. "Don't think I don't know! You have a lot left to tell me, Mr. Jordan. You, too, have motives and excuses. No one is all bad. There is good in all of us."

"Not in me."

"In you too. Once you mentioned how much your stepdaughter resembled another girl. Who was this girl? What did she mean to you?"

He noticed I paled and a muscle in my face began to twitch. Immediately he said, "We're in no hurry, Mr. Jordan. I just wanted to show you that you only spoke of events. You have never touched on the roots of your life. I am very sure that, for instance, this girl is one of the roots of your life. This girl—not your stepdaughter who is so much like her."

I stared at him.

One sentence in one hundred and eighty pages mentioned Wanda. And right away he had recognized the truth.

Wanda.

I've said her name now. For the first time in many years. And I had sworn I would never say her name again. And I never wanted to even think of her—

Wanda.

What is Professor Pontevivo doing? He is right. It all began with Wanda. When she—

I don't want to talk about it.

I must. I must force myself to talk about her. I must confess that I—

I cannot.

Perhaps one day I will. Perhaps one day I will be able to.

Wanda—

No, I cannot. Not yet.

2

"Third?" I asked Professor Pontevivo and touched my twitching cheek.

"Thirdly, I noticed that more and more of your past comes into your story."

"What do you mean?"

"For instance. You say Dr. Schauberg bore an uncanny resemblance to your father."

"He did."

"Perhaps he did. Perhaps the resemblance was not great. Perhaps the resemblance in reality was very minor. But what is reality? Whatever one experiences, right? Perhaps, in retrospect, you believed the doctor to have this resemblance so it would be easier to talk about your father. You had a difficult relationship with him."

"Yes."

"You are reluctant to talk about him. He, too, is part of your real past. You also have a need to talk about him. Subconsciously you then built yourself a bridge by insisting on his resemblance with Dr. Schauberg."

Professor Pontevivo smiled. "There are many such instances, dear friend. It shows we are on the right track. Your brain is not damaged, the first tapes prove that."

"I'm not crazy?"

"If you were, there would not be so many logical connections in your confession." The muscle in my cheek ceased to twitch. "You are fighting a very difficult inner battle. You are attempting to resolve something in a few weeks which you haven't been able to all your life."

"Namely?"

"Your life. When you have exposed the roots of your existence and you realize that your life could not have been any different under such conditions, then you will be cured of your need for alcohol. Now, be patient. Can the damage of twenty years be undone in eleven weeks? Well, you see. So, go on telling your story. What took place after the twenty-seventh of October, Mr. Jordan?"

3

The next morning, Professor, I awoke at seven and took the pills which were due then. I showered and ate breakfast and took the pills due at eight. Finally I called my producer in his hotel in Düsseldorf. I found out that he would not be in Hamburg until the following afternoon. My examination was for the morning. He had obtained permission to shoot the movie in the locations he had chosen. Since there was nothing important scheduled for the morning, I requested the afternoon off.

I took a few more pills and went to the polyclinic. I had dressed as inconspicuously as possible. In the waiting room were half a dozen people. My turn came very quickly. A nurse asked: "Name?"

"Hanz Wolfram, Bendesdorf, 4 Schlangenbaumstrasse." I received a number which was called.

They gave me the electrocardiogram in a sealed envelope which Schauberg opened as soon as I arrived. It was a cold, foggy day.

"How does it look?"

"Not too good, dear Mr. Jordan," said Schauberg. He did not look too good either. He was nervous. His smile was as forced as the irony in his voice. He gave me injections and drops and pills and examined my heart repeatedly. He examined my blood and tested my urine. Once I felt very sick but after a large whisky from my black bag I felt much better.

"It's drastic treatment," said Schauberg.

For dinner he opened cans of goulash, heated them on the stove, and served them with bread and beer.

"Would you like another beer? By the way, the Mousetrap has your blood in group."

"Who?"

"Don't you know her? Olga from the Herbertstrasse."

"Ah yes. I remember. When were you there?"

"Last night. I had to arrange for the medicines."

"I could have taken you into town!"

"No, we must never be seen together. It would be best if we were to meet tomorrow in the Herbertstrasse. The girls there all know me. I sometimes treat them."

"I understand."

"It won't be unusual if I'm there. The Mousetrap is a little anemic. So I'll do another bloodcount. We'll use her urine too. You have made an excellent impression on Madam Misere."

136

"I'm so glad."

"Käthe thought you were charming, too." His tone was expressionless; Käthe obviously meant nothing to him.

I thought Madam's house was ideal to telephone Shirley who would be waiting at Gregory Bates' for my call tomorrow morning.

"Call tonight and have Käthe reserved for—when are you to have your examination?"

"At nine."

"For eight then. I'll be there to give you the blood and urine you'll substitute. We'll have to watch the time; blood does not keep long. I'll give you the injection for your heart and you'll go straight to the doctor." His talking seemed to have exhausted him. He was very pale. Dark circles were suddenly under his eyes; his breath was labored. What if suddenly, halfway through the movie, he became ill or died?

"I know what you're thinking," he broke in. There again was the cold intelligence, the man who knew how to live with his addiction.

"You thought: If Schauberg has treated me three or four weeks, half-way through the movie he can demand more and I'll have to pay him—just so he'll give me more dope."

That was a new thought. I was silent.

"But, dear Mr. Jordan, after this movie you will have to go to a clinic. They will ask you who drugged you so unscrupulously. You could tell them and they could catch me in Europe, right?"

"Correct."

"You see, we are both in the same boat."

"I didn't complain. I knew we would have to trust each other."

I did not tell him what I had thought but after lunch I was reminded of it again. He became very sick and had to lie down. He was very embarrassed. Blamed it on the fog, and asked me to take a little walk.

The fog had become so dense I could only see a few feet ahead. The foghorns on the Elbe vessels were hooting. I walked up and down, reflecting on the uncertainty of the entire business.

When he called for me, he was once more as ironical and blasé as he had been the night before. Soon I had forgotten my apprehensions.

I returned to the hotel about ten and made my reservation with Madam. Such a charming lady!

4

The brightest sunlight next morning, though a cold day.

Everything had a clear, crisp look in that early light. The Herbertstrasse was quiet, the windows bare, the pimps asleep. Several well-dressed men arrived simultaneously with me.

The gentlemen for the early morning shift!

Madam's house was quiet too. Two gentlemen were greeted lovingly by their "reservation" and led up to the second floor. Käthe was in a black dress which had been fashionable for teenagers before the First World War. Button boots, stockings with embroidery and again a bow in her hair. I admired her dress. Madam, I was told, had bought at auction the entire stock of a theatrical costume company.

The table in the drawing room was set for breakfast. Flowers made it look attractive. The scent of lavender hung in the air.

"Has Dr. Schauberg arrived?"

"Not yet."

"I have to make a call. Is that possible?"

Käthe led me to Madam's office and I arranged for the call to Gregory Bates in Los Angeles. If my letters had arrived, Shirley should be waiting there. It was eleven o'clock at night in Los Angeles.

. We left the door open and sat down to breakfast. Madam had been generous. Champagne, which I refused because I had to go to the doctor, and caviar, Käthe's favorite food. Her face glowed as a child's seeing a Christmas tree. "I'm so terribly happy, Mr. Jordan! Walter told me he is working for you!"

"Yes, that's right."

"He said in only a few weeks we'll get married and leave Europe."

"Yes," I said for the second time. I ate rolls with butter and jelly and thought of how Schauberg would leave the blonde helpless Käthe once he had the fifty thousand.

"Many times, after I fled to the West, I wanted to kill myself. I was desperate. And now everything will be all right. It's like a fairy tale, I can't believe it!"

I could not either. Poor Käthe!

"Why did you leave the East?"

"Because of seven eels."

"Because of what?"

"I told you the other day how stupid I am. Something like that can only happen to me. You know I was conductress on a train in Leipzig. And one Friday night two drunk, but nice young men, got on my tram. With a huge basket full of eels. But I'm sure you're not interested in that."

"Go on. The telephone call will take a little while to come through."

"But the eels belonged to the state."

"I see."

"From a fish collective. Those two guys were supposed to take them to the state-owned store at Goetheplatz. One of them got a little fresh and to appease me they gave me seven eels."

"And you took them?"

"I was very happy to! As soon as I got home I ate one.

139

They were smoked eels. Well, the next morning the bell rang. State Security Police." She drank more champagne. "Or the waiter will drink it. You'll have to pay for the whole bottle anyway. Somebody in the tram had denounced me. And the eels were property of the people, right? So they took me to the fish factory and all the workers had to line up outside. They demanded I identify the two who had given me the eels. Those poor guys were white as sheets with fear."

I heard a door open and voices.

"There he is."

"Who?"

"Schauberg. And the Mousetrap. First he'll go to her and then he'll come down here. So I walked up and down."

"Where?"

"In the fish collective. I just told you about—"

"Oh yes. And?"

"I told them it was not one of those here. They let me go then because I had to go to work, but at night they came back. And asked and threatened. And they came back every night. I still had six of those eels and they confiscated them." Käthe's face reflected sadness and indignation. "Eel is very rich! I couldn't eat all of them in one night. They told my landlady I was an enemy of the German Democratic Republic. She was in Dresden and was burned by phosphorus, and ever since then she has been funny. She was so afraid, she told me to move. The tram authorities told me they would have to transfer me to a tractor association if I couldn't remember who had given me those eels. And those guys from the State Security Police came every day! Sometimes they went through my things before I got home. Questions, questions! So I finally fled. Now tell me. Only a stupid person can get in a mess like that, right?"

"How do you mean?"

"Any normal person would have pointed out those two guys and that would have been the end of that, right?"

The telephone rang. It was my call.

"Gregory? This is Peter! Did you get my letter?"

"Yes, I did. I just mailed one to you, Peter."

"Something went wrong?"

"I'm afraid so."

"Shirley?"

"Shirley is all right. She is right here. You can talk with her in a moment. Something else . . ."

"What happened? Tell me!"

"It's very difficult on the phone. I have to be careful."

"Tell me!"

"I see only one possibility. You'll have to ask Joan and Shirley to come to Hamburg right away."

5

From Gregory's letter and later from Shirley, I found out what actually had happened in Los Angeles.

Shirley had received my letter and, according to my instructions, had called Gregory. He, following my request, had called Joan. He told her he wanted to hire Shirley. Since he was going to need documentary material, he wanted to look at old newsreels at the Fox archives. Because it might get late, could Shirley stop by for him at his apartment before driving to the studios. Smart Gregory. He thought he had thought of everything.

6

On this twenty-eight of October it was hot in Los Angeles. Shirley drove to Gregory's house in Clarence Park.

Gregory was a little older than I, tall, slim, and prematurely gray. His good nature, his wealth and his charm made him one of the most sought-after bachelors in Los Angeles. He had known Shirley as long as I had. During the war he had been a bomber pilot. The fragment of a German anti-aircraft gun had left him with a permanent limp.

"Now, Shirley, don't worry. Your old Uncle Greg has arranged everything."

They drove to the busy Romaine Office Building at Santa Monica and Holloway Drive.

The express elevator took them to the twenty-third floor. They walked past open doors. Through one they saw an auctioneer accepting bids for a surrealistic painting.

The sign on the door said, PAUL ARROWHEAD, M.D.

The young nurse who opened the door looked pale and disturbed. Shirley and Gregory, nervous themselves, did not notice. They also did not notice the nurse's eyes trying to warn them of the young man standing close behind her.

"Hello, nurse. We have and appointment. My name is—"

"I know, sir," the nurse interrupted. "Please come in. The doctor is expecting you."

Gregory was still unobservant.

"There's no one ahead of us? This young man?"

The young man was just waiting for a certificate. The nurse opened a door.

In Dr. Arrowhead's office stood two men in shirtsleeves, shoulder holsters holding forty-fives under their left arms. A third, older man in a sweat-stained shirt sat behind a white desk. He was smoking a pipe.

An open door led to an examination room. There, among heat-ray lamps, instrument cupboards, and operating table, perhaps half a dozen girls and women, stiff as statues, stood silently, scared and embarrassed. No one spoke. On a white couch near the window sat a man in a white coat, his head in his hands. He was the only one who did not look up.

It was Dr. Arrowhead.

7

Everything happened very quickly. The young man from the waiting room was trying to push Gregory into the office. "Go in, please. The inspector will—"

He could not finish. Gregory realized what was going on. He turned and hit the detective who stepped back, stumbled into a chair, and fell.

Gregory pushed Shirley toward the office entrance. Shirley ran. Gregory followed slamming the door before the detective reached it.

"Not to the elevator. Over there!"

Shirley ran to the open door of the gallery. She heard Gregory call, "I'll follow later . . ." Slowing down, she half-turned and saw Gregory disappear through a door of a plastics company. Shirley heard voices and steps in the hall.

"Howard, Hughes! Down there!"

Shirley moved carefully away from the door.

"This is number one-fourteen in the catalogue. 'The End of the World' by Lazarus Strong . . ." The auctioneer went on.

"They can't have gone very far!"

Steps. Voices. Shirley stood still. No one had taken notice of her.

We'll never get away from here. They'll find us, Shirley thought. Slowly she continued to move along the wall toward the rear of the large crowded gallery.

"Why don't you watch out?" She had bumped into a

lady in a salmon-colored dress sitting in the last row. Artificial fruits adorned her hat.

"Beg your pardon," whispered Shirley.

8

"One thousand dollars, ladies and gentlemen. Do I hear twelve hundred?"

"Twelve hundred!" cried the lady with the hat and raised her hand.

"Thirteen hundred!"

"Fourteen hundred." Other hands were raised.

"I'm bid sixteen hundred. Do I hear sixteen fifty?"

"Sixteen fifty."

"Seventeen. Anyone else?"

There was uncle Greg!

She saw him standing by the door looking for her. What if they could get away?

"Eighteen hundred. Who bids eighteen hundred for 'End of the World'?" The auctioneer raised his head.

"Uncle Greg," called Shirley softly.

"Sh . . ." said the lady with the hat furiously.

Gregory had not heard. Shirley waved to him. He nodded and made his way toward her.

"Eighteen hundred once, eighteen hundred twice . . . Sold to the young lady on the right in the last row. Thank you." All faces were turned to Shirley who still held her arm extended. An employee of the gallery came to her. "Will this be cash or check, Miss?"

"What? Me? Why? For what?"

"The painting, of course. It was just sold to you. You bid eighteen hundred dollars."

"But I only waved to this gentleman."

"What's the matter, Watts?"

"The young lady says she doesn't want the painting."

The auctioneer in black suit, white shirt, and silver tie said sharply, "What do you mean?"

"A misunderstanding, gentlemen. Allow me to—" But they did not let Gregory finish.

Someone said, "Call the police!"

"Not necessary," said a deep voice. The inspector and the detectives stood in the entrance.

9

"And then?"

Gregory had been talking most cautiously, but I could visualize exactly what had happened. In Madam's office I held the receiver in both hands. I was very calm, as if all this had nothing to do with me.

"They took all of us to the precinct on Wilshire Boulevard. My lawyer came and they released us at six after I had raised bail."

"Yes?"

"All the women were examined."

"I see." Now they knew Shirley was pregnant.

"They will be examined again in four weeks' time. And then once more. You understand?"

"Yes." It meant no one in the entire country could help Shirley now.

"They preferred charges against the man we went to see. With witnesses. You understand?"

"Yes."

"The police wanted to call Joan . . ."

"Joan!"

". . . Until my lawyer told them I was the one . . ." That he was the father of Shirley's child.

"I don't know if they are going to be satisfied with that. My lawyer says any day now someone could go and see

Joan. That's why I think it best if you have Joan and Shirley come to Hamburg as quickly as possible."

"But if Shirley is supposed to be examined again . . ."

"My lawyer says as long as I'm here he can take care of it. You'll have to stay in Europe for a while. A lot of things happen there which cannot be ascertained from here. Right?"

"Yes, Gregory. And thanks."

"Call Joan today. Time is of the essence. Here is Shirley now. Bye, Peter. Take care."

"Thanks again."

"Peter?" When I heard Shirley's weak voice I realized the enormity of the crime I had committed.

"My sweet . . . trust me . . . I love you . . . I love you. I'll call Joan today. . . . You'll come over here . . . as quickly as possible . . ." I could only talk haltingly.

"Yes, Peter."

"We'll make it . . ."

"Yes, Peter."

"Everything will turn out well . . ."

"Yes, Peter." Her voice was low. "But it will have to be soon. I can't stand it much longer."

"You'll be here with me in a few days."

"Yes, Peter. Yes."

Then I sat staring at the telephone. I could not think. And now this. It was too much. Any moment the police might talk to Joan. Perhaps they had already. Perhaps she already knew.

". . . matter, Mr. Jordan?" I only heard the last few words of the sentence. Schauberg looked at me. "Trouble?"

"Yes. No. Yes."

"Listen, you'll have to pull yourself together! In half an hour you'll see the doctor."

"Yes, Yes, of course . . ."

"Damn it all! Did you have to telephone this morning of all mornings?"

146

As if I had suddenly lost my reason, I yelled, "Yes I did, if you don't mind!"

"Dear Mr. Jordan, let's not have a scene," he said with contempt. He extracted a metal case from his jacket and took out a syringe and ampoule. "Take off your jacket and push up your sleeve." He gave me an injection and massaged my arm. "I've done all I could to help you. Now it's up to you. I'll wait here for your call. You'll come to the camp in the afternoon."

"Why not sooner?"

"I'll have to buy myself some clothes." Schauberg handed me two test tubes filled with blood and one with urine. "You know what to do?"

"Yes."

He looked at his watch. "You'll have to leave. I'll take care of the bill here and you'll square it later." He slapped my back. "Good luck."

Carefully I stowed away the tubes. I went to the Reeperbahn where my car was parked. Sanitation trucks were cleaning the streets.

I had promised him and myself not to drink before the examination. As soon as I sat behind the wheel of my car I knew I could not keep that promise. The talk with Gregory and Shirley had drained me. I was convinced I could not even drive unless I had a drink. Just a little drink. Everything would look better then. I opened the black bag.

10

With a furious cry the huge movie producer seized the heavy bronze lamp. In vain, I tried to evade him, to protect my head with my hands. The base of the bronze lamp came whistling through the air onto the back of my head. Without a sound, I collapsed on the gray carpeting. A dark red stain quickly spread underneath my head. I did not move any more. This was November second, 1959.

"Cut! Thank you," said the director. "Excellent. Just to be quite sure we'll do it once more."

"Lights!"

"Make-up!"

Thirty people began to talk and move around the entrance hall of a house which had been built in studio two of the Alhambra Studios outside Hamburg. I got up. Henry Wallace, who played the American producer, carefully placed the lamp with the bronze base of foam rubber on a table. The stained gray carpet was replaced. A large funnel was refilled with "panchromatic blood," a mixture of mineral oils and vegetable coloring. A thin rubber hose connected to the funnel led underneath the carpet to where my head was supposed to fall.

The first day of shooting. We had shot the scene three times and only the third time had Thornton Seaton been satisfied. To be able to choose the best take he wanted me to be murdered for a fourth time.

I have just passed over four days in my report, Professor Pontevivo. In those four days, most important events had taken place. I had passed my physical. Our movie was insured. I had telephoned my wife. She and Shirley were to arrive on November third.

The insurance fraud had been easy. Dr. Erasmus Dutz's office was in an old house on Hallerstrasse. From there one could see the dead grass of the ballfields of the Hamburg Sports Club. Street musicians, surrounded by a crowd of watching people, were at the entrance gates. Girls, holding boxes with white envelopes, were walking about. The martial music could be heard in the doctor's office.

At this early hour I was the first patient. A pale, cross-eyed nurse was assisting Dr. Dutz. She was very blonde and friendly, and it occurred to me that, most probably, she had chosen this profession devoted to

Christian charity because of her eyes. One could be cross-eyed or look like Marilyn Monroe—it would not matter if one were helping sick people.

Dr. Dutz said my pulse and my blood pressure were normal; my heart seemed to be all right.

"Your heart is not the way it ought to be," said Dr. Dutz. "We'll take a look at a cardiogram." The nurse took the cardiogram. "Now we'll do ten little knee bends, Mr. Jordan."

So I did ten little knee bends and became quite dizzy. After all my blood pressure had been reduced artificially.

"Now we'll lie down again, Mr. Jordan."

Dr. Dutz studied the cardiogram and I calmed down slowly.

"It's not good, but not nearly as bad as I thought," said the slim Dr. Dutz. "You have some heart there, Mr. Jordan." And some injection too, I thought. "But what are you doing?"

"What do you mean, Doctor?"

"You're so wound up."

Schauberg had warned me of this and had also supplied me with an answer. "It's been rather hectic since I arrived in Hamburg."

"Women?"

The nurse blushed.

"Women. Whisky. Not much sleep. Two weeks of parties."

"If I were you I would stop that. It's the best way to get a heart attack. Does that hurt?" He had applied pressure to my liver, and, although I had been prepared, the pain caused me to dig my nails into my palms.

"No."

"Your liver is very swollen, Mr. Jordan."

"I just told you I've been living rather . . ."

"Yes. Surely." His reply was automatic. "We'll have to make some blood tests."

Just as Schauberg had, they filled test tubes with blood.

The nurse left the laboratory door opened. I watched what she was doing with the test tubes.

"We're doing the blood tests here. Professor Ihrt will take care of all the other tests." An insurance company is very cautious.

"But you just said my heart was not too bad . . ."

"I'm not worried about your heart. I'm worried about your liver."

"Now look, Doctor. I'm perfectly fine! I've never been sick a day in my life!" Schauberg had told me to become annoyed after the blood test. "That is simply ridiculous! You are going to insure me, aren't you?"

"If your liver is all right, naturally."

"Every time I drink too much my liver swells!" Another part of Schauberg's counsel. "A little congestion, that's all!"

"Very probably it is, Mr. Jordan. A congestion, hm, hm. Just to make certain we'd better take a look at your urine." Jovially he patted my shoulder. "It is probably all right. When did you see a doctor last?"

"It's been so long I can't even remember."

The test tubes of blood, now labeled, had been placed in a holder.

The telephone rang.

"Excuse me. Good luck with your movie. I'm happy to have met you." Smiling he shook my hand. "Nurse, will you show Mr. Jordan to the bathroom?"

Then I stood in the laboratory and, through the closed door, heard the doctor talk on the telephone. The nurse gave me a vial and showed me to the bathroom. I locked myself in and filled the vial with the urine Schauberg had given me. I stepped on the toilet seat and unhooked the float in the water compartment. Schauberg's instructions again. Once disconnected, there was no control of the water. It ran over the edge of the bowl.

I hurried to the adjoining laboratory.

"I'm afraid something's happened . . ."

The nurse ran into the bathroom and threw up her hands. "Oh dear, something got loose. Put the vial on the table here. I'll take care of this."

"If I can help—"

"No, no! I'll have it done in a moment."

She balanced on the toilet seat as the water began to run into the waiting room. I went quickly to the lab, placed the vial on a table, poured the contents of the test tubes down the sink drain, refilled them with the blood Schauberg had given me.

The nurse was mumbling in the bathroom. The doctor was still on the telephone. Schauberg had not only told me about the toilet float, but had made other suggestions which would distract attention from me.

The flushing stopped. The nurse returned for a pail and mop.

"I'm so sorry . . ."

"But it wasn't your fault! No, no, that's quite unnecessary!" But she took the ten marks and we parted amiably.

My car was parked at the Harvestehuder Weg. Just after leaving the doctor's office I turned down another street. Schauberg stepped from a doorway. In the harsh light of the morning his shabby clothes looked even more disreputable. Yet his bearing was almost regal.

"I thought we were not supposed to be seen together."

"An artist's interest in his work," Schauberg said. He fell into step with me. "It was stronger than I. Everything okay?" I nodded. "How nice. Then I get two thousand marks from you."

We were walking toward the Hamburg Sports Club and heard the music and saw the pretty girls carrying the boxes with white envelopes. A black-haired girl in a dufflecoat said to us, "We're playing music for you too, gentlemen, and we ask for your contribution. Won't you buy a lottery ticket?"

"We don't pay for martial music," said Schauberg

151

gruffly. Behind the musicians was a large board with the name of the charitable organization.

"Our organization is well-known for the good it does," said the girl shaking the envelopes in her box. "Today we are collecting for the poor in Africa."

Schauberg sneered, "You don't say? Interesting. For a hundred years, in the name of Christian love, our moral Occident world exploited Africans, enslaved them, deported them, let them die by the millions in the colonies and now, just because the nasty Russians are at our door, our unhappy brothers suddenly have need to get steak, steel from Krupp, and foreign aid!"

I could not comprehend the meaning of his words. I had been perfectly calm when I exchanged the blood, but now came the reaction. My legs were shaking, I felt dizzy, and with great longing I thought of the black bag in my car.

"There are many winners." The girl insisted. "You receive your money right away. Perhaps you pull a winning ticket." They were playing the Hohenfriedberger March. The screaming of the three jets over the Aussenalster drowned out the music.

There was a menace in this suddenly aggressive Schauberg. The cynic, always seemingly controlled, should have remembered how inadvisable it was to attract attention to himself, was in a rage. His jaundiced face had become purplish. He yelled, "Is it starting again, this swindling of the people?"

I took hold of his arm. "Stop it!"

He pulled away and threw one hand up to the sky lit by a pale sun. "There! There they fly, the poor of Africa!"

"Don't talk such nonsense," I said. If only he would come along! Bystanders began to notice us. Schauberg did not care; he cried, "You people were not here! But we were! We've been through all this once before! Lottery tickets and collection boxes, stamps and badges! At first, only once a month! Then, every damn weekend. Winterhilfswerk. For the poor. The same deceit!"

"Give the communist one on his kisser!" called a man.

"No, he is right!" cried a woman.

"I sure am right! I was in Russia!" yelled Schauberg and his hand went to his beret. This stupid fool was capable of showing his scar. I turned with the intention of leaving him. Schauberg's hand dropped but he continued, "And what did your money buy? Goering got his Luftwaffe, Hitler his German Wehrmacht—and German women got widow's weeds!"

The girl became indignant. "We are a nonpolitical, independent organization!"

"We are a nation of idiots!" yelled Schauberg. Now a crowd had ringed around him. A few were of his opinion, the majority protested. The girl said to me, "I swear it is for the poor in Africa. This man only knows hate. But God wants us to love one another. Grant His wish. Maybe then one of your wishes will come true."

It was a point, I thought.

"How much is a ticket?"

"Fifty pfennigs."

"I'll take ten."

"Bravo!" called Schauberg and applauded. "A piece of a rocket is already yours."

"Ah, just be quiet," I said and, pulling the girl with me, left him.

"Maybe one of your wishes will come true . . ."

One of my wishes.

I had an important one.

11

Our insurance contract was dated October thirty-first and cost over four million marks. It was an impressive document with five pages of "General Conditions" in small print. They enumerated everything I had to abide by and everything I was prohibited from doing. For instance, I was not allowed to take planes, boats, climb mountains, join expeditions or safaris, compete in races, parachute jumps and many other things, or become pregnant!

The premium was paid on October thirty-first by Jorkos Productions. Our film was safe, a financial difficulty averted even if I were invalided or died.

To reduce this unpleasant possibility to a minimum it was necessary for me to pay fifty thousand marks to Schauberg of which he had already received five thousand in payment for the insurance fraud.

In fact, to be precise, it was fifty thousand and five marks I had to invest in my comeback. The ten tickets of the charitable organization had cost five marks.

To be even more precise, the total was less. For one of my tickets had been a winning one. I had promptly received six hundred and fifty marks which must be deducted from the fifty thousand and five marks!

Schauberg had compared the lottery to the collection tricks of the Third Reich. I could rest easy; I had not helped to finance a German jet bomber. And if the young girl had spoken the truth not one hungry child had received a piece of bread by my five marks donation.

"God wants us to love one another. Grant His wish. Maybe then one of your wishes will come true."

Well, despite the rockets, the jet bombers, the poverty of black humanity, my wish had come true. It would be interesting how Shirley's Father Horace would have explained this. Or any other priest. Or anyone else who believed in God.

12

I called my wife without waiting for the evening of October thirty-first and with the certainty of knowing my fraud had been successful. Joan and Shirley had to come to Hamburg irrespective of whether or not *Come Back* would be made. Every day counted. Any day the police

could arrive at Joan's. So I called her the evening of the twenty-ninth. I had spent the afternoon with Schauberg. He gave me injections and intravenous infusions, and lamented his bad manners in the morning. "I behaved like a bloody idiot. You were perfectly right in leaving me, dear Mr. Jordan."

"Whatever got into you?"

"Without morphine for too long! Right away one's intelligence fades."

I said, "It takes expertise to live with addiction." Apparently he had not recovered sufficiently because he took my remark seriously.

"Quite right. Praise be I came to my senses at last and told the people I was conducting a test for the Ministry of the Interior. Survey: How does the man in the street react to communistic agitation?"

"And they believed that?"

"Every word after I casually waved an old MD identification and yelled at two of those who had agreed with me earlier. I bought a few tickets and praised their unexampled, their wonderful organization. But, I said, if contributions were made to underdeveloped nations it was also very necessary to do more for the Bundeswehr. Bravo! After all they had formed their Volksarmee first! Right! And we had to defend ourselves. Applause and general shaking of hands. I went into the nearest house and gave myself an injection. I am always prepared. Nothing like this is going to happen to me again!" He was now wearing a new, almost black suit, black shoes, a shirt, an unobtrusive tie.

The injections gave me enormous self-confidence and callousness. Schauberg's treatment seemed to have frozen my heart but had set my mind vibrating. Friendliness, charm, words of love, the longing quality in my voice when I spoke to Joan came from my mind precise, inexorable, and obviously effective.

"Joan, darling, this is Peter. I guess you are surprised that I'm calling . . ."

No answer.

Next to the telephone stood a drink. Just to see it there gave me assurance.

"Joan! Can't you hear me?"

"Yes, I can."

Nothing else.

"Did I wake you?"

"No, it's already ten o'clock."

I took a drink. Perhaps the police had been to see her. Perhaps she already knew everything.

"Is Shirley up?"

"No."

"Aren't you glad to hear from me?"

"Yes. Naturally. It was just so unexpected. Are you ill?"

"No."

"Is something wrong? With the movie?"

Another drink.

"I'm calling because I want you to come over here, to me."

"You want . . . me . . ." her voice trembled.

"You and Shirley. Right away."

"But . . ."

"I thought about our last conversation. What you said about Shirley; that she was destroying our marriage; that you wanted her out of the house." Joan was silent but I

156

could hear her quick breathing. "Darling, we were all nervous and irritable. After all, we have lived together those last ten years. I like Shirley. She is your daughter. I wouldn't want us to do something which we might regret . . ."

"Oh, Peter! It's wonderful to hear you say that. You have no idea how that had distressed me."

"I think I know. We'll just have to give ourselves another chance. In new surroundings. We're three adults. I'm sure with some effort we can solve the problem. You've never been in Germany. Neither has Shirley. She can work at her job here. I've already spoken to Kostasch." One more lie. What did it matter? Besides, Kostasch probably would hire her.

"Peter! You don't know what that means to me! After all, I love Shirley . . ."

"I know, darling."

"Sometimes I hoped you would ask me to come alone. But that you want both of us to come is so wonderful! Oh, Peter . . ."

Again I sipped at my drink. Then I said sternly, "Tell Shirley this is the last attempt to settle everything."

It really was. Comes the time when I have to tell Joan the truth I can say: "Here in Europe I had tried to end my affair with Shirley and return to my wife. I had not been successful." Unfortunately.

Joan interrupted my thoughts. "I feel as if I were young again, as if we had only just met."

"Yes, Joan."

"I feel it. We'll make a new start. I know. Europe will be good for us, for the three of us!"

"Let me know when you'll arrive here."

"I love you. I love you. Oh, God, how happy Shirley will be. I'm sure this is the greatest surprise of her life."

"Yes," I said. "I'm sure it is."

Later in the evening the effect of the injections wore off but I felt better after I had emptied half a bottle of whisky. It occurred to me that the same thing had happened to me that had happened to Schauberg when he had not had his usual dose of morphine. We both had become too sober, too much ourselves. That is why I now had a sense of shame over my trickery to Joan, why Schauberg had raged over rearmament and its implication of war.

Or rather was it not the other way around?

Morphine and alcohol and drugs showed us how we truly were: he, unscrupulous and cynical; I, egotistical and deceitful.

Yes. Surely. That was it.

13

Joan's telegram read,
ARRIVING NINE-FIFTEEN PM—
NOVEMBER THIRD LOVE JOAN.

14

November 2, 1959

Dear Peter!

Le jour de gloire est arrivé. Today is our first day in the studios. You know that it was my idea to make our movie Come Back, *your comeback. You know why I brought you to Europe, why I want you to make this movie: because I believe in you.*

Many difficulties lie ahead. Still I dare say that with a little luck Come Back *will be an unusual, exceptional movie. But even if everything should go wrong, even then I shall say what I say now, on this our first day: It has been a pleasure and a great honor to have met you, to*

*have worked with you and to have had only the best inten-
tions. Very sincerely yours,*

Herbert Kostasch.

15

The waiter brought this letter while I was eating breakfast on this our first day of shooting. The letter was nice.
It partly reassured me.

I took my coat and the black bag, which I had replenished last evening, and physically uneasy left the hotel.
The lights were on, cleaning women still busy. I handed
my car keys to the doorman. He smiled at me; he knew
where I was going. Frequently movie people stayed at the
hotel and if they were up this early they were shooting.

"Your car will be here in a moment. Good luck, Mr.
Jordan."

I stepped out on the street. It was still dark and very
cold. I recalled the mornings my mother and I had waited
on such deserted streets for a studio car to pick us up.

The Nazis, in the name of Germany, in the greatest of
mass genocides, were guilty of the death of six million
Jews; guilty of a war in which sixty million people of all
nations and races died. The guilty were undisturbed by
conscience. The dreadful events passed. Whatever doubts
their countrymen had were fleeting as a dream, about as
permanent as a night watch. Feverishly the world was
preparing for a new, even more dreadful war. Since my
days as a child star nations had advanced, even philoso-
phers had become activists; satellites circled the earth; a
few cobalt bombs were sufficient to atomize the earth. All
this had happened in the past twenty years, ever since I
had last stood waiting for a car to take me to my work.
Once again I was waiting: freezing, alone, afraid of
failing, of being inadequate.

I drove north through the desert streets, passing freezing laborers waiting at tram stops; newspaper delivery men and boys on bicycles. I passed the dismal Eppendorfer peatbog swamp above which screeching crows circled. There were no more dwelling places here. I saw blacksoil, occasional farms, and rotting meadows. A scene of desolation. I would drive this route to the studio for the next few weeks usually at this early hour. As I was playing the lead and would be in most takes, I had insisted that those scenes be shot first. Wardrobe, hairdressers, make-up took an hour for preliminaries. That meant a daily morning arrival at the studios by seven-thirty.

I turned off into a country lane and slowly drove the car toward a dilapidated barn. Behind it, hidden from the road, stood an old Volkswagen. I left my car and opened the door of the other.

"Good morning," said Schauberg. "Get in."

I did. He wore a new camel-colored flannel overcoat and a new blue suit. During the last few days I had seen him many times at the camp. Schauberg treated me daily and conscientiously. I received injections and medication for my circulation, my liver, my heart. Now he gave me an intravenous injection. He wore a new beret and smelled of cologne. He must have taken morphine; in time he seemed relaxed, confident, in good spirits. While giving me the shot he whistled the *March of the Toreadors*. Then, "Take one of these tablets now. Take the other two only when it is absolutely necessary. The first few days are the most difficult ones. I'm quite satisfied with you. When do you have lunch?"

"From one to two."

"Come back here then. And I'll be here again after six. You know you can always call Käthe should you need me. Apropos." He reached over to the backseat and picked up a bunch of asters. On the attached card was written in awkward letters "Good luck—Käthe Mädler."

160

"I wish you the very best too," said Schauberg, "because I still have forty-five thousand marks coming from you."

16

Professor, when you asked me to record my experiences you said and said more than once, "I want everything."

Well, I have been conscientious, hiding nothing while I play monologist to the insensitive audience of this electronic mechanism. Its only response to the revelations of my most tormented experiences, my most agonizing secrets, is a routine, indifferent whirr and, as a variation, a click to warn me that the tape has come to its end.

I'll tell you everything—but it would be unfair to you if I included the details of shooting in the studio. You wouldn't really care to know, would you, how often the signal sounded for silence, how often the slateboard listing the scene was held before the camera, what the script girl recorded, which takes were printed, which rejected, which of the film rushes were printed.

Surely you know, if only generally, how films are made; how actors, directors, producers, technical men behave on the set. Surely you can imagine how bravely, how amiably we began; how earnestly we hated each other after weeks of work on the set.

Most of what I will tell you about those days in the studio is what you will want to hear. The moments of creation and failure, of frustration and despair—of death and resurrection.

The Alhambra Studios were floodlit. There was the usual intense activity, the suppressed hysteria that precedes a first day's shooting.

A white-haired man approached me as I entered and

directed me to my dressing room, murmuring that it was the most comfortable in the studio. He was pretty old but genial, and he remained genial through my most difficult days.

There were the usual telegrams offering good wishes and flowers too. After a quick look I murmured my thanks. Then, for an hour I went through the ordeal of make-up.

17

Not unexpectedly, the first quarrel came early. The production manager, Albrecht, thin, bent, grim-faced, limped into the room. He shouted at my make-up man. "What's going on, Otto? Olga says Miss King still has her curse!"

Otto, Olga's husband, replied as loudly, "We sent you a notification in plenty of time. Now don't tell me that's not true! I have the carbon."

Kostasch came in. "Don't yell like that, Albrecht! What's the trouble?"

Still shouting, Albrecht explained.

It seemed at first a silly argument over just when there would be close-ups of Miss King, then hardly in condition to have them taken. Somehow I sensed that the argument had been designed by Albrecht. He had some reason for disliking me. The quarreling trio finally agreed to hold the close-ups until later. Instead, shooting would begin with the difficult scene between the second lead, Henry Wallace, who was to play Miss King's husband, and me. Thanks, Albrecht, I thought, you managed that cleverly.

I finished dressing and went to the set. I held Shirley's little cross tightly.

Wallace who was about to murder me in a violent scene, already on the set, put out his hand in welcome.

Seaton, the director, clapped his hands. "We'll run a test." A moment's pause while everyone froze in place. "Ready," said Seaton.

Wallace seized a bronze lamp. I tried to evade him. He held its base high and sent it whirling at me. It struck the back of my head. Soundlessly, I collapsed on the thick carpet.

For a few seconds there was silence. Then Seaton said, "That was quite good." He took Wallace and me aside, told us what he wanted changed. We played the scene three more times before Seaton was satisfied.

"Ready," said Seaton.

Then, for the first time in twenty years, I heard the words, the melody of my childhood.

"Sound!"

"Sound okay!"

"Camera!"

"Camera ready!"

"Four twenty-seven, take one!" The take slate clicked.

"Action!".

An hour later the first of what was to become four hundred and thirty-three takes had had the director's approval.

18

In the next take Belinda King, playing Henry Wallace's wife, entered, discovered what had happened. The scene was long, but since her close-ups had been rescheduled we made more progress this morning than had been planned.

I was playing dead on the floor. After a long argument with his wife, Wallace had called the police. The distressed couple were waiting for the homicide detectives to arrive. Then the camera moved in for another close-up of me, swung away, and focused on a script I had brushed off a table before my death. The camera lingered on it. *Come Back.* This shot was to be the last frame of the completed movie.

"Break for lunch!" called an assistant director.

Kostasch and Seaton came to me.

"Great," said Kostasch.

"Well, I don't know," I said.

"No, really," said Kostasch. "Your expression was great. Am I right Thornton?"

"Perfectly," said my director. "You were first class, Peter. I can't remember when I last had such a beautiful corpse!"

"That's very nice of you," I said. Seaton had been one of Hollywood's greatest directors. He had one serious weakness: young boys. As young as they were, they had blackmailed him. In 1949 there had been a scandal; Seaton's arrest and trial. His lawyers had in turn blackmailed the boys and their parents. The verdict was favorable to him but, after the trial, women's organizations were vociferous in their disapproval. No studio dared employ Seaton for the next nine years. He had had lean years writing scripts under a pseudonym or working as a cutter for television. Hopeless about his future as a director, he was suddenly rehabilitated when engaged to direct *Come Back.* He was known as a superb director—and he was now available for a relatively low fee.

For this man, now past sixty, our film was as desperately important as it was for me. This was his last chance too. All his energies were focused on what had to be a triumph.

But Kostasch was worried. He had mentioned to me that Seaton had been seen in nightclubs with his young German assistant, blond Hans, positively cute with his bright blue eyes and silky lashes.

I left the studio quickly and drove to the dilapidated barn where Schauberg was waiting.

After lunch we went through the rest of the sequence we had been shooting. Wallace knew that I had deceived him with his wife. I declared that I hated him, always had, and why. The scene began calmly, intensified, and climaxed with the murder.

Everything went well. I made no mistakes. It astonished me that I was so confident before the camera. If Miss King's close-ups had been shot we would have been finished for the day. Now two hours remained. An earlier scene which I had not expected to play until the following day was to be shot. For me, what followed then was disastrous.

19

About halfway through a rather long scene, I shouted at Wallace, "You think with your goddamn money you can buy everybody!"

We were rehearsing when I saw Albrecht whisper to Kostasch. Kostasch whispered to Seaton who then called Wallace and me to one side. It seemed "goddamn" was frowned on by the American movie code.

"You know how it is," said Seaton. "We'll have to change the word later if we don't do it now. You'll say 'miserable' instead of 'goddamn,' Peter. Okay?"

"Okay."

We rehearsed it once. In the take everything went well until I came to the altered sentence. I yelled, "You think with your goddamn misery——"

"Cut," said Seaton.

"I'm sorry," I said.

"It doesn't matter. We'll do it once more."

This time I cried, "You think with your money you can buy all miserable——"

"Cut."

"I'm terribly sorry. It will be all right next time."

"Well, of course!" said Seaton.

The next time I spoke the line correctly but fluffed the next sentence.

"Cut."

I began to perspire.

The make-up man dabbed my face and Seaton said amiably, "Just keep calm. It doesn't matter even if we have to do that take ten times!"

20

After I had ruined the tenth take most of those on the set avoided looking directly at me. A few did smile encouragingly in the manner of hospital nurses comforting a very sick man. I had gone through the dialogue with only minor slips but, in the last three takes, I had ruined the end of each scene. Nervous concentration on my role had exhausted me, left me quivering.

Preparing for the eleventh take Wallace was whistling. Albrecht was cleaning his fingernails.

Seaton asked me, "Perhaps we should leave the 'goddamn'; would that help? Then we'll have to synchronize the word later on."

"That won't make any difference now," I said and looked at Albrecht. He smiled.

"Peter boy, even if you ruin three kilometers of film—doesn't matter! I've never seen anyone perform the way you do!" cried Kostasch. I did not notice then how often he praised me.

"I swear, next time there'll be no slip!"

I kept that promise.

Then Henry Wallace slipped up.

At each new take he had been waiting for the moment

when I would make a mistake. In his malicious eagerness he had missed his own cue.

Scene 421 for the twelfth time, the thirteenth, the fourteenth. Now we took turns making mistakes.

Albrecht said to Kostasch, "May I remind you that in ten minutes we'll be through for the day?"

"Shut up," Kostasch replied. And to Wallace and me, "Will you try one more time?"

I nodded. Wallace, his smile blinding, said, "But as often as you like, dear Mr. Kostasch! I've been in the business long enough to know how patient one has to be with child stars!"

"You dirty son-of-a-bitch," I said to him.

21

Kostasch and Seaton exchanged glances. I knew then we would have to repeat 421 until midnight if necessary. The action called for Wallace and me to hate each other. Now we really did. Our dialogue would sound very convincing.

There had never been any love lost between us. In America his reputation was lofty. He had received two Oscars, ardently pursued James Joyce research, collected early Indian art, corresponded with Jean Cocteau and Bernard Buffet, and was the author of a book on atonal music.

He would never have become my acting partner, never would have played opposite me in a movie, had it not been to his advantage to come to Europe for a year in an effort to straighten out his tax problems.

Disagreeable. Arrogant. An intellectual snob. Yet a most accomplished actor.

"It is now five to seven," Albrecht said.

"I told you to shut up! If we don't finish 421 today

we'll be behind on the first day and tomorrow's schedule will be upset."

"That's hardly my fault, Mr. Kostasch!"

"We'll try it again," said Seaton. I swallowed the two red pills Schauberg had given me. We did the sequence again. And again. I had fluffed the line.

A buzzer sounded. It was seven o'clock, the end of a workday.

"Overtime!" called Kostasch.

"It's not my money, thank goodness," said Albrecht, smiling at me.

Half an hour later I was bathed in sweat. Black spots, fiery wheels before my eyes. I overheard the stagehands making bets.

"Make-up softening," reported the man who made me up.

"Ten-minute break!" called Seaton.

In his room he quickly restored the facial work, talking to me while his deft fingers moved. Yet I heard nothing: something was stirring the pit of my stomach.

The fist.

I just made it to my dressing room. I abruptly ordered out the man assigned to help me. Now I was staggering; I could hardly walk. Bells reverberated in my ears. My hands shook as I struggled to open my black bag.

I did not bother to lock the door or close the rattling window; the storm had returned during the past night. I pulled the cork with my teeth and drank from the bottle. I drank and drank, and then slumped into a chair, the bottle in one hand, the other pressed to my abdomen in an attempt to keep that fist from reaching my heart.

22

The whisky restrained the fist. Whisky alleviated my fear but not my desperation. Twenty-three times for number 421. If we were to go forty-six takes—I could not do it. And if I could, what, after all, did that signify? Today was only the first day of the forty-three days scheduled for the movie. The work was too demanding. I would not be able to keep it up. Never. Shirley was coming. Joan was coming. Shirley was expecting a child.

The child. The movie. Another forty-two days. In a hotel together with Joan. The child. The doctor. Shirley. It was too much.

Whisky.

I drank leaning back, my face to the window. Startled I spilled some whisky and sat rooted to the chair.

An elephant was coming toward me.

It was huge. Its ears flapping in the storm. It walked slowly up the road leading to my dressing room. It came closer, grew larger step by step.

From the light of the streetlamps I could see its fissured hide. Its small, black, shiny, cunning eyes were looking directly at me.

I knew those eyes. Fear gripped me. They were the eyes of the dead seagull I had seen on the balcony of my hotel suite, the morning of my first attack. The gull which had vanished when I had wanted to show it to Natasha.

23

Closer and closer came the huge animal. I couldn't escape its eyes. Gull's eyes staring at me. How can they?

I'm sitting here in this brightly lit room. How can those eyes look at me?

But they do. I can see them.

Closer. Closer. Closer.

No one is outside. Only the animal. The trunk swings. The ears flap. The elephant leaves the road and steps on the lawn outside my dressing room. A wall. A gray wall. There is no way out any more. I'm closed in. I'm going to suffocate. I'm going to die here. Just as it happened once before.

Drink.

The gray wall moves, wrinkles. The elephant bends down and his left eye looks into my room. The eye. The all-knowing eye. The pitiless eye of the gull which seems to say: Blasphemer. Liar. Scoundrel.

24

I screamed.

I jumped up and threw the whisky bottle at this eye which quickly moved and disappeared. Glass from the broken bottle and window fell on the grass outside.

The view was clear again. I felt hot. I felt cold. I staggered to the window, looked out. The animal had disappeared. Had it ever been here?

"Mr. Jordan?" A knock at the door.

I must pull myself together.

"Come in!"

My dresser entered. "Now, if we—" He broke off. "Don't you feel well, Mr. Jordan?"

"I'm all right. I just had a fright."

"The window—"

"Yes. The . . . the storm ripped it open. And slammed it shut. It broke the glass . . ." The whisky was working. I had drunk a lot.

The whisky. Damn, I have no more whisky. Idiot. Why hadn't I thrown a book, a shoe, a brush? No more whisky. I had thrown away my best friend. Idiot!

My man finished helping me dress just as the loudspeaker announced, "Mr. Jordan! Will Mr. Jordan come to the studio, please."

I asked. "What other movie are they shooting here—what is your name?"

"Harry, Mr. Jordan. Old Harry."

"What else are they shooting here, Harry?"

"Only a war movie. In Studio Two."

"No circus movie?"

"What makes you think that?"

"I've read it somewhere."

"That's right too. There was a circus here. Tigers, lions, elephants!"

So there. Of course. Naturally.

"But they finished shooting two weeks ago. Good God, Mr. Jordan, are you sure you are all right?"

25

"Four twenty-one. Take twenty-four."

Wallace and I finished the scene without one mistake.

"How was it?" asked Kostasch.

"Okay," said Seaton.

"Sound okay!"

The camera man was silent.

"Well!" said Kostasch to the young man who blushed, got up, and cried despairingly, "It's my fault! Only my fault. I didn't watch the footage!"

"Do you mean to say," Kostasch almost whispered, "that you ran out of film during the scene?"

The young man nodded.

Wallace laughed hysterically.

I sank down on a box and pressed my hands to my face. Behind me, bets were made and accepted on another failure. But they lost those bets. The twenty-fifth take was perfect.

One scene of four hundred and thirty-three scenes of a movie miles long. We had used three hundred and thirteen meters of film for a scene hardly thirteen meters long . . .

"That's all for today!" yelled the assistant director.

"It was worth it, Peter boy!" said Kostasch. "I'm happy. Very happy. You were—"

I left him standing there. If I did not see Schauberg quickly I would break down in the studio.

Ten minutes later the man with the beret was sitting next to me in the Mercedes parked behind the old barn. A storm was raging. I had not stopped to change or take off the make-up. Shaking, I sat behind the wheel. Tears of exhaustion messed up my make-up. Schauberg was silent. He pulled off my jacket, pushed up my sleeve, and gave me an injection. Then he said, "I'm giving you what I gave you in the camp. Do you remember?"

I nodded and wanted to reply but the moment the needle punctured my skin I collapsed and everything went dark. I heard him talk, but did not understand; I heard myself talk unintelligibly. Then I heard no more and an overpowering feeling of peace, warmth, and contentment came over me.

I opened my eyes. Schauberg was there, smoking. I felt as good and strong as I had when he injected me the first time in his camp.

"Did I faint?"

"Just for a second." He smiled. "Nothing of any consequence. Your blood pressure drops easily. After all you are an artist. An artist lives the sensations of his body. August Strindberg made a will every time he had the flu."

"Did I say anything?"

"Yes."

"What? About Shirley? The child? Joan?

"It was rather confused," said Schauberg. "It had something to do with God. He's tormenting you, is He?"

"One can't be tormented by an entity one does not believe in."

"I see," he said in a tone of satisfaction.

"What do you mean: I see? Do you believe in Him?"

"You feel fine again, right?"

"Answer me."

"I like to give good value for good money. Don't be afraid, we'll pull you through."

"I want you to answer me!"

"Well, Mr. Jordan, I believe in nothing at all. I think. Few people think. If they can't think or won't, they have to believe. Or they can't function. God: for all of them, belief is the remedy, as many different concepts as there are different people, without any sense—and naturally animals too. Elephants, for instance, surely have their own elephant God."

"What makes you think of elephants?"

"Because I saw one a little while ago."

"You saw—"

"An old, huge elephant. What's the matter with you?"

"Where did you see an elephant? When?"

"Half an hour ago while I was waiting for you. When I took a stroll on the road over there."

"Where did he come from?"

"From the film studios. Why are you so interested? He was in a movie there."

"That was three weeks ago! The movie has been finished, the circus moved on!"

"Yes, the keeper told me that too, but some scene with the elephant had to be shot again. So they brought him back for that. The poor animal. Imagine! A three-kilometer walk to the next railroad station. The animal looked exhausted. He was probably angry with his elephant God. Well, that's the way it is, Mr. Jordan. Even if inanimate objects had consciousness, they would prefer believing to thinking. Triangles for instance would imagine their God to be triangular . . ''

26

The next day passed without any disturbance. All went according to schedule. Schauberg's injection had a long-lasting effect. I played my part easily and without fear. Henry Wallace apologized. "I'm sorry about yesterday. You're all right, old boy."

Kostasch beamed. "I knew it! All you needed was one day to adjust. Now things will go swimmingly."

And Seaton, "I wouldn't have thought you could adjust so quickly, Peter!"

Yes, it was a pleasant day. Such friendliness, such charm!

After we finished shooting, Kostasch and I went to the screening room to look at the rushes.

Walking through the rain to the building which housed the cutting and screening rooms Kostasch took my arm.

"When are your wife and daughter arriving?"

"At nine-fifteen."

"I'll be there."

"No!"

"But yes, I'll be there. I want to be the first to congratulate your wife and to tell her how happy we all are about the way the movie is going."

At a quarter past seven we were in the screening room: Kostasch, Seaton, his blond blue-eyed assistant, the camera man, and I.

Seeing the scenes we had played the day before was very exciting for me. Kostasch sensed it and patted my shoulder. "There's no business like show business, eh?"

We saw Henry Wallace murder me with the bronze lamp and Seaton chose the second take.

"Very clear picture," said Kostasch to the camera man.

"Yeah."

We saw several copies of my close-ups.

"Marvelous," said Kostasch. "Just great, Peter boy. People will cry their eyes out when they see that."

Seaton nodded agreement and said to his assistant, "We'll print the fifth take."

"Yes."

The scene between Wallace and Belinda King and the scene we had played twenty-five times followed. The lights went on. Kostasch and Seaton beamed at me as if they had just won a million.

"Just great," said Kostasch and touched wood. "I've never seen better!"

"Peter, let me thank you," said Seaton. He rose and shook my hand.

"Okay, okay."

"You have no idea how good you really are," said Kostasch now turning to my director. "You know, Thornton, I've noticed something about Belinda King I'd like to talk to you about . . ."

I glanced at my watch.

"If you don't need me any more I think I'll leave."

"Sure, Peter boy. I'll see you at the airport!" Kostasch shook my hand. "And thanks a million."

"Ah, nonsense," I said, feeling very happy indeed.

I left, closing the soundproof door. The heavy iron door to the projection room stood open. Light fell through the small windows in front of the massive projector from the room where Seaton and Kostasch were. I climbed three steps and looked through a window. They could not see me. I could see them—and was shocked. A moment ago they had been happy and optimistic. Now I saw two troubled men. Kostasch walked to and fro; Seaton rested his head in his hands. Kostasch said some-

175

thing. Seaton raised and dropped his shoulders. What were they talking about? I had to know!

I was familiar with the standard equipment in projection rooms. I turned a few switches until at the third one I could hear Kostasch's voice clearly. ". . . a disaster! A first-class catastrophe! Or do you mean to tell me you are going to play even one more scene with this man?"

"These were the first samples of the first day of shooting," groaned Seaton. "You have to give him more time. He hasn't made a movie in twenty years. He is unsure, inhibited . . ."

"Inhibited? What about this melodramatic scene where he dies? Straight out of a silent movie! What am I saying? Silent movie! It's nothing, less than nothing! I can do it better! Anybody could!" Breathing heavily he stood before Seaton. "Admit it!"

"Admit what?"

"That you made a mistake. I admit it too. It's my fault as much as it is yours! Jordan is a dilettante, a joke, a zero!"

"Oh, stop it," said Seaton. His hands shook visibly as he lit a cigarette. Haltingly he said, "I've seen Clark Gable carry on as a strolling player would. They were going to recast Spencer Tracy once. The fools fired Tyrone Power in one of my movies. Kostasch, I have faith in Jordan!"

"After all that?" cried Kostasch, indicating the empty screen. "Then you are a fool!"

"Even after that. I warned you of that possibility. And you? You promised, Kostasch, you gave me your word you would inspire the poor man with courage no matter how bad he was!"

"God Almighty, how could I have known how really bad he would be!"

I was standing behind the little window hearing all that; and through the night and the rain, somewhere above the

Atlantic a plane was nearing Hamburg, would soon land, carrying Joan, carrying Shirley . . .

"I did my best!" Kostasch cried in desperation. "As bad as I felt I slapped his back and congratulated him all day yesterday! And today too—in spite of the fact—you have to admit—that today he was even worse than yesterday!"

"Let's wait for the next few samples!" Seaton raised his head. He looked tired and defeated. "The man needs time. At least three more days!"

"And then what?"

"Then what?"

"Then he'll act the way we want him to. Then we'll shoot the first days again!"

"Reshoot five days? Do you know how much that is going to cost? The distributor is not going to give us a nickel! The Wilson Brothers will be furious if we go beyond our budget!"

"Then what would you suggest?" Seaton asked very calmly. He stepped on his cigarette. "Discontinue the movie? Recast Jordan?"

"Naturally."

"Do you have another actor?"

"There were a few other child stars in your country."

"But only one as good as he was."

"I've been thinking of him since yesterday."

Seaton said sadly, "Do you think I haven't?"

"Well, then?"

"We can't get him."

"Why not?"

"He got two years. Drugs."

"He . . . he's in jail?"

Seaton nodded. Kostasch groaned. He dropped into a chair, stretched out his legs and rubbed his face with both hands. The white-haired, gentle Seaton sat next to him. Kostasch dropped his hands. Quietly he said, "Four million. The distributor. The Wilson Brothers. Thornton, I can't sleep any more. If this movie goes phut, I'm ruined."

With grave dignity Seaton said, "I have directed important movies. I've worked with the most famous actors of my time. I am no fool. I have tested Jordan. I tell you: This man is a good actor." Kostasch laughed mirthlessly. "I promise you: He'll be okay in three days. But we have to encourage him; he has to have confidence in himself. If he finds out how we feel he'll never make it. It would be the finish!"

"But what about the others? Belinda, Wallace! They've all noticed . . ."

"No one will say anything. They have promised."

So that's why Wallace had apologized. That's why they were so nice to me. Who had talked to them: Production manager Albrecht, perhaps?

Kostasch sighed. "And he? What if he notices himself?"

"He won't. You've seen yourself how pleased he was when we looked at the samples."

They looked at each other silently. At last Kostasch said, "All right. Three more days. Then I'll have to tell Horwein and the Wilsons the truth." And now came something that gave me a profound shock. He folded his hands, lowered his head, and murmured, "Help us now. Please. Help us." I thought of Schauberg's comment: And if he had been a triangle he would have believed Him to be triangular.

27

"Attention please. Pan American announce the arrival of their flight 517 from New York. Passengers will go through customs at Gate 4!"

178

"Dear Passengers! Our building has become too small and we have to expand . . ."

I had had a few drinks in the car, still under the shock of what I had overheard before seeing Schauberg. Now in the airport restaurant I had again ordered whisky. Even the bar was under construction. The place smelled of steel, cement, and wet sand.

I had been drinking heavily but the injection had prevented me from becoming drunk. I was just slightly confused.

Now I passed many doors with airline signs. Ahead of me a door opened suddenly and I collided with a woman in a beige-colored flannel coat just as she was turning around.

"I beg your—"

Surprised, I stared at the slanted eyes of the beautiful young woman. A flash of recall—the seagull, the elephant.

"Good evening," said Dr. Natasha Petrovna.

28

"Good evening . . ." As I bowed slightly I lost my balance and realized that I was drunk after all. "What . . . what are you doing here?"

"I'm here about my furniture." Her answer was as calm and friendly as the look she gave me just as if the scene in my hotel had never occurred. "Unfortunately most of the things have already been flown out."

"I . . . I thought you were in the Congo!"

"I was supposed to be there." She smiled. "It seems the reverse of what we plan always happens. Terrorists have burnt down the hospital in Leopoldville. Didn't you read about it in the papers?"

"No."

"It will be at least a year before I can go to Africa. Now I'm stuck in an empty apartment and my furniture is in Rome, Dakar, or God knows where." Natasha laughed.

"You . . . you are going to be in Hamburg for another year?"

"Yes, I am." Her eyes narrowed. "You don't look at all well, Mr. Jordan. I read that you started on your movie."

Before I could answer Kostasch's voice said, "Peter, for heaven's sake, where have you been?"

Massive shoulders bent forward—a boxer on the offensive—bouquets of yellow and red roses in his hands, he came hurrying toward us. "The plane has already landed! I've been waiting a half hour for you! Excuse me, ma'am . . ." He pressed the red roses into my hand. "Come on, let's go!" He pulled me along by my arm.

"Good-by," I stammered, stumbling as I turned around. Natasha looked serious and now I could not see her eyes behind the thick glittering lenses of her glasses.

Kostasch hurried ahead of me up the stairs at the end of the hallway. "Why did you disappear so quickly after the viewing? We would have liked to have split a bottle of champagne with you! After those samples!"

You bastard, I thought. You miserable bastard. You poor, poor unhappy bastard.

The stairs led to Gate 4, a long, freezing room which immediately reminded me of Schauberg's barrack. The wind and rain came through the wooden slats of the temporary walls. The floor was wet and dirty. The room was very crowded. People waved, called, laughed, cried. The long line of passengers inched forward to customs and passport control.

"Hey, Charley! Over here," Kostasch yelled at our photographer holding a camera and flash. He looked very angry. "Don't make such a face, I'll pay you overtime!"

"Peter!" I heard my wife's voice. Now I saw her at the customs. Shirley stood next to her, Joan waved. Shirley did not. Joan's face was flushed. Shirley's was very pále. Joan gesticulated and laughed. Shirley stood perfectly still.

Joan wore a mink coat. Horrified, I saw that she had dyed her hair blonde. It made her look years older. What had made her do that? She probably wanted to look younger. To please me, to be more beautiful, more desirable . . .

"Oh, Peter, Peter!" Her arms were around me and she kissed my lips, my cheeks, my forehead, my lips again. I noticed it right away. She was high. Not embarrassingly so and not without charm. But I could hardly believe it. For the first time since I met her, my wife was tight. My cool, self-controlled, reserved wife.

Tight.

29

The photographer took our pictures, his face grim. I held the giggling and laughing Joan in my arms. She had dropped the red roses and continued to kiss me. "I'm high, Peter! Just a little. I was so excited! And happy. We had fun in the plane and the champagne tasted so good. Oh, Peter, I'm so very happy!"

Shirley stood behind Joan and I looked at her over Joan's shoulder. She looked at me over Kostasch's shoulder who, most fatherly, embraced and kissed her.

"Welcome, darling," I said to Joan.

"You're not angry I'm tight?"

"I think it's very becoming."

"And my hair? Don't you think my hair is too?"

"It's lovely."

"I knew you'd like it. Don't I look at least five years younger?"

"At least."

She whispered, "I have to look younger for a younger man! Marcel says I don't look a day over thirty-eight."

"Who is Marcel?"

"My hairdresser. He's a genius! Oh, it's wonderful to be a little high!" Her blonde hair. Her flushed face. The smudged lipstick. The wrinkles on her neck. The happy, slightly wet eyes. "How come no one ever told me? One ought to feel like this all the time!"

Kostasch was making some room. "Excuse me . . . just a few photographs . . . this is Peter Jordan, the famous American actor . . . please step back . . . thank you . . . Come on, Charley! Peter, kiss your wife!"

So I picked up the red roses and we kissed again. Now two more photographers from the airport had arrived.

"Now kiss your daughter, Peter!"

I turned. There was Shirley in a white sheepskin coat, black stockings, black shoes, a slim black wool dress, her pony tail pulled forward over her shoulder. Her green eyes were luminous but the hand I held was as cold as ice.

"So kiss your daughter!" cried Kostasch.

"Go ahead and kiss," called Joan laughingly.

I kissed Shirley. She was cold and stiff; unresponsive. Kostasch and Joan insisted we all take one another's arm. We smiled and laughed and the photographers snapped our pictures while Kostasch was talking incessantly. "Your husband is a very talented actor, Mrs. Jordan . . . One of the best . . . We're making a movie here they are going to talk about fifty years from now . . . I'm very proud to be the producer of such a movie . . . and of working with Peter!"

Joan began to kiss me again. "My husband! If he tries he can be the best actor in all the world!"

"Come on, Joan."

"Aren't I right? Isn't that so, Mr. Kostasch?"

"That's right, Mrs. Jordan," said the poor unhappy man.

Joan's eyes were damp. Impetuously I squeezed Shirley's arm and felt her nails dig into my hand.

"Well, let's go. Charley will take care of your baggage."

Kostasch pushed through the crowd toward the stairs. Holding Joan's and Shirley's arms, I followed. Joan was laughing and stumbled once. Shirley looked straight ahead. Then I noticed that she was looking toward the stairs. On its uppermost step stood Natasha Petrovna staring at us. She continued to stare.

"I just knew the movie would go well!" cried Joan. "That's why I had a few drinks. To celebrate."

"You had a few drinks, Mrs. Jordan?"

"Don't tell me you hadn't noticed!" Joan and Kostasch bumped each other foolishly and laughed.

"Peter."

"Yes, Shirley?"

"Who is that woman?"

"Woman? What woman?" Joan still laughing looked at her daughter.

"The one who is looking at us from the top of the stairs."

Joan turned her head. "At the stairs? I see no woman!" She giggled. "You are high too, Shirley darling!"

I looked back once more. Natasha was still standing there. Many people descending the stairs were now between her and us.

"Who is the woman, Peter?" Shirley repeated.

"No idea," I answered. "I've never seen her before."

The Fourth Tape

1

"This is the best champagne I've ever had! Isn't it the best, Shirley?"

"Yes, mommy."

"I've never enjoyed champagne as much as tonight! What are we drinking, Peter?"

"Pommery Demi-Sec, 1949," I said. And with emphasis, "The third bottle."

It did not make the slightest difference.

"But you ordered four!"

"One is still in the cooler."

"Then open it," said Joan. She was very drunk now. I had never seen her like this before; she seemed a stranger. A charming woman. A gay woman. A perfectly unfamiliar woman. Her awful blonde hair had become disarranged. Her eyes were glittering; her face, shiny. Her hands moved ecstatically, her expensive bracelets jangled. She talked too much. She repeated herself. She was just another person who had drunk too much. "Oh, I'm so happy! I love you both so very much! You two are all I have! Do you love me too? Tell me you love me, Peter."

"I love you too, Joan," I said and took the fourth bottle from the cooler.

"Tell me you love me too, Shirley."

"I love you too, mommy."

Joan jumped up, kissed me, ran to Shirley and kissed her. "I must kiss you! I must embrace you! I'm so happy I could embrace and kiss the whole world!"

It was late; the three of us were more or less drunk each in our own peculiar way: Joan was happy and gay; Shirley, off balance by an unaccustomed quantity of wine; I, depressed and fearful of what could happen to us in this condition.

One careless word.

One heedless look.

Then what?

It was madness, but how could I have prevented it? I, a drinker, was almost helpless; watching Joan drink because she was happy, watching Shirley drink out of desperation. Luckily Joan was too occupied with herself and her happiness to notice anything wrong with Shirley. How much longer? When would she become aware of it?

"Can I help you, darling?"

"No, thanks. I can manage." The cork would not move. I wound the napkin around the cork and tried again. Joan wore a silver-gray cocktail dress; Shirley, a gold-brown one. Joan had insisted on changing once we had arrived at the hotel. "Of course, we'll make ourselves look beautiful for our Peter! And we'll have another drink. I'm not at all tired. Are you tired, Peter?"

Shirley had said, "He has to be up early tomorrow."

But that, too, had made no difference.

"Just tonight, please! Starting tomorrow, I'll be reasonable and understanding. But today is the happiest day of my life. Our little family is together again. And Paddy's movie is going to be a success! Kostasch says everybody is delighted. Touch wood, but you'll see, this movie is going to be your comeback! Is that no reason to celebrate, Shirley?"

"Yes, mommy," she had answered. "Mommy is right. We'll have to drink to that."

188

It is impossible to stay sober among drinkers if one is not happy. Shirley had begun to drink too; she could not bear to be sober on this evening. And so we drank an excellent champagne in our charming apartment in a luxury hotel.

Others were drinking elsewhere: in dives, underneath bridges, in cockpits of patroling planes flying above the Arctic, A-bombs on board, with the pilots painfully aware of them; they were drinking in king's palaces, consulates, central committees, on yachts, in steel foundries and laboratories; they drank whisky, wine, sake, vodka, cognac; poor and powerful, rich and miserable, rulers and ruled; hunters and hunted, those who feared people, and those who are feared; all drinking to escape, even though each knew there was no escape.

2

Suddenly, so quickly I could not stop it, the cork popped out. A stream of white froth shot out of the bottle and over Joan who stood in front of me. I grabbed a glass, but my wife's dress was soaked. It made her laugh. "Peter! My awkward little Peter! Do you know, Shirley, Peter never could open champagne bottles?"

"And all his life he remained an awkward little boy," said Shirley.

Joan laughed again. "I must take this dress off." She stumbled into her bedroom, separated from mine by the living room.

Joan left the door partly open and we could hear laughing and chattering. "Really, every time he opens a bottle . . ."

Shirley and I stared at each other.

Hoarsely, she said, "Your friend Gregory sends his regards."

I went over to her, placed a hand on her shoulder and bent down to kiss her hair when she hissed, "Don't touch me!"

"Shirley!"

"If you touch me, I'll scream!" She was as drunk as Joan.

"Pull yourself together!"

"I can't. I can't. I feel I'm going to go mad if things go on this way. I feel as if I'm going to vomit. I have been feeling sick for weeks now. Give me another drink."

"You've had enough."

She snatched the bottle from my hand, spilling half a glass. She glared at me as though I was her worst enemy, the epitome of all she hated. She whispered, "Peter, I love you but I cannot stand this any longer!"

From her room, we heard Joan. "This darned zipper! Shirley, could you—" She laughed. "Now I've torn it. Ah, well, doesn't matter!" We heard her tripping on high heels into her bathroom.

"Have you found a doctor?"

"Are you mad? She can hear every word!"

I had stepped away just before Joan returned. She had changed into a light, short black robe. As she wore no shoes, I had not heard her enter.

"This stupid dress!" Joan stretched. She had not noticed anything. Had she? "How nice to get out of my clothes. Why are you looking at me that way, Shirley? I've been married to this man for the past thirteen years." She kissed me and laughed happily. She went to my bedroom and switched on the radio. A combo played jazz. Joan dropped onto my bed.

"Bring me my glass, Peter."

I took it to her.

"Come in here too, Shirley."

Shirley came into my bedroom too.

"Such nonsense," said Joan.

"What is?"

"To have two bedrooms. Can you explain to me why we should need two bedrooms?"

"I have to be up at six."

"So? Do you think I can't do that too?"

I was silent. Shirley sipped her drink. I thought: She must stop drinking. We all must stop drinking. Now. Before something happens. I told myself I had to say something, do something. I did nothing. I drank.

"Well, do you?"

"Do I what?"

"Think that I can't get up at six."

"I know you can."

"You see. We'll use the other bedroom as a dressing room and—" She interrupted herself. Her dyed hair hung in her flushed face, her lips trembled.

"What is it?"

"Don't you hear it? They're playing our song!" And to Shirley she said, "Our song . . . when we met . . . when we were young. Shirley, some day you will know a love such as ours . . . Every bar we went to, we requested the band to play this song for us . . ." She took a drink and some champagne spilled onto her neck, on her robe. She took my hand and kissed it.

Shirley put her glass down. "You won't mind if I go to my room now?"

"I'm a little drunk . . . you don't like that, do you?"

"No, it's just that I'm very tired."

"We're just among ourselves. It isn't so terrible if your mommy has had a bit too much to drink. You're not going to tell on her, are you?" She repeated, "You are not going to tell on me, are you?"

"Joan," I said, "Joan, really!"

"You won't?"

"No, of course not."

"You swear? You swear you won't tell on me?"

Shirley looked as if she were going to throw up any moment.

"We swear," I said.

"That's good . . . then, I'll give you your presents . . ."

"No!"

"Yes . . . I was going to give them to you in the morning . . . but you are both so good to me . . ."

"Joan! Joan, it's very late."

"Just the presents . . . then we'll go to bed . . . I promise . . . Shirley, please go and fetch my jewelry case . . . and fill our glasses, Peter . . . I want us to drink to something . . ." I looked at Shirley and nodded. She left, I refilled the glasses, Joan sat up in bed and pulled her knees close to her body. Shirley brought the square black alligator jewelry case.

"Take your glasses," said my wife. Now she was talking slowly and fluently and forced a smile to hide her emotion. "It sounds silly to say it but I love you both. So much that I could not live without you. For years, I had to watch you hate each other. It made me very unhappy. I thought my marriage, we all would break. And now—" She broke off, rubbed her eyes and again spilled champagne.

"Joan . . . Joan, please . . ."

"No, wait. I'm almost finished. Now Peter asked us to come to Europe. Before we left I had a long talk with Shirley. She was so good, and agreed to try . . ."

"We all will," I said.

"Yes, we all will. And that's why, for the first time in my life, I got drunk. Now I know everything is going to be all right. Sometimes I thought I was just an old mother with two children who hated each other. Now, now I feel like a woman! I have a husband. I have a daughter. So let's drink to our little family. May God watch over us and may we always be together as happy as we are today. Cheerio, Peter!" Our glasses clinked and I too said, "Cheerio!"

"Cheerio, Shirley."

"Cheerio."

We drank. The champagne tasted bitter. Joan opened her jewelry case. She took the yellow envelope from the top and placed it to one side. She then extracted a gray case which she handed to her daughter. "This is for you."

Shirley opened the case. I knew the ring resting on blue velvet. It was a perfect five carat diamond surrounded by baguettes.

Shirley whispered, "No . . . no . . ."

"Your father gave me this ring. When I was five months pregnant with you. I was not going to give it to you until you were expecting your first child. But you have made me so happy, I want you to have it now . . ."

Shirley stared at the ring for a few moments; then, she began to cry. Her body was shaken by her sobs. She fell to her knees before the bed, "Oh, mommy, mommy . . . don't be angry . . . you must forgive me . . ."

This was it. The time had come.

"Forgive you? What should I forgive?"

"That I . . . I . . . mommy, I—"

I stepped behind Shirley and placed my hands under her arms. As I pulled her up roughly, I stepped hard on her foot. The pain brought her to her senses. She stammered, "Forgive . . ."

"But of course, mommy forgives you for crying. She knows it is because you are overcome with joy." Joan beamed.

I nodded, "She knows you cry because you're happy."

"I understand, Shirley. I cried too when I first received the ring!"

Shirley was sobbing hysterically.

I said to Joan, "Everything was too much of a strain." I was still holding on to Shirley or she would surely have fallen. I pushed her head down gently. "Give mommy a kiss." She did. "Thank her again."

"Thank you, mommy." She straightened up, still crying.

"She's overtired, overly stimulated and she has had too

much to drink. After that plane trip too." More words came from my lips, mechanically. "She has to get to bed. Right away."

"Yes, Shirley, yes . . . Paddy is right . . . go to bed, darling . . . good night!"

"Good night, Mommy . . ." stammered Shirley.

As I led her from the room, she leaned heavily on my arm. Joan was smiling at us. I was relieved when we reached the hall. Shirley began to whimper. Sharply I said, "Pull yourself together!"

"I can't . . . I can't . . ." She fell silent when a waiter passed us.

"Go to your room. I'll see you later."

Before running down the hall, she looked at me, a desperate, crazed expression in her eyes. I watched her enter her room. The key was still in the lock when she closed the door. I returned to Joan.

Joan was lying on the bed. Her eyes were closed but she was smiling happily.

"What is . . . the matter with her?"

"She's all right. Just nerves. But you really are out of your mind, Joan! To give her that ring!"

"Well, why shouldn't I?" she said sleepily. "She's my child . . . I won't lose her . . . we three will be happy together . . . now your present . . . the . . . yellow envelope . . ."

It was sealed.

"Open it . . ."

The document of many pages showed the letterhead of a well-known law firm in Los Angeles. Joan had given me, effective immediately, one half of all she owned. The other half was in trust for Shirley until she became twenty-one.

The document dropped from my hand. I stared at Joan. Her eyes were still closed; she was still smiling. Her speech was blurred. "Makes . . . happy?"

"Joan! You can't do that! You musn't!"

"I . . . love . . ."

My hands were damp with perspiration as I reached for the document once more. The letters were dancing before my eyes.

Joan was half asleep, "Movie . . . maybe necessary . . . money . . . you need . . . I need . . . only you . . ." Her head fell to one side.

I got up, turned off the radio and placed the document which had made me a millionaire in the jewelry case. I undressed Joan who was now fast asleep. Seeing the fragile, slight body I had once desired and which no longer stirred desire gave me a moment's sense of guilt. I slipped her into my pajamas, covered her, and left her in the darkened room.

In the hall I noticed how very drunk I was. The doors and shoes outside them seemed to move; the floor rose and sank. I knocked on Shirley's door. There was no answer.

"Shirley!"

No answer. I opened the door. It was dark. I thought that perhaps Shirley had already fallen asleep.

My head hurt. Damn champagne! I felt my way from the foyer into the bedroom. Apparently the rain had stopped. A wan moon of greenish tint faintly lit the room. The bed had not been touched. I turned to look in the bathroom. I had moved too quickly, became dizzy, and fell into a chair. That's when I saw Shirley. Her back toward me, she was leaning against the front of the balcony.

The wind was tossing her hair; the sheer curtains on the French windows fluttered wildly. She tottered back— Forward. Back. She leaned over the side of the balcony. Farther. I could not see her head. She straightened up and fell back against the closed part of the window. Suddenly, she moved fast. Holding onto the balcony, she swung a leg over the low balustrade. Her tight dress tore. I froze, holding my breath. Now. Now. She was going to jump.

3

She did not jump.

She drew her leg from the wall and staggered against the door. Her hands to her face, she swayed.

I jumped up, took a few steps to reach the French windows, and bumped into her trunk.

Clouds were covering the moon, the eerie light changed. I reached the door. Through the curtains, I could see her pale face, her large eyes gazing fixedly. She clutched the gray jewelry case to her breast. I held my breath, knowing that I had to reach her with one jump. Shirley staggered forward. She turned her head and then she saw me.

"No!"

Her scream jarred. I leaped and seized her arm. She had already lost her balance and her weight pulled me forward. I managed to plant my foot against the wall and pulled her back. We both fell; my head hit something. Pain flashed through me. Yet, holding her wrist, I rolled to one side and picked myself up. I dragged her into the room where she collapsed on the floor. I managed to close the French doors before I too sank down. We were both exhausted, speechless. I felt my aching head. She was staring at me; slowly she recovered.

"Oh, God," said Shirley. She sat up. I put my arm around her; she trembled and stared at the French windows. "I . . . I was . . ."

"Don't," I said. "It's all right now."

We were both sober again. I stroked her and held her close.

"I was so drunk. If you had come a few seconds later . . ."

"It's all over now," I said. I rose and pulled her up.

"I . . . I would be dead now . . ."

"Come away from here."

"I'm all right. You must not worry. I won't ever try it again. If I had done it right away! Now . . . Now . . . I can't even bear to think of it . . ." She sat on the side of the bed, green moonlight lit her auburn hair.

"I'll stay with you."

"No."

"Yes."

"You have to go back to her."

"I'm afraid to leave you."

"I won't try it again. I swear to God I won't. Peter. Peter. I love you. I swear by my love for you. It's passed now. Truly. Receiving the ring upset me. What . . . what did she give you?"

"Half of all she owns."

"What?"

"She gave half to me, the other half to you."

"No!"

"I'll never touch any of it but she has already been to her lawyers and . . ."

Shirley began to laugh hysterically, her body shaking between sobs and laughter.

"Stop it, Shirley, stop it!"

"All she owns . . . she gave—" She broke off. The reaction had set in. She ran to the bathroom and vomited. I followed her.

"Please . . . go away . . . I don't want you to see me like this . . ." But she fell to her knees; I had to support her. She was very weak; I helped her clean up and carried her to the bed. I had seen a vial of sleeping tablets in the bathroom. I gave her two. The vial I slipped into my pocket. I held her while she drank.

"Now you'll sleep."

"The child," she moaned, "it's the child too. I told you I'm always sick now."

"It will be over soon."

"Yes . . ."

"We must not drink this much again."

"No . . . Peter, she loves us! How can we ever tell her? I can never . . ."

"I'll tell her."

"You can't either. She trusts us. We're all she cares for. What if she killed herself—"

"She won't."

"How can we be happy if she . . ."

"She won't hurt herself."

Shirley's eyes filled with tears. She repeated some of the things Joan had said. "Now I have a husband again . . . a daughter . . ."

"Shirley! Stop it!"

"Your father gave me this ring . . ."

"Where is it?"

"What? Where is what?"

"The ring! Where is the ring?"

"In the case. I held it in my hand when—" She fell silent, closed her eyes, and remained quiet.

I got to my feet.

"It's late. There can't be many people on the street now. Perhaps it's on the street. Perhaps I can still find it."

4

I did not find it.

I searched the street and both sidewalks. Nothing. I looked up. The hotel had many balconies. The case could have fallen on one of them. I had to speak to the desk clerk. Suppose it could not be found on one of the balconies? What would we tell Joan?

Suddenly I felt very weak. Across from the hotel along the bank of the Alster was a bench. I sank upon it. The futility of it all overwhelmed me.

Someone was coming. I heard the muffled pad, pad of rubber-soled shoes on the stone pavement. I lowered my head. I did not want to see anyone. I did not want to be seen. Someone was standing before me. I looked up.

"Here is the case," said Natasha Petrovna.

5

I rose.

I took the case, opened it, saw the ring, closed it.

"This is a surprise to find you here."

"I'm taking a walk."

"This time of night?"

"I can't sleep. I live right around the corner. I'm always taking walks."

"Every night?"

"Every night."

In the moonlight her eyes shone large and luminous behind her glasses.

"And you always walk along the river?"

"Usually." She did not take her eyes off me. "Only tonight I walked past the hotel."

"Why?"

"You were on my mind tonight." She seemed most matter-of-fact.

I stared at her. "How long have you been walking here?"

"About an hour. Is your wife asleep, Mr. Jordan?"

"How did you know the case belonged to me?"

"I saw it fall." She looked up to Shirley's balcony. "I heard a scream and saw you and your daughter when I looked up. She is your daughter, isn't she?"

"My stepdaughter. What else did you see?"

"For a moment I thought your stepdaughter was going to jump and you pulled her back just in time."

"Why should my stepdaughter want to do that?"

"Possibly the scream had confused me."

"She screamed when she dropped the jewelry case."

"That is what I thought. That is why I picked it up and waited. You were bound to come and search for it."

We looked at each other in silence.

"Thank you very much," I said finally. "Now may I see you home?"

"No, thank you. I'm going to walk a little more. Good night, Mr. Jordan."

"Good night, Doctor Petrovna."

She took two steps, then halted. "I've lied to you, Mr. Jordan. I did not only see you and your daughter on the balcony."

"What else did you see?"

"I saw your stepdaughter alone too. I was afraid to call out, to cross the street, for fear she would then jump. I waited here behind this tree."

"I must explain . . ."

"You don't have to explain anything."

"Yes, I do. You see, my stepdaughter—"

"Good night." Her voice for the first time sounded severe. Then she did a strange thing. She stretched out one hand; made the sign of the cross before my face, said something in Russian, wheeled and walked away.

"S'bogom."

Today I know the meaning of those words.

S'bogom.

God be with you.

6

I looked in on Shirley curled up and sleeping peacefully. I placed the gray case on her bedside table and went to my suite. Joan was asleep too. Very quietly, I took my black bag from the bedroom and went to the suite's second bedroom. I had a drink while I undressed, got into bed, and called the desk to wake me at six. I turned off the light, drank some more whisky, but sleep did not come easily.

7

"My dear Mr. Jordan, I don't like the look of you at all."

"Well, don't take it so seriously, after all you're not going to marry me."

"Don't be funny. What's the matter with you?" Schauberg looked searchingly at me. He had just given me an injection after examining my heart. We were in my car parked behind the old barn.

"I've only had four hours sleep."

"Had much to drink?"

"Quite a bit."

Schauberg took off his stethoscope and shook his head. "Your heart never beat as fast as this before. Well?"

"Well, what?"

"Well, what happened? I told you in the beginning that you have to be completely frank with me. I must know what is happening to you."

"I . . . I'm afraid."

"That's the booze, dear Mr. Jordan."

"It's not that. It's something else!"

"What?"

I felt a dim misgiving about telling him. So I started again, "You'll have to give me something strong. I can't work like this."

"I have given you something strong. I can't start with the most effective drugs. What would we do in fourteen days?"

"It'll probably be all over by then."

"What do you mean?"

Instead of heeding my premonition, I told him of the conversation I had overheard in the studio. Finally he said, "Do you feel you played badly?"

"Now I do."

He looked at me in silence.

"What are you thinking?"

"I'm thinking of South America." He sighed and prepared another injection. "Very well then, I'll give you something to free you of fear but it will make you a little dizzy. Under no circumstances can you have a drink. Do you understand me? Under no circumstances. If you should have just a little drink, you would collapse and even I can't help you then. Will you be able to do it?"

"I must. I'll leave my bag with you." I felt truly heroic when I said that.

"You can buy all the whisky you want in the commissary," said Schauberg and gave me the shot.

"I won't."

"You know what will happen."

"Schauberg . . ."

"Yes?"

"There is something else I must tell you."

"Something else?" Nervously, he pulled at his beret. He was obviously worried. I was his last chance, just as the movie was my last chance. I realized that as I watched him try to control his twitching mouth. I had no idea then that what I had told him was to have so deep an effect.

Soon I was to find out how right I had been in hesitating to talk about the reaction of Kostasch and Seaton.

"Go on, then!" He barked impatiently. Then, with a distorted smile, "Sorry, didn't mean it like that. What else do you have to tell me?"

"There is a young girl. Could you help her?"

"How old is she?"

"Nineteen."

"How far gone, dear Mr. Jordan?"

"Two months, dear Dr. Schauberg."

"Do you know the girl well?"

"Yes."

"How well? It could not be a trap?"

"No."

"I have to be very cautious. I must see her identification. I must know who she is. Where from."

"She is my stepdaughter."

His mouth stopped twitching. He began to grin.

"Father knows best, eh? As long as it remains in the family," he said placatingly.

"You can help her?"

"I'll have to find someone to assist me."

"Another doctor?"

"Do you think I'm mad? A student! Give me until tomorrow."

"You'll be able to find one by tomorrow?"

"Easy. Boy! Now I need one. You don't mind?" He opened my black bag. I felt sick when I smelled the whisky. "Did you give me a fright!"

"I did?"

"Now look! First you tell me you are going to be fired from your movie. You look as if your dear little mother had just died and then you announce another disaster." He sipped his drink. "I thought it was something serious. And then it turns out a trifle." He laughed. "You are a peculiar fellow, dear Mr. Jordan!"

8

The secretary's transcript:

PROFESSOR PONTEVIVO: Please—a brief interruption—I came to see if the taping is not too strenuous for you.

SIGNORE JORDAN: Not at all.

PROFESSOR PONTEVIVO: Well, I don't think so either. Your blood pressure is normal. I'll leave you to your work. Just one question: You did not know what kind of drug Dr. Schauberg gave you on that morning?

SIGNORE JORDAN: No.

PROFESSOR PONTEVIVO: Did you have a taste of salt after the injection?

SIGNORE JORDAN: That's right.

PROFESSOR PONTEVIVO: I see. And it calmed you?

SIGNORE JORDAN: I felt a little dizzy; Schauberg had said I would, but I felt no apprehension before the camera. I made no mistakes. I thought I acted the scenes very well.

PROFESSOR PONTEVIVO: Did you still receive much praise?

SIGNORE JORDAN: Yes.

PROFESSOR PONTEVIVO: But it did not make you suspicious?

SIGNORE JORDAN: No. Kostasch and Seaton appeared to be genuinely relieved—I even found the courage to ask Kostasch to hire Shirley as an assistant cutter. He said, "I'll be happy to, my dear Peter."

PROFESSOR PONTEVIVO: It was a good day then.

SIGNORE JORDAN: A wonderful day. I was so absorbed in my work I did not even think of whisky.

PROFESSOR PONTEVIVO: At night you viewed the rushes again and listened to Kostasch's and Seaton's conversation?

SIGNORE JORDAN: They agreed that the rushes were even

worse than those of the preceding days. But Seaton insisted that Kostasch keep his promise to give me another two days. He would agree to only one more day. He then said he would have to inform the Wilson Brothers and the distributor. You can imagine my despair when I left the studio. I drove to see Schauberg but controlled myself so he would not again become upset. He returned my black bag replenished, and told me I could drink again but cautioned me to go to bed early.

PROFESSOR PONTEVIVO: Did you drink then?

SIGNORE JORDAN: As soon as I got into my car. All the way back to the hotel. My wife and Shirley were waiting for me. I told them I felt tired and we had dinner in my suite.

PROFESSOR PONTEVIVO: How were the ladies?

SIGNORE JORDAN: Considerate and solicitous. They recounted their sightseeing and shopping. Joan whispered how well Shirley and she got along. They had had a busy day too and at ten we were all in bed.

PROFESSOR PONTEVIVO: Did you share a bedroom with your wife?

SIGNORE JORDAN: No. My wife was very considerate. It was her suggestion we have separate rooms. She said she was afraid of disturbing me.

PROFESSOR PONTEVIVO: Did you have another drink when you went to bed?

SIGNORE JORDAN: Yes, as usual. I fell asleep quickly. That night, for the first time, I had a dream which was going to recur again and again. The dream frightened me to such an extent that many times I tried desperately to stay awake. In my dream . . .

9

. . . I crossed the foyer of my hotel and in the elevator pressed the button for the sixth floor. In this dream I had been living in this hotel for many years. I had taken that elevator uncountable times, with its ceiling lights, worn velvet-covered bench, its mirrors repeatedly duplicating my image.

When the elevator doors opened this time, instead of the red-covered hall, I saw a gray wall. It seemed strangely wrinkled, streaked and mottled.

Perhaps the elevator had stopped between floors. I pressed the white number six button. The elevator did not move. Suddenly a memory rose in me and I punched the gray wall. It felt rough, hard, as would the thick old hide of a large animal, an elephant . . .

Alarm.

Hurriedly, I pressed the red button. Through the intercom came a distorted voice I nonetheless recognized as Natasha's. She spoke calmly and friendly as always, "Yes?"

"The elevator is stuck, Dr. Petrovna."

"The elevator is working perfectly."

"No, it isn't! I'm stuck between floors! Please help me!"

"Who are you, sir?"

"Peter Jordan, Doctor. You know me!"

"I'm sorry, I don't."

"Dr. Petrovna! You examined me! Don't you remember!"

"My name is not Petrovna. You've made a mistake," said the calm voice.

"Then who are you?"

It was Natasha. It was her voice. She did not answer

my question. I pressed the alarm button once more. No answer.

I sank down on the little bench. I saw my image in the mirrors. I could not stand it. I stared at the gray wall of elephant hide.

"Hello?"

I started, "Yes?"

"I've made some inquiries. There is no Peter Jordan living in this hotel."

"I've lived here for the last ten years! I'm well-known here!"

"I asked. No one knows you. Anyway, where did you want to go?"

"To the sixth floor. I live there."

"You can't live there."

"Why not?"

"This building only has four floors."

There was a click, the intercom was silent. I was panic stricken. I began to pound against the mirrors, the wood, the elephant wall. I cursed. I begged. I screamed. There was the voice again.

"Yes?"

"The elevator is stuck, Dr. Petrovna—"

The conversation began again, was interrupted, continued, interrupted.

Hours passed; days passed, weeks, months, years passed. Hundreds of years passed.

I cowered on the little bench staring at the grating of the intercom through which Natasha had once spoken to me.

The grating of the intercom!

It took thousands of years—thousands of years too late—for me to recognize: this latticed coverplate represented God. I had to kneel down and pray. Then perhaps Natasha's voice would speak to me again.

I kneeled, folded my hands in prayer and bowed in reverence before the grating.

10

I awoke, drenched in perspiration, gasping for breath. It was eleven o'clock. A drink! Even whisky did not help. I tried to open the large window but it was stuck.

The fist.

I could feel it moving, pounding.

My one thought was to get away from here.

I dressed. In my hurry, I stumbled and fell on the bed. I was unable to tie my shoelaces properly.

I staggered through the living room. Joan was sleeping. Shirley was sleeping. Neither of them knew what was happening to me; what I was doing.

The fist was pounding in me. I walked down the six floors. I knew that I could never, ever again, use the elevator.

I went to the bar and ordered a double whisky. Neat.

The bar was crowded. People talked loudly to be heard above the din of the band. A young woman near me was telling her friends, ". . . and I said now there are two uncles who want to marry your mommy, Teddy. Which one do you like best? And very seriously he said, 'Let's take Uncle Martin, then we'll have a Mercedes.' Isn't that cute? And he is only five!"

I drank my whisky and asked for another double. After that, I left. In the cold, slight rain, I walked. And walked.

"I live just around the corner," she had said. "I always go for a walk at night."

Not tonight.

I would not have been able to say why I was looking for her. The raindrops felt like icy needles on my skin. I walked along the two narrow roads on either side of my hotel. In the second street, I found the plaque.

NATASHA PETROVNA, M.D.

All the buttons above the tenants' names were white. Only the superintendent's button was red. Below this button was the latticed cover of the intercom . . .

Natasha lived on the third floor. It was abstruse, absurd, inexplicable. I rang the bell. In a moment there was a click; the same sound I remembered from my dream.

"Yes?" said Natasha's voice.

"Peter Jordan."

Silence.

"I'm . . . excuse me . . . it's very presumptuous of me . . . I thought . . . I wanted . . ."

"Yes, Mr. Jordan?"

"You said you took a walk every night. I've been looking for you . . ."

No answer.

"I searched for you along the Alster promenade . . ."

"Why?"

"I don't really know. I'm probably drunk. I'm sorry to have bothered you. Good night." I had taken three steps when I heard, "Mr. Jordan . . ."

I returned to the intercom. "Yes?"

"I'll be down in two minutes."

"But . . ."

"I intended to go a little later tonight. Tonight I—" She halted. "Is it still raining?"

"Yes."

"Do you have an umbrella?" Her voice sounded happy. Had she had a happy experience tonight?

"No."

"Two minutes, Mr. Jordan."

Click.

The intercom had been switched off. I stood in the doorway; the whisky warmed me. In a little while I noticed that I was stroking the cold, wet, brass grating of the intercom.

We walked an hour through the rain; we hardly spoke a hundred words. Natasha smiled and offered her hand when she came down. She wore a brown sheepskin coat, a scarf over her hair. She had brought two umbrellas.

"This is all I could find. My things are still God knows where. It's a crazy situation." One of the umbrellas was a child's umbrella. I took this one although she wanted me to take the larger one.

We walked down the Jungfernstieg and the pad, pad of her low-heeled shoes was as reassuring as the sound of the raindrops on our umbrellas. Without looking at me, Natasha asked, "You are very worried?"

"Yes."

"I'm so sorry. You know, I've had a wonderful experience today." But she did not talk about that, and I did not mention my troubles or my dreams. Then, we went on in silence, once in awhile looking at each other and smiling.

We walked away from the hotel. I could not have found a reasonable explanation for this stroll with a strange woman, had I been asked. Neither could I have said what made me feel calm and at peace alongside Natasha, nor could I have explained anything else I did or what took place.

We passed through one of this city's oldest parts, the Nicolaifleet, once the main estuary of the Alster. We stood on the Hohen Brücke looking down at the narrow canal where hundreds of years ago Hanseatic ships had anchored, now packed tightly with barges. On one side of the fleet are ancient timbered houses. They had been painted pink, pale yellow and light green. Now the paint was peeling; they looked dilapidated. Beneath the pointed gable of the nearest house to the bridge I read:

THE TIDES ARE THE
TRADERS' WEALTH
1647
MAY GOD PROTECT US ALL

"Down here began the great fire of 1842 which destroyed a fifth of the city," said Natasha. "And a hundred years later bombs destroyed it again."

On the other side of the fleet were ruins overgrown with weeds. In the distance the pointed, black, gothic tower of the destroyed Nicolai Church was silhouetted against the even darker sky.

Natasha was thoughtful. "The tower is going to remain as a memorial to the war dead and as a reminder of the crimes of the Third Reich."

It was raining hard now and we left the bridge. Shortly after midnight we were at Natasha's house. I returned the umbrella.

"Thank you."

"Thank you for what?"

"You know for what," I said.

She did not take the hand I held out to her.

"Do you remember I told you I had had a wonderful experience today?

"Yes, I do."

"I'd like to show you something. Would you like to come to my apartment for a moment?"

"Certainly."

She unlocked the door. I followed, having forgotten Shirley, Joan, my dream, and that I had to be in the studio in a few hours. The elevator was not working. We walked up to her apartment.

We passed through one room which contained only one bed and chair. Suitcases were overflowing and coats and dresses hung from a few wall hooks. In the second room Natasha switched on a little bedside lamp standing on the floor. A little red oil lamp flickered beneath a few old and beautiful icons. Next to the eternal light hung a little earthenware vase with flowers.

A small bed stood in one corner of the room. A blond child, hidden by blankets, was asleep in it. A few toys were strewn around the room and the entire wall behind the bed was covered by a child's colorful and imaginative paintings and drawings. I was strangely moved.

A little foot protruded from the blanket and Natasha gently pushed it under the bedclothes.

I could not see the face of the child. I took one step forward and inadvertently tipped over the bedside lamp. The crash echoed in the almost empty room; Natasha looked up and smiled at my dismay.

"He didn't hear anything."

"I hope not."

"He couldn't have heard it, Mr. Jordan. He is deaf."

"Deaf?" I said, horrified.

"And dumb, Mr. Jordan. Deaf and dumb."

12

"What is his name?"

"Misha."

"How old is he?"

"He is four years old, Mr. Jordan," answered Natasha. "And deaf and dumb since birth."

We had left the child's room and entered her office. An old-fashioned oil painting of a troika hanging behind the desk was a strange contrast to the instruments which glittered in glass-fronted cupboards. On a white table stood a tape recorder.

"A colleague was supposed to rent the office. That's

why everything is in order here. Now the poor fellow might have to wait a year or two. Who knows? Who knows anything anyway?" She took off her scarf, busied herself with the tape recorder, and out of context said, "I told you once that you reminded me very much of a man in my life."

I nodded.

"He was Misha's father. I mentioned it once before: he was a hopeless drunkard. He died in an institution. We had lived together many years."

"How long were you married?"

"We were never married."

"You were—"

Almost gayly she answered, "No, never. His wife had left him but she would not agree to a divorce. When she found out about me, there was a big scandal. You can imagine the consequences in a town as proper as Hamburg."

"You lost your patients?"

"Many. I was investigated by the Doctors Association. I was ignored by many influential people. Many peculiar things happened . . ." There was a strange smile in her eyes. She was the first Russian woman I had met and at that time I knew nothing of the world in the East. Today I do. Through Natasha.

There is a universal belief that Russian women are sentimental. The woman of the East is not sentimental; she is melancholy. To sacrifice herself seems almost a pathological joy to a Russian woman in love. She would give endlessly. I was to have that experience with Natasha.

13

"When the child was born its father had already died," said Natasha. She pushed back her glasses.

"Misha paints beautifully, doesn't he?" she said. "At the moment he is sad. His paints and crayons are all packed in one of the trunks which have been shipped. He inherited his father's talent—and something else too."

I stared at her. I could not speak.

"You understand what I mean, Mr. Jordan?"

I nodded. I wet my dry lips. Finally I managed to ask, "You . . . you mean alcohol is the cause of this?"

Natasha did not answer.

"But why——" I began and fell silent.

"What were you going to say?"

I shook my head.

"You were going to say. 'You are a doctor. Why didn't you prevent such a man from fathering a child?' That's what you were going to say, weren't you?"

I nodded.

She answered, "Because I was selfish. I knew the man would die. I wanted to keep something of him when he left me forever. I ignored the facts. I counted on the law of averages. Even with the heaviest drinkers, congenital defects rarely are as tragic as this. I hoped to be lucky. But people have little luck."

My father had said that. Now Natasha said it. We were silent in the large office. I heard a clock strike once.

"How do you make yourself understood?"

"We use sign language. Isn't it lucky he is not blind too?"

"Isn't there some treatment——"

"There is nothing I have not tried. The best hospitals; the most accomplished specialists. There is a new theory that a constantly high temperature and a certain air pressure are beneficial. That is why I accepted the offer to go to Africa."

"I see."

"Still, I had very little real hope. I had come to terms with the fact that my little boy would never be a healthy human being—until tonight, Mr. Jordan," she said and her eyes were shining behind the glasses; her face flushed with joy. "Until tonight."

"What happened tonight?" I asked, thinking that possibly all this, the empty apartment, the child were a figment of my imagination, of madness.

"We were having dinner tonight and he was telling me a story." She switched on the tape recorder. "He was so excited, more than usual and then suddenly . . ." Natasha pushed back her glasses; the tape recorder hummed. "For the first time in his life he produced sounds! He was very excited and I switched on the tape recorder and he tried again—" From the tape recorder came a hoarse sound, "Orrr . . . orr . . ." Natasha was ecstatic. "Did you hear it?" I nodded. "Wait . . . again . . . there!"

"Rraa . . . rraaa . . ."

"Isn't it wonderful?" said Natasha. "Isn't it a miracle? It's a beginning, Mr. Jordan. I know he will be able to talk. He will be able to hear! When I was a little girl I once saw a scorpion inside a circle of fire. I often dreamt about that. Many times during the last few years I felt that my little boy and I were inside such a circle from which there was no escape."

What did those last words remind me of?

"We did escape the circle. Listen!"

"Rraaa . . . rraaa . . ."

She replayed the tape,

"Orrr . . . orrr . . ."

"I held his hand to the tape recorder and he must have felt the vibrations. He was so excited and laughed and

cried and at last I had to give him a sedative to calm
him . . ."

"Orrr . . . orrr . . ."

"I listened to the tape, again and again until you rang
the bell. Now do you understand why this is the happiest
day for me?"

"Rraaa . . . rraaa . . ."

14

The next morning in my car again. It was still raining.
"Today you seem much better," said Schauberg.

"I feel better too."

"Still afraid? I'd rather not give you another one of
those injections you had yesterday."

"I won't need it."

"Bravo! Better that you have a drink if things get
rough. How is everything? How were the rushes?"

"Worse than ever."

His mouth began to twitch again. I did not care. He
was afraid of not getting his money. I was afraid of losing
mine.

Schauberg managed a smile and patted my back with
the professional optimism common to doctors. "Just
nerves. You're just too sensitive. In a couple of days
you'll be fine, I'm sure."

"Okay, okay. Did you find a student for . . ."

"I've found two. They're demanding too much money."

"I don't care."

"But I do. One simply cannot ruin established prices!
Now I'm playing one against the other."

"Time is running out!"

"I'm sure you can wait until tonight, daddy. You can
rely on me."

"Schauberg——"

I looked at the road but not at him when I asked the question.

"Schauberg, is there hope for a deaf and dumb child whose father was an alcoholic?"

Irritated he pulled his beret. "Now look here, you'll really have to pull yourself together or both of us will end up in a nuthouse!"

"Answer me!"

"Don't think about it. The child is not going to be born."

"Damn, I'm not talking about this child. I mean a four-year-old boy whose father died of the d.t.'s."

"Very improbable."

"What is very improbable?"

"That the father's alcoholism is the cause. If the parents are drinkers the children may be feeble-minded or crippled but hardly deaf and dumb. There must also be a hereditary factor. Does the man have a history of deaf and dumb people in his family?"

"I don't know. Is there any chance of a cure?"

"It is not very likely."

"The mother says the child is producing sounds now."

"Adult deaf and dumb people can make sounds but they never learn to talk."

"Why not?"

"They can't hear. How could they imitate human sounds if they cannot hear them?"

It seemed reasonable.

"So you believe the case is hopeless?"

"Completely."

"But the mother doesn't! And she is—" At the last moment I stopped myself from saying "a doctor herself."

It would have made him suspicious. A doctor? I knew another doctor? Who was she? How did I meet her?

Half the sentence was sufficient to make him suspicious; "What is his mother, dear Mr. Jordan?"

"Intelligent. Very intelligent. And objective."

"I see." He was still not sure.

Quickly I carried on, "She knows the facts. And still she believes in a cure."

"Because she loves her child, Mr. Jordan. A mother will cling to the slightest hope. But there is no cure. One can live when deaf and dumb."

"What an awful life."

"An awful life," said Schauberg, "is still better than the most beautiful death."

15

The first take this morning was very long and heavy on dialogue.

According to the script I had been a child star. I was the lover of Belinda King, whose husband, Henry Wallace, wanted me to play the lead in a movie he was producing. According to the script, I had no confidence in myself and was not at all enthusiastic about resuming my acting career. Slowly I regained my confidence until at last I would have done anything to be allowed to act.

Our film told the story of how this movie was originated in America and Germany. I became famous, the movie was a financial success, I made my comeback, was hailed a star only to be killed by the jealous Henry.

Belinda and Henry played Evelyn and Graham Willcroft. I was Carlton Webb.

The author was among those once investigated by the House Un-American Activities committee. For what the courts agreed was contempt of Congress, they were jailed. The big studios did not dare employ them thereafter. Only lately had there been some change. Kostasch had been able to put the author under contract for a reasonable amount of money after his years of famine.

CARLTON (glass in hand, near a window, watching a car pull away. Shrugging his shoulders, he crosses to the bar and refills his glass.)

EVELYN (enters upset) Graham says you refused his contract?

CARLTON (drinks, growls) That's right. Sorry, baby. I've thought it over. I'm not going to play. Have a little drink?

EVELYN (hysterical) For goodness sake! You and your damn whisky! What do you mean you're not going to play? You must play! You know what it means . . . for you . . . for me . . . Carlton! You are an actor! This is your chance for a new career. A new life!

CARLTON It won't work, baby.

EVELYN Why not? (shouts) Stop this drinking! Why won't it work?

CARLTON (grinning drunkenly) For one, I can't stop this. (drinks) 'Second, because I'm no actor. I was a handsome child. But an actor? Never!

EVELYN That's not true. You're afraid. You haven't been in a studio for a long time. You'll get used to it again. Don't you see this is your last chance? For you and for me!

CARLTON No one has a chance. Not you. Not I. No one at all.

EVELYN (strokes Carlton tenderly) You'll be all right because you are brave and courageous. And talented.

CARLTON (pushes her away roughly) Courageous . . . and cunning, right? Yes. That's true. I'm as cunning and brave and courageous as the Rabbi of Krotoszin.

EVELYN What are you talking about?

CARLTON (walking up and down, glass in hand) That's a very . . . very edifying story. You want to hear it? So listen. The Cossacks returned once again to Krotoszin. There was another pogrom. They beat up the Jews and set fire to their houses and . . .

EVELYN Carlton! Please! You're drunk!

CARLTON (roughly) Shut up . . . and set fire to their houses. Finally they came to the rabbi's house . . . (sets his glass aside. Absorbed in story he acts the characters, thereby proving how good an actor he really is) . . . and looted it. And then the lieutenant arrived . . . (as the lieutenant) . . . and with chalk he drew a circle on the ground and said to the rabbi, "Stand inside the circle, Jew!" (as the rabbi) The rabbi stood inside the circle and while the Cossacks beat his wife and tore off his daughter's clothes the lieutenant said, (as lieutenant) "You will be silent no matter what you hear now. Whatever you see now. You will not move. If you as much as push your big toe outside this chalk circle you are a dead Jew!"

EVELYN (watching Carlton, fascinated and horrified)

CARLTON The Cossacks left the following morning and the survivors crawled out from the rubble of their homes. Loud laughter echoed from the house of the rabbi and they hurried there. Inside his pillaged home they found the sobbing, violated women and the rabbi still standing inside the chalk circle, and he laughed and laughed and laughed . . .

CARLTON (acting as the neighbors) He's lost his mind . . . He went mad . . . (as the insane rabbi) . . . and the rabbi almost choked laughing and finally he said, "The honorable lieutenant forbade me to step outside this circle no matter what I saw or heard. (laughs) But then, when he fell upon my youngest daughter and forgot about me I carefully . . . slowly . . . pushed my big toe outside the chalk circle! And you know what? He didn't notice it!

CARLTON (laughs, suddenly breaks off. Looks at Evelyn. Pulls himself together. Reaches for his drink. He is once again himself, weak, despondent, drunk.) Do you understand, sweet? All the world is a ghetto! And everyone stands inside his own chalk circle! No one can step outside it! Never. No one! And that's why I have my big toe where it is. And that's why I won't sign the contract. And that's why I won't act. It would be futile, senseless. And ridiculous ... (He drinks, glass slips from his hand. He sways. Whisky runs from his mouth. Evelyn stares at him. He smiles crookedly.)

Camera shows both of them in the luxurious room, each one helpless, alone, in his own chalk circle.

16

From the corner of my eye I saw the camera come to a halt. Automatically I counted the seconds. Twenty-one. Twenty-two. Twenty-three. To give the cutter sufficient footage for the following takes, the director always added thirty seconds to each take.

Twenty-four, twenty-five, twenty-six ...

The camera continued to run; it was still silent on the set; Seaton still did not call "Cut!"

Why not? I had not fluffed my lines. Belinda had not made any mistakes.

Twenty-nine. Thirty. Thirty—

"Cut!"

Seaton's voice sounded strange, choked. He stared at me. Behind his chair stood Kostasch, his mouth gaping, amazement in his eyes. I saw now that the entire staff was staring at me. Someone began to applaud. Another followed. Until all of them were applauding. Belinda King embraced and kissed me. Kostasch moved, shook my hand. Seaton slapped my back so hard I stumbled.

"Boy, oh boy, oh boy!" he groaned.

They were around me, congratulating me, telling me how marvelous I had been, and I saw that they honestly meant what they said. All of them, each one inside his own chalk circle, must have felt relief.

Seaton knew now that he would continue to direct this movie. He could hope to be hired for other movies.

Kostasch did not have to vindicate himself to the Wilson Brothers or the distributor. Important people, little people. I had freed them all of the worry for their immediate future. And that's why they were all smiling.

"Peter," said Seaton, "what did you think of when you played that scene?"

"Of my dialogue."

"No, no. There was something strange happening to you . . . what did you think of?"

"Yes, Peter," Kostasch joined in. "What was it? You suddenly seemed to be Carlton, this poor drunken fellow."

I said, "You know, I just realized that I played myself; the man hoping for his comeback. It was wrong. From now on I'm going to play Carlton, not myself."

"That's what you thought of?"

"Yes," I replied. It was a lie. I had thought of a mother and child for whom there was no hope. Two people inside a chalk circle. They had been the only thought in my mind while I was playing scene number thirty-seven.

A script, even the best, is but a script; a parable is only words, a movie is but a film.

Or had script, parable, words, film suddenly become vitalized since—for the first time—I had been moved by the sorrow of unknown people? Was that the reason why all those on the set, those strangers had applauded me?

Quickly I went to my dressing room. I called a florist and ordered thirty red roses to be sent to Natasha. The florist was to buy for me the largest box of crayons and a thick sketch pad. They were to go with the roses.

"Would you like to enclose a card, Mr. Jordan?"

"No."

They were most agreeable about my request.

I stared into the big make-up mirror. Suddenly I saw my future. I would complete this film. It would be a success. And it would be the end of me, empty, burnt out, extirpated, destroyed, unrewarded. Because, as had the rabbi, I—with the approval of my brothers in humanity—had also pushed my big toe across the chalk circle.

17

"What did I tell you?"

Seaton's voice sounded happy. Once more in the projection room I was listening to his and Kostasch's conversation after we had viewed the rushes. I did not have to listen, I knew. I knew that at last all was well: both of them had stopped praising me after the fateful thirty-seventh scene.

I hurried to Schauberg, waiting for me behind the barn. We drank together.

"Cheers, Schauberg. Everything is okay."

"What do you mean?"

"I found myself. They are satisfied with me."

"You mean: the movie is not going to be discontinued?"

"That's right. That's what I mean."

"Are you sure?"

"Quite certain. I gave a great performance today. The entire staff—"

His hand shook and he spilled half his whisky. He looked at me searchingly, his mouth twitched.

"You're not lying, dear Mr. Jordan?"

"I swear I'm not lying."

"I'm going to get my money?"

"Yes, Schauberg, yes. A miracle happened."

"A miracle happened," he repeated lost in thought, and took a long drink. "I have good news too," he finally said.

"Your student?"

"Charming person. Last semester. Demands a thousand."

"And you?"

"I do it for the sake of our friendship, dear Mr. Jordan. You're paying me enough. One hand washes the other."

"When can you do it?"

"Anytime. I only have to examine your stepdaughter beforehand."

"She is going to be a cutter at the studio."

"Can you bring her with you tomorrow morning?"

"I can arrange that."

"Excellent. Until tomorrow then. My respects to the young lady. Is she staying at your hotel?"

"Yes."

"How convenient."

"My wife is there too."

"How awkward. Too bad I can't ask you to give my respects to your wife too. She'll hardly come tomorrow morning."

"Good night."

"Good night, dear Mr. Jordan. And may I remind you that tomorrow is the end of the first week?"

"I'll bring you a check," I said and coughed.

"That would be nice. I'll bring a few nice new injections for you."

I coughed again. "I think I've caught a cold. You can also bring me something for my cough."

He threw himself back against his seat and laughed, laughed, and laughed as if he'd gone crazy. In between, he panted, "Something against a cough!"

"What is so funny?"

He continued to laugh.

"Schauberg!"

He composed himself. "Relief. That's all. I'm just relieved. Yes, all right, I'll bring something against your cough. I have a lot to help your cough."

And with that he began to laugh again.

For the first time, I felt sympathy for him. No, not sympathy—pity. The poor superman. He too had dared to break through the circle of his ruined life. He intended to go to South America. This morning it had seemed as if the lieutenant had become aware of this step. Now the danger had passed.

Yes, that is how I analyzed his laughter.

What an idiot I was.

18

The trumpet pulsated. The singer smiled at us as my wife and I danced past him. His voice was soft and low.

The bar, decorated in dark blue, was crowded. Candles glowed on the small tables; the lighting was intimate.

Joan nestled close to me. She wore her most expensive jewelry, her dress was so tight she could only take tiny steps. Now we were dancing past our table. Shirley was smiling at us. Tomorrow I did not have to be at the studio until nine o'clock. It had been my wife's wish for the three of us to go out together this evening.

"Doesn't she look adorable?" said Joan. Proudly she looked at Shirley in her white cocktail dress. Her auburn hair shone in the candlelight. "Our daughter is really beautiful, isn't she?"

"Yes," I said, "beautiful."

We continued dancing. As soon as Joan's back was turned to Shirley, her smile vanished and she looked at me steadily. Dark circles were under her eyes.

"I didn't think it was possible any more," murmured my wife.

"What was not possible any more?"

"That we could get along so well. She is so considerate. So tender. Sometimes I think it's a conspiracy."

"Conspiracy?"

"By the two of you."

I looked at her quickly but saw only love and trust in

225

her brown eyes. Her unnatural blonde hair was freshly set. She was flushed from champagne and the heat in the bar.

"A conspiracy to make me happy. Did you say anything to her?"

"No."

"Or write to her before we came to Hamburg?"

"No."

"Phone her?"

"Whatever gave you those ideas?"

Once more we danced past our table and Shirley smiled again.

"What made you think Shirley might change like this in Europe?"

"Intuition," I said, and continued to turn with Joan in a circle (in the chalk circle), away from the table where Shirley stopped smiling. "I just had this feeling."

Joan kissed me.

Shirley tipped over her glass. A waiter hurriedly brought another. Joan had not noticed anything. She pressed close to me. "It really hasn't passed, Peter. You and I. Shirley and I. We three. Your movie. All miracles. Now everything is all right, isn't it?"

"No," I said.

She started, horrified. "No?"

"No, Joan."

"What do you mean?"

"Your money."

"What about it?"

"You must take it back. Then everything will be all right."

"I don't want it. It is yours."

"I won't ever touch a cent of it."

"Then don't." She laughed heartily. "Don't touch it. Give it to the poor . . ." Again she pressed close to me. "Oh, Peter, Peter. That was all? You really did give me a fright."

"I'm sorry. But your money . . ."

"You won't touch a cent of it. I heard you, darling. My God, but you are adorable!" She kissed my hand and placed it against her cheek.

The song came to an end and the vocalist bowed to Joan who was applauding him. The musicians loved us. I had given them money so they would play the song—"our" song—when Joan and I danced.

19

The muted trumpet rose to a romantic cadence. The piano player smiled at Shirley and me as we were dancing past the band.

"What did she tell you?"

"How considerate and loving you are now."

"I try very hard. I promised you I would."

We passed Joan sitting at our table. Candlelight gave an extra sparkle to her jewelry. She raised her glass to us. We waved. She smiled. We smiled. Joan extracted a red silk kerchief from her evening bag.

"Turn around." Shirley's voice was quavering. "Quickly, turn around with me or I'll cry."

We whirled around. Now only I could see Joan carefully touching the kerchief to her eyes so as not to smudge the mascara.

"I'm so sorry for her. I'm so terribly sorry for her."

"I am too."

"Oughtn't we to—"

"No," I said loudly.

"No what? You don't know what I was going to say."

"I know. Don't talk about it. I love you. I love only you. I want to be with you. Always."

"I do too. But—?"

"We cannot undo what has happened. Nor do I want to. And you?"

Her lips were quivering.

"And you?"

"You know how I feel."

I held her tightly.

"Don't. Please don't do that. It drives me crazy when you do that."

"Tomorrow you're coming to the studio with me. Once you're working there we will have time to be alone."

"When? When will we be alone?"

"I'm not in all the scenes. You're not always working. We just have to be careful."

"Please. Don't let's talk about it, don't think about it . . ."

"We've almost reached the table again. Smile."

"I can't smile."

"You must."

Slowly we circled past Joan. She smiled. We smiled. Shirley even raised the hand with the diamond ring Joan had given her.

"There," I said. "Was that so difficult?"

"Sometimes I hate you."

"I know. I know."

"I mean it. Sometimes I think dreadful things of you."

"They are all true."

"Do you have to talk like this?"

"Like what?"

"You know what I mean. I wish you would say something nice, something good."

"A doctor is going to examine you tomorrow morning. After that it can be done right away," I said.

For a moment I thought she was going to slap me. Then she put her arms around my shoulders and clung tightly. My vision became blurred; the room seemed to float.

"At last. Oh, God, at last. When that is taken care of,

my nerves will improve. When that is done, I shall feel better again."

"I wonder if we have a guardian angel, in spite of everything?"

"Would I have found the ring if we had not? And the doctor? Would I have gotten the chance to make the movie?" I asked.

"Horrible."

"What is horrible?"

"That it makes me happy. Happy about a murder."

"Don't talk nonsense."

"But it is murder!"

"It's fortunate. And that's why you are happy. That's all."

Now everybody could be happy: Joan—because the three of us got along so perfectly now; Natasha—because her child had uttered a sound; Schauberg—because soon he would have money to go to South America; they all could be happy, as happy as I was, as was the rabbi, as—

I had to stop thinking this way. Now.

"Shirley, I love you."

Her eyes were moist and her lips soundlessly formed a sentence. I understood.

The vocalist bowed to Shirley who was applauding him. He loved us. The musicians loved us. I had given them money again, this time to play "our" song when Shirley and I were dancing.

20

It was a clear night, unusually warm for November. Moonlight suffused the Alster. For a few moments we stood outside the hotel enjoying the clean invigorating air. Two couples passed us. Then I heard another sound.

Pad, pad.

I saw her walking on the promenade along the water, her coat collar turned up, a scarf over her hair.

Pad, pad. Pad, pad.

She was walking slowly, not once looking over to us. Her steps died away.

"There she is again," said Shirley.

"Who?" asked Joan.

"The woman from the airport."

"Airport? What woman?"

"The one who was staring at us there."

Natasha disappeared behind the old bare trees.

"What is she talking about?" asked Joan.

"I've no idea."

"But I did ask you who that woman was!"

"Now I remember vaguely that you did ask me . . ."

"Peter! Who is that woman?"

"Shirley, are you high? What is the matter with you?" She pulled her arm from mine.

"You mean the woman who was walking along the promenade over there?" asked Joan.

"Yes, mommy! The same woman was also at the airport!"

Joan laughed. "Shirley, darling, we were also at the airport and now we are standing here. Coincidences like that happen in a large city. Besides, you're probably mistaken."

"I'm not mistaken."

"In this darkness! Really, I think you've had too much champagne!" Joan was still laughing. "Let's go, I'm getting cold." She walked up the steps. We followed. Shirley stared fixedly but said nothing.

Passing the newspaper stand I read the headlines of the just-delivered paper: Dike Breaks Near Amsterdam. Ten Thousand People Homeless. Martial Law in South Korea. Students Revolt in Istanbul. Camp Commander Herrle Accused of Murder of 30,000 Prisoners.

"Well, are you coming?"

Joan stood in the open elevator.

The elevator!

Seeing it, the fist made itself felt. No. No. I could not take the risk.

"I'll take the stairs. You take the elevator."

I had not used the elevator again after my dream, only the stairs. I knew it was ridiculous, cowardly, pathological. I did not care. Schauberg's injections were effective but I noticed they also had side effects. Possibly Joan and Shirley would think my behavior strange if nothing worse. That did not bother me. All this would be behind me in another five or six weeks. Then I would enter a clinic. Until then I had to try and avoid anything which would further frighten, agitate or unnerve me.

Joan laughed again. "You walk up six flights?"

"I always do. I don't get enough exercise."

"Well then, scale the Nanga Parbat, Mr. Hillary!"

"I'll go with you, Paddy," said Shirley softly.

"Well," cried Joan, "that's not for me. So long, heroes!"

When we reached the fourth floor Shirley said, "Of course you know that woman."

"I don't."

"If I had not climbed the stairs with you you would have met her again."

I shrugged my shoulders.

"Why don't you answer?"

"Such nonsense does not deserve an answer."

"Oh, thanks."

"Not at all."

"You have nothing to tell me?"

What could I tell her now? At the airport, when Shirley had asked me about Natasha the first time, I ought to have answered, "A doctor. She gave me an injection once when I did not feel well." Then, tonight I could have said, "Good evening, doctor. She lives right around the corner, you know, Joan."

Would Shirley believe an explanation like that now? Possibly she had seen Natasha return the jewelry case to me. Had she seen us walking together in the rain? Had she, by some idiotic coincidence, found out I had sent flowers to Natasha?

Shirley was an intuitive woman. The first time she saw Natasha she had just known—known what? What, after all, was there to know?

Women. Women's minds probably have antennas.

No. For then I would have to tell her the truth. About my breakdown, Schauberg, the whole story. Could I?

No. Never. It was too late now.

"You have nothing to tell me?" asked Shirley on the stairs.

"No."

In silence, we reached Joan standing at the door. She laughed, "The climb doesn't seem to have done you much good! How about a nightcap?"

"Not for me," said Shirley. "Good night, mommy." She kissed Joan's cheek. Joan embraced her.

"Good night, my darling. And thank you both for another lovely evening."

"Oh, Joan!" I said.

"Don't say oh, Joan! One ought to thank the people one loves most for every lovely hour. Who knows how long we'll be together? These are terrible times. Another war . . . illness . . . accident . . . death . . . Don't look so disapproving Why shouldn't an old lady be high once in a while? Good grief, that's the second time since we arrived here! Give Peter a kiss, Shirley."

Shirley kissed my cheek. "Thank you for a lovely evening," she said. Her eyes were mere slits.

21

Naturally she was not there any more.

It was crazy to hope she would still be there. Presumptuous to think that she would be walking up and down just to see me once more.

I was standing on the moonlit balcony staring at the empty street, feeling disappointment and pain because I did not see Natasha.

My wife was getting ready to go to bed. Shirley was surely asleep by now. I had been standing there for the last ten minutes, hoping that she might pass by after all.

Pad, pad.

It couldn't be.

Pad, pad.

She came from the direction of the Alten Lombardsbrücke, hands in the pockets of her coat, the collar pulled up.

Natasha saw me in the moonlight. She stopped directly under the balcony. I raised my hand. She raised hers. We looked at each other for a long time.

Suddenly she dropped her arm.

"Natasha!" My voice was subdued.

Quickly she crossed the street and disappeared into a net of bizarre tree shadows.

Why did she not look up once more, wave to me just one more time?

I bent over the balcony. The street was deserted. Natasha must have turned the corner. When I straightened up I saw Shirley.

22

She was standing on her balcony looking at me.

There were four balconies between us. The moonlight made her face appear a mask. She turned, entered her room. I heard her close the door. She must have seen us. Yet had she?

Now I had to tell her something.

"Are you coming?" My wife stood behind me in nightgown and robe. I left the balcony and closed the door.

Had Joan seen anything? What did she know, think, plan? I twitched nervously.

"But darling, I only wanted to kiss you."

Her lips on my cheek, she whispered, "I know you're tired . . ."

"Not at all."

". . . and preoccupied . . ."

"That's not true."

"But I see it. When I talk to you you don't listen. When I look at you, you don't notice it. You are thinking of something else. And I know what it is . . ."

"You . . . know?"

"Naturally, darling. I know and I can understand that you're always thinking of your work, your movie. But I . . ."

I looked at her. She lowered her head, as embarrassed as a young girl.

"I would like to go to sleep in your arms tonight."

I nodded, I could not speak.

"I've taken a sedative. I'll go to sleep soon. Just to go to sleep in your arms . . . after all this time . . ."

23

"She is one of my fans. What can I do? She follows me. She is forever at the hotel trying to see me."

"How do you know?"

"I talked with one of the doormen last night."

"I see."

"He saw her standing outside, waving."

"And he recognized her?"

"Yes, he did! She hangs around here since I arrived. He also said I had given her my autograph at some time."

"But you can't remember?"

"Naturally not! I've signed hundreds of autographs." I had not signed a dozen. "Now are you satisfied?"

"You're driving too fast," said Shirley. She was sitting next to me. It was seven-thirty. White frost covered the road. It was icy cold. Shirley wore her leopard coat and a black cap on her auburn hair.

"Are you satisfied now!"

"Why shouldn't I be?"

"Now listen——" .

"Watch out!"

I jerked the wheel over to the left to avoid a man. The car slithered on the slippery road.

"If you can't drive more carefully let me get out."

I clenched my teeth and eased off the gas. This was important and so I asked: "Then you don't believe me?"

"Why shouldn't I believe you?"

"Don't repeat everything I say!"

"Then don't yell at me! I haven't done anything to you!"

"Every actor has fans!"

"Who is arguing?"

"Don't talk like that!"

"I'm talking the same way you're talking!"

"Shirley, what's the matter with you? I love you!" And she loves me. Her behavior is perfectly understandable. "Perhaps you think I've deceived you with this lady?"

"Please. Please, let's just forget it!"

"I want you to believe me!"

"I do. Really. She is a fan of yours. A rather adult fan. She saw you with two women and, because she is tactful, she didn't speak to you so as not to annoy us."

"Right! Movie fans are poor, lonely people."

"But tactful! That's why she waved to you only when you were alone . . ."

"Yes!"

". . . and you, because you are also tactful, because you did not want to irritate us, did not wave to her until you were alone. Even though you had no idea who the lady was!"

That was logical.

"It's proof again of what a good person you are. It's perfectly clear to me. Why shouldn't I believe it?"

A logical woman. Jealous and logical.

I wouldn't have believed the story either. Now what?

I took the turn at high speed.

"Where are you going?" There was fear in Shirley's voice.

"The doctor is waiting for us up ahead." Out here the glittering frost had given the scenery a clean, fresh glaze while underneath the silver-bright surface it was dirty and rotting.

"Where is he waiting?"

"Behind the barn, up ahead." Now that I said it, fear gripped me. Why did Schauberg not come to meet me as always when he heard my car?

There—

A figure stepped slowly from behind the barn. Slid back. I braked suddenly. It had not been a man. It had been a young woman and I knew who she was.

236

I put on the brake, opened the door.

Shirley seized my shoulder.

"Let go!"

"Where are you—"

"Let me go!"

"But—"

"You stay here and don't move!"

I jumped out of the car, slammed the door. Promptly I slipped on the ice, fell, grazed my hand, got up again. More careful now, I slid and slithered until I had reached the barn. There was Käthe, blonde, distraught eyes reddened by tears.

"Thank God you came! I was so afraid . . ."

"How did you get here?"

"In a taxi . . . I sent it away . . ." Schauberg's girlfriend in only a suede jacket, high-heeled shoes and a thin sweater, was shaking from agitation and cold. Completely dressed, she looked almost obscene. Her pretty, vapid face was gray. Her lips were trembling. "I thought perhaps I was waiting at the wrong barn . . . or something happened to you too . . ."

I stiffened, alarmed.

"Too?" I asked softly.

She nodded, choked, and began to cry.

I whispered, "Schauberg?"

A flood of tears.

"What is the matter with him?"

"They arrested him. Last night," she sobbed. "In Reinbeck."

The Fifth Tape

1

The little cat in Professor Pontevivo's laboratory was completely drunk.

She stumbled through her special cage, bumped into it, meowed sadly. Her fur was unkempt, her body emaciated.

Today was the first time I had left my room in the clinic. Many days had passed in learning to walk again. Fearfully I had stumbled, physically weak, holding on to the bed, the window, the walls.

The mere thought of walking in a park, driving a car, speaking to strangers, going to a movie is agonizing enough for me to break into a cold sweat.

Professor Pontevivo told me that my physical condition had improved to such an extent that the time had come to cure my addiction.

"Today begins the second part of your recovery. Your tapes prove that your mind is functioning perfectly. It is necessary for you to know all we have learned about addiction and addicts so that you will be able to work with us in restoring your health. To help you remember, I would like you to report each session to your tape recorder."

"Very well, Professor."

"All right, the first lesson." He showed me photographs

of a little well-fed cat. "This was Bianca six weeks ago. We have used her in an experiment and now she is addicted to alcohol. I hope you are not a hysterical animal lover. Hysterical animal lovers are usually misanthropes. Those who cry for the animals used in satellites probably don't shed any tears about the Jews sent to the gas ovens."

"What did you do with Bianca?"

"We taught her to push a button to open a little door. Every time the door opened she found some fish, liver or cheese, everything little cats like. How do you feel?"

"Fair."

"Say: I feel fine."

"I feel fine."

"Bravo. We offered Bianca milk, and milk mixed with alcohol. She always drank the milk. She would rather go thirsty than touch the alcohol-milk mixture. Until we began to annoy her."

"Annoy her?"

"We connected a rubber hose leading to a small fan to the little door. Whenever Bianca pressed the button the fan was activated and, instead of the usual food, cold air blew into her face. Now if she pushed the button she never knew whether food would fall out or air would blow into her face. How would you describe what we had done?"

"You created a conflict for Bianca."

"Wonderful!" He beamed. "A mental conflict, right? Hunger drove her to push the button but with that her fear of the cold air increased. She alternated between fear and greed. Repeat, please."

"She alternated between fear and greed."

"She did not clean herself any more, she became restless, nervous, forgetful and irritable. One day she only found the alcohol-milk mixture. She sipped some. The alcohol befuddled her a little but appeared to give her courage too. She pushed the button."

"What happened?"

"A blast of cold air hit her face. The next day she found some liver. She never knew what to expect. Every time before she pushed the button, she drank some of the alcohol-milk to give her courage. She became more and more depressed. A few days later we placed a bowl of milk in her cage. We disconnected the ventilator and Bianca found food whenever she pushed the button. Still she preferred the alcohol-milk to the pure milk. She always takes a sip before she pushes the button. Now, Mr. Jordan, Bianca is addicted."

"Will she remain addicted?"

"It depends on whether or not she will lose her fear and distrust of the little door—and whatever is waiting behind it for her."

"Since no one can talk with her and since she probably cannot think she will probably die."

The professor rubbed his hands. "Bravo, Mr. Jordan, bravissimo. A human being can think and free himself of his addiction—if others will help him."

"Poor Bianca."

"Poor humanity. Experiments of this nature are still new. Only a short time ago we did not know why a casual drinker became a habitual drinker and why a habitual drinker became an alcoholic. Many reasons were given—character weakness, sybaritic tendencies, hereditary factors, the wish to escape. Today we know: Alcoholism is a disease, in most cases a neurosis. If problems can't be overcome, mental conflicts not resolved, one can become neurotic. Then it is easy to take to alcohol." The professor rose with extreme dignity. "This was the first lecture. Now I will escort you back to your room."

We walked along a corridor, its large windows sunlit.

Suddenly Pontevivo said, "Now you see the progress you are making. You walked by yourself. I did not help you."

Indeed. I turned to look at the long corridor. It seemed incredible. And I had not been afraid.

From the music room came the soft sounds of a piano.

"He plays beautifully, doesn't he?" The professor looked down at the park, enchanting with its profusion of colorful blossoms. "He has almost completed his concerto. There comes his muse." The wife of the composer, dressed in black as usual, a basket of oranges on her arm was walking sedately along the path.

"She always brings oranges," I said. "Can he eat that many?"

"He loves them. They are good for him." We had arrived at my room. "Tomorrow we'll talk further."

2

I must return to Käthe, waiting for me at the barn where I usually met Schauberg. Somehow I found my voice to ask, "What did he do?"

"He . . . he . . ."

I shook her. "Come on! Tell me!"

"He broke into a cough medicine plant."

"He broke into a what?"

"Into a place where they make cough medicine."

A pharmaceutical plant. Impossible. Things like that don't happen. I was crazy. The time had come: I was insane.

"Say that again! Where?"

"Into a place where they make cough medicines, you know?"

"What nonsense is that?"

"No nonsense. And he did it for you!"

I pressed both hands to my temples.

The gull. The elephant. The elevator. The voices.

No! I'm not giving in. I'll fight back. I can still fight back!

"Last night he burglarized that factory? For me?"

"No!"

"What do you mean, no?"

"He was arrested last night. The day before yesterday he broke in there!" Her breath formed white clouds every time she spoke.

"For my sake he broke in there? For me?"

"That's right! For you!"

"How do you know that?"

"Charley told me."

"Who is Charley?"

"The fellow who broke in with him."

"They didn't catch him?"

She sniffled, then came a new flood of tears.

I forced myself to be calm. We weren't getting anywhere this way. "Now they only have Schauberg?"

"Yes . . ."

"What about Charley?"

Tears. Sniffling.

"Answer me! Please, Käthe! Where does Charley live?"

"I don't know. I don't know! I've never seen him before! He called me at two in the morning at Madam Misere's." She imitated the conversation of two voices. "Can I talk to Käthe?—Speaking. Who is this?—Charley.—Charley who?—Just Charley. Listen. Your sweety just got caught. Burglary. Cough syrup factory. You know a Peter Jordan?—Yes.—He is the one he did it for.—He told me when and where to meet you, Mr. Jordan. Then he said, tell Jordan to send a lawyer for Schauberg. After that he is to pick up the box.—What box?—Don't ask stupid questions, Jordan knows which box. He is to get it right away!"

I heard a noise. I jumped back. It was Shirley. She had been listening but could not have understood anything.

"What happened? Who is that girl?"

245

"I told you to stay in the car!"

Käthe became hysterical. "Mr. Jordan, I've nothing to do with all this! I want to go back!"

"Shut up!" I yelled. Then to Shirley, "Leave us alone!"

"If you don't tell me right away what happened I'll scream!"

"For chrissake, I don't know myself what happened! Now will you get back into that car and wait?"

Shirley gave me a frightened look and backed away from me, stumbling, and got back into the car.

"Now listen, Käthe! I must go to the studio. Just for a little while. Stop crying and fix your face. Walk on the right side of the road toward town. I'll pick you up in about fifteen minutes. I need your help. Okay?"

Still sniffling she nodded.

I hurried to the car and dropped behind the wheel. The car leaped toward the road. Shirley was motionless. Käthe stumbled down the path on her high heels, sobbing, lost, without comprehension.

The tires screamed as I made the turn onto the road. Without taking my eyes off the road I said, "The doctor was arrested. She is his girlfriend."

Shirley began to laugh hysterically.

"What's so funny?"

"The doctor was arrested? This one too? That's what I had to come to Hamburg for!" She was still laughing.

"I must help the man."

"So you'll be arrested too?"

"They arrested him for something else. I promise, I'll explain it all to you later."

She looked at me, then shrugged her shoulders. "You'll never tell me the truth," she said in a low voice. "I know that now. You are in a precarious situation. Poor Peter."

"Shirley, I swear——" I began. But I did not explain. There was no time. The box. Käthe. A lawyer. I needed Schauberg. What would I do without him?

3

"What do you mean, Mr. Jordan, you have to leave?"
Albrecht, furious, glared at me. The skinny production
manager limped around his desk. He obviously hated me
but I did not know why. "How much time would you
like?"

"An hour. An hour and a half. At most."

"You're supposed to be ready for shooting at ten. It's
eight now. Or will all of us have to wait for you?"

I forced a smile. "Mr. Albrecht, you could do the takes
without me. The ones with Hoffmann."

"And change everything again for you? No, no!
Besides, Hoffmann is still at the radio station until twelve
o'clock."

Kostasch entered. He beamed when he saw Shirley and
me.

"How nice to see you!" He kissed her. Kostasch noticed something was wrong. Albrecht explained. Kostasch
decided the takes would be rescheduled. Albrecht was
furious, slammed the door behind him. We heard him
yelling for his assistant.

"Whatever is the matter with him?" I asked.

"Don't be upset. It's nothing personal. He just doesn't
like Americans."

"Why not?"

"He was in an American POW camp."

"That breaks my heart. How could we attack Nazi
Germany!"

Kostasch laughed. "There is more to it than that! Albrecht is an old communist. The Nazis first put him in a
concentration camp and then into a penal fighting unit for
probation. He was taken by the Americans in Normandy.
On one of those Liberty ships he reached the USA and

was stuck into some POW camp. His best friend was with him. They had been in the same camp at Mauthausen."

"Well, and?"

"Well, as was common in those POW camps, the Nazis were in command again. Complete with officer's administration, 'kangaroo' courts, and strangling anti-fascists at night. You know what went on in your country."

I was silent. I had heard about it.

"I bet it must have impressed the Americans how these blond, blue-eyed heroes sorted out the camp! One two three. One of those reds taken care of. Quite a few anti-fascists died. After Albrecht's friend had been strangled and he had been beaten and severely injured, a senator instituted an inquiry. Albrecht and other anti-fascists were then transferred to another camp. The food there, so he said, was not as good. Ah, well." Kostasch laughed. "You see, Shirley, such are the ways by which a man acquires prejudices!"

He had told the story while we were walking to the cutting rooms.

"Okay, Peter. Take off." He winked at Shirley. "Since yesterday I can't refuse him anything." He took her arm. "Come with me, I'll introduce you to the other cutters."

"I'll see you at lunch," I said to Shirley.

She did not reply. Kostasch and Shirley were already climbing the stairs leading to the cutting rooms.

4

The sun appeared a pale disc among the dirty gray clouds. Trees, bushes, paths, flowers, and grass were glittering with the past night's frost.

Käthe, still sniffling, was showing me the shortest route to Reinbeck, all the while lamenting her and Schauberg's fate. I drove fast, hoping not to attract the attention of a police patrol car.

"Mr. Jordan, you are the only person I can rely on. Now, that they've arrested Schauberg . . ."

"I must know exactly what happened if I am to help him. You understand?"

"Yes."

"For instance, did he really say he broke into that factory because of me? Did he really say that?"

"Yes, Mr. Jordan, he did."

We had reached the wall of the cemetery with its crooked gravestones. Here I had waited for Schauberg that first time.

Had he lost his mind? In my wallet was a check for eight thousand marks for him. He knew he was to get it this morning. Then why would he burgle a cough syrup factory? Why? Little by little I was losing the certainty, normal to a healthy person, that everything that happened was really happening. Day by day, not to mention the nights, my feeling increased: I am insane. What I seemed to experience were already phantasmagoria of a sick mind.

Käthe said, "Sometimes I think I'm crazy and I'm just dreaming."

"You too?"

"Excuse me?"

"Nothing. Tell me about Schauberg."

"He came to see me three days ago. You know what he did?"

"What?"

"He cried."

"No!" Schauberg and tears. Devil and halo. General and peace. "Why did he cry?"

"He had just seen you."

"Yes, that's right. So?"

"He was at his wit's end. He told me you had said your movie is not going to be finished. And he is not going to get any more money from you. He still has money to come from you, hasn't he? He never said what for and naturally I've never asked him. But he did say the movie was going to be finished. So I guessed it had something to do with that . . ."

There it was. My premonition had been right. I ought not to have told him about the conversation in the empty projection room I had overheard between Kostasch and Seaton. But I had told him. And this was the result.

"He said then he had to accept this job."

"This job was the burglary?"

"Must have been. He said there was money in that too. Not as much. But still. He said he was going to do this job and then he would leave Germany. He was going to do it with a friend, he told me."

"Friend Charley."

"Yes. Probably. Didn't you read about it in the papers?"

"What did it say?"

"In yesterday's paper it said, 'A truckload of cough medicine was stolen from a pharmaceutical plant.' "

A truckload!

That was the reason why Schauberg had laughed so heartily when I complained about my throat and asked him for some cough medicine.

Now did it make sense? No. None at all.

I stepped on the brake. We had arrived at the camp with its barbed-wire fences; the dilapidated barracks without doors or roofs.

"Get out. Käthe. Hurry up."

Barracks. Graves. Little lake, frozen. Dynamited shelters.

"Quickly! Hurry up!"

"I can't. My high heels . . . and I'm afraid. What if there are people here . . . policemen . . ."

"Only the dead are here," I said.

5

We pulled the heavy olive-green box from the rubble of the third shelter and dragged it back to the car. I felt better once it was locked into the trunk of the car and we were driving back toward Hamburg.

Nine-forty-five.

I thought fleetingly of Albrecht but more pressing things were on my mind and the film seemed almost unimportant.

"I'll let you off in Hamburg," I said to Käthe. "I can find my way from here. I have to hurry. I'll call Madam Misere. I'll see you tonight. By then we'll know more about Schauberg."

"You will help him, won't you?"

"I'll do everything possible. But you'll have to be smart now, Käthe. If the police question you, you tell them that you are lovers. You can tell them that you are going to be married."

"Yes, Mr. Jordan."

"You must not mention me or this box. They can't know that Schauberg and I worked together."

"I understand. I'll do everything you say."

"I must not become involved in this. The cough medicine job has nothing to do with me. Really. If they should ask you about me—it is most unlikely—or if they should show you a photograph of me, or supposing I arrive when they are there, you know me only as a customer."

"Only as a customer. Yes. Of course."

"You could say that I come to see you."

"Because you like my dialect, right?"

"Now, get out here. Don't cry. We'll get your Walter released. You'll see."

"I believe that, I really do," said Käthe.

6

Ten-fifteen.

I stopped at a park with a deserted playground where I opened the trunk and then the padlock of the green box. Schauberg had already given me a duplicate key the second time I saw him. "One never knows. Should something happen to me you'll take care of this box." I opened the lid and took out the sealed envelope. Carefully I locked box and trunk and entered a bar opposite the park. An unshaven but well-dressed man was the only other customer at this early hour.

I ordered a beer.

"And a cognac. The gentleman is my guest," said the unshaven man. I noticed a little package wrapped in newspaper on the bar near him.

"Thank you, but I don't care for cognac." I went to a table near a window.

"You don't want to drink with me, eh?"

"It's not that. But at this early hour—"

"Please, Doctor." The bartender appeared embarrassed and winked at me as if asking me to make allowance.

The unshaven one said to him, "You keep out of this." And to me, "You could tell right away, couldn't you?"

"Tell what?"

The bartender standing behind the man touched one finger to his forehead, still smiling. At the same time the other one pushed up his sleeve. On the inside of his wrist I saw several numbers preceded by an A. I had seen such tattoos in American magazines. The man had been in a concentration camp.

"Excuse me. I didn't know—"

"Then you are going to have a drink with me?"

"Yes. Yes. Of course." The bartender placed a drink

before me. We drank. The man had a very prominent forehead, almost no hair, and large melancholy eyes. His complexion was yellow. His hands shook. A 2 456 954.

"Really. I did not mean to hurt your feelings!"

"You didn't. It was only a test." He spoke with a cultivated and low voice. His dark searching eyes, seemingly filled with six thousand years of sadness, dominated his face. "I don't want to disturb you any further." I offered him my hand. He shook it and said, "Thank you."

I ordered the same again for the man, went to the table near the window. From there I could keep an eye on my car.

I broke the seal of the envelope and read the message written in single letters in Schauberg's small script.

Dear Friend,

When you read this letter I might have had an accident, escaped, be very ill, in jail, or dead. Most likely dead.

I am as ill as you are and just as afraid of death as you are. Since we are both men who have no faith in anything our fear is understandable.

Christian doctrine teaches us that our life in this miserable vale is merely the step toward something perfect, wonderful—to paradise, if only one had lived in accordance with God's commandments.

And yet!

In the many years of my profession I have observed that very often even men of the cloth and devout nuns, whose salvation was—so to speak—practically guaranteed, did not want to go to the land of bliss. One would have expected them to have rejoiced that the time had finally come. Elucidate for me the mysteries of Christian faith!

Being proper delinquents and heathens we won't rely on such people or even God's impenetrable ways. But I must do all I can to help you toward your goal in the event I should not be around.

253

You are no medical man.

Following is a precise bill of fare for your treatment using the medications in this box . . .

Schauberg was a conscientious man. He explained symptoms and drugs for treatment. He gave names, times, dosages. Instructions about how to inject myself and cautionary advice.

While I was reading, a workman entered the bar and the unshaven man again tried his test. The workman reacted as I had.

"The only difficulty would arise if you should ever again feel the way you did on that first evening at the camp and on the evening of your first day of shooting. You will probably remember that I then gave you an intravenous injection."

Yes, I remembered: The wonderful transition from paralyzing fear to peace, warmth, security.

"Should such an attack reoccur, another intravenous injection would be imperative. For that you would need a doctor or at least a trained nurse. I would advise you to try and find somebody you could trust since your survival would depend on him. The medication is in the yellow box which I have marked with a green circle.

"Hoping (for you and for me) that you will never receive this letter I remain your blasphemous associate."

I called the bartender to pay for my beer and the cognac I had not touched and the drinks for the unshaven man who was still talking to the workman.

"He's a poor, unfortunate man," said the bartender.

"Have you known him for a long time?"

"He's a regular here. He's been around the bars in Hamburg for years. Used to be a successful lawyer. Lost everything."

"What is he doing now?"

"He's drinking himself to death, as you can see. He still has some money."

"This 'test' is a crazy idea, isn't it? Even the most fanatic Nazi would not refuse to drink with him if he shows him the tattoo."

"That's what I keep telling him!"

"And?"

The bartender shrugged his shoulders.

The unshaven poor man had opened his little package. He showed the workman a pair of children's shoes.

The bartender said quietly, "He always shows these shoes once he's found someone who will listen to him. He was in Auschwitz. After the Russians came he returned once more and found a huge pile of children's shoes behind some barrack. The poor man had had a wife and a small child. They both died at Auschwitz. So he took a pair of those shoes. It's hardly likely they belonged to his little Monika. Still he has been carrying them around for the last fifteen years. He shows them to everybody."

"What about the people? Do they believe the story about the shoes?"

"Maybe one or two. They just drink his beer and cognac. He's well-known around here. They say he's crazy."

I rose and nodded to the man from Auschwitz. He bowed and I left the bar. I never thought I would see him again. But soon this man would figure in the most terrible episode of my life.

I returned to my car and opened the trunk and the green box. I searched a little, then I found it. If the worst should come to pass this was my only hope of survival—the yellow box with the green circle.

7

It was now ten-thirty. I was to be ready for shooting at eleven-thirty. Make-up would take an hour. And I was not even at the studio. Albrecht would be in a rage and rightfully so.

Fleetingly, but sincerely, I regretted the circumstances which had existed in some American POW camps in 1944. Had the anti-fascists received fairer treatment in Texas and Oklahoma fifteen years ago I might have had a friend in Hamburg, at least not an enemy.

That is the way of life. Our lives weave the fabric of existence, an inescapable web with a detestable pattern.

I made my telephone call to Madam Misere from a call box. Perhaps the police were already there. Possibly her telephone was being tapped. Why had Schauberg really been arrested?

"Käthe came to see me this morning."

"Yes, I know." Madam did not say, 'Yes, I know, Mr. Jordan.' One could rely on her.

"I'm sorry for the girl."

"It is terrible for her. She seems to love him very much. I hardly know him."

"I don't know him at all. What is his name?"

"Schauberg. He came to see her here several times. He made an excellent impression on me."

"I heard he is a doctor?"

"That's right."

"And a doctor breaks in somewhere?"

"I think the entire business is a tragic mistake which will soon be cleared up."

"Käthe begged me for help. I'd be glad to help her. I'd be glad to help her financially. Since I don't know any lawyers here I thought that perhaps you could . . ."

"Käthe is one of my best girls. I have already arranged for a lawyer. I like to be a second mother to my girls. Thank you for your concern."

"Well, if one can be of help . . ."

"Always on the side of the underdog," said the keeper of the bordello who apparently had been raised in the best English tradition. "I'm sure it is an error. It will be cleared up. The police will arrive at the truth. My lawyer will assist them in that."

"Well, then, if it is a question of money . . ."

"Thank you so much. It is not very often one meets such a generous and warm-hearted man such as you. I hope you will honor us soon with a visit. Please call first so I may make the best arrangements."

"Thank you, I will." Käthe should arrive there soon and announce that I would be there this evening.

Out of superstition I drove out to the old barn where I usually met Schauberg. There, carefully following his directions, I gave myself an injection. I broke the first ampoule. The injection was painful. If anyone had seen me there, clothes in disarray, contorted limbs and distorted face, they would have called a psychiatrist right away.

". . . Should such an attack reoccur you would need an intravenous injection . . ."

Who would give me that injection?

Natasha Petrovna? She would not do it. She would call the police. Or send me away.

Should such an attack reoccur . . .

There would be another attack. Why not? Then what? A person whom I could trust. No such person. No one would trust me not without reason.

Since man hopes so long as there is life in him, I hoped we could get Schauberg off quickly. Perhaps everything would turn out well. In spite of everything.

8

Naturally I was not ready for shooting at eleven-thirty. Tired out, I arrived at the studio just after eleven.

My dressing-room assistant told me Albrecht was furious. He had had to change the schedule because of my absence and had now advanced the lunch period. I took two of Schauberg's red pills and gradually felt calmer.

After make-up and dressing I went to the cutting department to talk to Shirley. She was not alone. The chief cutter, Jaky, and his very handsome German assistant were there too. Shirley was operating an editing machine. She did not look at me.

"Have a look at that, Mr. Jordan," said Jaky. To Shirley, "Show it to daddy." Shirley started the editor. Number 427 was rolling. I saw Wallace kill me with the bronze lamp.

I said, "What's the problem?"

"The sound stinks," said Jaky.

"This scene is supposed to be reshot," I said. "Just like the others we did in the first few days."

"Not this one," said the German assistant. He seemed to like Shirley. He was staring at her a great deal.

"That's right," said Jaky. "But where did you get that sound, man? Couldn't you find anything better than this?"

The good-looking assistant was offended. "We've tried other sound effects. This is the best they had in the archives."

"It has to be a real skull, a read head," said Jaky pensively.

"Why don't you use your own," said his assistant, annoyed.

Jaky ignored him. "I'll get enough skulls for three remakes. It will only take an hour."

The loudspeaker clicked. "Mr. Jordan, you are wanted in Studio Three. Mr. Jordan, please."

Shirley had said nothing. She had not once looked at me.

At three o'clock I had a few free minutes. In the cutting department was only one film splicer.

"They are all at the Sound Department." I found Shirley in Hall Three. She was squatting on the floor, a microphone above her. On the floor before her were six pig's heads. The heavy hammer she had used to smash the heads of those dismembered pigs was still in her hand.

"Okay, Shirley!" Jaky was pleased. "That sound is authentic. Wait a minute and we'll get the effect."

Jaky and his assistant disappeared. Shirley and I were alone. I helped her up. Her face was white; she looked ill and helpless as she sank down on a chair. I was moved.

"Were you sick again?"

She nodded. "What about this doctor?"

"I'll know by tonight. A lawyer is already looking into it." I lied. "And if he is not successful I have another doctor. Don't worry, darling. We'll help you. In a few days it will be over, I swear."

Now she looked at me and held her hand out to me. It was cold and narrow, and without strength. Her beautiful eyes, no longer burning with this morning's fury and jealousy, were dull, her voice apathetic. "I'm sorry about this morning."

"Shirley—"

"And for my behavior last night too. Please forgive me, Peter."

Seeing Shirley, seeing her brave struggling to overcome her despair, I was suddenly mortified. What had I done? Could this be love? Love which destroyed the loved one? Wasn't I only in love with myself? Had that woman been right who once had said, "You are incapable of love. You don't even know what love is."

"Shirley, tonight on our way home—" I began but realized that tonight I was to go to Madam Misere's. I started again. "Tonight at the hotel I'll explain—"

"Don't," she said. Her tired voice held no anger. "No, I don't want you to explain anything."

"But—"

She pressed my hand. "Let me talk. You'll be called back to the studio in a moment."

"Shirley," I said, "my sweet, my all, trust me. I love you. Please believe me. I love you. You're all I live for. I think only of you. Of the secrets between us, the letters we wrote, read and then burned. Our meetings. The small hotels. The telephone calls. Flowers without notes. All this forbidden life, this love. It is my only, my true love, Shirley . . ."

"Mine too." She lowered her head as if we were both talking of someone dead, someone to grieve for.

"The little bar. Our song. I love you Shirley. Believe me."

"I do believe you. But I also believe that you are in some trouble here in Hamburg."

"If you mean the blonde girl this morning—"

"Not only the girl. There are other things."

"Shirley—"

"I think you are very unhappy right now. I think you would have to lie if you were to tell me what happened here. That's why I don't want you to explain anything. I trust you. There is nothing I can do. I'll see what happens. I just don't want to be lied to any more."

"I would not lie to you," I said and thought: I'm lying right now.

"Yes, Peter, you would. All my life I've heard lies. From Joan. From you. From my friends. From boys. Many, many lies. I love you, too, with all my heart. I know you'll do the best you can for both of us. But I could not bear to be told any more lies."

I tried to put my arm around her, to hold her, kiss her. I did not care if someone came and saw us. Shirley pushed me away. "Please don't. Don't touch me. I feel nauseous at the slightest . . ."

I stepped back, suddenly feeling chilly. Was that love? Had we both come to this?

"Don't be angry, Peter. When the child is—"

"Yes," I said. "Of course."

"Now I've hurt your feelings."

"No, I understand," I said.

Jaky and his assistant appeared. The chief cutter showed his elation. "Boy, oh, boy, what sound! I must say I'm a genius! You know where we got those pigs' heads from,

Mr. Jordan? From the slaughterhouse in Wandsbeck. I hope you're not going to take offense now!"

"Why should I?"

"Because I thought of a pig's head as a substitute for your head!" He roared with laughter. "But to make sure we'll do it once more, Shirley."

"All right, Mr. Jaky." Shirley rose and, picking up the heavy hammer, she said to me, "That woman called."

"Excuse me?"

"This morning. You weren't here."

"But—"

"They transferred the call to me. I guess they think I'm your real daughter. Or they thought it was Joan."

"It couldn't have been this woman!"

"It was."

"How do you know?"

"She asked for you."

"Well, that's no proof."

"She gave me her name."

"What's her name?"

"Mrs. Petrovna."

I stared at Shirley.

"You see, Peter. That's why I don't want you to explain anything. You would have to lie."

Red and green lights flashed on.

"Ready, Shirley?"

"Yes, Mr. Jaky."

"Shirley, that's crazy! It couldn't have been that woman! I don't know a Mrs. Petrovna!"

"The mike is live, Peter."

I turned to leave when Jaky asked me to stand still.

"Okay, Shirley!"

Shirley kneeled down. She raised the hammer. The impact smashed the head.

"Marvelous!" Jaky's voice was ecstatic. I looked at Shirley. She shook her head and looked aside. There was nothing I could say or do. I walked to the exit.

Mrs. Petrovna.

Damn, why had she called? Resentment and anger rose in me. How could she? She was a woman. She had intuition. She should have known—

Known what?

What should she have known?

Nothing, nothing at all.

In the telephone booth outside the sound department I looked up her telephone number. Her serene, gentle voice answered.

"This is Jordan." I was still angry. "I'm at the studio. You called this morning."

"Yes."

"Why?"

"Good God, did I do something wrong?"

"Yes."

"I'm sorry. I had no idea your daughter was working at the studio too."

"What was it you wanted from me?" I asked. While I was talking I felt my anger and resentment abate under the influence of her gentle, soft voice.

"I wanted to thank you."

"To thank me?"

"For the lovely flowers, the crayons, the sketch pad."

The flowers and crayons. I had completely forgotten.

She had wanted to thank me. For a person like Natasha Petrovna that was the natural thing to do. If only she were here, I thought. Perhaps then I could have told her the true story I had to keep from Shirley. I had told lies all my life. For the first time I experienced the torture of not being able to disclose the truth to anyone. If Natasha were here now . . .

No!

It was madness. This line of thinking was folly.

"I must see you; I must talk with you, Natasha." I did not call her Mrs. Petrovna. I hardly knew her and I called her by her first name.

Her voice was calm. "When?"

"As soon as possible."

"Tell me when and where." Was her voice still calm? Was I wrong or was her voice breathless?

No, I was not wrong.

I said, "I'll meet you . . ."

9

Rome, April fourteenth, 1960.

Professor Pontevivo said, "Alcoholism is a prop for the mind. Most people in this day and age are unhappier, less free and satisfied than they will admit to, or rather than they are aware of. Albert Camus called this the century of fear. People try to banish fear with alcohol. That is why this is also the century of alcoholism."

"Don't you think, Professor, that in all other centuries people thought their time the most frightening?" I asked. "Don't you think that we too are just victims of this distorted historical view which makes the present appear worse than any past?"

"No, Mr. Jordan, I don't. The impact and resulting momentous effects are greater in our present than at any time in the past. We have objective human and scientific proof of that."

"The objective human proof?"

"In only twenty-five years, between 1922 and 1947, seventy million men, women and children were deported, uprooted or murdered. There were two world wars; revolutions and concentration camps are too numerous to count. Systematic brainwashing and mass propaganda are as much part of our everyday life as is the existence of the hydrogen bomb."

"The objective scientific proof?"

"Can be derived from findings of psychiatrists, theologists, and sociologists who have examined the behavior of people; above all, the artists of these decades. Shall we talk about the artist for a moment? It was the traditional duty of the artist throughout the centuries to shoulder all the fears, the guilt and the problems of humanity and, with his spirit, his talent, his genius, create a work of art which would bring understanding, relief and release to the viewers, listeners or readers. That was his role. For that, he was admired, revered—and paid.

"And the artist today? With abstract art and atonal music he intentionally destroys any recognizable reality and creates a world in which he is the master, for no one else can understand this, his world."

"That's why he is the master!"

"Certainly, Mr. Jordan. But why does he create this world which does not really exist? Only because he can no longer master the one he lives in. What do the writers do? For a long period, on stage, screen and in books, they could only work under the influence of psychoanalysis. Now they have begun to break the bridges between themselves and their audiences. They no longer want to move, to exalt, or release. More and more they try to involve their public in their own fears, their own inability to solve their problems. Artists no longer want to relieve their public of its fears, troubles, and doubts; they want to make their readers, their audience, their viewers as fearful, despairing, and helpless as they are themselves—and have to be."

"Do you think this inevitable?"

"I think so. We really live in a time different from any other time we know about. Past eras have been even more turbulent, more insecure, and more bloody—for instance the mass migrations following the fall of the Roman Empire, the era of discovery, the days of Galileo and Copernicus, or the industrial revolution. But our century is the product of the culmination of all those enormous changes. Our time, Mr. Jordan, does not only require us to accept a completely new world but also that we search it out. We are only at the beginning of knowledge. There has never been anything like this. The old religions, the old isms have failed. It is a critical situation. Who or what can seemingly relieve our many fears, the fears borne by many of us who cannot manage our lives—our life in this century?"

"Alcohol," I said.

He nodded. "This is the time of regeneration of our world. The new ideas are not yet accepted by the masses; they are not sufficiently tried or proven. There is still chaos. But this is the age of reason. So we fear chaos. The people of the Bible, especially the Old Testament, were living in the age of faith . . ."

Faith and thought. Thought and faith.

Oh, Doctor Schauberg!

". . . for them the question was not, 'Why does chaos exist?' but 'Why is there order?' "

"What answer did those people find?"

"In their daily living order was the fruit of their endeavor to be and do good. It was the natural result of that effort. We, in these chaotic days, must try to do something similar to accelerate the victory of clear thinking and order for humanity. That is only possible if we do not try to evade our responsibility—by using drugs, or drink, by self-destruction. Each one of us has something to give to another human being. It must be given and received. Plain thinking is the end of fear. I've said that before and I'll probably say that many more times." He shook my hand and walked to the door. There he turned and smiled.

"By the way—our little Bianca is much better."

"Will she recover?"

"I hope so. Some of my animals seem to think clearer than many of my patients." Had he been Schauberg he would probably have added, 'Which would hardly require any great exertion.' He merely said, "Good morning, Mr. Jordan."

This had been the second lecture.

10

"Please sit down," said Madam Misere. She indicated the couch in her office. Through the window in the upper part of the door I could see part of the bar. Even at this early hour of the evening many guests were already there. The undressed girls, getting in and out of the show windows, danced and screeched and laughed. Only the blonde Käthe appeared subdued. She was sitting on an old man's lap listening to the story he was relating.

Madam Misere, elegantly dressed in a cream-colored dress, her gray hair as immaculate as her make-up, noticed my glance. "The poor dear. She is so unhappy. I offered to give her today off but she thought working the evening shift would take her mind off this situation."

The old man whispered something in Käthe's ear. She took his hand and they walked to the stairs leading to the second floor. The red bow in her hair quivered with each step.

I sat down. Now I could only hear the noise from the bar.

Madam Misere served cognac. The drapes were drawn. On the nearby Elbe River tugs whistled and ships' sirens sounded. The night was foggy.

"Your health, Mr. Jordan."

"And yours, Madam." We drank. I held a lighter to her thick Brazil cigar she held between two ring-adorned fingers. The large diamonds sparkled. Exhaling a cloud of the spicy smoke, Madam said, "I'm sorry to have to tell you that things have not gone well."

From the bar I could hear snatches of verses of a song

telling of a nymphomanic innkeeper's wife who lived near a river called Lahn.

"My lawyer has been to court."

It was worse than I had expected. "He has already been committed to trial?"

"Unfortunately. The detectives have been in a great hurry. They were here for hours too."

"And?"

Solemnly, Madam said, "There is nothing to hide in my house." She could have said as readily, 'In my house and at the English Palace.' And with conviction I would have replied, 'More likely there, Madam'!

In the bar they had come to another verse.

"The lady also had a salamander who could do it ten times in a row . . ."

"I'm sure you understand that my lawyer is just as interested in his reputation as you are. It would not be good if the detectives saw you with him, and it also would not be good for my lawyer if—need I say more?"

"No, Madam."

"Not that the thought ever occurred to me that you and Schauberg were engaged in some unlawful business and that that was the reason for your interest in him. I know you are doing this for Käthe's sake."

"Yes, Madam."

"How touching. Then I might ask you to give me ten thousand marks. Tomorrow will do; I'm sure you don't have that much on you right now."

"Now, listen—"

"Mr. Jordan, I, too, have my reputation to consider. If I am to be the go-between, something not without risk, for you and my lawyer, in which case both of you remain perfectly anonymous, then, according to the most elementary laws of economy—"

"You have studied at the university?"

"Three terms; the risk must be covered by a sum in the

event of failure. It is just like an insurance. You know how insurance companies work, Mr. Jordan?"

More and more I came to respect this cathouse madam.

"Two thousand."

"Ten thousand."

"Madam, a lady does not blackmail a gentleman."

"Mr. Jordan, a gentleman does not bargain with a lady. Give me eight thousand and we won't talk about it any further."

"Five thousand."

"Five thousand, all right. But I'm a little disappointed in you. Are you a man who would risk his reputation for a mere five thousand marks?"

". . . then the salamander stood upright and whistled the Marseillaise," they were singing in the bar.

11

"Now."

"Schauberg and this Charley stole five thousand liters of cough medicine. In glass containers of fifty liters each. Three truckloads. The drivers helped load. The cough medicine has been recovered. The drivers are in jail. Charley too. Schauberg sang like a canary."

"He must have lost his mind!"

"I would not say that." Madam savored the smoke of her cigar. "He could have made a lot of money with the cough medicine. And he needs money."

"I know that."

"Exactly. And it seemed to me he was afraid that dreams, connected with you, would not come true. Am I correct?"

"Yes."

"That's what I thought. I know nothing about pharmaceuticals but this cough medicine—a new kind of cough medicine, it was just coming on the market—"

"Don't say cough medicine any more! The word is driving me mad!"

"—well then, this syrup supposedly contains a particular chemical substance, codeine, caffeine, I don't know which, one cannot know everything. This substance is reputed to have a similar euphoric effect upon many morphine addicts."

"The syrup was to be sold to addicts?"

"That is what my lawyer was told by the detectives of the narcotics division. Every year hundreds of new nonprescription medicines are marketed. Addicts test their effectiveness. They know right away if one particular medicine has the desired effect or not. It would take months of work for doctors and chemists in laboratories or hospitals to discover it. Then there is a run on the product. The narcotics division becomes suspicious only when pharmacists notice how well any such new product sells. The medicine is then added to the list of prescription drugs; the addicts look around for something new. It is a game without an end. Dr. Schauberg obviously thought to make a killing with this syrup."

"What an idiot!"

"Don't say that. He was worried about his future. Don't you know what one is capable of then? My lawyer thinks that the police would like to keep our friend in jail as long as possible, hoping to get together sufficient material about other dark incidents in his life. You know the German proverb 'Time brings wisdom'?"

"No."

"I would say the police think, 'Time brings betrayal.'"

"You mean, someone Schauberg betrayed will rat on him?"

"Man is his own worst enemy, Mr. Jordan."

"Can we have Schauberg released if we post bail?"

"Yes."

"How much?"

"Thirty thousand at least, says my lawyer."

"If bail is put up—does anyone ask where the money came from?"

"No. Of course you realize that even if the doctor is released he will have to report to the police regularly. He will be under close surveillance which will make his business with you not exactly easy. And, naturally, his investigation will be continued."

"It makes no difference," I said. Since I had drunk the cognac I had not felt well. I thought of Schauberg still behind bars, of myself and the instructions that dealt with a boxful of drugs. I had a sense of panic. Another attack. Then what? "It makes no difference," I said. "We must get him out."

"You would risk the money?"

"Yes."

"Very well."

"Just supposing your lawyer is asked about the origin of the money?"

"I am prepared to say that I lent it to Käthe; because she is my best worker; because I feel for her as a mother would; because I am convinced of Schauberg's innocence. Either the investigation is dropped or he is arrested again. In both cases the money will be returned to me. Or do I look like a woman who could not afford thirty thousand marks?"

"You look like a woman who can afford thirty thousand marks and at the same time make five thousand," I said full of admiration.

"When can I have the bail money?"

"Tomorrow."

"There is still the possibility bail will be refused or at least delayed." She rose, her smile benign. "But we must keep our spirits up. God helps the courageous! Since you will be coming to see me more frequently I would like you to spend at least half an hour with Käthe upstairs.

Just to alleviate any doubts any informer here might have that you are coming here for your amusement."

She simply thought of everything!

We could not find Käthe. The Mousetrap, a beautiful dark-haired girl clad in only a bra, tiny pants and silk stockings told us, "She is in her room."

"Alone?"

"Yes, Madam Misere." The Mousetrap did not wear shoes; a few of her toes were bandaged and she limped.

"Room seven, monsieur."

I climbed the creaking stairs to room seven on the second floor and knocked. There was no answer. I opened the door. Käthe, in a very short yellow robe was kneeling before a picture of the Madonna hanging above the bed. The only light came from a red-shaded bedside lamp.

Käthe had not heard me. Her hands were folded in prayer and her voice low and fervent. "Please, dear Mother in heaven, help my poor Walter. I'll do anything you want. Help him. Let him be free again so we can get married and go away, away from here. Please, please, dear Mother of God, please, please, please."

I gently closed the door.

12

Rome, April sixteenth.

The little white cat, Bianca, has had a relapse. After drinking milk for five days she again drinks the milk and alcohol mixture.

She does not eat; her eyes are glassy and her fur unkempt. Professor Pontevivo told me the reason for her relapse. Virginia creepers cover the walls of the clinic. Below the windows of the laboratory where Bianca's cage stands a pair of swallows that have built a nest. Bianca can hear the chirping of the young birds. Being a cat and not being free, she now suffered by her captivity.

The professor said, "The pathological urge to destroy and the drive to create; the intention to do good or bad—if thwarted—usually ends with alcohol."

The professor and his beautiful assistant carefully moved the nest to an old tree in the park. Now Bianca cannot hear the chirping of the young birds any more.

"It was a test for Bianca, a temptation," said Pontevivo. "You will be tempted and tested too, Mr. Jordan. Don't be discouraged by setbacks. They exist to be surmounted, to be learned from. We shall see if Bianca is able to do that."

"What do setbacks teach, Professor?"

"That no human being and no animal can always be happy. So long as they live they will again and again be tortured, be hurt. To grieve, Mr. Jordan, is the beginning of illness."

13

The sun was brilliant in a very blue sky. A gusty wind blew from the northeast. White crests crowned the waves of the restless, many-hued water. The sides of the ships we passed reflected the hard bright light. Our little boat danced on the waves.

Misha was holding the wheel while the young skipper steered.

Natasha and I were seated in the cockpit. The wind blew fine spray into our faces. We were going up the Elbe on a Saturday afternoon, westward past the shipyards at the Kuhwärder harbor. We saw ships of many nations on which men were busy with pneumatic drills and others, with loading coal. We passed the Maakenwärder harbor, Altona and its picturesque little houses; to the Parkhafen where foreign ships were tightly berthed. We turned in the harbor where oil was being pumped onto tankers. An Iranian tanker came toward us, its wash foaming.

Misha looked at his mother from under the arm of the helmsman; his eyes shone and his fingers made a quick sequence of signs.

Natasha too, moved her fingers; the boy beamed and laughed soundlessly. Surprised, he looked up at the skipper who had gently brushed back his hair. In the wake of the Iranian ship our boat tilted and Natasha was thrown against me.

"Misha says he loves it out here and he is not afraid," Natasha translated. "This is the first time we have taken a sightseeing trip. Every time I suggested it he told me he was too afraid."

He told me?

She spoke of her deaf-and-dumb child as if he were perfectly normal. For her, Misha did talk—with his fingers. She had become used to it.

"I told him today we had been invited. He said if a man was coming too it would probably be all right."

I had suggested the trip to Natasha when I had called her from a telephone booth, after I had spoken to Shirley.

"I must see you, I must talk to you, Natasha!"

"When?"

"Right away."

"Tell me where and when."

"I am free tomorrow afternoon. Shall we meet at three? At the piers near the Hafentor subway station. We could charter a boat and do a little sightseeing." It was safe on a boat. No one would recognize us there.

"You know Hamburg very well."

"I've taken sightseeing trips before."

"I usually spend Saturdays with Misha. Would you mind if I brought him along?"

"Not at all."

That had been on Friday.

Saturday morning I talked to Kostasch. The hundred thousand marks, part of my fee, was paid in three instalments. The second part was not due for another ten days. I needed that money for Schauberg's bail and asked Kostasch for an advance.

"Sure you can have the thirty thousand, Peter boy. But—"

"But what?"

"It's none of my business. It's your money."

"Exactly."

"But don't you think you're spending rather a lot here in Hamburg? You know, you're like a son to me. I'd hate to think you're buying diamonds for some starlet. Those girls do it for nothing and—"

"There is no girl."

"Okay." While he was telephoning the cashier, a telegram was delivered. Kostasch opened it, read it, suddenly grabbed my shoulders and, yelling and shouting, danced me around his office. The telegram came from Hollywood.

"Rushes excellent. Thank you. Carry on. Wilson Brothers."

After Kostasch had calmed down somewhat I confided, "By the way, I'm going to look around for movie locations with the assistant producer. In case my wife calls . . ."

"Of course, Peter boy. You can rely on me." His wide grin froze. "So there is a girl!"

"But I swear she is not what you think!"

He looked at me, doubtful.

"Really!"

"I believe you. Boy!" He seemed genuinely relieved. "Do you know I had suspected you of being weak enough to be carried away through some affair? Don't get mad but I was really concerned. You seemed troubled those last few days." He cleared his throat. "But you are a decent fellow. Your wife should be very happy."

"Why?"

"No loves. No affairs. Like me. Always a new girl. One, two, three, finished. You know, there are some men who have affairs that last for years? Our wives don't really appreciate us. Looking for a location, eh? For how long?"

"Early evening will be sufficient."

"Okay. Have fun. But," he began, "if you're going to give her money——"

I set his mind at rest. Then I called Madam Misere. "I cannot post bail until Monday," she told me. "Over the weekend hardly anyone is at court. A few gentlemen are having breakfast here just now."

"How is Käthe?"

"She is very unhappy but she pulls herself together. I've had no complaints about her, the poor little thing."

"Give her my regards, please. Until Monday then, Madam Misere."

We finished shooting at one o'clock. I drove Shirley back to the hotel where Joan, Shirley and I had lunch. I told Joan that I had to spend the afternoon looking for a suitable location to shoot a part of the movie. In the car I had told Shirley, "I have some things to take care of. Possibly I can get the doctor out on bail." I could not tell whether or not she believed me. She had only replied, "Yes, Peter."

"Don't you believe me?"

"Please. Not again. I'm sure you'll do the best you can for both of us." Was she smiling? My nerves became increasingly worse. Naturally, she was not smiling.

While we were having lunch she received a telephone call.

Joan watched her leave the room smiling. "I think our little daughter is in love."

Surprised I dropped some food. She had not noticed. "In love? Shirley?"

She nodded. "Isn't it sweet?"

"What makes you think so?"

"A blind man could see it. But not you! Your mind is so occupied with your movie or you would have noticed how frequently she is called to the telephone. She has gone out twice at night too."

"At night?"

"You were already asleep. I saw her leave." Joan smiled again. "I see quite a lot. I'm not as unobservant as all that. I see what I see."

What did she see? What did she know? Was there a reason for all this? Had I been so wrong about her? Was she the most prudent of the three of us? Could she really be different from what I had always thought her to be? Was she not the woman beset with the fears of aging, quietly suffering, the deceived? Or was she really the spider of the web in which we were enmeshed? The spider, cruelly, untiring, watching its victims become more and more entangled in its web?

"Did you . . . did you talk with her?"

"I'm waiting."

"You're waiting?"

"Well, after all, she is nineteen!"

"So? Are you going to wait until she—"

"Until she becomes pregnant?" said Joan softly. "Darling, don't be so melodramatic. If you could only see yourself!" She laughed out loud. "What a face you're making!"

"Very comical, I'm sure."

"Are you jealous?"

"Jealous?" The spider. Careful now. "Why should I be jealous?"

"After all she is not your real daughter. She is only your stepdaughter. And what a pretty stepdaughter! When I came to see you at the studio I could see she had already charmed the production staff." That was true. The young men were, to a man, after Shirley. Mostly that fresh kid Hennessy, chief-cutter Jaky's assistant. Was it Hennessy? Who could it be? Was it at all probable that

Shirley, in her condition, even felt like flirting with a young man? Or was it a trap? A trap Joan had set for me?

Had Joan seemed suspicious these past few days? She had gone shopping, modeled her new dresses for me, come to the set when we were shooting. She had had tea with her cousin, a high-ranking member of the American Consulate. Joan's relatives, wealthy, famous, influential, could be found in all parts of the world.

Suspicious?

No.

Yes! Now I remembered something. Twice, on days I did not have to be at the studio early, I had been at the hotel when the mail arrived. Each time Joan had swooped down on it, preventing me from seeing the mail first as though she were expecting some secret message.

What could that be?

"Peter!"

I started.

"Yes?"

"The waiter wants to know if you would like more meat."

"No. Yes. No, thank you."

"What is the matter with you?"

"Nothing. Why?"

Joan smiled. "Your movie, right? You just can't think of anything else but your film, I know . . ."

A spider?

Shirley returned.

"I'm sorry . . ."

"Who was that?"

"It was nothing important, Paddy."

"Who was it!"

"My goodness! What's the matter? Why are you shouting at me? It was Hennessy."

"Hennessy. I see. What did he want?"

"I had locked up the latest rushes in the cutting room. But they have to make the plane to Hollywood tonight."

"So?"

"By mistake I took the key with me. He'll stop by later to pick it up."

I stared at Shirley.

"Really, Peter," said Joan. "That's the second time you've dropped your French fries. Do artists always have to be sloppy like that?"

14

At three o'clock I was waiting for Natasha and Misha who were coming by subway. Misha's skin was as fair and clear as his mother's. He had also inherited the slanted, black, luminous eyes and wide cheekbones. He bowed as he offered me his hand. Then moved his fingers quickly.

"Thank you again for the crayons and the sketch pad," translated Natasha.

Misha laughed soundlessly and nodded. He wore a gray fur-lined coat over a blue suit. To his delight I rented a boat, and mentioned Misha's condition to the young skipper.

"Well then, I must let him steer the boat a little." He smiled at Misha as he helped him aboard. The little boy seemed a little afraid as we entered the rougher waters of the Elbe River. The skipper explained how the motor worked and how to steer and soon the child had forgotten his fear and beamed at the skipper; "talked" to Natasha.

"He says the skipper is wonderful."

Although the skipper was not familiar with the sign language he and Misha appeared to understand and enjoy each other.

Leaving the Neuen Petroleumhafen we once again entered the rougher waters of the Elbe. Silvery, screeching seagulls circled above, frequently diving down onto the water.

I opened the black bag anchored between my legs and fixed two large drinks. Natasha and I looked at each other before we drank. Her beautiful eyes were moist but she smiled.

We entered a maze of narrow canals and the water became calm once again.

"I know," said Natasha.

"Know what?"

"What you are going to tell me."

"What am I going to tell you?"

"That you don't love your wife, that your daughter is jealous, that you've defrauded your insurance company, and that we must not see each other any more," answered Natasha. "Was I right?"

"Yes," I replied. "You were correct."

"Just by observing you these last few days it was not difficult to guess." She had guessed as much as I had wanted to tell her. I felt relief. There was nothing to worry about. I finished my drink and bent down to pour another. Just then the boat swayed; Natasha was pressed against me and for one second our cheeks touched.

I know that this moment, when Natasha's face touched mine for the first time, is the one I treasure and relive in my memory.

15

A moment of desperate hope while I wished this trip on the shimmering water would never end. I said, "It's true, I have defrauded the insurance company, I am going to divorce my wife, and my stepdaughter is jealous." For a moment I wanted to confide everything to Natasha but it passed. While our little boat and other vessels were waiting to enter a lock I said, "My stepdaughter thinks I . . . that you and I . . ."

"That we are lovers?"

"Yes."

Natasha blushed and looked straight ahead. Her little son signaled and she answered. "Misha thanks you for inviting us on this trip." I waved to him. He waved back. "I thank you too. Could I have another drink?" I refilled her glass.

The gates of the lock opened and once inside it was shady and cold.

"I told Shirley that I did not know you. I explained that you were probably a fan of mine. Please forgive me."

She did not reply.

"Shirley now knows your name. If she should contact you, would you . . . would you stay with my version? A lot depends on it for me."

"I promise. Your stepdaughter is in love with you, isn't she?"

"Excuse me?"

"You heard me. She is very beautiful and young."

"Nineteen."

"And she looks very unhappy."

The boat had reached the other gates of the lock. Misha, his face flushed with excitement, asked to sit between us for a little while. When he made sounds Natasha's eyes became moist.

"He produces sounds more often now. And louder too. I'm taking him to another specialist in two days."

"I wish you success, Natasha."

The gates of the lock opened and through a canal we re-entered the Elbe.

Misha held our hands; he smiled and his eyes were shining. To all appearances we were a happy little family.

Natasha translated for me. "Misha would like to draw a picture for you. I have told him I will mail it to you." She did not look at me. "And then I will tear it up."

"Save it. Don't throw it away."

"Why not?" Suddenly she turned her face to me and I saw tears in her eyes. She hugged Misha closely so he would not see her tears and repeated, "Why not? So I'll be reminded of this hour?" She took off her glasses and dried her tears. Misha's fingers were moving quickly. Natasha shook her head.

Misha looked at me sadly.

"What did he say?"

"Nothing."

"What did he say?"

"He asked if we were going to surprise him. If you, perhaps, were his father and would stay with us from now on. I have told him his father is on a long trip." Her eyes were moist again. Misha's fingers were making signs. Fiercely she said, "Don't listen to him! Don't listen to him!" She held the boy closely and the inarticulate noises he made sounded sad.

We had come back to the piers crowded with people on this pleasant afternoon.

"We'll take the subway," Natasha said to me as I helped her off the boat. The young skipper lifted Misha onto the pier. When I paid him he remarked, "You're very fortunate to have a child like that."

"But I told you the boy is deaf and dumb."

"What does it matter?" he replied. "I'm married too. Our child was born dead. My Marie can't have another. Can you understand why God allows that?"

"No," I said, "I don't know."

He told me where to find him if we should ever decide on another trip. "I would like to see the little boy again. What is your son's name?"

"Misha," I said.

At the subway station I said good-by. Misha made signs. Natasha translated, "Could he kiss you?"

I bent down. His silent lips kissed my cheek. I kissed him too. His little arms encircled my neck but in a moment Natasha freed me from his embrace. "We must go now. Please nod. He asked if we are going to see you again." I nodded. His smile was bright and with his thumb and index finger he formed a circle.

"That means Auf Wiedersehen," said Natasha.

I also made the sign.

"Don't worry. You can rely on me."

"Natasha—"

"No," she said, "I can't stand any more." And she quickly pulled Misha along to the subway entrance where he turned and made the circle with his finger and thumb. I did the same. Auf Wiedersehen.

I would never see them again I thought as I watched them go down to the subway. Not Misha and not Natasha. We might, perhaps, meet by chance and then only to say hello. It was all finished. I picked up my black bag and left. I had parked the car on a side street. It was quiet there.

I sat in the car and drank. I dreaded the drive back to the hotel, back to Shirley and Joan. More than that, I was disgusted with myself and my life.

16

"Hennessy? No, he was not here this afternoon." The guard at the gate of the studios shook his head. He did not notice that I was quite drunk. The more I had drunk the more I had thought of the telephone call at lunch.

"Are you quite sure?"

"Sure. He left at one, when everybody was leaving. What would he do here on a Saturday afternoon?"

"He was supposed to pick up some rushes but somebody had taken the keys to the cutting room by mistake and he could not get them."

"That can't be. The keys are always left here. I've been

here since eleven. I would have noticed if a key had been missing. But I'll check."

Hundreds of numbered keys were hanging from nails on an enormous board inside the guardhouse. "There you are! And that's where it was at lunchtime." He laughed, "Now I even remember who left it here, Mr. Jordan. Your stepdaughter."

17

What did I do when I saw Shirley?

What would you have done, Professor Pontevivo? I did nothing. Shirley had lied to me. Deliberately. Since she had been capable of doing that with such blatant assurance I could expect her to continue to lie to me if I questioned her.

Now she had her secret as I had mine. She had been gone four hours on this Saturday afternoon, Joan told me. I had also been away for four hours. It was grotesque. Shirley did not ask where I had been. I did not ask her where she had been. She lied. I lied. I was determined to find out whom she met and why. Were it Hennessy or some other character, I had to be careful. I had to watch her. Did she watch me too?

Perhaps she was equally determined to find out my secret?

It was inconceivable that Shirley, tormented by pangs of conscience, tortured by fear and suffering constant nausea; a good and pious girl carrying a child could deceive me with another man. Was desperation driving her to such irresponsible deeds?

No, it could not be. She could not deceive me, not now, not in her condition. It was unbelievable. Was it? Was it inconceivable to Shirley too, that I deceived her with another woman—now, while she was with child?

Yes? No?

No? Yes?

That evening a small passenger steamboat took us to the Mühlenkamper Fährhaus. We dined in a lovely old room with a heavy-beamed ceiling and comfortable red leather chairs. I don't remember what we ate. Yellow-shaded table lamps shed soft light on the faces of the two women sitting before the huge window opposite me. Two faces; so familiar.

How familiar?

Thousands of lights were reflected by the dark water of the Alster. Small boats hurried by and, on the other bank, the opaque candelabra formed a long bright string of pearls.

"Shirley, you're hiding something from me. That story about the key to the cutting room is not true." I might have said that if I had wanted to stop lying. What would she have replied if she had not wanted to lie any more?

"And you're hiding nothing? You don't know a woman by the name of Petrovna? You have never talked with her?"

No, No. No.

I had neither strength, courage nor moral right to begin such a quarrel. It probably wouldn't have made any difference anyway. I had to find out what Shirley was doing and why. I had to devise a plan. I had to be patient now.

Joan was gay and carefree on this evening; Shirley, friendly but solemn. Once, when dessert was being served, she excused herself. When she returned she was very pale. I knew she had not telephoned nor seen anyone but had been sick again. Strange: on this evening, for the first time, I saw Shirley not through eyes of passion and jealousy but with pity and a curiously different sense of love.

Whatever she did: it was done in anguish. I felt that now. If she had deceived me it was deceit of a special kind. Perhaps I had already lost her to a man, here in

Hamburg, who could release her from the torment I had brought her.

What kind of man could that be? Not the handsome, vain Hennessy or one of his good-looking friends. I decided that I must find out.

At the hotel I took the stairs again. Shirley accompanied me. Joan, poking fun at me, took the elevator.

Suddenly Shirley stopped.

"Peter—"

"Yes?"

"Do you still love me?"

"Do you have to ask?"

"Tell me."

"I love you."

She kissed me and the sweetness of this kiss swept away distrust, jealousy, logic and proof of her lie, her deceit. She had never kissed me like that before. Her kiss was tender, gentle; a delicate emotional kiss.

Then she ran upstairs ahead of me. When I reached the sixth floor she had disappeared. Joan was waiting for me in the living room.

"Head over heels in love," she laughed.

"Who?"

"Our little one. Didn't you notice?"

"Oh, yes. No. Really? Do you really think so?"

"Peter," Joan shook her head. "Won't you ever grow up?"

That night for the second time I lived through the nightmare of being locked in the elevator for thousands of years. Finally I fell down and prayed to the grating of the intercom hoping to hear Natasha's voice again.

But I did not hear it.

18

I awoke shaking, soaked in perspiration. I slid from the bed, fell, and crawled to the closet; to the black bag. My teeth hitting the neck of the bottle, I drank whisky. Still the horror of the dream did not leave me.

I had to get away from this room which was merely another, larger elevator. I could not breathe. Away. Away. To the street. To Natasha.

No.

I could not see her any more. I sat on my bed, the bottle in hand, and gasped for breath.

Joan?

Just to talk to someone, not to be so alone, so terribly alone.

No, not to Joan.

To Shirley!

I loved her. She loved me. I would go to her. To hold her. To kiss her. To caress her. To love her. We had not embraced since—since when? Could I still go to her? Surely. Didn't I do everything I could for her, for our love? Of course. To Shirley. Yes, I would go to her.

You lied to me. Don't argue. Don't tell me any more lies. I know everything. You are mine. Only mine. Another man? Absurd.

To hold her. To embrace her. To hear her sigh. Yes. Yes. Everything the way it used to be in my bungalow. The same. Right away! Now.

At her door I raised my hand to knock. Suddenly I saw Natasha's eyes. They seemed to say: So you are going to do another vile deed. You are doing this for your sake. Not Shirley's. It has nothing to do with love. It is fear, desperation, desire, lust. You're doing this to a very young girl who is carrying your child. Does that mean nothing to you? Don't you care? Is there no decency in you at all any more?

My hand dropped. I returned to my room, sat on my bed and drank. Slowly I grew calmer.

Had I gone to Shirley I would have felt ashamed though Natasha would never have known. Did I suddenly have a conscience? What nonsense: a conscience by the name of Natasha.

19

Rome, eighteenth of April.

There is much agitation at the clinic. A dreadful discovery has been made. The hunch-backed Suora Superiora Maria Magdalena, as romantic as she is gossipy, as kind as she is curious, told me about it.

"Signore Jordan, I am most upset. And I thought it was love . . ."

Antonio, a very strong thirty-year-old Neapolitan attendant at the clinic had been fired. It was well-known that he loved fruits and sometimes took and ate some of the fruits belonging to the patients. Fruits could easily be replaced, and since his great strength was often called upon his stealing was tolerated.

Yesterday Antonio suffered a dreadful attack. At first it was thought he was simply drunk. He floundered about, babbling incoherently; then he foamed at the mouth and went into convulsions.

Professor Pontevivo examined him. He had had an overdose of drugs, later found to be dolantin.

After his stomach had been pumped and he had sufficiently recovered he confessed to having stolen seven oranges from the young drug-addicted composer.

"He always plays better when his wife comes to see him," the romantic Suora Superiora had once told me.

Now the reason for his euphoria had been discovered. The oranges his wife had regularly brought him had been confiscated and tested by Professor Pontevivo. They were found to contain large doses of dolantin. Questioned, his wife confessed to having "filled" the fruit by means of a syringe.

"The little you gave him was not sufficient for Pierre!" she screamed at the Professor. "He could not have composed! He is a genius! His orders should be obeyed! He will live in his music when we are all dust!"

The genius has suffered a breakdown. Two attendants watch and restrain the pitiable human wreck screaming, gasping, fighting demons in this artificially produced delirium.

The piano in the music room has been closed.

Professor Pontevivo is very upset, Suora Superiora told me. "And I always thought it was love . . ."

20

It is extremely difficult to find ways to keep watch on someone, especially for a visitor in a foreign city and particularly if the interested watcher is working from morning to night. Living, as I was, in a hotel, I was painfully aware that perhaps I was being watched too.

At the studios and at the hotel I confided in a few older people: Harry, my dressing-room attendant, a guard, a sound man, a white-haired waiter, the chief telephone operator at the hotel, a woman in charge of the sixth floor.

It was difficult in spite of the tips I handed out. They all promised to help a man worried about his young, innocent daughter. A man who did not want his wife to worry.

Most of them probably hit on the truth. Stepfather. In love with stepdaughter. Jealous of a younger man. Guilty conscience. Very guilty conscience. Or he would not have given such large tips. Much too large.

It remained to be seen if they would help me. Would they tell me the truth even if they learned it? Perhaps Shirley had bribed them too? Or Joan? The three of us?

November fourteenth had been the Saturday I had said good-by to Natasha. Sunday it rained and I used that time to search out accomplices. At lunch Shirley again excused herself. She hurriedly left the room and I wondered how much longer before a mother would notice the recurring nausea. Sundays were the most dangerous days. They gave Joan the chance to observe her closely. I resolved there should not be another such Sunday. Or at most only one more.

Monday morning, before I drove to the studios, I delivered to Madam Misere her five thousand marks and the thirty thousand for Schauberg's bail. Shirley was not with me. She had told me, "Jaky said I need not be at the studios before ten. The bus is going to pick me up."

Really?

Jaky, when I asked him, had corroborated Shirley's words. But who drove the bus? What did Shirley do until ten o'clock? Why did Hennessy avoid me? Did he avoid me? Was I seeing things? All I could do now was wait. Shirley was being watched. Perhaps something would come to light.

I telephoned Madam Misere Monday evening.

"The lawyer is hopeful," she said.

He was also hopeful on Tuesday, Wednesday and Friday. But he could not get Schauberg out on bail. New difficulties arose every time. "*À la longue* they have to let him go," said Madam Misere.

Sure.

À la longue Shirley would be in her third month. *À la longue* the child could not be taken care of any more. *À la longue* . . .

À la longue my work became a severe strain although I

was treating myself according to Schauberg's instructions and had become quite expert at giving myself intramuscular injections. The green box was always in the trunk of my car. Wednesday the telephone operator told me Shirley had received a telephone call from a man. He had not given his name. They had made a date for four o'clock.

"Where?"

"They did not mention where. Mr. Jordan, I can understand how worried you are but this is terribly embarrassing for me . . ." But she pocketed the fifty marks and thereupon seemed less embarrassed.

The sound man and guard only knew that Shirley sometimes telephoned and left the studios when I was working and they were also very embarrassed. So was I. More tips with no results.

On the nineteenth of November I simply could not remember my lines. I was becoming increasingly exhausted. The drugs in the box would not be sufficient to see me through the movie. If Schauberg did not soon get out . . .

Kostasch and Seaton fell back on the old treatment. Don't upset the star, don't frighten the star, don't let him see how we really feel.

"So what, Peter boy? We'll use prompt cards if you can't remember the lines!"

I read the lines. It was fortunate I was not shortsighted too.

It was on the twentieth, a Friday, when I showered, that I first noticed the rash.

21

This rash began harmlessly enough.

Tiny red pustules had appeared between my toes, on my feet, and inside my legs. I blamed the excessive quantities of drugs my body had to absorb. But the rash could hardly be seen by anyone.

Supposing the rash spread to my chest, my neck, my face?

Schauberg!

They had to let him out on bail. They had to, had to.

Did they really have to?

Friday night Joan again asked to go to sleep in my arms. My self-control was badly lacking and she broke off when she saw the expression on my face.

"I know your movie is the most important thing in your life right now. I can understand that. I shall never ask you again. When your film is finished we'll take a vacation and catch up on everything." She kissed my cheek and quickly went to her bedroom.

While I was debating whether or not I should follow her I heard the key turn the lock. Joan had locked herself in . . .

Schauberg was still in jail on Saturday. I went to see Madam Misere and told her of my urgent need of a doctor.

"That is most unfortunate. The doctor who takes care of my girls is in the hospital with pleurisy. I'll try and find someone. I'm sure you won't mind waiting one or two days."

"But no more than that. Do you think you can find a doctor at all?"

"I hope so, Mr. Jordan. Doctors who are asked for services by people such as me are always suspicious since our business is under police supervision. But I will do my best."

I drove back to town; Shirley on my mind. We could not go on like this. Tomorrow was Sunday. Something had to be done. I had to confide in Kostasch. He was the only German I knew well enough.

There was no need for me to look for him. He was

291

waiting at the hotel for me. He was pale and his hands shook.

"Something wrong?"

He nodded.

"Just let me tell my wife and we'll go——"

"Both ladies are out. I wanted to say hello. Your wife was just leaving for a party at the American Embassy. I believe she is with her cousin."

"And Shirley?"

"No idea. Your wife didn't know either. Shirley made a call and left in a taxi."

"Excuse me. I'll be right back."

The telephone operator I had bribed was not in her usual place. It was her day off. I returned to Kostasch. I felt sick and told him so.

"You can't feel as sick as I do."

"Let's go to the bar."

The bar was empty at this hour.

"Whisky," ordered Kostasch. "Give me the bottle."

We went to a corner table in the wood-paneled room. Kostasch's hands were still unsteady as he poured the whisky. I had never seen him so unnerved.

"Peter boy," he said, "Jerome Wilson is arriving here tomorrow afternoon. I talked to him an hour ago."

"Coming to Hamburg? But why?"

"George is ill. Heart attack. Or he would have come. Cheers. Drink up. You'll need it. Unless a miracle happens, we are finished."

"The film?"

Kostasch hardly ever drank. Now he downed a large neat whisky.

"That's right. Our movie."

Kostasch explained. The subject of our movie had been an outstanding Broadway success in 1928. The man who played the lead had been a famous child star on the stage. He had even portrayed the now-aged child star in the movie, made in 1940 by one of Hollywood's chief studios.

The cast was headed by some of Hollywood's most renowned actors. The film had been an international triumph and a fantastic box-office. Reason enough for us to decide to make an updated remake of it.

"It's just a year ago since the star of that film died. Now his studio has decided to release his movies."

"Now? Now they decided that?"

"Now! Not a year ago when he died but now, now that we are in the middle of our remake! They have sold those movies to TV stations all over the USA!"

"Including the old 'Comeback,'" I said.

"Including the old 'Comeback,'" said Kostasch. He held his glass with both hands. His hands were shaking uncontrollably.

The Sixth Tape

1

The Wilson twin arrived Sunday at four p.m. Kostasch
had had the inspiration to bring along two very pretty
starlets to whom he had promised a small part in a movie
in exchange for their services.

"In our movie?"

"No! Some other movie. I don't know. I have other
things on my mind now!"

The girls, one blonde, one dark-haired, hurried ahead
to greet the dwarfish man dressed in black. His ears stood
away under his homburg. The expression on his parch-
ment-like face was grim. The photographer we had
brought along took pictures as the girls affectedly kissed
Jerome Wilson and offered him flowers. Jerome brusquely
pushed them aside. The girls, startled, tripped along, their
high heels clattering, staring at us helplessly.

"That's not Jerome," I said to Kostasch. "That's
George."

"How could it be? George is in the hospital. He's had a
heart attack."

"Maybe you made a mistake. Jerome is in the hospital.
This is George."

It was Jerome. We knew as soon as we were by his

side. "Was that your idea to bring the broads, Mr. Kostasch?"

"Of course, Jerome. Good grief, I thought you'd like that. Happy to make your stay a pleasant one, isn't that right, girls?"

The starlets giggled. They had visions of the movie parts Kostasch had promised them.

Jerome Wilson who could never pass a woman without visualizing her undressed grunted, "I have no time for that."

"Jerome!" Kostasch was thunderstruck. "What is the matter with you?"

"George is ill, right? Somebody has to look after the business. Send the broads away."

Kostasch told the girls to see him at the studio tomorrow.

The blonde protested. "I'm not going to be insulted by this old guy! You're not going to get away with it!"

Kostasch was embarrassed. People began to stare at us. The dark-haired girl started to cry.

"That's enough to make me sick," said Jerome.

Desperate now, Kostasch broke his rule of long standing. He pulled out two one-hundred-mark bills, one for each of the girls. Jerome was already walking down the stairs.

Driving back to town the little man who, together with his twin brother, always reminded me of Tweedledum or Tweedledee sat in utter silence. Kostasch had reserved a suite in a hotel opposite mine.

"It's the best suite in the hotel, Jerome," explained Kostasch. The business with the girls had visibly shaken him. Jerome was in a quarrelsome mood. "You call me Mr. Wilson! I don't call you Herbert, do I?"

"All right, Mr. Wilson. Sorry, Mr. Wilson."

Oh, Kostasch! Oh, money!

"The view is terrific!"

"You mean the rooms face the street?"

"Naturally! You can see the ships and the—"

"It's no good. Street noise keeps me awake. I want a suite facing the rear."

The only available suite did not please Jerome. "Great rathole. Thanks a lot, Mr. Kostasch. Thank you very much."

At least he talked to Kostasch. He had completely ignored me. From time to time he gave me a deprecating glance. Kostasch tried everything to placate him. He didn't want a rest, did not want to eat or have a drink. All he wanted was to talk business. Now.

It was unbelievable! This was the lecherous old man whose peculiar needs were talked about by the call girls of the West Coast. The little Jerome who for years had told me, "Money is no object. Be a good friend. I buy everything. Books, films, photos. But they must be different, you understand, Peter, different!"

Ah, well. Money is better than pornography.

I was not prepared to put up with the little voyeur's impudence and told him, "But I'm going to have a drink."

"You're back on the booze. That's nice. Very pretty."

I ignored him and rang for service. To the waiter I said, "Three double whiskys."

"I said I am not drinking," barked Jerome.

"I am not either," cried Kostasch.

"Three doubles," I repeated to the waiter. And to Jerome, "Now stop behaving like a little Caesar—" I knew his small stature bothered him and I added, "—a very little Caesar. We are in this mess just as much as you."

"George and I are only producers. You should have thought of the old movie and taken precautions!"

"And you didn't think it necessary?"

"How could we foresee they were going to throw that old movie back on the market!"

"It's something which happens very rarely. That's why

I find it very peculiar . . ." I said. Suddenly I had had a flash.

"You find it peculiar?" Jerome's eyes narrowed. I had the feeling I was on the right track.

Unfortunately Kostasch, walking up and down in agitation, interrupted me. "Just let's take it easy. We'll find a way." He extracted a cigarette from a case. "Do you mind if I smoke, Mr. Wilson?"

"Yes, I do. You'll be leaving soon and I have to live with the stink." Kostasch dutifully put away the cigarette.

I said, "Jerome, I have a few select books for you."

"Peter, please!" Kostasch implored. "We'll find a way." The huge man's voice was low.

"I've already found a way," said the short little man who had made millions from selling faulty war equipment. "It's quite a simple remedy." The waiter brought the drinks and Jerome barked at him to hurry it up.

"The remedy?" asked Kostasch.

"Three hundred thousand dollars," answered Jerome.

Kostasch's mouth was gaping.

"I went to see the president of that studio. It only took me five minutes to realize he was just trying to blackmail us. For three hundred thousand dollars he promised not to release this old movie and to give us all available copies."

That's when I downed the first double whisky. For a moment there was a dead silence.

2

"That's blackmail," Kostasch finally uttered.

"I call it a trap," said Jerome. "We walked right into it. We have ten days. Either we pay or he will sell the movie to television."

"Three hundred thousand dollars!" Kostasch stuttered.

"That's another third of our entire budget! That's a million two hundred thousand marks!"

"I know, Mr. Kostasch. I can multiply by four." The miserable little bastard was now as cold and hard as his brother. "I talked to Cosmos Distributors. There are two possibilities: discontinue the shooting—or pay the money."

"We could make a deal for less money," Kostasch offered.

"I've already done that. At first he demanded half a million. As I said, either we pay—or we stop production!"

"Then what happens?" Kostasch looked ill. I pushed a drink in front of him but he ignored it.

"Then Cosmos and my brother and I will sue you for breaking paragraph fourteen of our contract. But, naturally—"

"Mr. Wilson, please—"

"Would you kindly let me finish? Thank you. But, of course, we are not that cruel—"

"Aren't you?" I interjected.

"—and quite willing to help you. We suggest halving the cost. Cosmos and my brother and I will pay one hundred fifty thousand dollars. You will pay the other one hundred fifty thousand."

"How could we possibly get that kind of money in the next ten days? Right in the middle of production?" yelled Kostasch.

"Don't shout, Mr. Kostasch. I don't like that at all."

Obediently Kostasch lowered his voice. "What . . . what happens if we can't come up with the money?"

"If you split it it's only three hundred thousand marks for each of you."

"Yes, yes, I know. What happens if we don't have the money?"

"In that case," Jerome's voice was gentle, "to salvage the film, we—Cosmos, my brother and I—are prepared to pay the entire sum. Naturally, gentlemen—you will understand this——it means that we will become the sole producers with all rights."

That's when I drank the second whisky.

"Unfortunately you interrupted me a while ago, Kostasch," I said.

"I did? When?"

"Mr. Wilson remembers when."

The little man's eyes narrowed again.

"When I said I found it very peculiar they should want to release that old movie right at this time. Just a moment, Jerome, this time I won't be interrupted! Wouldn't you think it a strange coincidence, Kostasch? We have finished one third of our film. We have regularly supplied our partners, the Wilsons, with the rushes. The Wilsons even sent us a telegram because they liked the rushes so very much." I was now sure my suspicion had been correct. Jerome tried to interrupt but I ignored him. "The Wilsons and Cosmos are pretty sure of a success. A financial success which they would have to share with us. Isn't that annoying? It might not have been a bad idea if someone suggested to the president of that studio to release a certain old film!"

"That's a terrible accusation!" Jerome screamed, his face wrathful.

Kostasch caught on at last. He clenched his fist, lowered his head, as a pugilist on the offensive.

I said, "I'm sure neither Mr. Jerome Wilson nor his poor sick brother George went to see the president of the studio. Hollywood has many excellent lawyers. One can remain anonymous."

Kostasch towered above Jerome. His voice, a mere whisper now. "So that was the idea? You knew we couldn't pay. You'd get rid of us and then it's all yours."

"If you don't stop . . ." Jerome broke off when he saw Kostasch's raised fist.

"Now you can call him Jerome again," I suggested.

Kostasch whispered, "You son-of-a-bitch!"

"Get out!" whispered Jerome.

Both of them were whispering as angry men do under extreme tension.

I asked, "How much did you promise them? Twenty percent?"

"How dare you!"

"Fifteen? You are misers. For such service!"

"I forbid you to—"

"Kostasch, would you believe it? They actually only offered them ten percent!"

Jerome got out of his chair whereupon, standing before the massive Kostasch, he was even more physically insignificant. "Enough of this. Get out of my room," he said.

Kostasch's finger jabbed his chest at which he fell back into his chair.

Jerome cried, "I'm not going to be insulted by you. I must not get excited. I have a weak heart—"

"I thought your brother had a weak heart?" I said.

"The way I see it you are not in a position to pay the hundred fifty thousand dollars . . ."

Then the room began to sway. Kostasch and Jerome continued to argue but I could no longer understand what was said.

3

The way I see it . . .

You bastard. Not in a position to . . . You son-of-a-bitch. You can have the hundred fifty thousand. You cheat. You can have three hundred thousand. A million.

You can have it.

You could have.

My wife, my wealthy wife.

She had given me half of all she owned. Take that into consideration, you lecherous little bastard.

"Your money. I won't ever touch it. Not one cent." I had said that.

"Then don't. Throw it away! Give it to the poor!" Joan had answered.

Give it to the poor. Why give it to the poor? Give it to the rich! Give it to the president of that studio! The film. You must finish the movie. Your future is at stake. You are a scoundrel. You know that. It really would be idiotic if now you would not behave as one.

"Not one cent . . ."

Actually, why shouldn't I?

"To fall asleep in your arms . . . After all this time . . ."

No. No. No.

Impossible. I cannot do it. In one month at the latest I must tell Joan that I'm going to leave her and of my love for Shirley. I can't take the money. I am a scoundrel. Fine. But one without the necessary format. I'm nothing. Nothing at all. We are finished. Jerome is taking command. He really managed that beautifully. Now I can—

"What . . . what is it?"

"Are you deaf, Jordan?"

"I . . . I was lost in thought . . ."

"Thoughts! I've already told you twice the call is for you and you just sit there and stare at me! That's what I always say. That's what booze does to you!"

I quickly took the third glass of whisky and the receiver Jerome held out to me. "Hello . . ."

"Mr. Peter Jordan?"

"Speaking."

"I have a long distance call for you from Mr. Gregory Bates in Los Angeles."

Something must have happened or Gregory would not call me. What?

"Peter?"

"Gregory! Just one moment." Kostasch and Jerome were staring at me. "This is a private call . . ."

"Take it in the bedroom," said Jerome.

304

I sat on the bed. "Now I'm alone. What happened?"

My friend's voice sounded distressed. "You remember . . . this deal?"

"Yes."

"Well, they held the first hearing."

"Did you have great difficulties?"

"I'm afraid so. They wanted to know where Shirley is."

"Are they looking for her?"

"I don't think they are any more since I—you're sure no one can overhear us?"

"Quite sure."

"I told them I was the father. Also that Shirley had gone to this man at my request."

"Grègory . . . I don't know how to thank you . . ."

"Never mind. That's not why I'm calling. I am going to have to pay a stiff fine. Shirley too when she returns. That is not so important. Tell me, how is your wife?"

"She is fine. Very happy."

"Peter, I don't know how to say this. I'm afraid Joan is putting on an act."

"What do you mean?"

Something stirred in my chest. I paid no attention to it. I sipped my third drink.

"Paul came to see me an hour ago."

Paul was my English valet. He had been with me for fourteen years and was absolutely devoted to me. Paul resented Joan. We had lived carefree bachelors' lives until I married.

"Paul?"

"He was very embarrassed. He told me he had carefully considered all aspects but he thought it his duty to speak to me as your best friend. He was afraid to write to you. The letter might have—"

"Yes. Yes. What did he tell you?"

"That detectives came to your house."

"Detectives?"

"On October twenty-ninth. He remembered the date

exactly. They asked for you. Paul told them you were in Europe. Then they asked for Shirley. Shirley was at the studios. Then they asked for Joan. She was at home."

The glass dropped from my hand. I gasped for air. I could not speak. The spilled liquor made a dark, weird pattern on the light wood of the floor.

"This is the operator. Do you wish to continue?"

"Yes. Yes, Operator! Gregory?"

"I couldn't hear you for a moment."

"We were cut off."

"Or does someone listen in?"

Did someone listen in? Perspiration covered me. In the next room? Kostasch? Wilson? The hotel operator?

"Did the detectives talk to Joan?"

"Yes, they did."

"What . . . what did they say?"

"Naturally Paul does not know that. All he could tell me was that Joan was very upset when the men left an hour later. She was crying and locked herself into her room."

Locked herself in.

She had done that here in Hamburg too. Just a few days ago.

"What . . . what do you think they told Joan?"

"What do you think? Good God, Peter!"

What could they have told her? That Shirley and Gregory had been arrested in the course of a raid on a gynecologist's office and afterwards she had been found to be pregnant?

"Supposing they told her that, why doesn't she tell me, Gregory?"

"That's what I'm worried about. Do you know if she received any unusual mail? From a lawyer?"

"I don't know."

Mail!

My cheek began to twitch. Now I knew why Joan

swooped down on the mail each morning. She was expecting a letter.

"She should have told you something. Whether she believes I'm the father or not."

"But she didn't!"

"Then there are two explanations for her silence."

"Which are?"

"Either she spoke to Shirley secretly so as not to worry you while you're making your movie and they are going to clear up the matter between them."

"She did not speak to Shirley. I would know about it."

"Then it must be the other one."

"Which is?"

"Your wife believes you to be the father."

4

The fist.

It hit the pit of my stomach, hot yet cold, with such force that I dropped the receiver and reared up groaning.

The fist.

Now I would die.

And even if I did not die right away it would be the beginning of another attack. If I did not have the injection then I would die. It was unrealistic to think otherwise. I staggered to the drawing room, crushed the glass I had dropped underfoot.

From the moment I opened the door it seems to me now that I went through the pangs of temporary insanity, of dreadful fear—and a desperate compulsion.

Huge Kostasch. In my way. Tiny Jerome. Disappears. Carpet sways. Walls slope. Open mouth.

". . . with you?"

"Back . . . a moment . . ."

"Peter boy . . ."

"Doctor . . ."

"Air . . . let me go . . ."

Door open. Hall. Elevator.

No. No elevator!

Race down the stairs. The fist, rising. Dying. Foyer, street deserted. Sunday. Only car mine. The yellow box with green spot. Trunk compartment. Seize it. Only one person can give me that injection now.

Drive. Drive madly. Can't drive. Kill people. Must drive. Screeching tires. No people. Sky, air, houses, all black. Go faster. Why don't I die? Must live. Borrow life through an injection.

Natasha. Faster. Hit the curb. Hard braking. Engine stalls.

Yellow box in hand. Stagger. Fall. Sticky. Blood on my cheek.

Door. Jacket tears. Door open. Stairs. Steps, second floor.

Fall. Pain between eyes.

"Hel—"

Cry for help. No sound. Crawl. Third floor. Crawl on all fours. Dying animal. Gasping. Kneel. Ring bell. Again. Again.

Nothing. No answer.

Gone out. Futile. All for nothing. Fist opens. Closes around heart. Closes.

I fell forward and dove into a red flaming eternity. I died a second death. It was not to be the last one.

5

Rome, April twenty-fourth.

In his laboratory Professor Pontevivo lectured. "The human brain, as well as the body, develops until its twenty-fifth year. After that a gradual degeneration begins."

Bianca, once more recovered, was permitted to run free in the laboratory. She was drinking pure milk again and her fur was becoming smoother.

"I would like to familiarize you with the mind," said the professor. "The subject is much too complex. So, I will deal only with its simplest factors: those two parts which are interdependent; the conscious and the subconscious mind."

Bianca jumped on my knees and licked my hands. When I stroked her she curled up in my lap. I felt glad that she had come to me.

"Everything you have experienced since earliest childhood leaves a memory trace, reinforced when it is connected with an emotion. Whatever makes you happy or unhappy, scares, depresses, or tortures you is stored in the archives of your mind. The conscious and the subconscious are constantly interacting. Your conception of father, mother, wealth, poverty, disease, travel, profession, love and so on has left a trace, an engram which has been stored in a subjective archive. Subjective since engrams represent memory traces of experiences you have had from birth to about your twenty-fifth year. Each engram therefore has a definite emotional value—either pleasant or unpleasant."

Bianca suddenly jumped from my lap.

"You feel sad because Bianca left you?" The professor inquired.

"Yes, I do."

"You like cats."

"I always have. My mother did too. Even when we were very poor we had a cat."

"Thank you for your help, Bianca," the professor bowed to the little animal.

"Help?"

"I was just about to say: Each situation which involves your emotions is checked against what has already been stored from a similar previous experience. The subconscious impulses travel in fractions of a millionth of a second. You have loved cats. You loved your mother. So now you are sad because Bianca deserted you. Do you understand everything I have been explaining?"

"Yes."

"On the basis of past experiences, even long-forgotten ones, a person reacts to each situation with either negative or positive feelings. An alcoholic has had negative experiences which, as soon as checked, again torture and depress him. It is easy to see what he will do."

"Continue to drink."

"Exactly. Alcohol blocks the connection between the memory center and the mind. Alcohol can chemically change negative feelings into—"

"Positive ones?"

"At least for a period of time. It removes inhibitions, prejudices, tension, shyness, fear. It creates a situation an alcoholic can master. Initially it does something positive. The ideal medicine—at first. Then it becomes poisonous. Given time it destroys the mind."

"Actually," I said, "then everybody should drink. It seems impossible that there are people who have no engrams of an unpleasant nature."

"There are no such human beings. People are of stable or unstable personality. Artists are generally considered to belong to the latter group. Some people are broken by conflicts which others handle easily."

"And, I assume, there are many such conflicts."

"No," said Pontevivo. "There are only a few. According to the known mental diseases there are only about four or five basic types. Each one of us believes himself to be unique, different from others. But that is an erroneous idea. All of us are similar in our reaction and in our conduct."

"What are some of the conflicts?"

"Politics. Money. Work. Disease. The desire to dominate. Relating to the opposite sex . . . I could name a few. Not many."

"That is why you want me to talk about my life. You hope to find the conflict I cannot master and which made me an alcoholic."

"That's right, Mr. Jordan."

"Have you found it?"

"On one of your tapes you once mentioned a girl. You said your stepdaughter bore a great resemblance to her."

"Once I mentioned her! Only once!"

"Precisely. And I believe you will not yet talk about her—or will you?"

Wanda.

Wanda. Wanda. Wanda.

I felt great admiration for the professor.

Wanda. I shook my head.

"Take your time."

Bianca jumped back onto my knee. "You see, now she returned to you."

"Professor, you said the human mind develops until its twenty-fifth year . . ."

"That's right. Up to that time the prognosis for recovery is very good. Cures can be effected through psychotherapy by the use of electric shock, medications, or possibly group therapy."

"Professor," I was afraid to ask the question, "I am thirty-seven years old. I have been drinking for almost twenty years. Don't you think—"

"That your brain cells have been destroyed? No. You need not worry about that."

"But is there still a treatment which would help me? Or is it too late . . ."

"There is a way to help you. But I think it is a little too early to tell you about it. You must learn more about the mind and, for my part, I must know a little more about you. You think it is a little too soon to talk about this obscure Wanda. We both need more time. And patience. We must not be hasty. All I am going to say is: there is a method, an absolute effective method to cure you of your alcoholism—if you are prepared to help."

"I am."

"Good," said Pontevivo. "This was our third lecture. Just look at that cat! She really seems to be very attracted to you. Would you like to take Bianca to your room sometimes?"

"I'd enjoy that. It would remind me of my youth. It would—" I broke off. "That's why you suggested it, didn't you, Professor?"

He smiled and nodded. He appeared to be very satisfied.

6

The first thing I heard when I awakened from my second death were faint, light, chiming bells. I was lying on a wide couch in an antique furnished room. Dark woods, blue candles in silver candelabras, an icon near the window, a small triangular, carved cupboard beneath it. On it stood an old clock which had just chimed six.

I got up and took a deep breath. I felt relaxed, strong, confident, fearless. I did not have to look at my turned-up sleeve and the small patch on my arm to know I had received the injection I needed. From the adjacent room came Russian, melancholy music.

Natasha's furniture had arrived and the apartment was now comfortable. I felt at home in this room, its walls lined with Russian, French, German and English books. Asters in an old samovar. Several pipes and ornate china containers for tobacco on a shelf.

A door opened. Natasha, in black, silk, gold-embroidered lounging pajamas entered. Her beautiful face was serene and friendly as always.

"You are on your feet again," said Natasha.

"I thank you," I said. "I was afraid you would not be at home, I rang and no one opened."

"Misha and I were listening to records."

"But he can't hear the music!"

"He feels the vibrations when he places a hand on the record player. By the way, it was Misha who heard you first."

"Heard me?"

"Sensed then. He sensed you at the door and drew my attention to it. I opened the door. There you were."

"Unconscious?"

"Yes. You are rather heavy, Mr. Jordan."

"Whisky and water. Twenty pounds of edema." It was not a very wise remark; she turned away from me.

"Your box with ampoules is over there," she said.

"You want me to leave."

"Yes."

"I would not have come here. I could not reach the man who is treating me."

"The man who is treating you is a criminal."

"Natasha, I must finish that movie! Then I'll go to a clinic right away."

"If you are still alive then."

"It's not that bad."

"It is. You could die any day. Any time."

"Something upsetting happened today. That's all."

"You must leave, Mr. Jordan. We agreed not to see each other any more."

Her eyes were artless, incapable of lies or pretense. Fleetingly I thought of Jerome, Kostasch, Shirley, Joan and the detectives in Los Angeles. A sudden, burning, agonizing longing overcame me to be with this woman, just to be near her. Always.

"Couldn't I stay just for a few minutes?"

"No."

"Do you despise me that much?"

"Don't say things like that."

"You don't despise me?"

"You know that you must go. You know as well as I."

"All I know is that I want to stay with you. Just for a little while."

"I don't want to see you. I cannot see you any more. I—" She averted her head and pushed back her glasses in a typical gesture. "Don't you understand me?"

I picked up my yellow box with the green spot and said, "Good-by Natasha." She did not reply. The door was flung open and Misha, in a red gym suit and stockinged feet, his blond hair disheveled, ran to me. He threw his arms around my neck and kissed me. He made hoarse, happy-sounding noises and 'talked' with his mother. It was as pathetic as it was touching. Finally Natasha said, "He asks you to stay."

"Then I may?"

"Misha wants you to have tea with us and listen to some records. In his room. I told him that you had to leave. He asked for half an hour." Abruptly she said, "What we are doing is wrong and bad. It will have serious consequences."

"Thank you," I said to the little boy. "Thank you, Misha."

7

The record player was on the carpet of Misha's bright, cheerfully furnished room. We drank tea and listened to melancholy Russian records.

It was growing late. Misha sat between us on the carpet and above his head Natasha's and my eyes met again and again. At last it grew so dark in the room her face was visible only as a pale patch.

The half hour had passed a long time ago. Kostäsch and Wilson were surely looking for me. Shirley and Joan probably too. After all, I had stumbled out of Wilson's suite like a madman . . .

I did not care. The injection had freed me of worry and responsibility.

Misha held his left hand to the record player. He sat motionless, his eyes closed, his face serene.

Natasha pulled matches from her pocket. She was getting up but I took the matches and lighted the candles in a candelabra on Misha's bedside table. There were many beautiful candelabra in the apartment. In Misha's room alone were three. When I lighted the candles in the third candelabra Natasha quickly extinguished the third candle. She smiled apologetically.

"An old superstition."

"Three burning candles are bad luck?"

She nodded embarrassed. "Three in one room."

"Why?"

"In my country it is said that a loved one dies. Naturally that is nonsense. But if one has been brought up like that . . ."

Schauberg would have said, "All the nonsense in the world is perpetuated through the centuries." Schauberg! Right now I did not even care that he was still in jail.

Misha made some excited noises. Laughing silently, his hand still pressed to the record player, he pointed to the record.

"It's his favorite song," said Natasha. "Even though he can't hear the music he recognizes each song. This is called 'The Crimson Silk Scarf.'"

The candles flickered. The record circled. A woman sang a love song.

When the record had stopped spinning Natasha said firmly, "Good-by."

I bent down to Misha who embraced me again and left the room. He came running after me, a paper in his hand. His gestures made it plain: he had almost forgotten to give me his present.

It was the drawing he had promised me. A little boy holding the hands of a woman and a man in a red boat. There were many other boats. A black bag stood in front of the man and he held a glass in his hand. The man was much taller than the woman, larger than the entire boat. Misha, it was obvious to see, longed for his father who had gone on a long trip.

Misha pointed to the boy and then to himself, to the man with the glass and to me, and to the woman. He turned and I saw Natasha standing in the doorway of his room. He pointed to his mother. He was very serious now.

"Go away," said Natasha. "Go away quickly. And don't ever, ever come back."

8

They were waiting wide-eyed for me in my suite. Joan flanked by Kostasch and Jerome.

They were composed and I was out of breath after climbing six flights of stairs. I had a sense of the ridiculous. No doubt it was the effect of this damn, wonderful injection. The ampoules were once more in the green box in the trunk of my car with Misha's drawing.

"Good evening," I said.

Silence.

"It's all right," I said. "That's right, Jerome, I'm alive. You're out of luck. I'm not a ghost."

"Where . . . where . . ."

"I think now you could stand a drink." I picked up the telephone and ordered. An hour ago I had thought I was dying. Now I felt like superman.

The movie? Finished. Discontinued. So what?

Joan? The detectives had talked to her. She knew of

Shirley's pregnancy. Perhaps she knew more than that. And even if she did, what did I care?

Joan said, "We were terribly worried about you."

Kostasch said, "We've looked for you all over town. Peter, are you out of your mind? Why didn't you tell us before?"

Jerome, with an obsequious bow, said, "I would like to apologize to you. I must apologize! We've said some terrible things. You accused me—unjustly—of some dirty work. I'm sorry that I became upset and lost my head. I did not want to insult you. Please forgive an old, sick man. I am happy, very happy, that everything worked out so well in the end."

"What worked out well? How?"

Kostasch was staring at me. Instead of answering me he repeated, "Why didn't you tell us before? Why did you leave it to your wife to tell us?"

"Yes, why?" cried Jerome. "I just don't understand you, Peter!"

Disconcerted, I looked at Wilson, then Kostasch, then Joan. She was not smiling. Were her eyes cold? She rose. "Come," she said to me. "I'm sure the gentlemen will excuse us."

I followed her to the bedroom, her bedroom. She was pale and, as always, perfectly groomed. As sentimental as she had been during the past few days, now she was cool and matter-of-fact.

All right, I thought, so you know everything. Or a great deal anyway. Now you are going to settle accounts. Did you plan it this way? Had you planned it with Jerome?

Let's get it over with. As long as the injection is effective, as long as I too am as cool and calm.

Joan was walking up and down. Her silence was unnerving me. She obviously wanted to savor her triumph.

Yet, was she not entitled to that?

I could not stand it any longer.

"You know everything?"

"Yes."

"Just tell me one thing: how?"

"Where were you all this time, darling?"

"First, tell me who told you, how you found out!"

"Kostasch told me."

I felt weak. I sat down.

"Kostasch?"

"Of course. Kostasch."

"But how . . . what . . ." I swallowed hard. Nausea was rising in me. It could not be. Could it?

She was acting.

She wanted to torture me.

"Don't look so thunderstruck. After you disappeared Kostasch and Jerome came here. Kostasch told me when Jerome went downstairs to take care of something."

"Told you what?"

"Why are you shouting? He told me about the hundred fifty thousand dollars you need to checkmate Jerome's plan to get rid of the two of you. And now tell me where you have been all this time!"

I could not believe it. Automatically I answered, "I've been walking around."

"But why?"

"Joan! One hundred fifty thousand dollars! We're finished! This goddamn son-of-a-bitch took care of us with his plan! I couldn't stand to look at him! That's why I ran out. Can't you understand that?"

"No, I can't. If Kostasch can't come up with his share of the money right away you will pay it for him. He will give you a few percent of his share of the profit. That much even I understand about business."

We were looking at each other. A cat-and-mouse game? A few hundred yards away. Natasha.

"That's what you told Kostasch?"

"I told him and that little sneaky rat that you have the money. I had to tell him that half of all I own belongs to you. You should have seen their faces!" She laughed out loud.

"Joan . . ."

"I understand, darling. You must have been very upset about Jerome's dirty trick."

I was certain she didn't know anything.

No woman could put on such a convincing act. After all it was her daughter!

"It's your money . . . I won't touch it . . ."

"Now don't upset your little Joan. And anyway, everything is settled."

"Settled?"

"I called my cousin at the consulate. You must hurry now and change. He invited us tonight."

"Your cousin?"

"Darling, are you high? That's what I'm saying!"

No. No. No.

She could not know. She did not know. Or did she? What about those detectives? Gregory's call? She must know! How far was she willing to go?

"Who is invited?"

"Both of us, Kostasch and Wilson. Don't you feel all right? Poor darling." She opened the door. "Has the whisky arrived, Mr. Kostasch? Would you please fix a drink for Peter?"

Kostasch's voice was breathless. "Right away, Mrs. Jordan. I'll fix him the largest drink he's ever had!"

"I think he needs it, too," Joan said very softly, leaning against the doorframe. Her smile was wiped away for the fraction of a second and her eyes were hard and cold. They were the eyes of the dead seagull, the eyes of the elephant, they were scrutinizing me, without mercy, without pity, with hate. And seemed to say: Liar. Blasphemer. Scoundrel.

She knew, I thought. It is worth a hundred fifty thousand dollars to her to torture me and get her revenge.

The next moment her brown eyes reflected love and tenderness. She handed me the drink. She kissed me.

"Cheers, darling."

Quite possibly this was one way to become mad.

"I asked my cousin to invite us for tonight. I thought since you have to be at the studio tomorrow again, this matter should be settled quickly."

"But I don't understand—"

"It's pure formality. The banks don't have your signature as yet. I think of everything, don't I, darling? Tonight my cousin will witness your signature on the check and that's it."

"On what check?"

"You poor darling, you really are confused, aren't you? The check you are going to write for the hundred fifty thousand dollars of course," said Joan. "Have you noticed Jerome's consternation? He can take the check and give it to this nice president." She leaned forward. "Didn't I manage things beautifully?"

"Yes," I said.

"Isn't it lucky I have all that money?"

"It is," I said.

"And a cousin at the consulate?"

"Yes," I said.

"And that I can help you, now that you could use some help?"

"Yes," I said.

"I always hoped that someday, somehow, when you needed help I could help you. It's been a very gratifying day for me! It's too bad Shirley won't be with us tonight."

"Why . . . why can't she?"

"She has gone out again. An hour ago. She told me she had a date. Isn't that sweet?"

I emptied my glass. Was this her revenge? Was she trying to see how much further she could push me?

"Just think, Peter, our little Shirley's first love. I wonder which of us will be the first to know who he is?"

9

I did not see Shirley that evening.

We, Joan, Kostasch, Jerome and I drove to Joan's cousin's. His villa in Blankenese had large grounds which fell steeply to the water of the Elbe.

Joan's cousin had also invited another official of the consulate to witness my signature of the check. My hands were unsteady and I had to write very slowly. Wilson, who still did not seem to have recovered from the shock, wrote out a receipt. Kostasch wrote that I had paid for his part of the payment to the movie company and the changes which would be made in our contract.

Business over, we spent a lovely evening talking and watching the ships pass on the Elbe.

About midnight we took our leave and drove back to town. Wilson and Kostasch got out at the Carlton. Tears were in Kostasch's eyes when he shook my hand. "I'll never forget this, Peter. Never. You saved our movie."

"Yes, yes," I said.

Wilson kissed Joan's hand and offered me his. I didn't take it.

"You're still angry with me."

"No, I'm not," I replied. "Just the same I'd rather not shake your hand."

"Peter, I swear—"

"Yes, yes," I said. "Have a pleasant trip. Regards to George."

The little man's lips moved, he was searching for words. Kostasch, trying to smooth over the situation, slapped his shoulder, "Let's forget the whole thing! You tried to gyp us and you didn't succeed. So let's end it right here. Are you tired, Jerome?"

"No, not at all. Why?"

"Then come along to the Reeperbahn."

Jerome's eyes lit up, as lecherous as ever.

"Sankt Pauli. All right? Tomorrow morning your knees are going to be knocking!" Kostasch laughed. They waved as I pulled away.

The subject came up a few days later. Kostasch shrugged his shoulders. "What do you expect? I gave him what he wanted—and more. I'm unprincipled? Sure I am. How would you know how a German producer makes a living? Last year three hundred movie theaters closed. A producer who borrows money from a bank today to make a movie has to guarantee repayment personally within nine months. Who can give such a guarantee? One reason why we have to co-produce with private money lenders. Preferably with foreigners, like the Wilsons. And I ought not to have gone to a cathouse with the little Jerome because of principles? I should not have taken him to some flagellating perverts, if that's what he wanted? I know he is a bastard; so is his brother. But do you think our industry is so grand? I tell you one thing; I'd do a lot to be able to continue to produce movies. You're an artist. You can't understand that. Besides: you have integrity!"

"Nonsense."

"That's not nonsense. I saw how bad you felt when you had to accept your wife's money. You walked around aimlessly for hours. I would have taken the dough right away. But not you! That's the difference between us. You have scruples. I'm unscrupulous. You have a conscience. I don't . . ."

10

As I mentioned before, this talk took place a few days later.

After Kostasch and Wilson had left us, Joan and I drove back to the hotel in silence.

As usual I took the stairs while Joan went up in the elevator. The drawing room was empty.

"Joan?"

"I'm in the bathroom!"

I undressed in my bedroom and went to my bathroom where I had hidden the black bag. I sat on the side of the bathtub and drank. Finally, after a half hour or so, I stowed away the black bag and returned to my bedroom.

The bedroom was dark. I groped for a switch when Joan said, "Don't turn on the light, darling."

From a dim light in the drawing room whose door stood slightly ajar I could see that Joan was nude.

She opened her arms.

"I want you, Peter . . ."

I sat on the side of her bed.

"Be gentle with me, darling. It's been so long . . . I've been dreaming of how loving you used to be once . . ."

She pulled me down to her.

"Kiss me."

I kissed her.

"Come . . . do all those wonderful things . . . come . . . come to your Joan, who loves you so much . . ."

She clung to me. Her hands in my hair pressed my head down and—down—

(Transcriber's note: Mr. Jordan's remarks here are interrupted by sounds that appear to be sobs.)

11

I had to be up at six the next morning.

Joan did not stir. In the bathroom, looking in the large mirror, I made a terrible discovery. The rash, which for days had covered my feet and legs, had spread overnight to my abdomen, chest and back. The spots were dark red, dry and hideous. It brought to mind something my mother had said, "One is always unclean inside first and then outside."

My thoughts, my deeds, my entire life should, according to the maxim of my unfortunate mother, have been the cause of the disfiguring rash and pestilential boils on my skin. My soul had long been putrid. Now, finally, my body was beginning to rot . . .

Nonsense!

Absurd. Enough of that.

I pulled the black bag from its hiding place, poured a drink and looked at myself in the mirror. In the movie I did not have to swim or undress. Only during the scenes at the steel mills which we were going to shoot on location would I appear naked to the waist. Makeup would still hide the rash provided it did not become worse. But as soon as the rash would appear on my face—

They would immediately call in a dermatologist. What would he say after an examination? I quickly drank some more whisky. I mustn't think about it.

But I had to!

I had to do something. But what?

When I asked for my car to be brought the doorman said, "Your car, yes. Oh, Mr. Jordan, the garage just called a moment ago about your car—"

"What is the matter with my car?"

Stolen? Burglarized? The green box was in the trunk . . .

"Something is wrong with the starter, the mechanic said. He asked if it would be all right if he drove out to the studio with you. He would then have it fixed. This way you could have the car back tonight."

"Yes, that will be fine. Tell him to come along."

The doorman was one of the people I had asked to keep an eye on Shirley. When I asked, he reluctantly told me that Shirley had come home the previous night at eleven o'clock. A tall, slim man in a black coat had accompanied her. They shook hands like friends and she had seemed somber and pensive.

He was very sympathetic. "Don't take it so hard, Mr. Jordan. I well remember the upsets and the troubles we had with our daughter when she was this age. Girls today are more impetuous, less restrained. But not Miss Shirley, Mr. Jordan! She is not like that. You don't have to worry about her."

"Thank you."

"A doorman has an eye for people. Miss Shirley would not do anything wrong." He answered the telephone. "Your car is outside now, Mr. Jordan."

"Thank you." I pressed a bill into his hand as I shook hands with him, then left.

My black Mercedes, shiny from the rain, stood outside. A man in a clean yellow uniform of the garage mechanic held the door open. He wore a beret and bowed slightly in the manner of a lord greeting his guests at his manor.

"Good morning, dear Mr. Jordan," said Dr. Schauberg.

12

"Wasn't that a great gag?" Schauberg was driving. The windshield wipers were moving quickly. "I ought to be a script writer. German movies would probably be a little better then."

"Schauberg!"

"I said, a little better."

"How did you get here? When did they release you?"

"Saturday." He was in high spirits.

"Saturday? Why didn't you call me right away?"

"My dear Mr. Jordan, don't forget that I was released —my thanks for the bail money last but not least—but that now I am surely under even more intensive surveillance than before. Can you imagine what the police would have thought if I, hardly free again, had come to see you?"

I did not answer. He laughed, very pleased with himself.

"No, no. Even though I had to do without morphine for quite a long time my brain functioned well enough to direct my steps to Madam Misere's establishment and to Käthe. Wouldn't the police think that a touching gesture of gratitude and love?"

"Why did you go and see Käthe?"

"First I gave myself an injection. Then—really, Mr. Jordan!"

"Don't talk such nonsense. I want to know how you managed to land here in the hotel!"

Now he was serious.

"Well, you see, even the smartest man can make a mistake. You frightened me out of my wits, I lost my head and stole this damn cough medicine. I swear: I'm never going to slip up like that again!" His gaze was searching. "The movie is going to be finished now, isn't it?"

"Yes."

"It was obvious that once I was released the police would watch me closely. Question: How could I treat you? Only if I was in your proximity. How could I be close to you without looking suspicious?"

"How?"

"Well, one of my cellmates—such coincidence is truly remarkable—happened to be a mechanic who had, until very recently, been employed by a hotel garage. He recommended me to the chief of your hotel garage. I know a lot about cars and the man did not ask too many questions. I was even given a small room in the hotel's staff quarters. How do you like that: I am, from now on, at your service day and night!" He laughed. "Isn't that a marvelous solution? The police are reassured. I am working. I have a place to stay. Now it is child's play to operate too."

"You are going to——" I began.

"In your stepdaughter's room, naturally," said Schauberg. "She couldn't be more comfortable! I'll bring my young friend to give the anaesthesia. Then afterwards I can keep an eye on her."

"When . . . when are you . . ."

"You can introduce us as soon as she arrives at the studio. I'll examine her then. It would also be best if your wife were not too close by when I operate."

"On the twenty-ninth, which is a Sunday, I'm going on location to Essen. Shirley can stay here. I'll take my wife along."

"Any time after Sunday then." He smiled. "By the way, I must congratulate you."

"Why?"

"Your stepdaughter. She is absolutely charming!"

"Be quiet."

"No, really. I'm green with envy."

"If you don't—when did you see her, anyway?"

"Last night. Outside the hotel. When I was picking up a car."

"With whom?"

"No idea. He wore a black coat. Tall and slim."

"Car?"

"No. They were walking. I asked the doorman who the girl was. The man left right away. They only spoke a few words. Now, don't make such a face. I don't think Shirley is being unfaithful to you. Perhaps she wants to make you jealous. Women are strange creatures."

13

Before I went to the make-up department Schauberg and I locked the door of my dressing room. He had taken the necessary medication from the green box and had seen that one ampoule was missing. I told him that I had had an attack. He asked me when and who had given me the injection.

"A doctor."

"Who?"

"I won't tell you."

"Then I won't treat you any more."

"Then don't!" I thought the time for a strength had come. "Get out of here. I don't want to see you any more!"

His face was ashen. I could see that he too was at the end of his rope. "I need the money, you know that! But I did tell you that I would stop treating you if another doctor——"

"Just leave me alone! Go ahead! Get out of here!" What would I do if he really left? But I felt I had to put him in his place.

He murmured, "My risk is increasing."

"So is mine. I paid thirty thousand marks for your bail."

"You can rely on this doctor?"

"Yes."

With sudden clairvoyance he said, "It is a lady doctor!"

"No!"

"It is, of course. And she loves you."

"No!"

"Yes. And you know it. Now I understand why you are so composed. Love is a heavenly force. Well, I guess then she will keep quiet. Just tell me one thing, dear Mr. Jordan. What do you think your future is going to be?"

"Just tell me one thing, dear Schauberg: how do I get rid of this rash?" While we had been talking I had undressed and he had given me injections.

"It's nothing serious. I'll give you something to take care of it. It's from all those injections."

"I know what it is from. It has already spread to my

328

chest. Once it spreads to my face, that's the end of the movie."

"I'll give you some powder for your body. As a preventative I'll give you aureomycin ointment for your face." He gave me directions for its use.

"You do sleep alone?"

Thanks to the cream and the protective towel he recommended I would have to manage that from now on, I thought. A man with an unguent on his face. A man with a toothache towel. A ridiculous man. One should be thankful for small mercies.

"Dear Mr. Jordan, I won't conceal the fact from you that your condition had deteriorated somewhat."

"Somewhat?"

"I'm afraid so. Your work is taking its toll. And I guess you've had some upsets."

"Enough."

"Exactly. How many more days do you have to work?"

"Twenty-seven."

"Hm."

"What do you mean, hm?"

"I shall have to use some new medicines."

"Such as?"

"More effective ones. Perhaps a little arsenic . . ." Schauberg looked dejected. My condition must have been poor indeed if he could not conceal his worry over me. Maybe he thought of his money. Suddenly he brightened. "Don't worry. It will be easy. Now that I'm living at the hotel I can treat you much easier."

"Mr. Jordan to the make-up department, please." The voice from the loudspeaker.

"I must go," I said. "My daughter will be here about ten o'clock."

"I shall wait."

"Good."

"I still have money to come from you."

329

I handed him two checks of eight thousand marks each which I had been holding for him.

"But one week I was not here . . ."

"You gave me the medication and instructions for self-treatment."

"That's very generous of you." He actually blushed. "Really most generous, I thank you."

"All right. Sign a fictitious name when you cash the checks."

"Certainly."

"Schauberg?"

"Yes?"

"I'll be leaving Hamburg on Sunday . . ."

"Once I've treated your stepdaughter I can come to see you as your chauffeur. Don't worry."

"That's not what I meant. Shirley will be alone in Hamburg. She might . . ." I stopped, feeling ashamed. "Possibly she will meet this man again. Or the man will come to her."

"I see."

"I must know who he is. Can you help me find out?"

"Surely. I have many friends. What would you like to have done?"

"Nothing. Both of them must not be aware of being watched. I merely want to know who the man is."

"I'll take care of it. That reminds me, on top of the green box was a child's crazy drawing. Did you put it there?"

Misha's drawing!

As if I'd lost my senses I suddenly yelled, "Leave it there! Don't touch it!"

For the first time since I knew him I saw pity in his pitiless eyes. He sighed.

"Why are you sighing?"

"Because I feel sorry for you, Mr. Jordan," he said. He stuffed his stethoscope into his mechanic's uniform. "You are a poor slob."

330

14

This had been on the morning of November twenty-third.

At ten o'clock I introduced Shirley to Schauberg. He examined her in an unused cutting room while I was before the camera. During lunch Shirley came to my dressing room. She said the examination had not taken much time.

"He said it would be easy. He drove away in your car. Why are you looking at me like that?"

"Don't you have anything to tell me?"

She looked directly into my eyes and shook her head. She was pale and somber and her beauty stirred me.

"Nothing at all?"

"No. You?"

"Excuse me?"

"Don't you have anything to tell me either?"

"No. Oh, yes!" I told her about Gregory's call. "I think we can assume that Joan knows everything."

"She would have said something to me, at least to me."

"She set a trap for us . . . she is waiting . . . waiting . . . for us to tell her . . ."

"Some day we shall have to tell her."

"But surely not that you are expecting a . . ."

Quickly she interrupted, "Do you still have my cross?"

"Shirley!"

"Do you still have it?"

"Naturally."

"Show it to me."

I showed her the little golden cross she had given me at the airport in Los Angeles.

"Could I have it? Just for one day?"

"No."

"Please! I'll give it back to you."

"Well, all right then." Sudden fear of a new attack rose in me. I felt very weak and dizzy. I did not feel up to all this. Were both women sticking together? Was each one deceiving me in her own way? But who was I to reproach them; I who deceived everybody?

I sat down on the couch and held my head with both hands. I felt Shirley's hand on my hair and heard her say, "You think that I'm deceiving you."

I was silent.

"I know that you believe that. I'm not deceiving you. But there is somebody I must meet sometimes."

"It's all right," I said.

"But I'm not unfaithful to you. It has to do with us."

"All right," I repeated.

"With us and our love, our future. Soon I'll explain everything to you. But you must have a little more patience and not ask me any questions. I haven't asked you any more questions either, have I?"

I was silent.

"When the baby is gone I'll tell you everything. Will you trust me until then?"

"All right," I said.

I spoke softly and did not move. I thought I would not have another attack if I did not move, not become excited and spoke quietly.

And I did not have another attack. By the time I felt better Shirley had gone. She had taken the little cross of gold.

15

After the day's shooting our first camera man gave a party to celebrate his winning of a lawsuit in the States. The cafeteria was crowded with people who drank, were merry or sad, each behaving characteristically.

Thornton Seaton drank with his blond, blue-eyed assistant and told a secret, "Hans is coming to the States with me. I'm going to find him work in television."

Henry Wallace was upset and argumentative. The Internal Revenue Department had attached his collection of French impressionist paintings in Hollywood.

Hennessy was apparently drinking to work up courage. When he was quite drunk he blushed and announced his engagement to the cutter, Ursula König, and his intention of—hic—marrying her in the very near future.

Everybody applauded and congratulated him. When I shook his hand he said, "Your daughter also has auburn hair. She reminds me a great deal of Ursel. Perhaps you noticed that I often stared at her."

"Yes, I had noticed that."

"Every time I saw your daughter I was reminded of Ursel. It drove me absolutely crazy so that I finally thought: It must be love then! And now I am going to marry her!"

Now I could forget Hennessy. Even if he was lying to me: he could never have lied to the red-headed Ursula and been believed.

Then who?

My wife, who happened to be there too, was drinking with a merry Kostasch whose movie had been saved.

Shirley had excused herself. "Don't be angry if I drive back to town. I have to see someone."

She was not aware of Schauberg following her. The next morning, when he gave me my injections, he told me that she had taken a bus and then a taxi. He lost her when he had to stop for a red traffic signal. "Never mind. We'll find out where she goes."

"Who is we?"

"My student and I. When I work at the garage I can't always get away."

The twenty-third was also the day I applied the aureomycin for the first time. I wound a towel around my head and must have looked a caricature. Joan could not stop laughing.

During the lunch period of the twenty-fourth Shirley returned the little golden cross to me in my dressing room.

"What did you need it for?"

"That's my secret. Please, don't ask. I hope the cross will continue to bring you happiness."

"I am doing everything for you. And you lie to me. And you deceive me——" I had said exactly what I had wanted to avoid.

Nerves. From day to day they were growing worse.

"Shirley, I . . . I . . . I didn't mean it like that. Please try to understand. We've never been like this; we shouldn't behave like this."

"Like what?"

"Arguing . . . disturbing each other . . . drifting apart like this. We . . . we only have each other. We love one another! Everything is still the way it has been."

"No, it is not," she said gravely.

"What do you mean, no? You don't love me any more?"

"Yes, I do, Peter. I still love you. But it is not the same as it was."

"What do you mean?"

"I can't tell you."

I lost my self-control. "Because you are deceiving me! Because you are lying!"

"I speak the truth."

"Swear it! By your God!"

"By my God," she said. "I love you the same as I always have." Harry stuck his head through the door and I shouted at him to get lost but then I went to the door and called out an apology to him. Shirley was standing by the window, her hands buried in the pockets of her black workcoat.

334

"If you did you would tell me whom you meet so secretively!"

"I shall tell you."

"When?"

"As soon as the child is gone. Then I'll tell you everything. Everything."

She began to cry and ran out of my dressing room. I ran after her but she had disappeared. Finally I found her sitting on a roll of cable in an unused studio. She was crying uncontrollably.

I tried to calm her; I stroked her. She only repeated, "You must believe me. I love you. I am not deceiving you. I can't tell you where I go. It is something to do with us. When you return from Essen I shall explain everything." She looked at me through her tears, her body shaken by sobs. "Please trust me, Peter. If you love me you must trust me now."

The boat trip on the Elbe, Misha, the afternoon I had spent at Natasha's flashed through my mind. What arrogance, what presumption to have her watched, to pressure her, to play the righteous, jealous lover.

So I answered, "I do trust you." That was a lie.

I left her in the studio. She said she needed time to calm herself and fix her face.

It had begun to snow. I walked through the whirling snowflakes and felt very giddy. Schauberg was treating me with arsenic to stimulate me. Perhaps it was the arsenic.

Perhaps it was my mind that was as sick as my body, covered with rash. Perhaps all this was happening to an insane man or had not really happened at all, or had happened differently—the creation of a disturbed imagination.

For instance, the notion that Shirley was deceiving me, that she was meeting another man. Perhaps I even imagined that I was having her watched. Could it be that I had already died? Or was I still alive and in a clinic where I was dreaming all these awful things I believed to be my life? Perhaps—

Squealing tires tore me from my thoughts. Hennessy in a little red sportscar had pulled up sharply beside me. "Can I give you a lift?" His smile showed his beautiful teeth.

"No, thank you. I like to walk."

"Okay!"

He stepped on the gas and the car shot forward. Automatically I looked at the license place. HH–HC111. An easy number to remember.

I had a few drinks from my black bag in my dressing room before going back to face the camera. But the disquieting thoughts returned in spite of the whisky.

The next morning I was still at the hotel when the mail arrived. Again Joan hurried to take the letters. Two letters were for her. She opened one.

"From the bank. About the hundred fifty thousand dollars. They really ought to have addressed the letter to you."

"And the other letter?"

"Oh, it's just an invitation to a fashion show," Joan answered. She placed the bank statement on the table and took the second letter to her bedroom.

It was not an invitation to a fashion show. I had glanced at the official-looking envelope and read the printed return address: City of Los Angeles. Police Headquarters. Criminal Investigation Department.

16

I waited.

I sat at the breakfast table and waited. Joan had to leave her bedroom sometime and if she did not tell then I would ask. I had no idea what kind of revenge she had planned but at least I could see to it that it did not continue forever. I'd provoke her. I'd force her to talk. She would lose her control. Then finally I would know what she knew.

When after half an hour she had not returned I went to her bedroom.

"Joan?"

"In here, darling." Her cheerful voice came from the bathroom.

She was in a bubble bath.

"I was waiting for you."

"But I told you I was going to take a bath. Didn't you hear me?"

"No."

"I'm sorry. Was there something you wanted to tell me?"

It was hot and humid and sticky in the bathroom. I looked at Joan. She smiled. Without make-up her face looked years younger. Why did she use make-up? Why was she smiling?

"This other letter," I began.

"What other letter?"

"The one you just took to your bedroom."

"You mean the invitation?" She raised one leg above the bubbles.

"It was no invitation. Where is the letter? I want to see it!"

"Darling, have you gone crazy?" She was shocked. "Of course it was an invitation!"

"For a fashion show, eh? They're sending you an invitation to Germany so you can see their show in the States, eh?"

"They don't know that I'm in Germany. You know that all my mail is forwarded to me from Pacific Palisades!"

"Where is the invitation?"

"On my dressing table. Really, Peter, if you could see your face—"

Three steps took me to the dressing table. On it was an envelope, a card. It was indeed an invitation. I tore open the drawers of the dressing table, I searched the wastebasket, the shelves of the cupboard, ashtrays and the corners of the room. I had not made a mistake. I knew what I had seen.

Joan had received the invitation earlier. She had hidden the letter received from police headquarters. Where? Where? I pulled dresses from the closet, searched drawers of lingerie, opened handbags. A noise made me snap around. Wrapped in a bathtowel, barefoot, Joan stood in the doorway. She was staring at me.

I dropped the lacy garment in my hand, stammered, "Nerves . . . overtaxed . . . forgive me . . . see you tonight," and stumbled from the room.

In the inside mirror of the open closet I caught sight of Joan again. Water dripped from her. She was looking at me. Her lips suddenly twisted into a smile of triumph.

17

The next morning at the studio Shirley asked, "Did you have a fight with Joan?"

"Why?"

"She intimated that much. You had carried on like a madman."

"She received a letter from the Los Angeles Criminal Investigation Department and denies it. I saw the envelope. I was searching for it."

"Did you find it?"

"No. Why are you looking at me like that?"

"You are working too hard, Peter."

"Shirley, I swear I saw the envelope! And what about Gregory's call?"

"He must have misunderstood. You must have made a mistake. If Joan knew anything she would have said something a long time ago. It's just not possible that my mother—your wife—would remain silent if she knew what we had done."

"She doesn't necessarily know everything."

"Even if she knew only part of it."

"She is shamming! She is lying! Just like you!"

Shirley said very softly, "And you? Do you speak the truth? I think—"

"What? What do you think?" Perhaps I could provoke her.

"Never mind," she answered. "I have to go back to the cutting room."

The twenty-fifth, a Wednesday, was Schauberg's day off. After he had given me the usual injections he drove to the casino in Travemünde. Three of his friends went along also. He gave each of them four thousand marks which they changed into chips but did not use to gamble. Feverish activity reigned at the crowded casino.

A few hours later Schauberg who had gambled a little pro forma had his friends return all the chips to him. He took the twelve thousand marks worth of chips to the cashier where he himself had exchanged two hundred marks. The cashier congratulated him on his large winnings. Schauberg tipped him a hundred marks and asked for a check which he cashed the following morning.

He explained the reason for all this. "I had no money when I was arrested, right? If I suddenly have money now somebody might ask questions. Then I can prove that I had won it. It's not necessary to do this with the money I'll still be receiving from you. Only with the capital I'm starting out with."

"Starting what?"

"Well, I need a forged passport. As soon as your movie

is completed I'm getting out. Now I can leave Germany only with a forged passport. After all, I have to report to the police every day."

Thursday I developed a large boil on my thigh. I was still applying aureomycin every night. The powder did not help. Meanwhile parts of my body had the appearance of raw meat. Schauberg desperately tried injections. Some of the spots had begun to discharge, too. Schauberg said, "The boil is no problem. The body is not important. It is important that we keep your face free of the rash. You ought not to eat so much, dear Mr. Jordan!"

"But I'm always hungry!"

"That's the effect of the arsenic. You must control yourself!"

"What if the rash does spread to my face?"

"It won't. Aureomycin is a miracle drug. Just like penicillin." He was trying to reassure me. But I also noticed that he himself was worried. "I'm going to discontinue the arsenic. Or you are going to put on too much weight. I'm going to try something else. But then I have to have you under constant observation."

"Which means you're going to have to come to Essen with me."

"If you remember I already mentioned it: You only have to request me to be your chauffeur."

"What about Shirley?"

"You are leaving Sunday morning, right? I'll drive you down. Takes about three or four hours. Then I'll return to Hamburg and take care of her. At night I'll come back to Essen."

"The distance—"

"Merely a few hundred kilometers on the Autobahn. Which reminds me: Somebody has to take the rushes to be copied from Essen to Hamburg, right?"

"That's right."

"Marvelous. Then you can suggest to Mr. Kostasch that I do that. That will also give me the opportunity to look in on your stepdaughter during the first two days—it is not really essential because she'll be all right by Monday morning."

"You've really thought of everything."

"I really would like to get out of Europe, dear Mr. Jordan."

I admired his resourcefulness. "By coming each day from Essen you can also register daily with the police."

"Exactly. Incidentally, they are most satisfied with me since I lead such a respectable life and work so conscientiously as a mechanic."

This was early Thursday and we were talking outside the hotel. Schauberg had just brought the Mercedes from the garage. It was snowing again. Schauberg brought a newspaper. The headlines said: "Bloodshed in the Jungles of Laos. Native Pilots Mistakenly Bomb Own Troops."

"Voilà, progress," said Schauberg.

"Progress?"

"In warfare. Once it becomes popular to bomb one's own troops and towns—imagine how much gasoline and how many lives could then be saved!"

18

"I changed my mind," said Joan.

It was Friday evening.

"About what, darling?"

"If Shirley stays in Hamburg I'll stay too. What would I do in Essen? You won't be with me anyway."

So I met Schauberg in a bar. He thought the situation very amusing. "This is turning into a comedy. There is only one thing to do: Your stepdaughter will have to come to Essen. We'll do it there."

So I called Kostasch.

"You know I have this girl . . ."

"Still?"

"Yes. And Shirley must have noticed something. I'm afraid she is going to find out more when I'm in Essen. Couldn't we take her along?"

"There's no work for a cutter there."

"It's just for those few days. Surely, you could think of something!"

"Of course I will. You know, I'd do everything for you."

"The suggestion must come from you, though. You know my two women—"

"Stick together. Mother and daughter. Naturally. Leave it to me, I'm famous for being tactful."

Saturday morning Joan declared that she had changed her mind again: "You're so overworked. I'd rather not leave you alone. I'll come to Essen with you."

So I went to the studio and told Kostasch to forget the whole thing. He merely tapped his temple with his index finger. On this morning they again had to make use of the prompt cards for me.

Midday I called Schauberg from my dressing room. I had finished for the day.

"We have to call it off."

"But why?"

"My student cut his finger. Danger of infection. He can't assist me." Shirley, who stood next to me and had listened began to laugh hysterically. Her face twisted convulsively. I slapped her hard, she stopped laughing, said, "Thank you" and began to cry.

I held her close and tried to calm her. When I did not succeed I gave her two of Schauberg's red pills and told her to lie down and rest. I had to view this day's rushes. Half an hour later I came back to my dressing room. Shirley had left.

Harry, my assistant, told me: "She went into town."

"Alone?"

"Somebody gave her a lift. I looked in to see if you needed me. She was telephoning just then."

"To whom?"

Harry blushed. "Really, Mr. Jordan—"

"She is my daughter! I worry about her. Now then!"

He pocketed the twenty marks.

"I only heard her say: 'Right away. Yes. Please. Right away.' She heard me come in then and did not say anything more until I left. A moment later I heard her ask one of the set men if he could give her a lift to the station."

"Which station?"

"The main railway station. Mr. Jordan, you really shouldn't worry about Miss Shirley. She is so sweet, so decent, she wouldn't do anything bad . . ."

"All right, all right."

Shirley was not at the hotel when I arrived.

Joan was unconcerned. "It's Saturday afternoon! She is probably with her boyfriend!"

"Joan, tell me, aren't you at all worried?"

"Peter, you really are a sweetheart! Now you are worrying about her like a real father! What am I saying? Like a lover!" She laughed heartily. "Yes, indeed! Like a deceived lover! I think that's perfectly charming!"

The telephone rang. Was it convenient for me to interview the chauffeur I had engaged for the trip to Essen.

Schauberg arrived; dark gray suit, elegant as always, wearing his beret. He bowed to Joan asking her in fluent English to excuse him for keeping his beret on. "A wound from the war."

"Oh, God. This terrible war!" Joan, who seemed to like him right away, was now especially charming. "I'm certain you were not always a chauffeur, Mr. Schauberg?"

"No, ma'am."

"What is your actual profession?"

Schauberg smiled.

"May I guess?"

"Please, do."

"A physician?"

Schauberg did not bat an eyelid. "What makes you think that?"

"Your hands. You have beautiful hands."

"Pianist, ma'am," said Schauberg, smiling even more ingratiatingly. And to me, "If you would come to the garage now, Mr. Jordan. There are some papers you are required to sign."

I walked out to the hall with him.

"What's the matter?"

"Do you have your checkbook with you?"

"Yes, why?"

"I found another student."

"Does that mean you can operate tomorrow after all?"

"Yes. Come to my room."

He opened a door which read, "Personnel Only." Behind it was a spiral staircase. The door separated two worlds. The luxurious one of the guests and the messy one of the staff. Plaster falling off the walls, staircase badly rusted, halls low-ceilinged, dark and dilapidated. Some doors were open. The rooms were obviously lived in, some had several beds. This was where maids, apprentice waiters, and extra help lived.

Schauberg had a room to himself. A sloping wall, with a half-round window that started from the floor. One had to bend down to look out. An iron bedstead, a cupboard and a shaky table completed the scene. I sat on the bed and wrote a check for one thousand marks.

"You might as well write out my weekly check," said Schauberg. Something in his voice made me look up. He was white. His lips trembled. He swayed and fell on the bed next to me. He stammered, "Cupboard . . . case . . . quickly . . ."

I tore open the cupboard, found a case containing a syringe and several ampoules. I broke one open, filled the syringe and handed it to Schauberg.

He jabbed the needle through his trousers into his thigh and depressed the plunger. Then he sighed deeply and fell back. He was resting quietly now. Only his slim, beautiful hands still twitched; the hands Joan had admired; the hands which in a few hours were to touch Shirley's body . . .

19

Rome, May third, nine-thirty p.m.

The little white cat is sleeping, curled up in a chair next to my bed. It is a warm, lovely night. Through the open window I can hear the steps of the carabinier who is guarding me. Behind the old trees I can see the illuminated façade of the Colosseum. The fragrance of the flowers in the park fills my room.

Professor Pontevivo came to see me after dinner. We discussed what he had told me about the functions of the mind and he continued, "I can explain the functions of the mind to a drinker. I can explain the reason of an inferiority complex, the problem he believes himself not able to handle. One thing I cannot do. Do you know what?"

"Yes. You can point out the difficulties in his life which made him a drinker but you cannot remove this difficulty. I thought about that. I imagine that is also the reason why—I once read this—about ninety percent of so-called cured drinkers suffer relapses and are actually incurable."

"You are perfectly right. If a man of forty drinks because he cannot progress in his profession, no longer loves his wife, desires another woman, is convinced that his talent will never be recognized—I cannot obtain for him the woman he dreams of or release him from the one he hates. Neither can I suddenly make him a successful businessman or a Nobel prize winner. I cannot change his basic circumstances."

"Well, then! Ill-bred children. A bad marriage. A wasted life. Enough to drive a man to drink! No matter how well you explain it to him: All he knows then is why he drinks. You are not able to do any more for him."

"Yes, I can."

"You can?"

"I can—" The slight professor interrupted himself. From below we heard noises and men's voices, muffled but still audible in the stillness of the night.

"Non così lentamente!"

"Attenzione, idiota! È sul mio piede!"

"What is on his foot?" I asked.

"The coffin probably," Pontevivo guessed. From the window we watched two men in shirtsleeves struggling to haul a coffin up the steps from the basement of the clinic to a waiting hearse. The coffin swayed dangerously.

"Who died?"

"Our composer. Yesterday morning."

It upset me to hear that.

"We usually remove our—hm—departed ones late at night. Many patients would be shocked to witness such a transfer. Do you possibly belong with these people, too?"

I was silent.

"Mr. Jordan, people are dying all over the world. In a hospital death ought to be a regularly expected event. Don't you agree? Why are you sad?"

"That he died without having completed his concerto."

"All of us are saddened by that," said Pontevivo.

Apparently not all. From below we heard this dialogue.

"È un compositore. Dicono che ha fatto una sì bella musica!"

"Musica, merda! Il mio piede!"

Finally the coffin was placed in the hearse and they drove away. We watched until it disappeared in the darkness, in the void, where all of us would disappear one day.

"By the way, toward the end he also became very pious," said Pontevivo. "It happens frequently. He felt ill

346

and almost daily demanded the priest and extreme unction. All in all he received it seven times. Yesterday morning he told the masseuse to come back at eleven since he had just received extreme unction. By eleven he had already died . . ." Pontevivo led me away from the window. "Where were we?"

"I said you could do very little for a drinker because you could not change his circumstances."

"Right. And I said that I could!"

"How can you do that?"

"I can change his attitude to life. I can—improbable as it may sound—correct his engrams; his experiences as it were. I can effect changes in his subconscious stemming from early, unpleasant experiences with mother, father, poverty, wealth, sickness and so on. I can transform his inferiority complex into a normal emotion. There would then be no more reason for him to drink."

"Then you can change a person?"

"A person, yes. But I can only do that if the patient is agreeable. The patient must cooperate. He must agree to my treatment."

"Which is?"

"Hypnosis," said Pontevivo.

"You can cure alcoholism through hypnosis?"

"In the last two years I have had many successful cures, only a few setbacks. Please consider if you are prepared for this kind of treatment. Good night, Mr. Jordan."

This had been the fourth lecture.

20

On Sunday, the twenty-ninth of November 1959, at exactly four p.m., a pale young man with close-cropped black hair and dark-framed glasses entered the office of the foreman of the hotel garage and asked for Walter Schauberg.

"He just got back from Essen," answered the foreman. "He's driving for a movie company now," he added genially while he looked at the seemingly nervous young man carrying a heavy attaché case. "He's supposed to drive back there tonight."

"Yes, I know," answered the young man. "We were going to see a movie."

The foreman sent a mechanic to fetch Schauberg from the sub-basement. Schauberg was wearing a dark gray chauffeur's uniform. Together with the young man he left the garage and went to a nearby cinema. He bought two tickets for the four o'clock performance. He aroused the cashier's anger by insisting that he had given her a fifty-mark bill and not a twenty she insisted he had given her. After a lengthy argument Schauberg "discovered" his mistake, apologized and entered the movie theater accompanied by the cashier's, "That's a new trick, is it? I'm going to remember your face!"

"I hope so," said Schauberg softly. They waited until the newsreel was shown and left the movie theater, whose only usher had left, by a side exit. At the hotel they used the delivery entrance and service elevator. Shirley, very pale in a black robe opened the door as soon as they knocked. They entered in silence. While the young man took off his shabby coat and pulled up the sleeves of his blue turtleneck sweater Schauberg hung a card on the outside of the door. In four languages it said: DO NOT DISTURB!

Schauberg now locked the door from the inside. Still not a word had been said. Rain beat against the windows. The young man's hair was damp. He put on a white surgeon's cap. Schauberg did the same after he had removed his beret and Shirley had gasped at the sight of the horrible scar.

All I have described and will describe I know from Schauberg's report.

Both men moved the large table to the window. Schauberg spoke for the first time, "Where is the pail?"

"In the bathroom," answered Shirley.

"Get it." Shirley brough the pail she had bought the day before at Schauberg's request.

"The sheets and the other things?"

Shirley pointed to the bed. On it were three new white sheets, sterile cotton wool, sterile gauze, and sanitary napkins. The men spread two sheets over the table and Schauberg took off his jacket and also rolled up his sleeves. He said to Shirley, "You can get undressed now."

"I'm only wearing the robe."

The young man meanwhile had spread the contents of his attaché case on another smaller table. He lit a kerosene burner held in a tripod. On it he placed a chromium bowl he had filled with water. He placed a number of surgical instruments in the bowl. Now he spoke for the first time. "Has to boil ten minutes." He couldn't have been more than three years older than Shirley. He looked undernourished, sad and nervous.

Schauberg said, "Now you can call the operator." He went to the bathroom where he began methodically to scrub his hands and arms.

Shirley instructed the operator. "This is Shirley Bromfield in six-eighteen. I don't feel very well and I'm going to take a sleeping pill. Please don't accept any calls for me until I call you again."

Schauberg returned and threw a razor and shaving brush into the boiling water.

"What's that for?" The young man's watery eyes blinked fearfully behind his glasses.

"I'll take care of it. Wash your hands."

"Why shave her? Iodine will do."

"You shut up."

"That's crazy! Shaving too! As if we have that much time!"

Schauberg looked threatening. His voice was low, "I worked ethically for twenty years like any decent doctor, and I'm going to work properly today too. You understand me?"

The young man shrugged and went to scrub his hands. Schauberg told me later, "Naturally, iodine would have done as well. But—ridiculous I know—just then I remembered that I had no license to practice any more. I did it out of stubbornness. Stubbornness and . . . and longing for my profession, probably. Ridiculous, isn't it?"

Shirley lay on the towel on the bed and he shaved her carefully. "Now you can take off your robe and lie on the table. Feet to the window. We need light."

"Can I have a pillow for my head? The table is so hard."

"No. You have to lie flat. You'll be sleepy in a moment and you won't feel anything." Schauberg injected Shirley's vein.

"What's that?"

"Evipal. By the way, your stepfather sends his best regards. Move forward. Farther, to the edge of the table." Shirley obeyed apathetically. The injection was taking effect. "Let your legs hang down." Schauberg pushed the pail close to her legs. He turned on the radio.

"Music drowns out noises. Spread out your arms."

Schauberg tore a long, wide strip off the sheet. He tied one end around Shirley's right wrist, pulled the strip underneath the table to the other side and secured Shirley's other wrist. Her stretched out arms were now fixed as those of a crucified person.

"Pull your knees up. Higher!" he said louder. Shirley was mumbling, not reacting to his request. He pushed her legs up against her body. He placed a wide long strip of the sheet underneath the backs of her knees and fastened the strip tightly behind the girl's neck. He went to the

350

bathroom where the student was still brushing his hands and began to scrub again. The instruments were rattling in the boiling water and melodies of a Lehar operetta came from the radio.

"How is her heart?" asked the student.

"It's okay. You have Cardiazol?"

"Yes."

"Good."

"Why should you need it if her heart is okay?"

"One never knows. It's always good to have handy." Both men went over to Shirley. The student placed the mask on her face.

"Count, please."

Indistinctly Shirley began to count, "One, two, three . . ."

"Breathe deeply," said the student. He slowly dropped ether onto the cotton wool of the mask. Schauberg bent over Shirley.

". . . four . . . five . . ."

"She's out," reported the student.

"All right," said Schauberg. "The rings, please."

As he inserted the first the telephone began to ring.

21

The music emanating from the radio was sweet and sticky as honey.

Schauberg straightened up.

The telephone shrilled.

"It will stop in a moment," said Schauberg.

The telephone stopped ringing.

"You see," said Schauberg. "The next ring, please."

The telephone started up again.

The student dropped the ring.

"Stupid," said Schauberg. The student picked up the

ring and threw it back into the boiling water. The telephone continued to ring.

"I can't stand that," groaned the student. His face was green.

"If she doesn't answer they'll stop ringing. She said she didn't want to be disturbed."

The telephone stopped.

"There you are," said Schauberg.

The telephone began again.

Schauberg said, "It must be something important."

"If it is they'll send someone up here."

"The sign is on the door."

"That won't stop them if it is important," the student cried hysterically. Schauberg shrugged his shoulders and walked toward the telephone.

"You can't answer that!"

"Why not?" asked Schauberg, supremely confident. "After all, I am her stepfather's chauffeur. I could have brought her something from him." He turned off the radio, Shirley moaned and moved her head.

"God . . . forgive . . ."

"Give her a little more."

The student dropped a little more ether onto the mask.

Shirley quietened.

Schauberg lifted the receiver. He did not say anything. A woman's voice said, "Miss Bromfield, I'm terribly sorry to disturb you. You said you did not wish to be called. But an inspector from the police is here and he says it is urgent. Just one moment I'll connect you . . ."

The Seventh Tape

1

Infernal noise, while the steel block, glowing blue-white, shot out from under the resounding electric hammers of the pressure rollers. It sped to the furiously rotating cylinders of the rolling mill.

The light in the workshop was so intense that all of us, workmen and movie staff used goggles. There was no escape from the noise of the gigantic machines.

Two hundred men had started on the nightshift at seven p.m. this twenty-ninth of November. They were stripped to the waist, wearing the usual costume of boots, protective helmets and goggles. The heat was almost unbearable despite the huge ventilators forcing fresh air into the mill.

This is where we would be shooting for the next five nights. We had permission to shoot only at night for, during the day, five hundred men worked here. We would have been in their way.

What was to be filmed now was a segment of the career of Carlton Webb, the drunken weakling played by me. The brutal, sweaty world of tough manual laborers, into which he was suddenly thrown almost destroyed him. But painfully, stubbornly he fought through to a personal victory.

The background of this "movie within the movie" was the daily lives of working men. Among them and their families the hero came to know "real" life, "real" problems, "real" men and—a dramatic essential—a beautiful working girl, later to be his sweetheart, and Evelyn's rival.

After Carlton Webb's salvation (as it were) through honest toil he would be killed by Evelyn's jealous husband.

The two hundred men of the night shift were more than just extras. They were real men—not players. After talking and working with them I had a greater awareness of that other world, more solid and lasting than my world of luxury apartments, corruption and depravity.

Joan, Schauberg and I had left Hamburg at eight o'clock Sunday morning. We reached Essen by eleven o'clock. In the afternoon two foremen instructed me in routines I would need for the scenes that night. I had an hour's rest before starting work at seven p.m.

The scenes in Essen were the most dreadfully taxing ones, psychologically and physically. Workers were on four-hour shifts but we—under pressure by our deadline—spent eight or nine hours in the heat and noise of the mill. Those were five nights I would not soon forget!

On that first Sunday night the make-up artists were horrified when they saw my body covered with spots, pustules and scabs. Seaton, Kostasch and Albrecht had been summoned.

Soon half a dozen people were staring at me, shaking their heads all the while I was insisting that the rash was a harmless allergy; that I was already under the care of a dermatologist in Hamburg and that he had said make-up would conceal the rash but not irritate it. Schauberg had told me, "You can apply any amount of make-up. Considering the large doses of aureomycin you've had it's simply impossible to get an infection! Just to make sure I'll give you another one to carry you through until I get back."

356

He had done that, and left at twelve noon. Now it was ten p.m. While we were shooting perspiration was rapidly washing away my make-up. As though I was really a workman I pushed the white-hot steel bouncing past us, with a long iron bar along the rotating cylinders. I had a double for a few dangerous scenes (such as a fist fight on a narrow bridge above the rolling mill) but I played in most of the takes.

The camera man told me not to worry about the melting make-up. "We're using panchromatic film. The glowing metal will photograph so bright, you'll all appear as silhouettes. Close-ups are on your face and that is free of the rash."

A buzzer sounded. Two hundred exhausted men left. Two hundred fresh men started work.

Eleven p.m.

Schauberg had been gone eleven hours. What was keeping him? It was seven hours since he had operated on Shirley.

Something must have happened! Something went wrong with Shirley. Or with Schauberg. Or with both of them. What had happened?

I played my scenes. The fear did not leave me. My arms grew weak; I could hardly hold the iron bar, my head ached, my back hurt, and along with the perspiration I felt my strength ebb. At midnight we paused for a half hour.

Still no sign of Schauberg.

I was lying on my cot in a portable dressing room. Harry had wrapped me in blankets and I asked him to bring me a telephone. He rolled in the telephone with a seemingly endless line rolling off a drum on wheels. With shaking hands I dialed my hotel in Hamburg.

"This is Peter Jordan. I'd like to speak to my daughter, please."

"I'm sorry Mr. Jordan, Miss Bromfield left word that she did not want to be disturbed."

"When?"

"At four o'clock. She said she did not feel well."

"You have not heard from her since?"

"No, Mr. Jordan. She said she was going to take a sleeping pill."

"Well, connect me anyway."

"But—"

"Connect me! It is important! The worst that can happen is that we wake her!"

I heard the phone ring.

"Miss Bromfield does not answer."

"So I see."

"She must be fast asleep."

"Yes." Perhaps she was dead.

"Shall I send someone up?"

Perhaps she really was asleep. Perhaps Schauberg was still with her. Perhaps—

"No. No, don't do that! I don't want to disturb her if she is sleeping that deeply. Thank you, operator."

Twelve-thirty a.m.

Where was Schauberg?

Why didn't Shirley answer?

If something happened to Shirley, if Schauberg had injured her . . . if she had bled to death . . . if this old morphine addict with his shaky hands had killed her . . . if he was already on his way to the frontier . . .

"Good God in heaven!"

I suddenly realized that I had spoken aloud. I believe I had never said those words before!

A knock. The door opened.

"And a very good evening, or rather good morning." Schauberg looked pale and tired but he smiled.

I started.

"How is she?"

"Everything is fine. She's sleeping. She'll have to rest today but tomorrow she can work again. Sends her best regards."

358

Suddenly the room spun, my hand went to my throat and I fell back on my bed. "Can't . . . can't breathe . . ."

"Where is the box?"

"Under . . . bed . . ."

He quickly locked the door, pulled out the box. Yellow box, chrome-plated steel, injection. Then peace, calm, serenity.

I breathed deeply. Schauberg stowed away the box, unlocked the door. Not a moment too soon. Seaton's protégé, the blond Hans, looked in, "We're ready to resume in five minutes, Mr. Jordan."

"Rest another five minutes," said Schauberg, his smile benign. "Everything went off smoothly, dear Mr. Jordan."

"Swear it!"

"You know that I don't believe—"

"If Shirley is not all right, if you are lying, I'll see to it that you'll never leave Germany, that you'll never get a chance of a new start, that you're going to rot here—you understand?"

"Perfectly."

"Why are you so late?"

"I ran out of gas right after I passed Hanover. I stood and waved for almost three hours before I got a lift to the next gas station." Hans looked in, "Mr. Jordan, are you ready now?" And was gone again.

I got up. I felt reborn. Now I could take on another dozen such nights!

"Schauberg, those injections are fantastic."

"Are you telling me?" He looked worried and held on to my arm. "Listen, dear Mr. Jordan, there is something wrong with your wife."

"What do you mean?"

"You're paying me. So I'm on your side. I don't care about your wife. This afternoon we very nearly ran into some trouble . . ."

Door open. Hans.

"Mr. Jordan—"

"Get out!" I yelled. He did, offended. "What kind of trouble?"

"Well, just as we were about to start the telephone rang. Your stepdaughter had left word not to be disturbed but some stupid bitch called anyway because it was the police."

"The police?"

"Yes, an inspector."

"Who talked to him?"

"I did."

"You?"

"What else could I do? The girl was already anaesthetized. I said I was your chauffeur. Miss Bromfield could not answer the telephone since she was taking a bath."

"And he believed that?"

"Apparently. He really didn't want Miss Bromfield, he wanted to see her mother."

"My wife?"

"I told him she was staying at the Königshof Hotel in Essen. He said he would call the police here and have them send someone to the hotel. Tomorrow morning. That is, this morning."

"Did he say what they wanted my wife for?"

"He was very polite. It seems the German police don't want anything from her. But the American police seem to have asked the German authorities for help."

This time it was Seaton who opened the door. "Peter, we're all waiting for you. You really must come now!"

I left Schauberg and followed the director. Seaton gave me instructions, "Now in the next scene you are certain that Maria knows everything. You are panic-stricken, desperate, at the end of your rope. But you must pull yourself together. No one must know. No one. Okay?"

"Okay."

"It's a difficult scene, I know."

"It's quite easy," I said absent-mindedly. "You'll see."

2

At eleven o'clock, after six hours of sleep, I was up again, breakfasting with Joan.

"Shirley called an hour ago."

"Anything special?"

"No, just to see how we were. She said she had caught a cold and was resting in bed, reading."

"Something interesting, I hope?"

"Exodus."

Now I felt relieved. *Exodus* was the word we had agreed on. If Shirley was reading *Exodus* everything had gone well and she was feeling all right.

The telephone rang on the table behind me. I picked up the receiver.

"This is the operator. I have a call for Mrs. Jordan."

"All right."

"Just a moment please. I'll connect you with a phone booth."

A man's voice. "Mrs. Jordan?"

"This is Mrs. Jordan's husband."

Joan caught her breath. "Who is it?"

I motioned her to be quiet.

The man asked, "Could I speak to your wife, Mr. Jordan?"

"Who are you?"

Joan had jumped up and hurried to me. She pressed her ear to the receiver.

"I'm Inspector Munro. Hamburg asked us to talk with Mrs. Jordan. They had been asked by the Los Angeles police to help. It would be best if I could explain it to you personally. May I then—"

Joan's lips quivered. She was deathly pale.

"Come on up. Room five-eleven." I replaced the receiver.

"He'll be here in two minutes," I said.

Joan covered her face for a moment with both hands. Her eyes were enormous.

"Now the time has come," she said.

I said nothing.

"Two detectives already came to see me in Pacific Palisades before I left for Hamburg."

I remained silent.

"Then they wrote to me . . . to the hotel in Hamburg . . . you saw the letter . . . you looked for it . . . I lied to you . . . I told you it had been an invitation for a fashion show . . . You remember?"

"I remember."

"I was going to tell you everything right away! Right after arriving in Hamburg. I . . . I was so upset . . . that's why I drank too much in the plane . . . I didn't think I'd be brave enough to tell you . . . and then I was tight and lost my courage altogether . . ."

One more minute and the inspector would be here. How odd that the final catastrophe should take place before another person, a witness, a stranger, this Mr. Munro.

"And then . . . then I thought I'd forget all about it . . . Hamburg is a long way from Los Angeles . . . but they sent that letter . . . and now the inspector . . . one cannot escape them!"

No, one could not escape, I thought. Why did the authorities go to Joan, not to me or Shirley? Apparently they had not believed Gregory's statement that he was the father. Obviously they hoped to make me confess in this way.

"Peter, you must forgive me!"

"Forgive you?"

"Yes. I've done something terrible . . ."

"What?"

"You had already left for Europe . . ."

"I had already left for Europe . . ." I repeated as if I had been hypnotized.

"On Sunset Boulevard . . . my foot slipped off the brake onto the gas pedal and I hit a car about to park. I think I did quite a lot of damage . . . it was very late . . . I had been drinking . . . I came from a party at the Lexingtons' . . ."

"Lexingtons' . . ."

"And I was afraid of a blood test. So I drove away." Now she was crying. "On the next day the detectives came . . . They thought at first that you had driven the car but when they heard you were in Europe they asked me . . . and I did the second stupid thing . . ."

It was fantastic. It was unbelievable. But true.

"I told the detectives the Cadillac had been stolen. I said I had only just noticed that it was missing and that I was just about to report it!"

"I don't understand . . ."

"Well, I abandoned the car after the collision . . ."

"Where?"

"In some street . . . I only drove a little way and left the car. I ran and ran until I found a taxi . . . I told you, I just lost my head . . . I told the detectives the car had been stolen from the street in front of the house . . ."

"Yes, and?" That was all I could manage to say. I still did not have complete control over myself.

"They believed me at first. They had already found the Cadillac and our fingerprints in it . . ."

"What happened then?"

"Nothing. Until they sent that letter . . . they wrote they had found paint chips and tire marks and some witnesses . . . and I don't know what else . . . I was to go to the German police and make another statement . . . tell the truth . . . they were threatening hit-and-run charges . . ."

"Why didn't you go to the German police?"

"I thought it might be just a threat, a trap. I wrote them that I had nothing new to add . . . I meant to tell you . . . later . . . but not while you were working . . . you are so nervous right now . . . and we never had anything to do with the police . . . they are going to take me to court . . . in Los Angeles where everybody knows us . . ."

There was a knock at the door. I opened it.

A short, slight man, hat in one hand, a brief case in the other, bowed politely.

"Come in, Inspector Munro. My wife just confessed the entire business. I knew nothing of this." Behind me I heard Joan cry. "She did a very foolish thing and committed a punishable offense. At least no one came to any bodily harm."

"Well, it's not a capital offense." The inspector spoke good English. "Good morning, Mrs. Jordan. Please calm yourself."

"I'll be taken to court!"

"Well yes, but—"

"And I'll be sent to jail!"

"It is possible. Perhaps a suspended sentence. Or a fine. Naturally your driver's license will be revoked. Please, Mrs. Jordan, you must calm yourself. I'm very sorry, but my orders are to question you once more."

"Yes, darling," I said, "you must stop crying. Try to be reasonable now."

Joan slowly stopped sobbing.

"I'm so ashamed," she whispered. I offered her my handkerchief. "What I've done is a criminal offense, a terrible thing . . ."

Inspector Munro in his correct school-English tried to pacify her while he pulled paper and pen from his brief case.

"Excuse me for one moment, please," I said. The black bag was hidden in a cupboard of my bedroom. I drank from the bottle until I fell on the bed gasping for breath.

3

(Transcriber's note: At this point Signore Jordan interrupted his taping for three days because of influenza. It enabled me to catch up with transcribing his report and to hand the entire manuscript to Professor Pontevivo. The following was taped on May eleventh, 1960.)

PROFESSOR PONTEVIVO: Have you come to a conclusion regarding the treatment by hypnosis?

SIGNORE JORDAN: Yes. I agree to it.

PROFESSOR PONTEVIVO: Good. We'll discuss the details tomorrow. It will take several sessions. While you were ill I caught up on your last tape transcriptions. Now for weeks you had lived in fear of your wife knowing all about you and your stepdaughter. It proved to be without foundation. In fact she had been afraid that you might find out about her car accident.

SIGNORE JORDAN: That's right and yet that's not all of it. At the time of our filming in Essen I was already so exhausted that I could hardly think straight. Logically, I now had no more reason to be afraid. But the fear was still with me! I would say that after Inspector Munro's visit my fear increased. Perhaps I knew; I sensed that all this could not come to a good end. I had prepared myself for the long overdue catastrophe. I had almost wished for an end of this torture, no matter how dreadful the end might be.

PROFESSOR PONTEVIVO: I understand. And now, once more, your situation was as it had been in the beginning, with a loving, trusting wife . . .

SIGNORE JORDAN: You can imagine that when she confessed her "crime" to me, my reaction made her feel even more affectionate. She thought I was the best husband in all the world. She kissed and hugged me even while the inspector was still there.

PROFESSOR PONTEVIVO: And the prospect of having to talk to your unsuspecting wife ...

SIGNORE JORDAN: You can understand how I felt, can't you? It would have been easier if she had suspected something, if she had mistrusted me! The fact that she was so happy, so relieved made my life doubly difficult. Right after the inspector left she went out and bought me a gold cigarette case. And before I left for the night's shooting—(unintelligible)

PROFESSOR PONTEVIVO: You completed your shooting without any kind of breakdown?

SIGNORE JORDAN: Yes. Schauberg now used medications which must have been very strong. I frequently had dizzy spells while I was working; I vomited a few times, I often had intolerable headaches. To counteract those symptoms Schauberg gave me more and more drugs.

We left Essen on a Friday, December fourth. For me there were another fifteen days of shooting. The scenes I did not appear in were to be shot later. The most difficult ones had been completed.

PROFESSOR PONTEVIVO: Your stepdaughter was all right again after you returned? How did she seem to you?

SIGNORE JORDAN: She seemed very friendly but preoccupied. I often felt she did not recognize me when we talked. She was the same with her mother. She did her work, was pleasant and polite—and very reserved.

PROFESSOR PONTEVIVO: She had promised you to explain her behavior once the operation had been performed.

SIGNORE JORDAN: I did ask her about that. She asked me to be patient for another few days.

PROFESSOR PONTEVIVO: Were you intimate?

SIGNORE JORDAN: Not once since she had arrived in Europe. She seemed so strange that I did not even dare kiss her any more. Besides, I already mentioned it, Schauberg's medications were making a physical and mental wreck of me. Often when I walked, I thought I was falling. Again and again I dreamt the dream that I was locked in the elevator. Sometimes tears would be streaming down my face or I caught myself talking to myself. I tried desperately to control myself so as not to become suspicious.

PROFESSOR PONTEVIVO: But day after day you were in front of the cameras.

SIGNORE JORDAN: I had to finish the movie. As I think of it now, I had only one wish: to finish. Just to complete that movie.

PROFESSOR PONTEVIVO: Did your stepdaughter still see that man secretively?

SIGNORE JORDAN: Yes. Schauberg and his student were still watching her but they never found out who he was or where Shirley was meeting him. She always eluded her pursuers.

PROFESSOR PONTEVIVO: But you did find out the truth. When did it happen?

SIGNORE JORDAN: On the twelfth of December. Things might have turned out differently if Schauberg had not asked me to be a witness to his marriage.

PROFESSOR PONTEVIVO: Witness to his marriage? For heaven's sake, he was going to marry?

4

"Witness to your marriage?"

It was early morning on the fifth of December. Schauberg and I stood in the darkness outside the hotel entrance. It was snowing again and the exhaust from the Mercedes looked like a shivering white snake. Schauberg had just brought the car.

"Witness, that's right," he said.

"Surely, you're not going to marry!"

"But I am."

"Whom?"

"Käthe, of course."

The sudden shock made me slip on the snow and I came to rest on the fender.

"Why are you staring at me, my dear Mr. Jordan? We'd like you and Madam Misere to be our witnesses. You are my choice, Madam is Käthe's. The wedding will take place on the twelfth of December at twelve noon. That's next Saturday. You'll be finished at the studio by then. Will you do us the honor?"

"Now tell me the point of the joke."

"It's no joke. Käthe and I want to marry." He smiled and once more reminded me of my father. His disarming smile, his elegance even in his uniform.

I rose.

"Your drugs have done it. I'm crazy. Do you know I just heard you say that you're going to marry Käthe?"

"That's what I did say."

"Then you're the crazy one. It's the morphine!"

"What's so crazy about my wanting to marry Käthe?"

"I can't believe it. Do you know why I admired you?"

"Why, dear Mr. Jordan?"

"For your perfect cynicism, your incorruptible frigid reason. I saw you as a man who had no false ideals, no empty talk. A man who would never fall victim to a treacherous, undefinable feeling . . . let alone love."

"I'm sorry to disappoint you, dear Mr. Jordan. Apparently I have."

"You can't possibly love anybody!"

"Yes, I can. One person. Käthe. You admire my perfect cynicism. Thank you. Well—"

"I said I admired cynicism. It can't be perfect."

"Why not?"

"It would make love impossible."

"On the contrary. It proves very useful to my love. Were I an honorable, moral idealist—I could not marry a whore who is working in a bordello: a woman who is dumb, primitive, simple, uneducated. Käthe is all those things, isn't she?"

I was silent.

Schauberg said, "For a cynic such as I am there is also a second Käthe who is more loyal than any woman I have ever met. In spite of what she does, she has retained a child-like innocence. She never lies; she will never betray me. She has stood by me when things were at their worst. Many times I have hurt her feelings, have offended her. She always loved me."

Now he did not remind me of my father. "I want to get away from here. I want to start anew, in spite of everything. I can't do it alone. With Käthe, who will stand by me, who will always be truthful and who does not have to fear evil because her innocence is stronger than evil—with her I will be able to succeed."

I was silent.

"You believed, naturally, that I would abandon Käthe."

"Naturally,"

"It's understandable. It would have been the logical, reasonable thing to do. Of course, at first I thought that too. But in time, weeks, months, I discovered that I loved her. In her artlessness, her simplicity she did things . . . little things . . . which touched me . . . things I admired."

"Such as?"

"Two men in Leipzig gave her seven eels which they had stolen. When pressure was put on her she escaped to the West just so she would not have to betray those men. She left everything, her home, her youth, Would you have betrayed those men?"

"Probably."

"I would have too. You see what I mean. What is love, Mr. Jordan? To go to bed together? To writhe, to groan with lust, to copulate in the manner of animals? How long

369

does that last? How long can it last? Two years? Three years? A month? And what follows then?"

"What?"

"Mostly nothing. Sometimes a human relationship. One needs the other. One trusts the other. Trust and need—that's probably love. And that's why we are going to marry."

"I understand."

"And you're terribly disappointed in me," said Schauberg. He was still smiling and straightened his beret. Snow, crystalline and clean, fell on us, still clean because it had not yet come in contact with our dirty world.

5

Luck had been with us. We had worked so steadily that we were a day and a half ahead of our schedule. I talked to Kostasch in good time. He said, "If you are supposed to be at City Hall at noon you'll have to leave here at eleven. We could do a few scenes in which you don't appear and you can take Saturday off. You look as if you could use it. A day off will do you good!"

"I asked that all my scenes would be shot first. And it would give me enough time if I left here at eleven-thirty."

"No, no, you take Saturday off. Present from the boss. I already mentioned to Thornton that you look a little under the weather and he thinks so too. We don't want you to drop in your tracks during the last two weeks. You boozing too much?"

"No. No, I'm not."

"Then it's something else. I don't want to know. But we've all noticed something is wrong."

"If my work is not—"

"Something is wrong with you, I said. Your work is

okay. You are worrying us, Peter boy. Is there anything I can do?"

"I'm just tired, that's all. Don't worry. I'll finish the last two weeks. And if I can really take Saturday off . . ."

"I told you you could!"

"Thanks."

So they had noticed that something was wrong with me. Two more weeks. Only two more weeks. Just to get through those two weeks was what I most wanted now.

At ten o'clock on Saturday, the twelfth of December, Madam Misere gave one of her fabulous champagne breakfasts. Eleven of the girls joined us at breakfast while the other eleven were permitted to come to City Hall for the wedding ceremony.

Business could not be completely interrupted.

While the "first party" was breakfasting the members of the "second party" in their rooms above us were being noisily merry with some early guests.

Madam Misere, Schauberg and I were dressed in black. Käthe wore a blue suit; three orchids pinned to the lapel. For the first time since I met her she seemed a mature woman, not at all an adolescent. She wore little make-up and I was surprised how pretty she was. Her blonde hair was pulled back, her blue eyes were sparkling and from time to time she had to dab her nose. She sat at the head of the table, radiant with happiness.

Soon Madam was reminding us to get ready to leave. A few of the girls were already high. Thereupon, the breakfast party went upstairs to work and the other eleven, unfamiliar in their best clothes, came giggling down the creaking staircase.

We were ready now. At that moment two foreign women, with the imperious manners of the spoiled rich, announced loudly why they had come. "We want two big blondes with two big 'godemiches'." Madam assured them that both were available in several shapes and forms. The two foreigners made their choices from among the girls of the "first party" while Madam went in search of the key to the cupboard where she kept such accessories. The key could not be found.

Madam became nervous. The girls grew restive. It was twenty-five to twelve. One of the women had chosen Käthe but when told that she was about to leave for City Hall had said, "To marry a man? What a shame!" Käthe suddenly burst into tears and Schauberg tried to calm her.

"Let's go some place else," said one of the women.

Madam soothed the ladies, urging patience. At quarter to twelve the Mousetrap found the key in her room and had her face slapped by Madam Misere as a reward. "Got drunk afterward and forgot to return it, eh?" Madam opened the cupboard in her office and showed the two women a truly imposing collection.

"Boy, oh boy!" said one of them. "I think I'll take that one."

Then, hurriedly we left by taxi and in my car.

We had to wait in an anteroom. Two couples, ahead of us with their parties, eyed us suspiciously and whispered together although the girls were behaving most demurely.

Half an hour later Walter Schauberg and Käthe Mädler were called and we entered an office. A small organ, chairs for the couple, for visitors and witnesses, a table draped with a red velvet cloth.

An old man played the organ. The eleven girls began to cry softly. It was contagious; even Madam succumbed. "It reminds me of my husband, may he rest in peace," she whispered to me.

A friendly registrar in a black robe passed out a few routine jokes as he checked the marriage papers. Then he went into a brief formal address. The family, he said, is the foundation of the state; marriage, the most perfect bond between two people. He concluded, "Man and wife are complete in their togetherness, the happiness of marriage is an essential condition for your future. This is the happiness I wish both of you."

We rose and Schauberg's "yes" in response to the registrar's formal question about his acceptance of Käthe as his wife was very solemn.

Käthe tried twice; her response was a sob. In a third effort she managed an almost inaudible "yes."

When they exchanged rings Käthe's hand shook so much that Schauberg dropped the ring. I picked it up.

We signed our names to several documents and then a general kissing began. It was an emotional spree. Even the registrar had his share of kisses.

The Mousetrap could not seem to control herself. I led her to the empty dark anteroom where I gave her a drink from my pocket flask. The overwrought girl calmed down gradually while the other guests left the registrar's office.

Suddenly Schauberg, very excited, appeared by my side. "Follow me, quickly."

He pulled me into the registrar's office. A telephone receiver was lying next to the phone on a desk. "My student is on the phone. The registrar was nice enough to leave us alone for a few moments."

"What's the matter?"

"Your stepdaughter. This time he didn't lose her."

I picked up the receiver.

"Yes?"

An anxious voice inquired, "Mr. Jordan?"

"Yes. Speaking."

"I hope I'm not going to get into any trouble if I tell you . . . listen, I would deny everything if the police got onto this!"

"You'll get money if you tell me! You'll get trouble only if you don't talk! Where are you?"

"Lietzenburger Street, corner of Laeiz-Allee. They parked the car a little farther down the road. The man and your . . . and the girl went into the house there."

"What does the man look like?"

"I only saw his back. Still young, I think. He drives a red Jaguar. My taxi driver said—"

"What?"

". . . that he drove much too fast. Once——"

"Hold it! The car. Can you read its number?"

"HH–HC111."

"I'll be there as soon as I can. Stay where you are. Only if they leave the house are you to follow them." I dropped the receiver and ran from the office without a word to Schauberg. I hurried down the stairs. Started my car. I realized that I'd just gone through a stop sign.

Jaguar. Red and small.

HH–HC111.

An easy number to remember.

The car belonged to the good-looking Hennessy, Jakv's assistant: The man who was going to marry the cutter Ursula König who reminded him so much of Shirley.

6

He was standing on the corner in his thin worn coat, his nose red and swollen. He sneezed often. "Down there." Schauberg's friend pointed with his chin.

The street was a wide busy street with many new buildings. Between them, spared by the war, a few old low-storied houses. Traffic was heavy. Streetcars, cars and buses raced past us.

It was snowing large watery flakes. The sky, the street, the houses, the lights were gray and dreary. Slush covered the street. The dirty brown water collected in many places and every time a car went through one of those little lakes fountains sprayed in all directions.

"They're still inside," said the student.

"Which house?"

"The green one."

The little one-storied house about a hundred yards away was squashed between two modern high-rise buildings of steel and glass, lost, pathetic, unable to breathe. Many years had bleached and eroded its pale-green paint. Gates were on all its windows, each with sheer curtains. There was a small door within a larger green wooden door. Both were closed.

"How long have they been there?"

"Since twelve-forty-eight."

A half hour.

"How did they get in?"

"You see the old bell pull? The young man rang and somebody opened the little door."

"Who opened?"

"I couldn't see that." He sneezed again. "Do you still need me?"

"No." I gave him some money. "Go to bed. Drink a hot toddy."

He nodded sullenly and slunk away, his head bowed, his shoulders bent. I walked down the street. Traffic had become heavier. Thousands of people were going home. The weekend had begun.

There was no name under the old bell pull. No name anywhere. It was a house from a different time, a time long past, a house without life. A dead house.

I was going to ring the bell but I felt strangely uneasy and I did not. I leaned against the green door and waited. A church bell chimed one-fifteen.

7

I was still there at two o'clock.

The traffic had not abated. It was snowing more heavily and the snow did not melt. I was cold. Ten minutes past two my patience was exhausted. Just as I reached for the bell I heard the voices of two men and Shirley's too.

Laughing. They came closer. Steps approached the other side of the door.

I dropped my hand from the bell and stepped to the left. The little door within the large one was on the right. It opened. Laughing, Shirley and Hennessy stepped out. Shirley said, "Auf Wiederschen. And thank you very much."

Young Hennessy, his face a healthy pink, said, "Bye, Thomas."

I could not see the man they were talking to. I only heard his voice. "Take care, you two."

It was a young voice.

The little green door closed. Shirley pushed her arm through Hennessy's. She was wearing her white lamb fur coat, black stockings and black, low-heeled shoes. She had tied a black scarf over her auburn hair.

Hennessy said, "Shall we have a quick cup of coffee?"

Shirley began, "No, I have to get back to the hotel. My stepfather—" They turned to leave and Shirley saw me. Hennessy took a step backward. His ruddy complexion had become very pale. Shirley said softly, "How terrible."

"Is it terrible?" I could hardly speak.

"It's too soon. It's just too soon!"

A passing bus splashed us.

"What's too soon?"

"I did ask you to be patient for a little longer . . . just a few more days . . . I would have told you everything . . ."

I was silent.

"Now look, Mr. Jordan—" began Hennessy.

"If you don't keep quiet I'm going to knock your teeth in!"

"Well now, just a minute!"

He was taller; he was younger; he was stronger. I did not care. With my left hand I grabbed the front of his coat and pulled back my right fist.

"Peter," screamed Shirley.

"You have it all wrong, Mr. Jordan." Hennessy was

very pale. He made no move to defend himself; his arms hung down his sides.

"You're meeting secretly. You disappear together for hours. This has been going on for weeks. But I have it all wrong, eh?"

"Yes," said Shirley. "Oh, my God, why didn't you give me a little more time?"

"What did you do here?"

"We came to see my brother."

"You have a very hospitable brother. Saves you going to a hotel."

He blushed and his hands too were fists now.

"Don't," said Shirley to him. "Please, don't, Werner."

Werner!

I hit him.

He crashed against the green door. His nose began to bleed. He was going to lunge for me but Shirley threw herself between us. People stopped and watched. A little boy was delighted. "Mommy, look! Look at those two guys!"

Shirley pushed Hennessy back. "Please . . . leave him be . . ."

"If he thinks he can beat me up—"

"I'll give you some more in a minute!"

The little green door was opened again by a man of about thirty-five, slim, tall, with closely cropped hair. "What happened? What's going on?"

"I'm sorry. Please forgive us!" Shirley's voice quavered. "This is my stepfather. He . . . he waited for me here. I have to explain a lot to him . . . and to you too . . . Peter, this is Father Thomas . . ."

"You . . . you are his brother?" I stammered.

"That's right, sir," answered the slim young man in the black garb of the Catholic priest, "I'm Werner's brother."

8

"He lives in the little house. The old church is in back of it, one street over. You can't see it from here. The new high-rise building blocks the view of it," said Shirley. It was ten minutes later. We were sitting in a modern ice cream parlor opposite the green little house. It was still snowing and traffic was still heavy. The parlor was empty save for a very young couple far too much in love to be aware of us. Their bookbags were on chairs next to them. From the jukebox came the screeching voice of a German juvenile recording star. "This is the rhythm of our time . . ."

I remember everything exactly: the giggling couple, the reverberating music, the colorful steel furnishings, the tiled floor, the newspaper on the next table. Alarm at the Riviera. Dam Bursts at Fréjus. Three Hundred Fifty Dead. Mass Grave under Mud. Town Threatened by Epidemics.

Hennessy had returned to his brother's house. His nose had bled furiously. I had apologized to him and to the young priest. Then I had said to Shirley, "Let's go to the place across the street."

Now we sat by a window.

"So," I said.

Her eyes were pleading. "You . . . you won't let me have a few more days?"

"No."

"And if I swear—"

"Shirley, you must tell me. Now. Here. We are not going to leave here until you've told me the truth."

"The truth will be painful for you."

"It doesn't matter."

"I don't want to hurt you."

"You'll hurt me more if you don't tell me the truth."

"My God," said Shirley. "Good God, why did You let this happen?"

"What?"

"That you found us. That you force me to tell you today. Must I really?"

"Yes," I said. "You must. I know you won't lie to me. The truth, Shirley. Right now."

"The truth," she repeated helplessly. "The truth is very simple." She had taken off her coat. Her black wool dress was one of my great favorites. Her auburn ponytail fell forward over her right shoulder. "But I could never tell it to you."

"Why not?"

"You would have forbidden me to come here. You forbade me to see Father Horace at home too."

Fear made me freeze. Hoarsely I said, "You confessed to the priest?"

The waitress came.

"A chocolate milk," ordered Shirley.

"And you, sir?"

"Whisky."

"I'm sorry, we don't serve alcohol here."

"Something else then."

"Excuse me, but something else—"

"Something else! I don't care what!"

"Another chocolate milk," said Shirley. The waitress shrugged her shoulders and left. "Why are you shouting at her? It's not her fault."

"I asked you a question."

"No, Peter, I did not go to confession. Never. I wanted to many times. I almost did the day . . . the day the child was . . ."

"What stopped you?"

"You."

"I?"

"I had promised you not to go to confession, you remember? That time I called you at the hotel. You told me: Don't tell anybody. You must not go to Father Horace! You must not go to confession! Do you remember?"

I nodded.

"I never did. I never will. Because I promised you; because I love you." The hand she placed on mine was cold yet in her green eyes I saw boundless love.

The waitress served us.

"I'll always love you, Peter. Never another man. Only you."

"I love you too, Shirley! I love only you. Just a few more days, a few insignificant days, then our movie will be finished, then we'll talk to Joan and leave her. Then we'll live together, for always."

"No, Peter," she said.

"No, what?"

Looking out into the swirling snow she whispered, "Why do I have to tell you today? Why today? I can't . . . it's too soon . . . what if something happens . . ."

"Shirley, come on! Tell me!"

"I was going to tell you when you had finished your work. When nothing else could go wrong with the movie."

"What were you going to tell me then?"

"That I'm leaving you."

"You . . . what?"

"I'm leaving you. We're not going to see each other again."

I tipped my glass. The chocolate milk spread over the table.

"Shirley, you are crazy!"

"I'm very much sane."

"You said that you love me! Only me!"

"Only you. Always you."

"Then why would you want to leave me?"

She mumbled something.

"I didn't hear what you said."

She blushed, embarrassed. "I can't say it out loud."

"Tell me!"

"I promised God," she answered almost inaudibly.

"You—"

"Because you are so ill," she said.

"I am what?"

"You know what I mean."

The waitress came and cleaned up the spilled drink. She mumbled. Now she was angry too.

9

Buses. Streetcars. Trucks.

The snow was falling even heavier now.

I am very calm.

Perfectly calm.

I am truly ill. I hear words which are not really spoken. I experience scenes which are not really happening. It is one of those dreams. One of those dreadful dreams which recur more and more frequently. I hope it is a dream.

It is a dream!

Shirley and I are talking in a dream. I have spoken with Natasha in my dreams. In dreams one talks with many people.

Is it a dream?

"I noticed how different you were as soon as I arrived in Hamburg," Shirley said.

"Different—in what way?"

"You were so tense, restless, nervous, and you did not look well."

"Did Joan notice that too?"

"I don't know. She never mentioned it to me." She swallowed hard, again looking out of the window.

"Go on!"

"It's so difficult . . ."

"Go on!"

"Then . . . then this Mrs. Petrovna . . ."

"Petrovna?"

"Dr. Natasha Petrovna."

"What do you know about Dr. Natasha Petrovna?"

"Everything." She stroked my hand. "You only denied knowing her so that we would not worry, that we would not find out."

"Find out what?"

"Peter . . . Peter, I . . ."

"Tell me!"

She spoke haltingly. "After that night, when you so surreptitiously waved to each other, the doctor and you . . . after that night I began to ask a few questions around the hotel . . . the maid . . . the doorman . . ."

You too? You too, then?

"You know how people are. A tip here, a tip there . . . then I'd found the busboy who had brought you the whisky, and who had put you back in bed—"

"Which morning are you talking about?"

"You know . . . it must have been dreadful . . ."

"What do you mean?"

"Your attack . . . the fainting spell . . . when you fell out of bed . . ."

"The busboy told you that?"

"Yes. And I asked him about the doctor who had attended you. He said it had been a Dr. Natasha Petrovna who had been substituting for the regular doctor."

"Why didn't you talk to me about this then?"

"Talk with you? You said you didn't know this woman! And still you met her secretly."

"No!"

"Yes, you did!"

"When?"

"Peter, please." She suddenly blushed. "On a Saturday afternoon near the harbor. Her little boy was there too. You rented a boat."

"You spied on me?"

"Yes."

Outside the snow was falling very thickly now.

The girl and boy were whispering. He rose, threw a few coins into the jukebox and music played again.

"Yes, I did spy on you. I also discovered the box."

"What box?"

"The green one in your car. Please! I told you I knew everything. I saw how you injected yourself . . ."

"When? Where?"

"I was in the old dilapidated barn . . . I listened outside your dressing room when Schauberg examined you. I knew everything about you. I knew the movie was your last chance and how difficult everything was for you . . . could I talk to you then? Would you have told me the truth?"

I was silent.

"You would have become very upset. Perhaps you would have had another attack . . ."

"Attack?"

"After Schauberg had operated on me he talked about you to his student . . . they thought I was still unconscious . . . I was only half awake then . . . Schauberg was concerned about you . . . if only you would not have another attack he said . . . Oh, God, dear God, and that is exactly what I wanted to avoid!"

"What?"

"To discuss all this before the movie is completed. It must upset you."

"No. It doesn't."

"I'm sure it does."

"No! It upset me much more to think that you were deceiving me with another man."

"Did you really believe that?"

I nodded.

"Then you can't believe that I love you."

"Lately I haven't believed it."

Now I knew that this was not a bad dream. It was reality. It was happening.

"And now you believe me again?"

"Yes, Shirley."

"You believe that I love you . . . that I could never deceive you?"

"I believe it. Go on. How did you come to this . . . how did you get here?"

"I felt so alone . . . so desperate . . . I couldn't talk to Joan . . . I didn't want to talk to Joan . . . To me she was what she always was: a stranger . . . and one day Werner asked me—"

"Werner?"

"—Hennessy, the young cutter, why was I always so sad."

"And?"

"I told him I had some problems. And he—please don't be upset!—he said that his brother was a priest . . . a very young, modern priest . . . would I perhaps like to talk to him sometime . . . At first I didn't . . . these days I was always going to churches . . . many different churches and prayed for you . . . I begged God to let you complete your film . . . but I was alone . . . and I couldn't talk to anybody . . . and when Werner, when Hennessy said that I ought to come and see his brother I came."

I glanced at the little old house hardly visible through the densely falling snow.

"I . . . I trusted Father Thomas immediately. He knew intuitively that something was troubling me. He took me for walks. We talked . . . for hours . . . he wanted to help me . . ."

"He wanted you to confess!"

"He never said that! Not once! And I never would have confessed . . . I couldn't have because of the child . . . Naturally he would have said the child had to live. That would have been the very first thing he would have said!"

She had begun to cry softly. She wiped her tears away, sipped her drink—intense love gripped me.

"If you could not confess—why then did you keep coming back here to him?"

"I ... I always felt better after talking to him ... at least for a while ... and calmer ... he speaks fluent English, you know. And I liked the things he said."

"Such as?"

"For instance that when we are in love most of us are egotistical at first. We want our partner all to ourselves. It is the wrong kind of love if one wants only what is best for one's self."

"What is the right kind of love?"

"If one does what is best for one's partner. That's when I first had the idea."

"What idea?"

"Wait. Father Thomas once said that it was not the most important thing that one confess. One can repent without confessing and not even repentance was the most important."

"What then?"

"Making amends. And if one has done wrong it is not enough to do good which takes no effort. The good one does must be difficult to do, must be a sacrifice. The sacrifice must be in relation to the amount of forgiveness and understanding one asks of God."

"Said Father Thomas."

"Yes."

"And what else did Father Thomas say?"

"A great deal more ... much more ... and also that I could always come to him whenever I felt very desperate. I did ... a few times ..."

"I know."

"No, you know nothing. You don't know how much I love you. I did everything you asked of me. I have been silent. I have never asked. I gave up the child. Because I love you. I have never confessed. Not even after the operation . . ." She was crying again. Tears from those beloved eyes. "And you . . . you became increasingly more nervous . . . you had this rash . . . the make-up people were talking about it . . . I saw them put up prompt cards because you could not remember your lines . . . my fear grew and grew . . . do you remember the day when I asked you to give me the little golden cross?"

I nodded.

"I immersed it in holy water. And on that day at the altar in Father Thomas's church I made a vow."

"A vow?"

"Now please, be calm. Please, Peter. I didn't want to tell you until the movie was finished. But now you force me to."

"Yes, I do."

"The cross was to protect you. The greater the plea for forgiveness the greater the sacrifice has to be, Father Thomas said. And if one truly loves, one does what is best for the other."

"Yes?"

"Since I asked God to protect you and for forgiveness for both of us I had to sacrifice what meant most to me."

"What did you promise Him?" I asked but I already knew. With hatred I thought that there was no escaping the One whose existence I had always doubted.

"I vowed that I would leave you if He would help you to complete your film. I promised God that I would never again kiss you . . . never again embrace you . . . not even in my thoughts . . . I promised God never to see you again if He would protect you."

She had been stirring her chocolate milk while she had been talking softly. She did not raise her head. She looked at the brown sticky drink and cried while from the jukebox came the sound of Harry James' trumpet.

"Shirley, my sweet . . . my darling .. that's pure, utter insanity!"

"You are becoming upset. I knew you would. I was

afraid of that. Why didn't you let me have a little more time?"

"I'm calm. I'm perfectly calm. So you promised God. And now what are you going to do?"

"I'll do what Joan suggested before we came to Europe. I'll leave Los Angeles. I'll go to another city. I'll go East. Maybe New York. Television. I don't know. All I know is that I must go away, away from you—forever."

"Never!"

"I must. I swore. I cannot cheat Him a second time!"

"A second time?"

"You know what I mean. Joan will never know. Never. She will never find out."

"But I don't want to live with Joan any more! I'll leave her as soon as the movie is completed!"

"Maybe, Peter. Perhaps you'll become reconciled once I have left. No one knows what will happen—not even during the next second. Only He knows. And He has protected you. You will finish the movie, Peter, and you will regain your health. You'll make the comeback you want so very much."

"Stop it."

"It's . . . it is unfortunate that you know now . . . now I cannot stay with you any longer . . . I must leave now . . . today . . . tomorrow . . ."

She tried to stem her tears but even more came. "And yet it is best for you and for me."

"It is not! It is a philosophy of madness! Your thinking is all wrong!"

"No," she said seriously. "It's right. Do you honestly believe we could be happy together—truly happy—after all the things that have happened? After . . . after the child? With Joan who will grow old alone somewhere—or who will possibly do herself some harm? No! Never. This is the right thing to do, Peter. And I have promised." She averted her head and looked out. Across the street the small door within the larger one opened and, spectral in the snow storm, Hennessy and his brother came out.

Shirley rose.

"What is it?"

"I . . . I must go now . . . I cannot stay here with you any longer . . . I can't bear it. We have to pull ourselves together before Joan."

"Where are you going?"

"Werner will take me back to the hotel. I'll see you later." She kissed me and her tear-stained cheek met mine. "I love you. All my life I will only love you."

Quickly she reached for her coat and hurried to the door. I was pinned in by the table. Now I jumped up.

"Shirley!"

I sensed the waitress, the young couple staring at me. It did not matter.

This was no dream, no delusion, no hallucination. This was reality.

I yelled, "Wait!"

She was already outside.

I ran after her.

Snow hit my face, blinded me for a moment. Then, indistinct in the driving snow, I saw Shirley's auburn hair, her white coat, the black stockings.

"Shirley!"

I shouldn't have yelled. As if she meant to escape me she ran out onto the road. Suddenly, through the thick swirling snow, a huge bus loomed up. Brakes screeched, tires squealed, the bus went into a skid. In a second of calm I clearly saw the driver desperately grappling with the wheel. Too late.

The bus collided with an oncoming car. Frantic sounds of glass splintering, metal in friction. A tire exploded. People converged on the scene through the whirling snow as though avenging furies, the Erinyes. Horns blared, streetcar bells clanged, women screamed hysterically.

I fought my way through the crowd. My flailing arms hit other arms, umbrellas, bodies.

"Shirley! Shirley! Shirley!"

I had reached the bus.

I was still yelling. People shrank from me. The driver had left his cab. Desperately he repeated, "I couldn't help it! She ran directly into the bus! I couldn't help it!" Then I saw young Hennessy. He was kneeling next to his brother on the dirty ground. Shirley, her face looking up, was lying underneath the bus. Her eyes were open. Her beloved face had not been injured. Not a scratch, not a spatter of dirt was on it. She was lying there, her green, staring eyes looking up to the sky. Her ponytail had come undone, her auburn hair encircled her.

Then I saw her crushed body. I saw a torment of clothes, flesh, bones and blood, blood, Shirley's lifeblood flowing from the torn body, flooding the street, mixing with the dirt, the dirty snow. She must have run directly in front of the ponderous machine before the heavy double wheels had crushed her.

Her face was clear and clean, beautiful and pure. It had never been more beautiful.

Hennessy noticed me and rose, staggering. From his lips came unintelligible sounds.

I kneeled alongside the priest.

He looked at me. Then he closed Shirley's eyes. His suit was wet and dirty. He said, "She must have died instantaneously."

The Eighth Tape

1

The large room was dark except for a pale yellow spot that glowed dimly yet without giving light to the surroundings. Inside a hollow globule no larger than a fingernail burned an electric lightbulb. The globule was suspended almost above me by a wire. I was lying on a cool leather-upholstered couch. It was raining in Rome on this May seventeenth, 1960. The drops beat monotonously against the windows covered with thick drawn drapes.

"Look into the globe," said Pontevivo close by. "Directly into the globe!"

To look at the mirror I had to stretch and raise my already raised head since the globe was hanging a little behind me. To see it took a distinct physical effort.

I thought: Was this the way I was to fall into a hypnotic sleep? Tired? I was not tired. I was very much awake. I just can't be hypnotized. I knew it. The professor is out of luck—and so am I. As much as I'd like to, Professor, it won't work!

"Even though it it difficult, Mr. Jordan, you must keep your eyes open."

"It is not difficult at all."

He spoke softly, in a monotone. "Yes, it is. It is difficult for you. You would like to close your eyes and not look at the light. The globe is in an awkward place. You must strain your neck. It is unpleasant, I know. But it is necessary. You must not become sleepy. You must not close your eyes."

Those words aroused my resentment. What did he mean: I must not become sleepy? I must not close my eyes? As far as I knew hypnosis always began by the patient being told to close his eyes and go to sleep!

I felt Pontevivo's hands now. One hand applied slight pressure on the back of my neck while the other touched my forehead. The fingers began to massage my head. The feeling was pleasant.

"Relax your shoulders. Breathe deeply."

I did.

"It feels good, doesn't it?"

Yes, it does.

"It would also feel good to relax and to go to sleep, wouldn't it?" inquired the monotonous voice while gentle fingers massaged my temples.

Yes, it would have been pleasant. Slowly I began to long for that. To lie relaxed. Not to look at that mirror.

"Breathe deeply. Very deeply. Relax your shoulders. I know how difficult it is for you not to fall asleep . . . I can see it . . . your eyes are closing . . ."

They really did!

". . . but you must not fall asleep. You must not. It is necessary for you to remain awake for a little longer . . ."

The rain beating on the windows. The gentle fingers. The darkness. The voice in a monotone.

"You must not become tired . . ."

And why not? What if I did and went to sleep? Then what would he do? Naturally then he could not hypnotize me.

But this was putting me to sleep. It could certainly not be what he wanted me to do or he would not forbid it. And my indignation was aroused once more.

Who did the professor think he was?

You must not fall asleep.

Why shouldn't I?

I could hardly keep my eyes open now. I had never been this tired before.

From far off I heard him say, "Now you close your eyes. You cannot open them any more. You cannot move your arms. Your shoulders feel very heavy. But you feel well. That's right, isn't it, you feel well?"

"Yes," I replied.

I felt very well. I did not try to move or open my eyes. I exhaled deeply. I don't even remember breathing in again.

When I awakened I was alone and daylight flooded the room. It was raining heavily. I looked at my watch. It was two-thirty p.m. The first "session" had started at ten a.m. I felt as refreshed as if I had slept soundly for ten hours.

I ate lunch in my room but hurried to continue recording even before the waitress picked up my tray. I sat by the window close to the tape recorder and watched the rain falling in the park. The tapes were turning slowly. I talked and talked and talked. It grew dark. It was night. The façade of the Colosseum was brightly lit. I was still talking. I had too much to talk about. I could not wait.

I don't know what had taken place on this day between ten a.m. and two-thirty p.m. All I knew was that I had been under hypnosis. I, who had thought it impossible to be hypnotized.

I don't know what Professor Pontevivo told me, I remember nothing. When I awakened I had one very strong urge: I had to talk about Wanda.

The truth.

Once before to a woman in Hamburg on a white winter's night, I had told the true story of Wanda, of Shirley and me.

2

"May I tell you? The truth about Shirley, me and . . . and somebody else?"

"Certainly you may tell me. But you are very upset. I wouldn't want you to reproach yourself later for having told me."

"Natasha," I said, "you are the only person I can tell. And I must tell! I feel I'll go mad if I don't tell how everything happened . . ." We were walking through the snow on this night of December fifteenth. It was a Tuesday and this morning we had buried Shirley in the cemetery of Ohlsdorf.

It had been snowing steadily for the last three days. The snow had stopped now and it was calm. The city looked very clean. Benches, railings and candelabra were wearing thick hats and blankets of snow.

We were walking toward the old Lombardsbrücke. Our steps were muffled and we talked quietly.

Joan at first had wanted to bury Shirley in Los Angeles but had changed her mind. "We don't have a family plot there. Someone would have to accompany the coffin. I really don't want to leave you alone just now, I want us both to be present when she is buried. As long as she remains in our thoughts it does not matter where she is buried."

We interrupted production and all members of the production, down to the last assistant, came to the funeral. Schauberg and Käthe had come too; they kept themselves in the background.

We were standing near the open grave and snow fell on us and the many flowers and wreaths.

Father Thomas spoke. "I am the Resurrection and the

Life. Whosoever believeth in Me shall live though he be dead . . ."

Father Thomas spoke and everybody heard what I had told Joan on that dreadful Saturday afternoon: "Shirley Bromfield often came to my church. To me she was not only a believer but she was also my friend as I was, I believe, hers. She was good, honest and very sad. I don't know why. Probably all those who are honest and pure of heart are saddened by many things they witness in this world.

"To many of us it may seem an incredible wrong, mean of God, to let such a person fall victim to a blind murderous accident; that Shirley Bromfield, before her father's eyes, blinded by snow, ran in the path of a bus. Why was she, of all people, not allowed to live? Doesn't our world need people like her?

"I said that Shirley Bromfield had been sad. She never disclosed the reason. But could not her sadness have been too much for her? Is it not possible to imagine that, in time, the conflict which tormented her would have proven too much for her? Did God perhaps take her for that reason—to save her from further suffering, increased sadness, even more despair? We shall never know. But all of us who knew Shirley Bromfield know that our world is the poorer for her death. Let us pray, each according to his faith, each to his God, each alone with his thoughts. Let us pray in silence."

In the hush I heard a girl's sob and knew it came from Käthe. Joan, next to me, her hands folded, her face a mask, her lips compressed, did not cry.

While the coffin was lowered Father Thomas spoke the litany to its end.

". . . receive the soul of this young girl and take it to God Almighty . . ."

Good-by, Shirley.

". . . May Christ Who called you, receive you, Shirley Bromfield and may angels lead you into paradise . . ."

What shall I do without you, Shirley?

". . . Oh Lord, grant her eternal peace . . ."

Peace. Not eternal. Just a little peace, a little happiness. It was not granted to us, Shirley.

". . . hear our prayers for her . . ."

You will never again hear me. I am alone. There, in the depth of your grave you will become dust, dust again. What can I do with dust? Can I talk to dust, love dust, your dust, Shirley, you who died because of me?

". . . Lord, forgive any who have sinned against her . . ."

Yes, Lord, if You are, forgive me, please. No, no, I know You cannot forgive me. No one could.

". . . your mercy and love, oh Lord. Amen."

"Amen," said Joan next to me.

"Amen," said the others.

I was silent.

Someone handed me a shovel full of earth and blindly I dropped it down into the grave. The soil sent up an echo as it struck the coffin. I handed the shovel to Joan and she too went through the brief ritual. Others followed. They passed by us, speaking words of sympathy. Joan's face remained a mask.

It was cold. It grew dark. People were leaving. I was trying to assist Joan as we were leaving but she said, "I can walk alone." She did not speak until we were driving back toward the city. Then she said, "It is my fault."

"What are you saying?"

"The priest said she had been so sad. She was sad because of me."

"Joan! You got along so well! You were so happy about that!"

"Shirley pretended."

"She did what?"

"To please me she pretended that she had forgotten all I did to her when she was a child . . . that I sent her away . . . to boarding schools . . . to camps . . . away . . . I was never a mother to her, Peter, never! And you, you were never a father to her. We only always thought of ourselves."

I said nothing.

"We thought she had fallen in love here in Hamburg. Instead of that she was looking for refuge with this priest—in her sadness, her despair. When did she tell you?"

"On . . . on the day she died." I went on to lie very convincingly. "She told me to pick her up at Father Thomas's. She was going to talk to both of us that afternoon."

"What about?"

"I don't know. She only said about us," I lied. It was so easy to lie.

"About us! That means about me! How can I live with this, Peter?"

You? I thought how could I, and answered, "It is a terrible thing to say, but today is the most difficult day. Each day following will lessen our distress and thoughts of Shirley."

"She asked you to meet her, not me. She always trusted you more than me, her mother."

"Joan! Please, Joan!"

"It was perfectly natural. You were nicer to her, more sincere. Even though she hated you for so long you showed more understanding for her. You never lost your patience." Abruptly she said, "I wonder if this young cutter could tell us anything else?"

"Hennessy? No, I already spoke to him. He knows nothing. Neither does his brother, the priest."

I had spoken to Hennessy and Father Thomas and we had agreed that it would be best, especially for Joan, if no one knew anything: nothing of the attack I had made on Hennessy, nothing of the scene outside the priest's house, nothing of my behavior, of my jealousy or the talk in the ice cream parlor. Father Thomas had said, "You have to go on living. You have to come to terms with all that has happened, all I can only surmise. I shall never coerce or entreat you. But then I shall never be able to help you either."

I didn't want him to. He couldn't help me. No one could.

Joan retained her composure until we reached the hotel. Then she broke down. She went through a crying fit and then suffered a heart attack. I summoned a doctor who gave her injections.

"She will sleep until tomorrow morning," he told me.

Schauberg, upstairs in his room, gave me an injection.

"Don't think about it."

"But I do. I shall always think about it. Always."

"You must think of your movie."

"I can't."

"You are in a very poor state of health. Very poor indeed. You have another seven days of shooting to go through."

"All I can do is think of how everything happened. How it had to happen."

"Would it make you feel any better to tell me about it? I'll be glad to listen. I am—I mean, I was a doctor. Many a time I have listened to unhappy people."

"I can't tell you. Schauberg. Not you."

He looked at me searchingly and finally murmured, "But perhaps . . .

3

. . . that lady doctor?"

I told Natasha. We had crossed the Lombardsbrücke and walked past snow-covered gardens to the Schwanenwik.

"He knows of me?"

"He doesn't know your name. He saw that someone

had given me an injection. When I told him that a doctor had given it to me he guessed immediately that the doctor had been a woman. He—"

"Yes?"

"He thought that the woman doctor might love me. That is why he thought the doctor would not betray me. Consequently he was safe also."

Natasha did not reply and we walked in silence through the snow.

"How is your wife?"

"She will sleep until tomorrow morning."

"Shirley and you were lovers, weren't you?"

"Yes, Natasha," I said, "we were lovers."

She was silent and looked straight ahead.

"I was going to divorce Joan and marry Shirley. I led her astray. I was not the first man in her life but I was her first true love . . . . The way Wanda was my first true love . . ."

"Who is Wanda?"

"The truth, I was going to tell you."

"Tell me the truth, Peter."

I stood still.

"What is it?"

"You . . . for the first time you called me Peter."

"Yes, Peter," answered Natasha.

And we continued walking through the snow.

"Wanda Norden is dead," I said. "I am as guilty of her death as I'm guilty of Shirley's. It is a terrible story. Do you still want—"

"Yes," said Natasha. "I still want to hear."

"This is not the first time that I am in Germany, Natasha . . ."

"You told me that you came over here as a soldier."

"That was the second time. The first time I came in 1938."

"Why?"

"My studio sent me on trips. My career as a child star

was finished. I was not making any new films so they quickly capitalized on the old ones. I was the living advertisement. They called me 'Ambassador of Good Will': 'Ambassador of Good Business' I should have been called! I traveled all over Europe and in January, 1938, I came to Germany. I had once been very popular here . . ."

"I know."

"The Nazis at that time were still seeking international sympathies—they wanted to show their people that foreign countries too were admiring them. And so I appeared in movie theaters all over Germany. In March I came to Berlin. It was the last stop of my European trip. I could have gone home. But I stayed."

"Did you like it so well?"

"The UFA wanted me to play in a movie. They made me an offer. They didn't care that I had grown! The UFA—the Ministry of Propaganda of course—expected a German Peter Jordan film to be a prestigious success. They offered me the best contract I had ever had."

"How old were you then?"

"Almost seventeen."

"And alone in Berlin?"

"The staff my studio had sent to accompany me on my trips returned to the States. Yes, I was alone. I had a suite in the Hotel Adlon. I drove a white Bentley. I lived like the young millionaire I was at that time. I was in no hurry. Hollywood was not waiting for me. The house in Pacific Palisades still reminded me strongly of my poor dead mother. And besides—"

"And you met Wanda."

"Yes."

"She was a Berliner?"

"Yes. Nineteen years old. Almost two years older than I. She had glowing auburn hair, green eyes, a pale, delicate complexion. She looked . . . looked very much like a girl who had not yet even been born. Shirley!"

We were walking along the other side of the Alster

now. It had become colder and our shoes crunched the snow.

"I . . . I was a very shy boy in spite of my wealth, in spite of my fame—perhaps because of it. I met Wanda for the first time at a race on the Avus. I overcame my shyness and spoke to her. She left me standing there. I followed her in my car and found out that she lived in a lovely old villa in the Grunewald. I spoke to her again. She was more friendly this time. We made a date. She said that she had thought me arrogant, a show-off who thought girls would fall all over him merely because he was Peter Jordan. Strange that I gave that impression . . ."

"The impression changed?"

"Yes. We fell in love. Her parents invited me. Her father, a melancholy man, was a professor of physics. In May . . . Wanda and I became lovers. That is to say: She seduced me. She was the second woman I knew. The first one too had seduced me the year before—Constance, the wife of an unemployed Hollywood director. But with Constance it had been an infatuation. With Wanda it became love. My first true love . . .

4

It was a wonderful summer! Day after day the sun shone. We drove to the Wannsee. We lay in the bulrushes. We loved one another.

We loved each other in our boat, in the lakeside hut, in the Adlon. We were crazy about each other. Wanda was as beautiful as she was experienced and passionate. I was as passionate as I was inexperienced. But she proved to be an excellent teacher.

I had my contract. I had money. As an American I was treated with respect by everyone.

Wanda and I went everywhere together. I was as proud

of her as any young man could be of his first love. We went to the most exclusive restaurants, nightclubs and theaters.

Wanda had finished school. She had a natural talent for languages and science but did not attend the university. In her child-like voice, which contrasted strangely with her womanly appearance, she said, "I don't know what I'm going to do. I have to think about it. Papa says we might go to England where his brother lives."

Wanda's father worked at the Kaiser Wilhelm Institute. He always seemed troubled and melancholy. During the summer months I noticed during my visits to the villa that the bookshelves became empty, furniture disappeared, carpets, tapestries and woodcarvings. "We'll probably go to England after all," said Wanda. And her father said to both of us, "Why don't you stay home a little more. Don't keep going out so much."

"Why not, Papa?"

"You know why."

Wanda shrugged her shoulders. "With Peter I can go wherever I want."

I did not understand this conversation at that time. As I told you, Natasha, I was seventeen years old, a guest in Germany and I did not know what was going on. The UFA had attached a Mr. Hintze-Schön to me. He was a slight, forever embarrassed man whose job seemed to be to anticipate my wishes, to reassure me when the script was not progressing so well, to arrange press conferences and to see to it that my photo appeared frequently in the newspapers—foreign papers too. (Peter Jordan, America's Famous Child Star Enjoying Himself at Schloss Marquart. "I love it here in Germany. I don't ever want to leave!")

And it was Hintze-Schön who one day opened my eyes. "Please don't misunderstand me, Mr. Jordan, we are happy to have you here. We are not telling you what to do. How could we? But between us, as a friend, I would like to point out something to you . . ."

"Please do."

"This Fräulein Wanda Norden . . ."

"Yes?"

"She is Jewish. Didn't you know that?"

"No. What about it?"

"Nothing, nothing! I only wished to inform you, Mr. Jordan, as your friend. You can associate with whom you wish."

I mentioned this talk at Professor Norden's!

"You see, Papa!" Wanda exulted. "They don't dare. Peter is too valuable for their propaganda. And even without Peter I keep telling you: they won't dare harm us! They need you—or you wouldn't be classified any more!"

"Your father is classified?"

"He is classified as a Jew essential to an organization committed to total war," Wanda explained, quite matter-of-fact. "A lot of Jews are classified like that. Father is a physicist. In 1933 he was working on a secret project. That's why they're keeping him."

"For how much longer?" Professor Norden asked softly.

"If things become worse we'll just go to England!"

"It won't get worse," I said.

"No? You don't think so?" asked Norden and smiled sadly.

"At least not for as long as I'm here! Just judging by myself, and not even taking the importance of your work into consideration, I must say I agree with Wanda. I really am a very good advertisement for them. Besides, I don't really think that anything serious will happen again. There has been no repetition of brutalities against Jews such as those of a few years ago."

5

At the end of October the script had finally been completed.

Embarrassed as usual, Hintze-Schön explained why it had taken so long. "Speaking confidentially, as your friend: The author was racially intolerable. We didn't want to trouble you with that problem. You do like the script, don't you?"

"Very much."

"You see! The new Aryan author is really much better!"

"What happened to the other one?"

"I believe he went to Paris. We don't want to create any difficulties for anyone who does not wish to remain here."

On November first, 1938, Mrs. Norden went to visit her sister in Zurich. Since she said she would return in a few days it seemed strange to me that she kissed me good-by. She had never kissed me before.

On November ninth Wanda and I ate out. She felt tired and I took her home early. The streets were unusually crowded as I drove to my hotel that night. Trucks with shouting SA men were everywhere. I heard blatant singing too. At Kurfürstendamm I saw men breaking the show windows of a department store. I heard the clanging of fire engines. Above the city the sky was red.

The porters at the Adlon merely shrugged their shoulders when I asked them if they knew what was going on in the city. They seemed embarrassed as they looked away. A man, breathless, came running into the hotel crying, "They are smashing the windows of Jewish stores! They're setting fire to the synagogues! The Friedrichstrasse is covered with glass . . ."

Two men in the uniform of the SA who had been sitting in the foyer rose and walked toward the man. He fell silent as between them they led him out.

Hurriedly, I found a telephone booth and dialed Wanda's number. There was no answer. I ran out to my car. The sky was red in several places. I heard the sounds of shouting and bellowing song, barking of orders, whistling, the ringing of fire engines, the breaking of glass.

Just as I was getting into my car a taxi stopped and Wanda got out limping. She was still in the ocelot coat she had worn earlier. While she was paying the driver I hurried to her.

"Wanda!"

She wheeled, frightened—and then she was in my arms, clinging, sobbing so that I could not understand what she was saying. I pulled her into the shadow of a tree. Trucks full of Nazis ready for action came rolling through the Brandenburg Gate. They were noisily singing.

Anxious people on the sidewalks were staring at them.

"What happened?"

"They . . . they came . . ."

"Where is your father?"

"Professor Hahn warned him . . . he didn't even come home . . ."

More trucks. The Horst Wessel song.

"Papa called . . . he told Franz to tell me that he had to leave immediately . . . I . . . I was to try to come to you . . ." Franz was their servant.

Columns of marchers. The flares of torches.

". . . SA marschiert mit ruhig festem Schritt . . ."

"Before I had time to do anything . . . to pack a bag . . . to take out a single dress they had already arrived . . ."

". . . Kameraden, die Rotfront and Reaktion erschossen . . ."

"They broke the windows . . . they came running through the garden . . . Judenschweine . . . Judenschweine . . ."

407

". . . marschier'n im Geist in unseren Reihen mit . . ."

"Franz delayed them. I climbed out of the kitchen window . . . when I scaled the fence I broke the heel . . ." She began to cry again and said—"I'll never forget it— . . . off my prettiest shoes . . . They were made especially for me . . . by Breitsprecher . . . to go with my dress . . ." She was still wearing the black silk dress she had worn when we had been together earlier.

"Stop talking about your shoes!"

"I made my way carefully to the Bismarckplatz . . . Nazis everywhere . . . breaking into the villas . . . until I finally found a taxi . . ."

More trucks. Anti-Jewish slogans.

Some people on the street turned away.

Others raised their right arm.

I had been living at the Adlon for six months. I was well-known there. Not all the staff could be Nazis. Furthermore I was still an American, still good propaganda for the ruling clique.

"Come with me!" I grabbed Wanda's hand and pulled her along. I knew my way around the Adlon. We used the service elevator. I had kept my room key when I left the hotel. Wanda clung to my arm, walking on tiptoe to conceal the broken heel of her shoe.

6

After the war, as a G.I., I was stationed in Berlin and worked six months at the Document Center of American headquarters. Thousands of official papers pertaining to the Third Reich and its leaders were collected there. One of the secret documents gave approximate statistics of the damage caused on the night of November ninth, 1938.

Destroyed: 815 buildings, 29 burned-out department stores, 171 private dwellings, 76 synagogues.

Arrested: 20,000 Jews, 7 Aryans, 3 foreigners.

Casualties: 36 dead, 36 injured: all Jews. One of the dead and two of the injured were Polish nationals.

7

"Professor Hahn arranged for an absolutely trustworthy man to take Papa to the Swiss border . . ."

Wanda was sitting on my bed. I had drawn the heavy drapes but we could still hear the chanting and shouting from the street.

"Papa told Franz to tell me that they would not dare do anything to me if I were with you . . . for propaganda reasons . . . You are quite prominent . . ."

"That's right."

"I am to go to Lindau. We have friends there. They will take me to Switzerland."

"Then I'll take you to Lindau in the morning."

"Yes, Papa asked if you would . . ."

"Naturally I'll go with you. I'll also go to the American ambassador! I'll tell them that we are engaged!"

"Oh, Peter, I'm so terribly afraid . . ."

"You don't have to be afraid. Not at all. No one will dare to do anything. Relax, Wanda, please, calm yourself! You'll stay here with me tonight and tomorrow morning—"

The telephone rang.

Wanda screamed. "There they are!"

"Nonsense."

As I picked up the receiver I heard the soft, obsequious voice; "Hintze-Schön, Mr. Jordan. I'm terribly sorry to disturb you this late . . ."

"What is it?"

Wanda was standing close to me. She was shaking uncontrollably.

I shook my head and held my hand over the mouthpiece. I whispered, "Only somebody from the UFA."

Almost fainting, she fell onto the bed.

Meanwhile the embarrassed voice said, "I must speak with you."

"It is almost eleven."

"I know . . ."

"I was just about to go to sleep . . ."

"I'm sorry. I wouldn't have come if it had not been important."

"Come? Where are you now?"

"In the foyer. I . . . I . . . I . . ."

Well, I thought!

". . . I must speak to you! Ten minutes! It is about our film . . ."

"What's the matter with the movie?"

"There could be difficulties . . ."

"Difficulties?"

"It is possible; I said could be. Ten minutes, Mr. Jordan, please."

"All right. Wait in the American bar for me." I hung up.

"It has nothing to do with you," I said.

"Yes! Yes it has! I know it!"

"The man's name is Hintze-Schön. He works for the UFA. Something seems to be the matter with my movie. I'll be back in a few minutes."

"Stay with me here!"

"Wanda, be sensible. I don't want the man to come up here. It might look suspicious if I don't go downstairs. Darling, I know how terrible all this is for you . . . but you must pull yourself together, you must control yourself—or we'll never make it to Lindau."

That was effective.

"All right. I'm calm. I'll try. I love you," she whispered.

I kissed her and walked to the door.

"Don't answer the telephone if it should ring. If someone knocks at the door——"

She cried out softly and terror was again in her eyes.

"No," I said. "I think it's best I lock you in or you might become so upset that you'd run away from me."

"Deutschland, Deutschland, über alles, über alles in der Welt!"

8

The American bar was crowded. Germans and foreigners, among them several international correspondents I knew, were discussing the events of the night. The timid Hintze-Schön was waiting for me at a corner table. At the next table two men were drinking cognac. They were talking and laughing loudly. Hintze-Schön was pallid. A large glass was on his table.

A waiter arrived at the same time I did.

"What will you have, Mr. Jordan?"

"What are you drinking?" I asked the short, slight man.

"Whisky." He blushed as if I had caught him doing something forbidden.

"No alcohol for me. Bring me an orange juice."

"I'll have another double," said the pale Hintze-Schön. His left eye twitched nervously. He pulled at his collar.

I placed my room key on the table and moved closer. The men at the next table laughed. They paid no attention to us.

"What happened? Is the movie going to be called off?"

"Perhaps."

"What do you mean, perhaps?"

It was very noisy in the bar; no one could hear us. The atmosphere was one of agitation. The American journalists frequently entered the telephone booths. From outside the noise and yelling could still be heard.

"Mr. Jordan, I am your friend."

"I hope so."

"I really am. I'm speaking to you as your friend, confidentially. I'm saying more, much more than I should . . ."

The waiter brought the drinks. Hintze-Schön gulped his. He leaned across the table. His bad breath hit me. "She is upstairs at your suite."

"Who?"

"You know who."

"I have no idea."

"There is no time to play games. From her house she came directly to you. Don't deny it, it's useless. Somebody at the hotel here saw her and called the Gestapo. That's when they got me out of bed." Lugubriously he said, "I always have to take care of these things. If you only knew how terrible it is for me . . ."

"I don't even know what you're talking about."

"You know exactly. Wanda Norden is in your suite. Her father is on his way to the border. A physicist at the Kaiser Wilhelm Institute! Doing research is extremely important to the state! A man such as he simply cannot be allowed to leave the country!"

"Perhaps he's already there."

"Then he will return."

"You must think he's crazy!"

"I say he will return."

"Why should he?"

"To save his daughter's life."

I rose.

"Where are you going?"

"To call my ambassador."

"Wait!"

"Let go of me!"

"No! No!" He pulled me down. "How old are you? Seventeen! A child! You're going to call your ambassador? What can he do? Of course he'll protect you. But you are in no danger! Will your ambassador protect Fräulein Norden? No, dear friend, please believe me. I am your friend." He spoke quickly and in a whining tone. "Professor Norden is a man who knows secrets which are of the utmost importance to the state. He must not leave Germany . . ."

"I know what happened here tonight."

"That has nothing to do with it. As your friend I want to caution you! If you are hiding Fräulein Norden we have the right to take certain measures against you."

"That I'd like to see!"

"You will."

"If you are so sure why don't a few gentlemen of the Gestapo go up and fetch Fräulein Norden?"

He was silent.

"I'll tell you why. Because they are afraid of a scandal here in the Adlon! There are still a few foreign correspondents here!"

"It makes no difference to us."

"If it doesn't why isn't the Gestapo here?"

"Because of me."

"You?"

"That's right. I really am your friend." His breath came in a foul vapor. "Suppose proceedings are instituted against you and—if you're lucky and nothing worse happens to you—you will be exchanged for a German held prisoner in America: what will happen to you? What about your UFA film?"

"I don't care."

"I don't believe that. When one is seventeen it does matter if one can make a comeback or not. Give me the key. Take a walk. Half an hour. Don't look at me like that. Fräulein Norden will not be harmed, I swear. Why should we want to hurt her? We merely want her father to return. We need him! Good God, what else can I say?"

"Nothing, you've said enough. And now I'm going to say something."

"What?"

"Not to you. Do you see the man over there, with the pipe? He's with United Press. The man in the tuxedo next to him is the Berlin correspondent for Reuters. They are my friends. I'm going to tell them of the suggestion you just made me . . ."

His forehead was beaded with perspiration.

"Over there are a few other journalists who work for prominent American papers. And tomorrow morning they are going to take a few photographs when Fräulein Norden and are leaving for Lindau." I called, "Hey, Jack!"

Jack Collins turned around.

"I've got a good story for you!"

"Be with you in a minute, Peter!" he called.

Hintze-Schön said quietly: "All right, then I'll have to see to it that the building will be canceled."

"Building?"

"The sets at the studios."

"You're lying. Nothing is being built yet!"

"Yes, they are."

"Since when?"

"Since today."

"That's a lie! We're not scheduled to start shooting until December."

He pulled out a letter. It was an official letter, complete with seals, which stated that at the request of the Minister of Propaganda the "Peter Jordan film project was to be started at the latest on November twentieth." Named were also the director and the female lead the minister had requested.

I dropped the letter on the table. Hintze-Schön put it in his pocket.

"I told you that everything depended on you when I called you. The film is going to be called off. Too bad. That lets the UFA off too."

"What does that mean?"

"Had the film been made you and the UFA would have been involved in the matter. You could have demanded to see Fräulein Norden daily while she was in protective custody."

"Protective custody?"

"Naturally after her father had returned she would have been released right away. The family would have been completely compensated. Any loss would have been made good." He leaned back. "All right. I've tried to make you see what is involved. If I leave here without your key two men of the Gestapo will be opening your room two minutes later with a master key. Then—"

"Then what?"

"Then your girlfriend will be on your conscience!"

He is lying. I know it. They are all lying. I've seen the fires, the destroyed stores. But what can I do? What purpose will it serve if I continue to resist? They'll force their way in. Then I won't be able to help Wanda at all. This way, if I make the film, I'll stay in the picture. If they'll let me make it. But the minister wishes it. They'll have to let me make it. I'll still be good propaganda for them. And I can make demands; I can demand to see Wanda, I can help her, protect her and her father. .

What would my ambassador do? He'd take care of me but not Wanda. What about my movie? My career?

"All right, Peter. Here I am. What's cooking?" It was Jack Collins, the reporter. When he saw my face he continued, "I'm sorry, am I disturbing you?"

I was silent.

"Well, I'll see you a little later. I'll be here a while longer."

I nodded.

"Something the matter?" he said softly.

I shook my head.

"Can I help you?"

I shook my head again.

"But you wanted to tell me a story!"

"I have no story to tell."

"Peter—"

"Go away," I said. "Please, go away!"

"Are you drunk?"

I shook my head.

"Hm." He gave Hintze-Schön a searching look, shrugged his shoulders and returned to the bar.

Slowly I pushed the key to my suite across the table.

"Well, at last," said Hintze-Schön.

He took the key and handed it to one of the men at the next table who had been so jolly. Both of them got up. Hintze-Schön said, "I'll take care of the bill here."

Both men left.

Hintze-Schön turned to me. "You'll go for a walk now. In fifteen minutes you can pick up your key at the desk." He grasped my unwilling hand. "I knew you would be sensible. It is best this way, believe me. Confidentially, you've just saved the girl's life. I'll see you tomorrow morning at the studios in Babelsberg. And please, don't forget. I am your friend."

I left the bar, crossed the foyer and went out into the street. The sky was still red in many places but the chanting had stopped and there were no more trucks with storm-troopers going by. I passed through the Brandenburg Gate and went into the park. The Tiergarten was dark and deserted. I tried not to think but my thoughts returned to what had taken place.

I was a despicable, weak, selfish bastard.

An hour later I returned to the Adlon. The desk clerk avoided my eyes when he handed me my key. All the lights were burning in my suite. Everything in its place. If there had been a fight it was not obvious now. Wanda's perfume still lingered in the air. Then I found the black silken shoe with its broken heel. I rang for room service and ordered whisky. "Bring me a bottle of Scotch."

Up to now I had never drunk whisky, only beer, sometimes wine and had not cared much for either.

I sat in the drawing room, soda and ice before me and drank. I emptied half a bottle. The glass was in one hand and the silken shoe from Breitsprecher, its heel missing, in the other. At first the aroma of the whisky nauseated me but then I became drunk and thought that it didn't really taste that bad. Hintze-Schön had probably been correct when he said that I was just seventeen and had no idea of anything as yet.

Then I became sick.

After I returned from the bathroom I continued to drink and finally fell asleep on the couch. When I awoke it was day. My head ached and I felt sick. I saw the black shoe lying on the floor.

I grabbed the bottle and began to drink and again I became sick.

I went to bed and stayed there. I was too weak to get up. At midday two men of the Gestapo arrived. They told me that I was to leave Germany within twenty-four hours and showed me orders and letters to that effect. I protested. I demanded to speak to my ambassador. They permitted me to telephone.

The ambassador was already informed. He was very cool. In view of the tense political situation I had behaved in a very imprudent manner, he said, and that he was unable to do anything for me. It had been inexcusable for me to interfere in a purely German affair and to resist the arrest of this Fräulein Norden.

"But I didn't resist it! On the contrary, I—"

"Mr. Jordan, I have here on my desk the sworn statements of two Gestapo officials and a certain Mr. Hintze-Schön. According to them you secretly hid Fräulein Norden in your suite and resisted her arrest leaving the officials no other choice but to use force."

"That's not true! That's a lie!"

"Do you have any witnesses?"

"Yes, Mr. Hintze-Schön! He would not dare—"

"According to the UFA Mr. Hintze-Schön has left on an extended trip. Mr. Jordan, in your own interest and to avoid further incidents I urge you to comply with the request of the Reichs government and to leave Germany. Good day."

I called the UFA studios. Herr Hintze-Schön had left on a trip. No, he didn't leave any message for me. No, his superiors had no instructions. They regretted what had happened.

How did they know what had taken place?

"It's in the newspapers."

It was indeed. One of the two Gestapo men, who had been with me while I was telephoning, showed me the newspaper.

American Ex-Child Star Misuses German Hospitality. Revealed to Be Agent of World Jewry.

I packed my bags.

At eight-thirty that evening I left for Paris. The two Gestapo men, who had not left me for a second all day, accompanied me . . .

9

. . . as far as the French border. They were very polite," I told Natasha. It was snowing steadily. We had once more crossed the Alte Lombardsbrücke and were walking alongside the Aussenalster. Church clocks chimed.

It was one o'clock in the morning.

Natasha suddenly gripped my hand. "Did you ever hear of Wanda or her father again?"

"Yes. Two years later in 1940. At that time many emigrants arrived in Hollywood: writers, actors, directors. One of them had been a friend of the Nordens. He did not know that I had known them. Unsuspecting, he told what had happened. The father did return from Switzerland in an effort to save his daughter. Wanda's mother had just died of a heart attack in Zurich. Wanda and her father were sent to a concentration camp. The Nazis did not need Professor Norden any more. They had merely wanted to prevent him from making his scientific knowledge available to an enemy foreign nation. The secret project he had been engaged on had been completed without him."

"Concentration camp," said Natasha. She let go of my hand.

"The actor who told me this in Hollywood also knew that Wanda and her father had died within a short time of each other in the spring of 1940." I stopped underneath a streetlamp and pulled out my pocketflask. "Excuse me."

Natasha pushed at her glasses and said nothing.

I raised the flask and took a long drink.

Then we walked on.

"I knew what I had done in Berlin. But no one else did. No one reproached me. Only when I thought about it . . ."

"You drank."

"Yes. When I was drunk I didn't think about it. Or dream about it. I drank heavily. And I rarely thought of . . . of . . . Besides, it is said that all things are forgotten in the end. I was hoping I would forget too.

"I became a G.I. in 1943. In 1944 I was in the invasion; 1945 I came to Berlin for the second time. The Adlon was a ruin, the villa in Grunewald had disappeared, the UFA did not exist any more, nothing but ruins . . . misery . . . hunger. Seeing Berlin this way assuaged my pain. It made me feel—how can I explain it—it made me feel that I, as a soldier, had made amends to some small degree for the dreadful deed I had committed there in 1938 . . .

10

"I returned to the United States in 1946.

"Then, in 1947 I met Joan. Her daughter was seven years old—a little redhead who grieved for her dead father and who hated me.

"When I married Joan, Shirley was nine years old. Her hatred of me diminished during the next few years and when she was thirteen she declared, 'Paddy sounds so childish.' From then on she called me Peter—for six years until her death.

"A lot happened during those six years. The plump child became a graceful young girl and then a beautiful woman. At first her voice irritated me because it reminded me of something. I could not readily remember. The voice remained child-like and high-pitched even when Shirley became seventeen.

"At first it was the voice.

"I had almost succeeded in forgetting the girl in Berlin. Now if I closed my eyes when Shirley spoke I heard Wanda. I was reminded of my offense and guilt.

"At first Shirley had hated me. Now I hated her. My wife was very unhappy because of it. Shirley and I argued, fought, insulted and avoided one another.

"I played golf, went into town, frequented bars, I drank. I came home drunk. Hollywood had written me off.

"Shirley's voice was only the beginning. With each new day she resembled Wanda more.

"Perhaps you are smiling now, Professor.

"Perhaps you think that my guilt made me imagine things different than they actually were.

"No!

"I have photographs of Wanda and Shirley. Wanda's

are in a safe in my house in Pacific Palisades. I have instructed my lawyer to open the safe and send me the photographs. When I show them to you you will agree with what I have told you, Professor!

"Shirley was beautiful now: a young goddess. I saw Wanda's clear, golden complexion, Wanda's narrow nose, Wanda's generous mouth, Wanda's green eyes underneath the dark brows so rare with redheads.

"Can you imagine how I felt?

"A beautiful young woman, who many years ago had died because of me, suddenly had come to life, living in the same house with me.

"Shirley's manner of walking, talking, eating, laughing—it reminded me of Wanda. She didn't merely resemble Wanda when she was seventeen: she was Wanda, risen from the dead to torment me, to persecute me.

"I already told you that I drank steadily during those years. You explained to me, Professor, that alcohol destroys clear thinking. How it can change unpleasant memory engrams into pleasant ones. This is also what happened with Shirley.

"I had always thought: each debt will take its toll, one cannot ever escape responsibility or punishment. Now, more and more often as I lay drunk on my bed thinking of Shirley and Wanda, Los Angeles and Berlin, I thought that perhaps it was not quite that way. Perhaps I could make some amends. Perhaps I could atone for what I had done to Wanda by being good to this rejected, resented, deprived child who hated me and whom I hated. A child who had never known a real home, had grown up among strange people in boarding schools and camps.

"I tried to be friendly to Shirley. I gave her little presents, spent time with her. I asked her opinions. I gave her books. I heard about her problems. I treated her as a friend and as an adult.

"The effect?

"Never before had a friend of Joan's paid any attention to Shirley. She had grown up, alone with her thoughts and troubles. Now suddenly there was a man who seemed interested in her and her problems. Was it surprising that Shirley fell in love with this new companion?

"She was well on her way to becoming a beatnik. She had already slept with boys, had spent many a night away from home. Now all this changed.

"She returned my friendliness with gratitude and devotion. She was very beautiful when she became eighteen. There was hardly a man who was not attracted to her, and I am a man too; I am only a man too.

"What happened now happened imperceptibly. When I noticed it, it was already too late. Imperceptibly the transition from the usual to the unusual, from the permitted to the prohibited took place. Imperceptibly the casual nightly 'Good night, Peter' kiss changed into a different kind of kiss. Slowly, slowly a handshake became more than just that, an embrace more than casual, a glance not a glance but a challenge, a provocation, a declaration and acceptance of love.

"One could not escape one's destiny.

"I believed that. Fate had sent Shirley into my life, had made her the image of Wanda so I could make good my sin. It was meant to be; I had to love Shirley, make her happy. Was it the alcohol which made me believe that? Was it my excuse to myself for all that had happened? Was it the easiest way out?

"What do you think, Professor?

"We now had our little secrets. We were already deceiving Joan. Furtively we met in small restaurants along the coast, wrote letters to each other and destroyed them after reading them, had secret signs, our songs, our words, our love.

"More and more frequently we met. More and more often my Cadillac was parked on lovers' lanes. More and more passionate became our kisses, our caresses. We both

422

knew how it would end. We did not care. We were wildly in love, beside ourselves with passion.

"Shirley—I mentioned it before—held only animosity for her mother. Perhaps she now felt that what was happening was a retribution for Joan's neglect of her as a child.

"What about me?

"I have no excuse. I felt no pangs of conscience. I only thought of her, her mouth, her eyes, her hands, her body, the body that was Wanda's. I wanted Shirley. And she wanted me.

"My marriage was falling apart. Joan still blamed Shirley for that: 'She hates you. She doesn't like you. That's why you are so irritable, because you can't stand to hear me fight with her. That's why you moved into the bungalow. That's why I now have to sleep alone. Oh, how I hate Shirley!'

"I had moved into the bungalow on the hill near the main house in the beginning of 1958.

"And this is where it happened for the first time. We had gone to the theater. Joan was in New York for a few days. When we came home the main house was lying in darkness, the servants asleep. We did not speak. Hand in hand we ran up the steep path to the bungalow. We were breathless. Shirley's ankle gave way and she cried softly.

" 'What is it?'

" 'My foot . . .'

"I picked her up. I carried her inside. Moonlight filled the living room. Down below, beyond the garden, the Pacific glistened. I gently placed Shirley on the oversized couch in front of the fireplace. She wore a black décolleté dress and black high-heeled shoes. We spoke breathlessly. Our hands moving swiftly, we pulled off her dress, her lingerie, my shirt. Passionately we embraced one another and I heard Shirley's moan.

" 'Come . . .'

" 'Yes, Wanda, yes . . .'

"I know that I called her Wanda. She did not hear me. I don't think she heard anything any more for what we did transported us to ecstasy again and again. Only tormenting passion had meaning then. There was nothing but the exquisite present.

"Hours passed. It was dawning. The Pacific was lead-gray, the air humid. Shirley dressed hurriedly to reach the main house before the servants were up.

"As she put on her shoes she discovered that the heel of one had broken off.

" 'It must have happened last night when I stumbled: Such expensive shoes. Custom made: What did you say?'

" 'Nothing.'

"As I kissed her I thought: I will make amends. I'll make up through Shirley . . .

11

". . . for what I did to Wanda," I said softly. Then I looked at Natasha. "Now you know the truth."

It was snowing more heavily now. We had walked around the Aussenalster for the third time. It was almost two a.m.

We went toward my hotel, underneath the old trees along the promenade with its bright, snow-capped candelabra.

"Can you . . . can you . . ." I could not say the words.

"Yes," she said.

"Yes, what?"

"Yes, I can understand you, Peter. I can understand it."

"Really?"

"Really!"

"I did want to make Shirley happy."

"I know what you wanted."

424

"Happy. I wanted to make her happy."

"That's impossible to do."

"It is?"

"Or very rarely. Not many people succeed."

"But there are many happy people!"

"How long does their happiness last?"

"I know some people who are always happy."

"Then they are happy from within. But for how long can one person make another happy?"

"Not for long?"

She shook her head.

"No, not for very long." And quietly she said, "Just think, Peter, if only it were possible—a happy world—a world of truly happy people . . ." We had reached the hotel. "You must go and sleep now. You have another day of shooting ahead of you."

"I'll see you home."

We walked to the next street corner. The street was deserted.

"How is Misha?"

"I took him to another specialist."

"And?"

"Don't ask. Please."

So the specialist told Natasha what Schauberg had already told me: that the sounds the little boy produced were no reason to hope, that there would not be a change in Misha's condition.

We had reached the door.

"Good night, Peter."

"I very much wish I could help you," I said.

"You—help me, now?"

I nodded.

"No one can help anyone. You know what they say: Everybody has to fight his own battles."

"Natasha," I whispered (why was I whispering?), "when I saw you in your apartment that last time you said to me: 'Leave now. Quickly, and don't ever come back here.' "

She did not reply and looked away.

"May I come again?

"May I?" I was more urgent now.

She was still silent as she stepped inside the opened door.

"Please," I said. "Please Natasha. Not often. Only sometimes. I'll call you. You say yes. Or no. But don't say no now. Leave me that one hope that I can see you again, talk with you again . . . go for a walk . . . talk . . . may I hope for that?"

She nodded quickly and a moment later the door closed behind her. I walked back to the hotel.

Joan was asleep when I looked in. She was still sleeping when I got up the next morning. Schauberg, who was giving me my injections in the drawing room, told me: "Your condition is not at all good, dear Mr. Jordan. I'll have to try to wash your blood."

"What's that?"

"Nothing dangerous. It will make you feel good and help you through those last few days."

It was a routine studio day. Everybody was friendly and considerate. It hadn't stopped snowing. At night, on my way back to Hamburg, my car was stuck in a drift from which strangers helped drag it. When I entered my suite Joan, in her bedroom, was packing her suitcases. She wore no make-up and seemed old, her face gray. Her excessively blonde hair was dishevelled. She did not return my greeting.

"What's going on? What are you doing?"

She continued carrying dresses to the suitcases and did not look at me.

"Joan, I asked you, what are you doing!"

Without looking at me she replied, "I'm going home."

"Home?"

"Tonight. At midnight."

426

"But why? What happened?"

Now she stopped, very close to me, and she stared. In her usually gentle brown eyes I saw hate, terrible, dreadful, burning hate.

"You want to know what happened? Really? Do you really want to know?"

12

Rome, May twenty-sixth, 1960.

Today I was hypnotized for the third time.

Now I fall asleep after only a few minutes. The glowing little globe is not necessary any more. It is sufficient when Professor Pontevivo speaks to me and massages my neck and forehead. After today's session we talked. I told him how remarkably successful he had been in overcoming my initially negative attitude by saying, "It is very important that you keep your eyes open."

"I wanted to keep them open, Professor! I wanted to keep them open to—"

"—to annoy me."

"Yes. To prove to you that I could not be hypnotized. But you said it was important that I keep them open. Your order confused me. I did not know what I could do to annoy you . . . and you succeeded."

"One can always succeed, Mr. Jordan. The exceptions are the insane. Insane persons cannot concentrate. The ability to concentrate is the only prerequisite for hypnosis. One reason why the patient must always be sober at a session. Most people doubt the success of treatment by hypnosis. Knowingly or subconsciously they also intend to resist the treatment, to show how strong-willed they are. As you have experienced, all that is taken into consideration. Your negative attitude helped me; it showed that you did not exclude the possibility of success. Else you would not even have assumed a negative attitude! It is most difficult with people who are indifferent."

"How long does each session last? What I mean is: For how long do you talk to me? I always seem to sleep for hours afterward."

"It varies, Mr. Jordan. I have to be very careful to prevent your dependence on me. I want you to be healthy. A healthy human being is not dependent on anyone or anything. Since you have told me about Wanda it has become much easier for me. I know your guilt complex."

"What will you do now?"

"I shall try to remove it. And what else?"

"I don't know."

"I shall try to give you another complex."

"Another complex?"

"Certainly, Mr. Jordan." The slight, rosy-cheeked, white-haired man said breezily, "You are actually missing one."

"What kind of complex?"

"You will see in time," answered the professor.

13

"You want to know, what happened?" asked Joan. "Really? Do you really want to know?"

"What kind of nonsense is this? Of course, I want to know!"

"Sit down."

Joan was suddenly a stranger to me. A woman I had never known, whose voice I had never heard. A woman who looked at me as if I were a murderer.

"This morning I was asked to come to the hotel office," said the woman to whom I had been married for ten years. "They were very polite. They told me that they had waited for days now but since we had not returned the key they assumed that we did not know."

"Know what?"

"Know about the safe."

"What safe?"

"Shirley had rented a deposit box in the hotel safe. The gentlemen wanted the key returned. I looked for the key among Shirley's possessions. It took a long time because she had hidden the key in the lining of a handbag. Yes?"

"I didn't say anything."

"When we opened the box I, Shirley's mother, was asked to take its contents. Do you know what the box contained?"

"No."

She placed on a small table the valuable ring she had given to Shirley on the eve of their arrival in Hamburg.

"Your ring . . ."

"Yes. It is my ring again. Do you know what else was in the box?"

"What else?"

"A package of letters. About fifty. They were all addressed to Shirley. They had all been written by the same man."

I was silent.

Joan's mouth twisted with contempt. She reached into the pocket of her robe and pulled out a letter. Her voice was without expression as she read, "Dearest Heart, I know exactly how you must feel when you read this letter. Let me say right now, before anything else: I love you. I have never loved anyone as much as I love you . . ."

It was the letter I had sent to Los Angeles on the day of my first attack. I had instructed her to destroy the letter but she had saved it. She had not destroyed any of my letters. Many times I had asked her, "Did you destroy my letter?" "Yes," she answered. "I burned it." "Do you burn all of them?" "Yes. All of them." "Right away?" "Right away." "Always?" "Always."

Obviously she had lied.

"Shirley, my All, you must now be brave and sensible," Joan read, her voice frigid and expressionless. "It is impossible for you to have this child . . ."

She continued to read. It was a certainty that she also knew the contents of the other letters. I had always destroyed Shirley's letters. But women apparently find it difficult to part with love letters. They rent safes and hide those letters as if they were treasures and do not consider that they might die, any day, any hour, senselessly and horribly, as, for instance, under the wheels of a bus.

". . . We shall have a child, Shirley—but not this one. I am also writing to Gregory Bates. You know him . . ."

One could not escape fate. Shirley was dead. I had thought that Joan would never find out the truth. Perhaps I would have left her. Perhaps not. Now, since Shirley was dead, that did not really matter. Perhaps we would have continued living together as we had until now. I had been certain that Joan would never have found out about Shirley and our love for each other.

". . . Shirley, dearest Heart, you know I'm making this movie here in Hamburg for both of us . . ."

Joan was still reading. I wanted her to stop but I lacked the strength to tell her to stop. Shirley, dead Shirley, had returned through my letters.

I remembered the words the priest had spoken at the grave. "I am the Resurrection and the Life . . . Whosoever believeth in Me shall live though he be dead . . ."

Shirley had believed in Him. She was alive, risen from the dead, and present here in this room.

". . . in my thoughts I am always with you—united with you on the beach, on our boat, in the bungalow and the dunes, everywhere where we were happy together. Soon we will be again. Forever. Peter." Joan dropped the letter. Her eyes burning with hate. "P.S.," she said without looking at the letter, "As always, destroy this letter at once."

I remained silent and withstood her look.

"She didn't destroy it," said Joan. "And she saved all the other letters too. I have read them all."

"Naturally," I said.

"I have already sent all the rest to my lawyer."

"Naturally," I said.

"I talked to him. I have instructed him to start divorce proceedings."

"Naturally," I said.

"I have retracted the declaration which gave you half of all I own. As soon as I am in the States I shall make a formal complaint against you. My lawyer quoted me the paragraph applicable to you from the penal code of California. It says . . ."

"I know what it says."

"Then you admit it."

"I admit everything."

"Shirley was expecting your child?"

"Yes." To anticipate her next logical question (strange that just then I should think to protect Schauberg and his student) I said quickly, "I would have spoken to you as soon as the film was finished."

"What would you have told me then?"

"That I wanted a divorce since I did not love you any more."

"Nothing else?"

"Nothing else."

"No," she said, "nothing else, of course. Too bad Shirley kept your letters."

"It is dreadful that she died."

"That's too bad for you." She put the letter back into the pocket of her robe and began to pack again. "It's better for me this way. It makes everything I intend to do much easier. Do you know what I am going to do?"

"Everything possible to hurt me."

"Everything to destroy you."

"I know."

"I was not aware of anything until today. I never had one moment of doubt, not one moment when I distrusted you. My God! The wrong I have done to Shirley—all her life! I thought she was destroying our marriage. I was going to send her away ... my child ... and all the time it was you ... you ... you seduced her—didn't you—or are you going to deny that?"

"No," I said, "I'm not denying anything. I seduced her."

"I swear to you: I'm going to avenge Shirley!"·

I thought: You, of all people, you want to avenge Shirley? You, who always hated her, sent her away, never loved her? No, you don't want to avenge Shirley, you want to revenge yourself! Which, after all, is your right and perfectly understandable.

"No woman could forgive what you have done. I cannot forgive you. Please go now."

I rose.

"I don't ever want to see you again. If you come back here tonight, if you should come to the airport, if you should try to prevent me from leaving tonight, I'll create the biggest scandal Hamburg has ever known."

"All right, Joan," I said. "All right. Good-by."

She held a cocktail dress in her hands and her back was turned to me. She did not turn around again. She spoke into the bathroom. "For as long as I live: You can be sure of my hate and disgust for you."

I looked at her once more, the slim woman in the elegant robe, the woman with the exaggerated hair, the sloping shoulders which now began to twitch convulsively. This woman, her back turned to me, had begun to cry, sobbing intensely. I left the bedroom and closed the door. I never saw Joan again.

14

Schauberg called it "washing blood." He did it for the first time on the evening of December seventeenth.

Now there was only one bedroom adjoining the drawing room. Joan's bedroom had been locked; a cupboard hid the door.

I was lying on my bed. Schauberg was working in shirtsleeves. He had brought a dialyzing unit, an apparatus to which I was to be connected by means of tubes.

"Where did you get that?" I asked.

"In a shop which sells medical equipment."

"Anybody can buy that?"

"Anybody. Strange, isn't it? You could go into such a store and they would sell it to you. Everybody wants to make money."

"But isn't what you are doing here unlawful? It's charlatanism!"

"Dear Mr. Jordan, if everybody were to apply such rigid ethical standards half the equipment used in modern medicine could not be sold."

He bound my arm and the very large needle he inserted hurt for only a moment.

"What's this equipment supposed to do?"

"It is going to wash your blood, filter out the impurities. It won't take long. A drink and a couple of sleeping pills afterward and you'll be good as new by tomorrow!"

"If you only knew how indifferent that leaves me."

"Then why did you ask for this treatment? If you don't care why don't you just simply give up?"

"I'm thinking of Kostasch. If the movie is not completed he will be ruined."

"Listen to an old, wicked man. Take my advice," said

Schauberg. "Don't do it for Kostasch. Do it for yourself. Think of your future."

"Schauberg! Shirley is dead. Whether or not I'll ever get another film offer is really a matter of complete indifference to me."

"Good grief, I'm not talking about your future as an artist. Just think: a little while ago you told me what had taken place between you and your wife. Today she is already in Los Angeles. Tomorrow she will see her lawyer. On the other hand it is also possible that she does not see her lawyer. Women are peculiar. Perhaps she'll forgive you."

"Never!"

"That's exactly what I'm keeping in mind! Most women have simply unbelievably primitive ideas when their daughters are seduced by their stepfathers. Now then! Do you know what the lady will do in her distress?"

"She'll drag me into court."

"That is the one thing she will never do!"

"What do you mean?"

"But, dear friend, that would simply be the most phenomenal advertising you could ever wish for! No, no, you can't hope for that. She will never do that!"

"I don't understand . . ."

"Well now, look! Suppose the proceedings against you begin after Christmas. Or later. About that time your film will be released. The newspapers will not fail to create a sensation. Peter Jordan's affair with stepdaughter. Stepdaughter expecting his child. Stepdaughter dies. Wife discovers truth. Jordan, the monster! Jordan, the teenage violator! and *Come Back* is being shown all over the country. Wouldn't that be marvelous? People will be pouring into the cinemas if only to take a look at that monster Jordan! No, no, that would be too good to be true. We don't dare hope that she will make that complaint. Her lawyer will make her understand that right away. She said she wanted to destroy you, didn't she?"

434

"That's right."

"There you are! Not to make you a success, a million-aire."

"I could be sentenced to jail."

"That would depend to a great extent on your lawyer! You might also be acquitted! According to that paragraph you quoted—and I'm sure you quoted it correctly—it is one of those elastic paragraphs which can be interpreted in different ways. What does it mean: guardianship? Did you adopt Shirley?"

"No."

"Bravo. Fortunately your subconscious must have been at work there. Was she always in the house?"

"No. She was very often in boarding schools or camps."

"Then how can the law talk about entrusted care and education!"

"But my wife hates me."

"Of course. And she will do everything possible to destroy you. She could do that easily. Suppose a court de-cided that you have to repay the hundred fifty thousand dollars—and you have not completed the movie."

That had not occurred to me.

"It should be easy for your wife to manage that. And then what? They'll have caught you with your pants down. No, you must think of yourself, not of Mr. Kostasch!" He looked at his watch. "Another few minutes and your treatment will be finished."

I hoped that the treatment would give me new strength which would help me through the next five days; another four days of shooting.

"The film is all you have right now, dear Mr. Jordan. You cannot fall back on your wife's wealth. You must re-gain your health. Your movie must be a success—"

"What if it isn't?"

"It will be—touch wood—a success. Too many wicked people have worked on that film, with too much deceit and trickery. Take just us two! No, no, projects which

435

result from any such devious methods always succeed. What's the matter? Why are you crying?"

"I don't want to cry . . ." I was lying. I did want to cry. I had to cry. I had caught a glimpse of my future. Without Shirley.

"I understand. You're thinking of Shirley. You'll forget her."

"Never."

"Yes, yes, you will. Another two minutes. There will be another woman."

"No."

"There is always another woman, another love if one has lost a woman, a love."

My tears were dripping onto the pillow and I spoke haltingly.

"I don't want another love. I don't want another woman. I'll never be able to forget Shirley!"

"You'll be going to a clinic for the next six months. You'll take sleep cures, two or three or four. You have no idea what you will be able to forget then!"

"No. No."

"Yes. You will see," he said. "You will forget whatever tortures you—doctors will see to that. To regain your health you must be able to forget. They will probably ask you to write about your life, or someone you trust will listen to you. In half a year things will look different to you."

"Maybe for a while."

"Naturally, for a while. Then you'll have a relapse and start boozing again. So? What are clinics for? You'll enter another one. You have the strength. You can control your addiction. You can—"

"Schauberg, you've already told me all that."

"Two minutes are up." Expertly and quickly he disconnected me from the unit. "We'll do this every day from now on. And stop feeling so sorry for yourself. Will you promise me that as one scoundrel to another?"

I nodded.

"Besides, you're not alone."

"That's very nice of you but—"

"I'm not talking about myself."

"Whom then?"

"You know who."

"I cannot draw this woman any closer into my life!"

"Why not?"

"I don't want to destroy her life too. She is so decent, so wonderful, she is—"

"There it is," said Schauberg. "You are already head over heels in love again." He gave me two sleeping pills and cleared away the equipment. "Where is the whisky?"

"The bag is in the cupboard."

He fixed two large drinks. I emptied my glass quickly and he refilled it. "You can have more to drink when I've left. But tell them at the studio to advance your close-ups."

"I've already taken care of that." The rash had climbed above my shirt collar and was visible on the right side of my neck. Aureomycin did not help any more. The pustules on my body had begun to bleed. My pajamas looked awful. Schauberg sat on my bed like an old friend, smiling with feigned confidence.

I said, "When I was a little boy my mother and I often went hungry. All I wanted then was an enormous steak. I dreamed about it." He smiled and poured two more drinks. "Then I became famous, we had money and I could eat whatever I wanted. Then I wished for only one thing: That my mother not have cancer."

"And, of course, it was cancer," he said and nodded. "I told you, that's life. Nothing lasts forever. Not the worst and not the best. Small wishes come true, big ones don't and everything is forgotten in time. You've forgotten your pain at the death of your mother, haven't you?"

"Yes. It does not hurt any more."

"You see," said Schauberg. "And there will always be

more pain, and it will also cease to hurt. And sometimes there will be joy, and joy is just as fleeting, and soon joy will not please. You forget the steak, you forget the cancer, that is life."

"I've had everything, Schauberg. Wealth and debts. Fame and oblivion. Even love."

"Then what else do you want?"

"I've never made another person happy. Somebody said to me: 'If each of us could make only one other person happy everybody would be happy.' "

"I could have said that," said the man with the beret, grinning.

"Schauberg . . ."

I was becoming tired and more and more giddy but I felt well.

"Yes?"

"Once . . . when I was a child . . . I said some terrible things to my grandmother . . . my mother's mother . . ."

"Why?"

"Because I was mad at her, because she had forbidden me to play on the street. I called her an old witch. You ugly old witch, I said to her, I wish you would die!"

"What a naughty, naughty little boy you were. Have another drink."

"My mother came and my grandmother demanded that she beat me. My mother did but without hurting me. After all, I was her spoiled little darling. Then she locked me into a room. I listened and looked through the keyhole. I saw how my mother, in tears, apologized to her mother. In spite of the punishment I had stubbornly refused to apologize. 'Daughter,' said my grandmother, 'this child has no heart.' And my mother, still crying, answered, 'And yet he is so beautiful'."

"You see," said Schauberg, "your mother was a clever woman!"

"Clever, why?"

"Well, you could also have been an ugly child without a heart."

15

Now it was snowing every day.

In Dortmund a gas explosion killed twenty-six people. There was a revolution against the dictator Stroessner in Paraguay. Belgian paratroops were fighting in Ruanda-Urundi. Bombs were planted in the South Tyrol. A German Air Force plane disappeared over Czechoslovakia. In one week in the Congo one hundred seventy whites and one hundred fifty-three Negroes were killed. Nothing important was happening in the world just now, Schauberg said. "Before Christmas everything calms down."

Christmas!

The show windows were brightly lit and festively decorated. Many streets were hung with glistening garlands of lights. The shops were overcrowded. On Saturday, December nineteenth, we, Natasha, Misha and I, went to the Hamburger Dom, the traditional Christmas market on the Heiliggeistfeld near the Reeperbahn.

The Dom has very little in common with the Christmas markets of other cities. It is rather more of a popular amusement in the manner of the Munich October celebration. Stalls line the streets. Everything to do with Christmas can be had there but also pancakes, barbecued chicken and beer. Rifle ranges, carousels, ghost rides and roller coasters. We walked through the long streets with their barkers, colorful placards, lights, Christmas stars. We bought a few small items and Misha, his eyes enormous, admired the Christ child in its crèche, the Holy Family made of plaster, the Christmas angels in innumerable quantities. We stood and ate pancakes from a stall and drank beer. Misha drank lemonade. When we walked the little boy took Natasha's hand and mine. He laughed soundlessly and when we swung him to and fro, raising him into the air, his little face would blush with excitement and he would make a few happy sounds. This did not excite Natasha any more. She knew now that it was of no significance. Misha would always make only those sounds.

I had told her about the developments between my wife and me. She had answered, "It must have been terrible."

"Yes, it was."

"I don't mean for you. For your wife."

Misha wanted to ride the roller coaster but I could not share this kind of amusement because I was afraid and because it always made me feel sick. While Misha and Natasha took the ride together I drank whisky from my pocketflask. At a shooting gallery I won a bear which I gave to Misha. While he was throwing balls at cans Natasha asked, "When will your movie be finished?"

"Tuesday."

"Then you will have to go to a clinic right away."

"Yes."

"Have you decided on one?"

"No."

"I know an excellent doctor who specializes in cases such as yours. But he is in Rome."

"That does not make any difference to me. What is his name?"

"Pontevivo."

"How do you know of him?"

"I sent Bruno to him."

"Who is Bruno?" It was a stupid question but my brain was functioning much slower lately. Frequently I could not find specific words. Then I would just say, "This what d'you call it?"

"Bruno Kerst," said Natasha. "Misha's father. He was in Pontevivo's clinic."

"He died there?"

She nodded.

Misha was still aiming for the cans. He had won a colorful fan. I paid for a few more games. Misha laughed happily.

"He went there too late. His heart was too weak to stand the d.t.'s. I flew to Rome to see Bruno once more. That is when I met Pontevivo. He is an excellent doctor. You would be in good hands."

"Perhaps my heart will give out too."

"Perhaps. Perhaps not. Shall I write to Professor Pontevivo?"

"Please, do."

"I'll send it off tonight. Would you go before Christmas?"

"As soon as the last scene is shot. Why are you smiling?"

"I just remembered something beautiful. Did you ever fly across the Alps?"

"No."

Street organs played and teenage idols screeched songs through loudspeakers. Blaring noise and busy crowds, which Misha happily ignored while throwing balls at the cans. He won an armful of worthless trinkets, to him a treasure. This was the world of a child.

"It was breathtaking, Peter. The sun shone on mountain peaks and enormous gorges. The sky was dark blue. The most magnificent scenery I ever saw. A blanket of snow, shimmering in rainbow colors. I sat at a window and—" she stopped.

"And drank whisky?"

Natasha smiled. "Cognac. As I looked down upon those unbelievably beautiful mountains I suddenly hoped for a miracle . . . that Bruno might recover . . . and that both of us might fly back together . . . above these thrusting peaks. He did not fly back with me and I took the train. But sometimes I relive that flight and . . ."

"And Bruno sits beside you."

"I cannot see his face as clearly as I could for the first two years. All I know is that a man sits beside me. And I love him."

"But you cannot see his face."

"No."

I was often dreaming of Shirley and I saw her face very clearly. But Shirley had died only a short time ago and Bruno Kerst had been dead four years. Would I still see Shirley's face in my dreams in four years?

"One of my most treasured memories is that flight above the Alps. It stirs one's spirit, it is so beautiful. I cannot describe it adequately. You must experience it yourself, Peter."

"Yes," I said. "I think I must." We drove back then. Natasha's time was limited. She still had patients to see that afternoon. Hamburg was in the grip of an influenza epidemic. She promised again to write to Professor Pontevivo that night and then added shyly, "If you would like to . . . will you come for tea tomorrow?"

I nodded and kissed her hand. Unaccountably, I was in tears again. I cried easily these days, without immediate reason. Embarrassed, I left them quickly.

In my room in the dark I sat by the window looking out, drinking. Snow was again falling steadily. I drank, I thought and I held Shirley's little golden cross in my hand.

16

Sunday morning Schauberg again "washed" my blood.

In the afternoon I drank tea with Natasha and Misha and we again listened to Russian records. Tired, I did not stay long.

At the hotel Schauberg examined me once more. I told

him that my last close-ups were scheduled. Not before time. The rash was spreading to my face but make-up would possibly conceal it for another two days.

The atmosphere at the studio, characteristic for studios when a film is drawing to an end, was one of irritability. People who had worked together for so many weeks were now nervous, exhausted, at odds with each other. My part in the film came to an end Tuesday. The others had another nine days to go. In between came Christmas and New Year.

Monday evening Schauberg again "washed" my blood. The close-ups had been an extreme strain for me. On several occasions I had been asked if I were ill. One more day. One more day of close-ups!

"We'll repeat this treatment in the morning," said Schauberg as I gave him his last check.

"In case something happens to me."

"Nothing is going to happen to you."

"I'd rather give you the check now."

He took it, thanked me and asked if I'd heard anything from my wife.

"I called a good friend. He is having her watched. She has not left her house since she arrived."

"What did I tell you!"

"But lawyers come to see her."

"That's perfectly understandable." He shrugged his shoulders. "You are going to enter a clinic now."

I told him about Professor Pontevivo.

"He is excellent. His clinic is the best place for you."

"When are you disappearing?"

"Thursday. We have wonderful false passports and other official papers." He became embarrassed.

"What is it?"

"I feel so straight-laced. Käthe asked me to invite you."

"When?"

"Wednesday. At Madam Misere's. We will have the drawing room to ourselves. Käthe would like the three of

443

us to have dinner. She would like to say good-by and to thank you . . ."

"That's not really necessary."

". . . and I would like that too. No one knows what will become of us, right? And we did get along quite well. Will you come?"

"I'd like to. Thank you."

After Schauberg had left, Natasha called to tell me that she had received a telegram from Rome. "The professor is expecting you December twenty-fifth. That would be Friday."

"Thank you very much, Natasha."

"Would you like to go for a walk with me later on?"

"I am very tired."

"Shall I come to you?"

"No. I'd like to be alone."

"Is there anything I can do for you, Peter?"

"No," I said. "There is nothing you can do."

Fortunately I had two bottles of whisky, water and ice in my room. That night I first dreamed of Shirley coming to my bungalow as she once had, and we loved one another as we once had. Then I dreamed the dream of the elevator. I awakened, drenched in perspiration, needing whisky.

17

I finished my last scene on the afternoon of December twenty-second.

I don't think anybody even noticed me as I left the set. Work was going on as usual for the others. Scene shifters removed a wall. Thornton Seaton explained the next scene to Henry Wallace and two German actors. Mr. Albrecht was arguing about money which had been spent on fresh flowers. Artificial flowers would have done just as well. "The vase is in the background! Nobody would have noticed the difference!"

I went to my dressing room and changed. I tipped Harry and he wished me luck. "It's been a pleasure working for you, Mr. Jordan. I say that quite honestly."

Perhaps he did. Perhaps he said the same to others. A wardrobe assistant works for many stars. Why should not other stars be nice to work for too. I did not say good-by to others because I intended to return tomorrow. It was not to be. Wednesday I was invited to Käthe and Walter Schauberg's. Thornton Seaton, Belinda King, Henry Wallace and I were to spend Christmas Eve at Kostasch's. I didn't know on Tuesday that I was not to see them any more . . .

Through the snow-cleared streets I drove to the cemetery in Ohlsdorf. The gates were still open. The guard told me, "We're closing in a half hour." I nodded. A few people passed me as I walked to Shirley's grave. It was dusk now. Snow covered the grave and only our wreath on the black wooden cross rose above it. I read the inscription on the white bow.

SHIRLEY BROMFIELD
BORN 11. 17. 1939 IN LOS ANGELES
DIED 12. 10. 1959 IN HAMBURG
REST IN PEACE

I spoke aloud. "If You exist, God, give her peace. She was good. She was so young. She was rarely happy."

Silently I communed with Shirley about my completed film, my plans of leaving for Rome to enter a clinic, and that I would probably never return to this grave, to this piece of sheltering earth with which she would sometime blend.

I thought: she cannot hear me; she already knows; she knows everything or nothing. I left the snow-covered grave and walked toward the exit. The bell of the small chapel tinkled vigorously.

The few people who had visited the cemetery were on their slow way to the exit. I saw an old couple. She was crying and he was comforting her and I thought how many more old than young people there were, especially in Germany. Then the thought of the black bag in my car made me quicken my steps. I overtook a man in a blue overcoat who was carrying a small package under his arm.

"Good evening," said the man as I passed him. I stopped and looked at his jaundiced, unhealthy skin, sunken cheeks, eyes filled with six thousand years of sadness. I recognized him at once, this former lawyer who had asked me to drink with him in that bar where I had gone to read the letter Schauberg had left me for self-treatment after his arrest.

"You don't want to drink with me, eh?"

He had pushed up his sleeve. On the inside of his wrist I had seen a tattooed number preceded by a letter.

The man from Auschwitz, always carrying a pair of children's shoes he had picked from a pile he had found in a field behind a barrack. The man who carried those shoes from bar to bar, to show them and to talk of his wife and little daughter. This haggard Jew of whom people in bars said that he was crazy. There he was.

"What are you doing here?" I asked.

"I come here often. Almost every day."

"Do you have relatives buried here?"

"No. But here are so many dead. Divided into religious denominations. There is also a Jewish section. I was born in Hamburg, you know. If my wife and Monika had not died in Auschwitz they would have been buried here too."

"But they are not buried here!"

"No," he said. "They're somewhere. The ashes were usually thrown into rivers. Perhaps they are in some ocean . . ."

"Then what are you doing here?"

"Way back in the cemetery is a section for suicides and

people who have been fished out of the Elbe. There are many headstones without names. I picked out two, one for my wife and one for my daughter. That's where I always go. Crazy, isn't it?"

I was silent.

"Well, I am crazy."

"You are not!"

"People say I am."

"They are crazy, not you."

We had left the cemetery and had reached my car.

"I'll drive you back to the city."

"No, thank you. I'll walk a little and take the bus."

"Would you like a drink?" His eyes lit up. "Whisky?"

"You have whisky? Here?"

"In the car. Would you like a drink?"

Softly he said, "I don't want to bother you."

I unlocked the Mercedes and he sat in the front seat next to me as I opened the black bag.

"You look troubled. You must have loved the one you visited here very much."

"Neat?"

"On the rocks."

"For me too," I said.

It was very dark now. At the entrance to the cemetery two lights went on. The guard locked the wrought-iron gate.

"We can stay here a little longer and drink," I said.

"Yes," he said. "We don't bother anyone here."

18

I remember everything clearly up this point. I had not felt well on that evening. I ought to have driven back to the hotel and called Schauberg. Everything might have been all right.

But I did not drive back to my hotel. I and the old man from Auschwitz sat in my car near the cemetery entrance; we talked and we drank. It was a mistake which was to be decisive. Since my blood was being "washed" I had lost my capacity to drink. Only I did not know that.

I also remember my long conversation with Doctor Goldstein. His wife Lizzy and his daughter Monika had first been taken to Bergen-Belsen and Theresienstadt before coming to Auschwitz. Goldstein told me of their suffering.

After the Red Army had liberated Goldstein and he was searching for his wife and daughter in Auschwitz he soon met some women who told him that both of them had been gassed. One of the women told him about the game the children had played the day before they had been killed. They played What Would I Like to Be Most? Little Monika had said, "I'd most like to be a dog because the guards like dogs . . ."

Goldstein told me many such stories and I poured another drink for him and for me too. That was my mistake. I stayed too long and I drank too much.

I was already drunk when I finally started the car. I don't remember what time it was. My head ached and I dreaded my return to the hotel. Making the movie had vitalized me. Now the movie was finished. There was nothing now to sustain me.

Had I had less to drink I might have telephoned and asked Professor Pontevivo to take me sooner. I would have booked a seat on the next plane to Rome. Had I been sober I might have been sensible. But I was neither when I drove back to Hamburg with Goldstein. I remember that I was afraid to hurt his feelings if I left him abruptly. He had been drinking my whisky. Did I not have to accept his invitation to a drink?

Goldstein apparently was known in the first bar we entered. People greeted him. We drank whisky with others and then drove to another bar. It was crowded. It must have been late by then. Perhaps nine o'clock. They were not serving whisky in this bar and we drank beer and cognac. That finished me off. I don't remember what Goldstein was saying. He was talking continually, happy to have found someone willing to listen to him. Every time I said I had to go home because I did not feel well he said, "Just another little one, you'll feel better then."

When we left the second bar I drove only to the next block. I was afraid of causing an accident. I was quite drunk. "Let's walk," said Goldstein. "I know a nice place near here. We can talk in peace there."

I hoped that a walk would make me sober. Instead the cold of this December night made me still worse. I don't remember where we went. I don't remember the bar either. I know it was not the last one for I remember that one perfectly!

It was a dreary place. Wood walls, a long bar, pictures of nudes on the walls. Red-shaded lighted lamps on small tables. The only bartender stood behind the bar. A jukebox blared out music. The bar and the dozen-or-so guests too looked a bit shabby. But they served whisky here which encouraged me. I still felt sick from the cognac.

Goldstein and I sat at the bar. By then I think we were already on familiar terms, making promises the way drunks do.

Then I wanted to telephone. I called my hotel and had them put me through to the garage where I asked for Schauberg. I wanted to ask him to pick me up here.

As soon as I heard his voice my drunkenness overpowered me. I could not talk, I could only mumble some nonsense. I did not know the name of the bar, not the location or street and I heard Schauberg call repeatedly, "Come to the hotel, good God! Come to the hotel at once, you fool!" When he called me a fool I became so infuriated that I hung up. I wanted to call Natasha then but the names in the telephone book blurred before my eyes and I gave that up.

I went to the bathroom and splashed my face with cold water. I suddenly realized that I had never been this drunk. I knew that I had to get to the hotel immediately or there would be a catastrophe.

Strange: that there would be a disaster. I knew the moment I returned to the bar to ask the bartender to call me a taxi. I did not have the time to do that.

I saw a large, muscular, bull-necked man in a gray suit push the haggard little Goldstein off his bar stool. Goldstein's face was very pale and he looked as if he were going to cry.

"That's mean," he cried. "Give them back to me!"

A few guests laughed but most were silent. The jukebox had stopped. The bartender tried to pacify the man.

A girl called, "Give him back the shoes, fatso!"

The shoes!

The fat man held the shoes Goldstein had found fifteen years ago in Auschwitz.

He must have unwrapped them to retell his story while I had been telephoning. His tormentor held them aloft; Goldstein, so much shorter, could not reach them. He jumped for them a few times. The man holding them, as drunk as Goldstein, not as drunk as I, merely laughed. His face was rosy-cheeked, not brutal but rather a pleasant, good-natured face. He was obviously enjoying himself by annoying a little, unhappy man.

"Give him back the shoes," ordered the bartender. "That's nothing to joke about!"

Goldstein, still jumping, still trying to reach the shoes fell. A few people laughed. The bartender said, "That's not funny! Give him back the shoes!"

But the fat man held them high.

He jumped back and forth, from side to side, before Goldstein who slowly got up. Goldstein followed him, stumbling, crying, "Please ... give back ... give back ... please ..."

A girl got up and said to the man at her table, "If you think that's nice—I don't." She extended her leg. The fat man tripped but did not fall. He crashed against a wall, then gave the girl two resounding slaps.

"You bastard!"

"That's enough now!" the man at her table said, got up and slammed his fist into the trouble-maker's face. He laughed at that and kicked his opponent who fell to his knees and groaned. He had been kicked in the groin.

Now the friends of this man leapt at the fat man who laughed at that and kicked his opponent who fell to his fight the four men. The girls screamed. The bartender ran to the telephone. Goldstein had caught one of the shoes, the other was lying on the floor near me.

I picked it up while I heard the bartender call, "Police patrol ... God Almighty, come quickly ..."

I held the shoe close to my eyes and stared at it. In faint golden letters the brand name was still visible: BREITSPRECHER BERLIN.

Breitsprecher, Berlin.

I seemed to hear Wanda's voice. "My pretty shoes ... broke the heel ... made for me ... by Breitsprecher ..."

The waitresses were screaming. Glasses broke. The bar was demolished. The brutal drunk seemed to have gone berserk. Men shrank back. The bartender hurried over.

"The police ... they'll be here in a moment!"

Guests grabbed their coats, threw money on the tables and hurried out.

Breitsprecher, Berlin.

I was still staring at the little shoe. Blind rage rose in me, overpowered me, robbed me of my senses.

Breitsprecher, Berlin.

Goldstein screamed. I looked up. The fat man had kicked him. Now he was beating him. "Judenschwein," he said quietly. He had just beaten up four men but his breath was even. "You dirty, little Jew . . ."

"No . . . don't . . . don't . . ." Goldstein whimpered trying to protect his head with his hands. The fat man was hitting him, pushing back the men who were trying to restrain him.

"I sit here quietly and peaceful and somebody like you comes. They forgot to send you to the gas ovens."

By now all the people left in the bar were trying to help Goldstein but the fat man was invincible. He shook off his adversaries with ease. Again and again he hit Goldstein.

"Six million—don't make me laugh! Two million at the most!"

Everything began to revolve around me. I saw Wanda, Hintze-Schön, my mother, Kostasch, Seaton, directors I had worked with twenty-five years ago, Joan, Schauberg, Natasha, all of them revolving, confused, above and below each other; I heard voices, boisterous singing, shouting; a voice screamed, "Peter! Peter! Help me . . ."

Faces. Flames. The sounds of breaking glass. The clanging of fire-engine bells.

"Die Fahne hoch, die Reihen fest geschlossen . . ."

"Peter! Peter!" That was Goldstein.

"Scene 321. Take eleven!"

The voices grew louder and louder, the images turned faster and faster. Something narrow and long flashed, blinded me . . .

"Peter!"

A siren. Steps. Voices. Screams. Many screams.

Then I recognized the narrow, shiny object: an ice pick, on a wooden board behind the bar.

I grabbed it.

I lunged.

Breitsprecher, Berlin.

Even the men who were trying to separate the fat man from Goldstein shrank back from me. This surprised him;

he lost his balance. He fell on Goldstein who groaned and I fell on the man's gross body. The images before my eyes moved quickly, out of focus.

I raised the arm holding the ice pick. I plunged it between the man's shoulder blades. The gray fabric of his suit quickly turned red. Somebody hit the back of my head with a heavy object and I lost consciousness.

19

"To the shelters! To the shelters! Enemy planes advancing on Berlin!" The voice jarred. Metal scraped on metal. A clamor of frantic voices.

"Get up! Rise and shine!"

"Get out of bed! To the washrooms! Hurry up!"

This is what I heard when I came to. Groaning, coughing, unintelligible sounds, shuffling feet, rattling of aluminum utensils, and again and again the beating of metal against metal and the jarring voice, "Enemy bombers above Mark Brandenburg. Full alert for Berlin!"

My head was splitting. Now I noticed the smell. Wherever I was, the stench was nauseating. I opened my eyes. I was lying on a hard bed enclosed in an iron cage. An old man in faded blue-gray pajamas rattled the cage and yelled, "Go to the shelter, man!"

At this point in my report it seems necessary to me to make one point clear so that you, Professor Pontevivo, and you, the judge at my future trial, will not interpret it as cowardice, evasion or concealment. Everything I reported up to now I remember clearly. After I awakened in the iron cage my memory was no longer perfect. It remained partially impaired for a time.

For instance: I said "cage." I remember a cage. Perhaps it was only an iron bed which reminded me of a cage. I lived in a shadowy world. A world which separates life from death, day from dream. What I am reporting now must have taken place this way. I have objective proof that it did; many people are my witnesses.

When I tried to sit up in the cage my head bumped into its roof. I sank back. I felt dizzy and nauseous. I looked around. The room held about forty beds crowded together. In the narrow gangways naked and half-dressed men were bustling about. I looked at myself. I was wearing pajamas too.

There was a closed door, three closed windows admitting a dim light. An adjacent room was also crowded with beds. Many had cages such as the one I was in. Men were lying motionless in some while in others men screamed and raged, rattling the bars. Attendants in white coats were ordering everybody to hurry to the washrooms. The attendants were large and powerful. Two of them were dragging an old, incredibly dirty man past me. He was shouting, "I don't want a bath! I'm two hundred and fifty-seven years old! I was in eight wars! I don't need a bath!"

A man next to me had dirtied his bed and proceeded to smear the wall with feces.

A boy of about eighteen was kneeling by the window praying. The man who had rattled my cage and announced enemy bombers suddenly fell to the floor in a foaming convulsion. Two men came and carried him to his cot. One of the men told me, "Welcome, sir. Don't worry about this. He always has a fit in the morning." Then he held the epileptic down so he would not harm himself.

The door opened and two attendants entered. One of them locked the door which had no handle. The other opened my cage and said, "Get up."

"I can't."

"Come on!"

"I really cannot . . . I feel very sick . . ."

The attendants looked at each other, reached for my wrists and pulled me up. I cried out with pain.

Assisted by the two attendants I was swaying.

"Where am I?"

He gave me the name of a place I did not know.

"I . . . I'm not in Hamburg?"

"No. You're far away from Hamburg."

"How far away?"

"I told you, quite a way."

"And what is this here?"

"What do you think it is?"

"I . . . I've no idea."

"A mental institution."

"A mental . . ." I staggered. "How did I get here?"

"There is no time to talk. Put on the slippers and robe." The second attendant indicated a chair. On it were a pair of old slippers and a clean but shabby robe which strongly smelled of disinfectant. "Quick, now. To the washroom. Then you'll see the doctor."

"Doctor?"

"New admissions have to see the ward doctor before eight."

The washroom, thick with steam, was crowded with about sixty noisy men. I was given a toothbrush, a washcloth and a cake of soap. "Brush your teeth!"

I tried and promptly vomited.

"Goddamn! Clean it up!"

I did, then washed myself. I had no recollection of the events of the most recent hours. I felt drunk and faint.

Near me, a man, one side of his face missing, was washing an idiot child. He was talking to the cretin with the intonation of telling a fairy story. "And then, you know, then I said to Eisenhower if you bomb Monte Cassino just once more you'll see what is going to happen! Then I'll get Stalin and we'll push you into the Atlantic."

"Atlantic! Atlantic! Atlantic!" cried the cretin.

"I want to get out of here," I told the attendant near

me. "I want to get out of here, right now! I can't be locked up with these crazy people! I'm perfectly sane!"

"Of course, you are," said the attendant. "It's also perfectly normal to want to stab somebody with an ice pick."

"Ice pick?"

"Come on now. Let's go!"

They held me, dressed me in the worn old pajamas and robe and took me back to the ward. The man who had rattled my cage was now running through the room, his arms extended sideways, loudly humming, imitating a bomber plane. A few patients were hiding under beds while others remained motionless.

The boy by the window was now doing exercises. This man who had restrained the epileptic said to me, "Going to be examined, eh? Be careful they don't poison you."

Suddenly a stark-naked dward, rags, broom and pail in hand, ran through the room and shouted, "Make way! Make way! Soraya is coming!"

One attendant opened the door, the other pushed me into a hallway with many doors and several benches. Some patients were sitting there, smoking. I saw only men. We passed a high, finely-meshed, grated door which closed off the stairs leading to an upper floor.

REFRACTORY WARD
TO BE KEPT LOCKED AT ALL TIMES

Two idiot boys were undressing in the hall, touching each other and one of them recited a counting rhyme. "This is the thumb, it shakes down the plums . . ."

I jumped as suddenly from the floor above came the most horrifying screaming.

"What . . . what's that?"

"Just one of the addicts," said one attendant as he pushed me along. "You'll get used to it when you've been here a while."

20

"What is your name?"

The doctor, pale and fatigued, sat behind a desk. He made me stand even though I was swaying. The window behind him was also secured by iron bars. I saw a bleak, enclosed yard, a few bare trees and black, grotesquely fat birds waddling on the snow.

"Why are those birds so fat?" I asked Dr. Trotha. I read his name on a name plate on his desk.

"What—" turned. "Oh, the crows. Many of our patients throw their food out of the windows. The crows eat everything. They are much too fat to fly; they can only waddle around. I asked you your name."

My head had cleared in the washroom and the mention of an ice pick had somewhat revived my memory.

Fleetingly I remembered the child's shoes. A bar. Goldstein. The fat man. Noises. Music. Screaming. "Police patrol will be here in a minute." A siren.

In the washroom I had touched the back of my head where I found a dressing. Now I could guess what had happened. Somebody had knocked me out. Then I had been brought here.

I had to be cautious now. If it became known that I, Peter Jordan, had been admitted to a mental institution—.

I needed time to think.

"Are you going to tell me your name?"

"You already know my name."

"If I did I wouldn't ask you."

"You took my suit. My passport was in the jacket." I hoped fervently that I was wrong. Often I changed suits and would sometimes forget to take my passport, even the car registration. If I was lucky now . . .

"We only found some money and car keys. Now, will you tell me your name!"

I was silent.

"You're not going to tell me your name?"

"Careful now. Think. Take your time. PETER JORDAN IN MENTAL INSTITUTION. Good God, if the newspapers were to find out!

"I'm not saying anything unless I have an attorney."

"You have no right to demand anything here. You were arrested by the police when you stabbed a man in a bar while you were completely drunk."

"Is he dead?"

"Severely injured. The blade glanced off the shoulder-blade."

"In that case I insist on an attorney. I'm not going to be locked up with these crazy people!"

He got up His voice was strident. "We have one doctor to every seventy patients. The institution is over-crowded. We cannot reserve a private room for each person brought here in an emergency."

"And you cannot lock me up with these mad people!"

"Why not?"

"Because I'm not crazy!"

"Are you quite certain?"

I was silent. I was exasperated.

"Why did you want to kill this man?"

"I'm not going to tell you anything."

"Not even your name?"

"No!"

A door opened. An older doctor, looking every bit as tired as Dr. Trotha came in. He nodded to his colleague and sat down. Dr. Trotha continued questioning me.

"Now, you are not going to tell me your name."

"No!"

"But perhaps you will tell me how much two and two makes."

458

"Sixteen," I said, rage rising in me. It was a mistake. He froze.

"You are misjudging the situation you're in. Will you let me test you now? Yes or no?"

"Test what?"

"The state of your mind. Even without a test I can see that you are an alcoholic. You're babbling."

What was he saying? I was talking rationally and distinctly!

"Your hands are trembling. Your body is shaking. I think you're verging on d.t.'s."

I looked down. He was right! "May. . . . may I sit down?"

"Please, do. The test will determine whether you are only an alcoholic or the degree of irreversible brain damage, if any. It will also determine which ward you will be sent to. As you see, the test is also in your interest. When you were admitted—at five in the morning—you were in no condition to be examined. And ward three happened to have had a vacant bed."

"Test me," I said.

The tests took about a half hour. I had to draw a tree, fit triangles to form a square, walk a straight line. I answered many questions. I made a few ridiculous mistakes, probably because I was still somewhat drunk and fatigued. I could not fit the triangles to make a square and when I walked the line I fell. He gave me a few words with which I was to form a sentence. I did and then I realized I had omitted one word. I tried to re-form the sentence. By then I had forgotten the words and I was embarrassed to ask for them again and gave up.

After a few more tests he called the attendants. I was very weak. Fear rose in my again. I could not think and I was grateful to the attendants when they helped me walk. We had to wait a while before we went into another room. The doctor who had sat silently while Dr. Trotha had tested me sat behind a table. Dr. Trotha was on his

459

left. On his right sat a male secretary. "Sit down." The attendants sat me down. "You know where you are?"

I nodded.

"You know how you came here?"

"Arl-arl-arl-arl . . ."

Dr. Trotha said something to his colleague, who nodded.

"You were arrested by a police patrol and taken to a station house. From there you were brought here by a fire department conveyance. They are responsible for emergency cases such as yours. Can you follow me?" I nodded. "Do you feel very sick?"

I nodded again.

Dr. Trotha said, "It won't take long. In a few minutes you'll be given a sedative."

The older man said, "My name is Dr. Holgersen. I have been appointed by the court. I come here every morning. It is my duty, on the basis of the results of the examination by the ward doctor and my own observation, to decide whether or not it is in the public interest that a patient who was admitted as an emergency is to remain in this institution." Holgersen looked at a paper. "Dr. Trotha's findings are very unfavorable. My own impression of you is no better. I'll ask you for the last time: Are you going to tell me your name?"

I shook my head.

"Do you have relatives?"

"No."

"It sometimes happens that people refuse to give their name because they are ashamed or frightened. But relatives search for them and in the end we find out anyway."

"Attorney," I said with difficulty.

"You want a lawyer?"

I nodded.

"You will see a lawyer."

Thank God.

"In about a month."

I almost fell off the chair, the attendants were holding me.

"I am ordering your temporary compulsory detainment in this institution."

"You can't do that!"

"I can and I must. As long as we do not know who you are, and considering your condition we cannot hold a hearing."

"A hear—hear—hearing . . ."

"It is Dr. Trotha's and my opinion that you are verging on d.t.'s if that means anything to you. If you are sensible now and do not resist the doctor's treatment we shall consider you further in about four weeks."

"Then what happens?"

"Under the law we can detain you here up to six weeks. By then a judge will determine your immediate future—on the basis of medical findings."

Something soft and warm was trickling down my neck. I touched it. It was blood. The wound on my head had opened.

"Where will the hearing be held?"

"Right here," said Dr. Trotha. "The judge comes here because we have so many alcoholics."

Holgersen said, "For the hearing a lawyer will be assigned to you. The judge will decide if you are to be cured here at the state's expense or if you are to be allowed to be treated privately. Then you will be tried for attempted murder. Have you understood everything?"

I was perspiring profusely. My hands shook. My pulse raced. I felt deathly ill. I vomited. This time I did not have to clean it up. Following that I passed out.

21

I was still dizzy and weak when I awakened. My eyes smarted, probably as a result of the sedative I had been given. The room was smaller. The windows closed and barred. It stunk.

The two old men must have been watching me sleep for they both began to shout as soon as I opened my eyes. Dizzy, I closed them again. Both men continued to talk excitedly.

They introduced themselves as Herrenkind and Schlagintweit, both Nazi bigwigs. Apparently one had destroyed a tank this very morning. Russians and Americans were fighting at the Elbe. What did the Führer say? When will he give the order for the Americans to attack the Russians? What were the new orders? Heil Hitler!

Meanwhile, thinking was difficult. I realized that Dr. Trotha or one of his colleagues had set this up as a trap for me. This was a test to see if I was disturbed or not. So two doctors, dressed as patients, put on an act for me. They made believe that it was still 1945, that the Russians were fighting to take Berlin—fifteen years ago. They wanted to see how I would react to such insanity.

Very calmly I said, "Stop this nonsense. There is no Führer any more."

That upset both of them. Was he dead? Who was his successor? We are loyal followers of the Führer. Especially the dead one! Adolf Hitler, Sieg Heil! They raised their arms in salute.

Still calm I told them, "Berlin was conquered by the Red Army fifteen years ago. There is no longer a Nazi Party, though there are still a lot of Nazis."

There, I thought.

The two disguised doctors looked at each other.

One finally asked, "Do you think we're idiots?"

"I think this kind of testing is idiotic."

"Testing? He destroyed a tank this morning—and you say the war is over? You can't think of anything better?"

The other man suddenly yelled, "He is a Soviet infiltrator! The Russians dressed him in our uniform—"

"I'm not wearing any uniform!"

"You're wearing the same uniform as we do!" The doctor's voice cracked.

No! This was going too far. Could this be a test?

"We'll have to kill the communist! Without delay!"

They both lunged for me. In a split second I realized that I had made a mistake. Those were no doctors. This was no test, no trap, no examination.

Weak though I was I managed to get off my bed, punch one or the other with my fists. They punched me. We rolled on the floor. Rolled over each other.

"Help! Help! Help!"

I yelled as loud as I could.

As soon as I had shaken off one the other would be on me.

"Sieg Heil!" they yelled while they were trying to kill me.

"Help! He . . ."

One of them was choking me. The door was thrown open. Two attendants ran in. I was still on the floor. They pushed back the two old men, pulled me outside. The door slammed shut. One attendant locked it. Dr. Trotha came hurrying down the hallway.

"What happened? Why was this man in room seventeen?"

"You gave the order yourself, Doctor!"

"Incompetents! I said sixteen. Sixteen!" He bent over me. "Are you injured?" I shook my head. "Those two in there were buried alive by bombs in 1945 . . . in Berlin . . . 1946 they were transferred here from Wittenau. Time has stopped for them, you know?"

"Leave me alone."

"It was a mistake. A regrettable mistake. One aspect of overcrowding and incompetent staff."

"Just leave me alone," I whispered. The fist in the pit of my stomach was stirring again.

No.

Not this too. Let it pass, Shirley.

It did. I did not have an attack.

22

"They are incredibly overburdened here," said the thirty-five-year-old architect, Edgar Shapiro. He was sitting on my bed.

Some men in room sixteen were sleeping, some talking quietly to each other. One was lying underneath his bed, another standing, his face to the wall. I had liked Shapiro the moment I saw him. He was polite, modest and charming. He had comforted me. My shock had subsided.

"This is one of the quiet, ordinary floors. Above us is the refractory floor. Twice as many people there. Even more patients in the women's section. Not enough attendants, not sufficient beds, not enough money."

"Dr. Trotha said one doctor for every seventy patients."

"Maybe on paper. In reality he has to take care of at least a hundred."

"That is too much."

"One of the reasons conditions are what they are."

Shapiro became enthusiastic. The official capacity of this hospital was fifteen hundred patients.

"Do you know how many patients are here now? About twenty-seven hundred! There are never less than twenty-five hundred!"

Extra beds had been placed in hallways and some day rooms. Because of insufficient space, old and young, addicts, degenerates, criminals, the harmless, and children were crowded together.

"It is criminal that children should be living among all these people!"

"How long have you been here?" I asked.

"Three years. Before I was admitted I used up to 50 ampoules of dope a day. I think I will be discharged this summer. I've been treated very well. This building dates from 1880. It used to be a barrack. Today there is no money to build new hospitals. Nowadays they have to build new barracks."

I was again startled when I heard the same terrifying screams from above that I had heard that morning.

"Why won't you say who you are?"

I did not reply.

Shapiro smiled. "I like you. You can use my electric razor."

"I have this rash . . ."

"Well, I do too. Look at me!" The light in the room was so dim that I had not noticed it right away. Shapiro's face was covered with eczema. The faces of some other patients were also disfigured. A man near the window looked the worst.

"The medication," said Shapiro. "Mostly from paraldehyde."

"Paraldehyde?"

"It's a sedative. That's the stuff you can smell everywhere here."

"Who is the man near the window?"

"King Washington Napoleon."

The man looked up and bowed politely when he heard his name.

"He's an artist. Fell from the high wire during his act. Head injury. He's engaged to the princess."

"Princess?"

"Margaret Rose. Of England. He writes her daily."

I met the other inmates of the room during the evening

meal. That consisted of sandwiches and herb tea. The cups and plates were dirty, the sandwiches unappetizing. When I pushed it away Shapiro said, "Eat it. Come on. Only stupid people throw it out of the window." He pointed to a pale, skinny man who was just throwing his food into the yard. I remembered the fat crows.

"You must eat. You must keep up your strength or you'll never make it. Go on—no matter how much you loathe it!"

I forced myself to eat. The tea tasted of saccharin. The man who had thrown his sandwiches into the yard had begun to drink at the age of fourteen, Shapiro told me. He used to be a pharmacist. Six times he had been in prison for raping minors. Now he was here permanently.

Kurt, the man who had been lying underneath his bed, had been a carpenter. As a result of alcoholism both his arms were paralyzed. Shapiro fed him patiently. Shapiro was well-liked. He helped where he could, he cleaned, he was always in good spirit. Dr. Trotha had permitted him to keep his small radio.

Then I learned about Butt-Dieter. He was the oldest, the one who stood facing the wall. He only said two sentences, "Today is my birthday. Have you a butt for me?"

Cigarettes! They were as important and precious as they had been for people in Germany after the war. We were allowed to smoke in the hallway where we were taken after the meal.

Two attendants led a troupe of children past us. I was horrified at the sight of these little human wrecks.

"Children of alcoholics. Even some of them have had withdrawal treatment. You should see their parents on visiting day!"

At eight-thirty we were sent back into our rooms. A young doctor accompanied by two attendants gave out medication. I was given an injection. Most of the patients received paraldehyde, a liquid of dreadful smell and taste which quickly induced sleep. I was beginning to adjust to the awful odor.

I was surprised that I did not have an attack. I had not had any whisky all day yet I did not feel bad, merely weak. Very weak. The lights went out at eight-forty-five. Shapiro's little radio played softly.

Butt-Dieter began to snore. The snoring became a rasping in his throat which in turn became a rattling cough.

Shapiro said, "I clean his phlegm up in the morning. Poor Dieter was in the firestorm in Hamburg—the air raid in 1943. He recognizes no one any more."

Now I had to think. Who was looking for me? Kostasch? Natasha? Had I been missed in the hotel? The police would accept a missing person's report only after forty-eight hours. Not even twenty-four hours had passed since my arrest. I had telephoned Schauberg just before that. He must be worried. But if Schauberg of all people—

I could assume that the police would not search for me before tomorrow night. Tomorrow was also Christmas. Would civil departments work at full strength? I wondered if the fracas in the bar had been reported in the newspapers? I had mentioned my name to Goldstein.

Had I?

I could not remember. The paraldehyde was as soporific as a potent sedative.

23

They had left me my watch.

I was awakened by Shapiro's panic-stricken dream at midnight. He was continually calling his wife not to let him drown because he could not swim. Attendants gave him a little more paraldehyde and he fell asleep again.

I was now wide awake. From the upper floor, and the women's wing as well, I heard screams, slaps, stamping, whimpering, crying, howling laughter. Sounds made by humans, but inhuman, idiot sounds. Members of the staff shouted and hurried about, bells clanged; twice a siren screamed. There was no letup. I finally fell asleep only to be roused by more shouting: "Time to get up! To the washrooms!"

December twenty-fourth was a dreary gray day. Breakfast consisted of sandwiches and tea. Two doctors accompanied by attendants made their rounds. With so many patients to see, the time with each had to be very limited. I was given a sedative and an injection. Before falling asleep I watched some patients leave for their daily chores: cleaning, helping in the kitchen. I slept till the afternoon. Shapiro sat staring on his bed. Butt-Dieter stood facing the wall. King Washington Napoleon was writing to Princess Margaret Rose.

From the women's wing came singing.

"Silent night, holy night . . ."

Attendants brought aluminum plates with fruits, chocolate, gingerbread cookies decorated with pine branches. They also brought opened letters and packages for some patients.

An attendant came in and pointed to me. "Come along!"

"Where to?" I was frightened.

"Quickly, hurry, before he gets rough," said Shapiro to me softly. I put on the old robe and slippers and followed the man to a door. VISITING ROOM.

He pushed me inside.

Two people were waiting there for me.

Dr. Trotha and Natasha.

24

Natasha came toward me. She bumped into a chair and dropped her handbag. Simultaneously Dr. Trotha and the attendant bent down to pick it up. Natasha pushed something into my hand. It was a hard object wrapped in paper. Immediately I put it into the pocket of my robe.

Both men had straightened up, Natasha took her bag and thanked them. She looked at me almost clinically, as if she had never seen me before. It took a desperate effort for me to do the same.

"Well, Doctor," asked Trotha. "Is he the one?"

Natasha shook her head.

"No," she said, "No, he isn't."

"You are quite certain?"

"I'm positive. Peter Jordan looks quite different."

"Take the man back to his room," said Trotha. Natasha turned away.

In my room again, Shapiro asked, "Visitor?"

"Negative. A woman looking for her husband."

I waited about fifteen minutes before I knocked on the locked door. When another attendant opened I asked to go to the bathroom. There I unwrapped the little package Natasha had given me. The hard object was a square-cut key that unlocked all doors and was wrapped in a typewritten note.

"You must get out of here tonight. Two thirds of the staff are off. I bribed the guard who is on duty tonight at 8 o'clock at the main entrance. He sold me the key. He will let you pass. I shall be waiting in a car around the corner of the first street to the right . . ."

There was a sketch that showed where I was to go once I left the institution.

"I'll have a change of clothes with me. The evening pa-

469

pers had a report of a man who, after a fight in a bar, had been sent to this institution. They also say that the man refuses to identify himself. By tomorrow morning, at the latest, someone from the studio will surely come to this place.

"Once your identity has been established you will no longer be able to leave Germany. But you must go to Professor Pontevivo. I have sleeping-car tickets for eleven-fifty. I shall be expecting you between nine and nine-thirty. It is your only chance."

I tore the letter into small pieces and flushed it away. Then I went out in the hall where the attendant was waiting for me.

The Ninth Tape

1

The voice announcing the arrival of the Alps Express reverberated through the loudspeaker in the quiet low-lying hall of the Hamburg Hauptbahnhof. It was almost midnight on Christmas Eve, 1959.

Only a dozen or so travelers standing in little groups were waiting for the train. A big Christmas tree, its lights and decorations glittering, stood at the head of the stairs.

Natasha was by my side. But for her support I would have fallen. The glistening railroad tracks, the tree, the few people, lights in the distance all seemed to sway. The overcoat Natasha had bought for me was too large, the suit too small, the new shoes too tight. A suitcase and bag were nearby. The express rolled into the station. Natasha helped me to a sleeping car. A porter brought the baggage. The entire train was almost empty. The talkative conductor, smelling of liquor, told us that he had already celebrated Christmas with his family that afternoon.

"Had a little drink too. Nothing much doing on Christmas Eve."

An announcer's voice wished us a pleasant trip and after a few gentle jerks the train started its long journey south.

I had sat down on a berth. We crossed a few bridges,

the lights of many ships reflecting in the black water. I felt ill yet elated. Despairing yet hopeful. The wish to die mingled with the wish to live.

Natasha had left the compartment. She returned with the cheerful conductor who brought soda, three glasses and ice.

Natasha opened the bag, brought out a bottle of whisky and prepared drinks. She first served the conductor. A toast, "happy Christmas," then he drank and left us.

We drank. I began to weep. Natasha comforted me. "It's all right, Peter. Go ahead and cry. I know, it's merely nerves."

I blubbered, "You remembered to bring whisky."

"You can drink all you want. It makes no difference now. The day after tomorrow you'll be at Pontevivo's."

The few minutes involved in a dangerous adventure had given us a greater intimacy than any other event since first we met. But our familiarity did not stem merely from being accomplices . . .

The train was moving fast through the snow-covered countryside. Natasha refilled my glass.

"Not so much."

"You'll sleep better if you have a few drinks. It's a long trip. We'll only have reached Munich by morning."

I drank, thinking that I was probably dreaming, that I was still on my bed in room seventeen. It was all too fantastic. In a moment I would be awakened by Shapiro's screaming during one of his attacks.

"Natasha . . . Natasha . . ."

"What is it?"

"I'm so afraid I'm dreaming."

"You're not dreaming. You're awake. We're on our way to Rome."

"I'm not . . . I'm no longer in that place?"

"No, Peter." Her look, her hand on mine was what I most needed for belief. Four hours ago I had still been there . . .

After I had read Natasha's note and stuffed the key in the pocket of my robe the attendant took me back to my room. The singing of Christmas songs came from all wards. Christmas dinner consisted of chicken and asparagus. The fat crows in the yard were having a special feast.

Once the plates had been collected we were sent out into the hall where smoking was permitted. At eight-thirty we received our usual medication. Another injection and again paraldehyde. Although I was nauseated by it I managed to keep it in my mouth until the attendants had left. Then I spat it under the bed. I dared not risk sleep.

The lights went off at eight-forty-five. I waited until I thought everyone in my ward was asleep. The screaming and yelling, stamping and crying from upstairs began and from afar I heard church bells.

My eyes were on my watch. I had but one fear: that Shapiro would have an attack. He did not.

Shortly after nine I rose silently, put on the robe and slippers and crept to the door. It opened soundlessly as I turned the square-cut key. Just as quietly I closed it.

The hall was empty and sparsely lit. I carried my slippers and hurried to the stairs. As I turned the corner I collided with the attendant who had taken me to the bathroom earlier. He promptly recognized me. I hit him, the key in my fist, as hard as I could. He fell forward, groaned and did not move.

As I raced down the stairs, I saw the light of the guardroom. The moment the guard heard steps he bent even lower over his newspaper. I crossed the foyer and ran past him. The entrance door was not locked. I was outside.

I ran down deserted streets to the first crossroad. In the scuffle with the attendant I had dropped my slippers. The snow bothered my bare feet. I turned the corner. In the narrow road the lights of a car came on. Its engine started, one of its doors was flung open. I dropped into the front seat. Natasha stepped on the gas.

"How far is Hamburg?"

"About thirty kilometers." A little later she stopped near some trees. "The clothes are in the backseat. You better change here."

I changed hurriedly and threw the hospital garb beneath a hedge. We continued on our way.

"Whose car is this?"

"I borrowed it from friends. We'll leave it outside their house." About three quarters of an hour later we left the car and walked in search for a taxi. Hamburg seemed deserted. Christmas trees gleaming behind windows. From radios came the songs and music of Christmas as we sought a cab.

"Where is Misha?"

"With friends. I told him I had to take a trip for a few days." Her voice was quite matter-of-fact. No hint of excitement, sentiment or fear. She had evolved a plan and was efficiently carrying it out.

We finally found a taxi to the railroad station. It was eleven-fifteen then. Outside we walked up and down. When I felt faint Natasha told me to sit on a suitcase.

"It is better we go to the platform at the last minute. Perhaps they are already searching for you. There are always police at the station."

"How will I get across the frontier? I have no passport."

"Yes, you have Bruno's." She handed me a German passport once held by Misha's father. I looked at the photograph. A man with glasses. A sensitive face.

"He doesn't resemble me at all!"

"I never said he did."

"Yes, you did. You said—"

"I said you remind me of him."

"But if I don't resemble him—"

She handed me a pair of glasses.

476

"Here. The lenses are plain glass. Besides you have this rash. The same short hair. It will be all right if you wear the glasses. You must memorize the dates."

Bruno Kerst. Born March 21st 1920. Profession—Artist.

"Shortly before I took him to Pontevivo he needed a new passport. It is valid until 1961. I did not throw it away. All lucky coincidences, aren't they?"

"Yes," I said, "all lucky coincidences indeed."

"Do you think that you injured the attendant badly?"

"I don't think so."

"Eleven-thirty," said Natasha. "Now we can slowly make our way to the platform."

2

The wheels of the fast train were pounding.

I drank and listened to Natasha. Her hand on my arm—that brought calm.

"We made it just in time. The film people think that you've met with an accident. At the hotel they thought you might have been the victim of a crime. They wanted the police to search for you even before the usual forty-eight hours had passed."

"How did you learn that?"

"I went to the hotel. I'm known there. That's where your friends were all waiting."

"Strange that no one thought I might be in an institution."

"That's not so strange. No one knew of the precarious state of your health. Only I. I became alarmed right away that something like that might have happened."

"Natasha—" I began but tears choked my voice.

"You must endure this trip, Peter. You must get out of Germany before a warrant for your arrest is issued."

"The man I stabbed—have you heard anything about him?"

"He is very ill but not critically ill."

"Don't you want to know why I did it?"

"You'll tell me," she said. "You'll tell me everything, Peter."

"He beat up a Jew."

"Later," she said. "Don't talk now. You've already had too much excitement."

"Natasha—"

"Don't talk." She filled my glass again.

"I must! You must not come with me. You must leave the train . . . at the next station. You must return to Hamburg. You'll be involved in this matter."

"I already am."

"That's why you must get off the train. If . . . if they catch me they'll not only try me for this knifing . . . there is also an insurance fraud . . . Shirley . . . the attendant I struck . . ."

"I know."

"Think of Misha!"

"I'm thinking of you now," she said. "Alone you'll never get to Rome. Someone will have to be with you. A doctor."

"But this is insanity! I don't want you to—"

She stroked my hair. "Have some more to drink, Peter. And get undressed. There are pajamas in the bag, a razor and everything else you'll need."

"Natasha . . ."

She had already left the compartment.

I staggered and swayed but made ready for bed. My face was now covered with pustules and eczema. I was sickened by my appearance.

Once more I filled my glass and emptied it looking at the snow-covered country outside. I went to my berth.

Natasha came in presently.

"Are you all right?"

"Yes."

"Wonderful."

"You are wonderful," I said.

"Would you face the wall, please?"

She prepared for bed and finally said, "Now you can turn around again."

The pale yellow pajamas could not conceal the lovely feminine lines of her body. She had brought in a clean and redolent fragrance.

"If you don't feel well wake me right away."

"Thank you."

She smiled at me. "You'll be all right. And everything will turn out well. As long as they don't arrest you and send you to some institution. You must get to Professor Pontevivo."

Quickly she ascended the little ladder to the upper berth. For a moment her legs dangled before they too disappeared. "Drink until you fall asleep. You can leave the light on if you're afraid of the dark."

"Yes, Natasha."

"Don't be afraid. I'm here with you."

"Yes, Natasha."

"Really, there is no need for you to be afraid. Not even of another attack. I want you to get to Rome. I want you to be well again. That's why I brought those ampoules along too."

"Ampoules?"

"You know the ones I mean," she said. "I have it all here, Peter."

Then we were silent. I drank and listened to the rhythm of the wheels.

Everything went well. We reached Munich. We had breakfast and lunch in the compartment. I stayed in my berth.

"My husband is ill," Natasha explained to the new conductor who had taken over the sleeping car.

It was snowing hard in Austria. The train remained

sparsely occupied, the platforms deserted. The rash was now so bad that I could not shave.

Natasha gave me sedatives and a few injections. The long train ride taxed my energy. At the frontier I put on the glasses. Natasha had drawn the shades and I was lying in my berth in semi-darkness. The customs officials came, examined our passports and left.

The howling of a blizzard at the Brenner Pass, the furiously swirling snowflakes and the dry heat in the compartment made me anxious, nervous. I felt hot, I felt cold. My pulse raced. My breath came quickly. Natasha took my temperature. It was high. She gave me medicine, more injections. She reminded me of Schauberg. Fleetingly, I wondered where he might be now. In Pernambuco? Still in Hamburg?

My thoughts wandered aimlessly. I thought of Shirley, my mother, Misha, Joan and the blonde Käthe. I wondered if I would die before we reached Rome.

Natasha looked fatigued but she did not leave my side. I was delirious and had nightmares from which I would awaken with screams. Natasha was always there, holding me, telling me, "You must pull yourself together. You must get to Rome. We must not attract attention on the train or they will put us off at the next station."

I tried desperately to control myself. Natasha gave me whisky but now whisky revolted me. In northern Italy it was snowing heavily. Names of stations: Bolzano, Trento, Rovereto were barely visible in the dense whirling snow. The turbulent snowflakes increased my dizziness. Sometimes I thought I saw little animals or columns of tiny people moving very quickly. Everything I saw moved fast and was very small. I told Natasha. She straightened her glasses, poured a glass of whisky and said, "Another eight hours. Only another eight hours."

That was the evening of December twenty-fifth. It was still storming. Suddenly I felt very uneasy.

"Natasha, I don't want to frighten you but I think I'm dying."

She took my blood pressure. The conductor knocked, looked in and asked how everything was going. Natasha smiled brightly and I attempted a smile too. She said, "He's doing just fine, thank you."

"We'll be in Verona in fifteen minutes, ma'am," he said. "Just in case your husband is not that well." He disappeared.

"What's my blood pressure?"

"One hundred."

"But it was 170!"

"Blood pressure fluctuates. You feel ill because it dropped."

She counted my pulse.

"How high?"

"One hundred thirty."

"Natasha . . ."

"Yes, darling, yes?"

"I'm afraid."

"You must pull yourself together. Please, please, do try. We must get to Rome."

"I won't see Rome. I'm dying."

"You are not!"

"Yes, I am. I'm so sorry. After all the trouble you've taken. I feel it. I'm dying. I'm dying."

I could not see but I still heard the howling of the storm. The train was rounding a curve and my bed tilted. Simultaneously that giant invisible fist I knew so well hit the pit of my stomach, rose and crushed my heart.

I could not see nor hear nor breathe. My body arched. There was only darkness. I plunged into bottomless depths. Ten minutes before we reached Verona I died again only to begin living my miserable, cursed life once more.

3

At first everything was out of focus. Then I saw that I was in a brass bed of an impersonal cheerless hotel room. Cheap modern furniture, linoleum flooring, a towel on the floor near the washbasin.

Last daylight fell through a small window. I again heard the storm and saw dancing snowflakes. Natasha in her blue suit was sitting by the window. Newspapers were piled on a small bamboo table.

I tried to sit up but I was too weak. I could hardly keep my eyes open. I fell back onto the soft, slightly damp pillow. The faucets were dripping. The drops were distressingly loud.

Natasha came to me. There were wrinkles and lines in her face. Natasha looked exhausted but she smiled as she sat on my bed and stroked my hand.

With difficulty I asked, "What time is it?"

"Six in the evening."

"Which day?"

"Sunday."

"Sunday? But . . . but we left Thursday!"

"We arrived here Friday. You've been sleeping since then. Thank God."

"Where are we?"

"In Verona. A hotel near the railroad station. It's a new hotel and the owner is very nice. When we dragged you in here . . ."

"Dragged me?"

"Two railroad men and I. You fainted on the train. Don't you remember?"

"Yes, I do now. Didn't you give me an injection?"

"Immediately. Soon afterward the train stopped. You were still unconscious. I did not dare leave you on that train. Now, when we brought you here the owner insisted that a doctor be called. I showed him my credentials. He was satisfied then. I think we can go on to Rome tonight. Anyway, I have reserved another compartment."

"I can't walk . . . not even a step . . ."

"We could use a stretcher. As I told you, the hotel is very close to the station. In Rome an ambulance will pick you up from the train. Before you have another attack you must get to the clinic."

"It was a very bad one this time, wasn't it?"

"You were extremely lucky. Your symptoms on the train all indicated that you were verging on d.t.'s. I was terribly afraid! Your trembling, the blood pressure, your pulse, when you said you saw tiny creatures . . ."

"Those things precede the delirium?"

"That's right."

"And then what happens?"

"Raving. Madness. Terrifying fear. The delirium is extremely dangerous. The agitation and nervous excitement are a severe strain on the heart, the liver. The heart could fail. Pneumonia could set in . . . and then it becomes very difficult to induce sleep. A patient with d.t.'s can only be successfully treated in a clinic, under constant care and supervision. I would have had to take you to the nearest hospital." She touched her glasses. "What happened was a miracle. Some divine spirit," she looked up, "must love you very much."

"A miracle?"

"You did not wake up after your attack. The delirium did not break out. You fell into a recuperative sleep."

"For two days."

"Naturally you've not recovered just because you've slept. We must get to Rome as fast as we can. Are you hungry?"

"No."

"I've been reading German newspapers. Very cautiously they mention that the man who escaped from a mental institution could possibly have been a well-known actor. In his flight he was aided by a doctor. They give no names. Naturally the police know. Now do you see how important it was to leave Germany that quickly?"

"If the police know . . ."

"Then your film company will know too, naturally."

"That's not what I meant. The police will be looking for you too."

"Of course. They'll also know my name."

"How?"

"When I went to the hospital I had to identify myself. I told Dr. Trotha that I had treated you once and would recognize you."

"But . . . then charges will be brought against you too!"

"All I want is to get you to Rome. Then I shall return to Germany and surrender to the police. Don't look so aghast!"

"Natasha," I said with difficulty, "why are you doing all this?" She lowered her head, her smile vanished.

"You know why."

"No. No. No." I said. "It's not true. It's because I remind you of Bruno Kerst. Because I drink too. Because you are compassionate. But not that, Natasha!"

"Yes," she said. "It is true. I love you."

4

It was very dark in the room. The storm rattled the windows; the faucet drip still loud. "I love you," said Natasha. Her hand covered mine. "Why you? I don't know. I love you. You will make me happy."

"I can't. You yourself said that no one can make another person happy."

"I said not for long. You will make me happy for a little while. That is all I want."

"Natasha," I said, "I'm no good. I have only brought unhappiness to the women I've known. I've driven two of them to their deaths!"

"That's not true!"

"It is!"

"I don't care."

"But I do! Because—I" I stopped. I almost said, "I love you too." Did I have the right to say that? Was it true? Had I ever loved anyone but myself? Was it really possible that I could love someone?

No.

And so I continued, "I don't want to make you unhappy too. I don't ever want to hurt you. Had we met ten years ago . . . Today it is too late . . ."

"It's not yet too late for a little while."

"A little while is not good enough! I love you too much to—to . . ."

"Now you've said it!"

"But it's not true! It's not quite true. It's not quite honest. Not honest enough for you."

"You're still thinking of Shirley."

"Yes, Natasha."

"I know. You've talked to her. In your sleep. But you also talked with me."

"What did I say?"

She shook her head. "Once something wonderful. But that's my secret."

"Natasha. Natasha. Why didn't we meet earlier?"

"Because God didn't ordain it."

"God?"

"Who else?"

"There is no future for us. I'll never be able to forget what has happened . . . again and again I'll talk in my sleep . . ."

"We will have to part soon. But we will have a little wonderful while together, Peter."

"What's a little wonderful while?"

"Everything," said Natasha.

"Nothing," I said.

"A little while of happiness—enough for a lifetime."

"But life goes on; one does not die. Loneliness, sadness, bitterness follow that little while of happiness."

"Let it."

"No," I said. "It's true. I love you too. But Natasha, I don't want to be the cause of your unhappiness. That's why I want to be alone, remain alone . . . to dream of you . . . to think how different it could have been had we met earlier . . ."

"I love you. And you love me."

"Because I need you."

"That's not true."

"You know it is."

"I'm so glad that you need me! You'll need me once you have recovered your health too, if only for a little while!" Her cool, beautiful hands stroked my face. "I knew it the moment I saw you on that first morning in the hotel . . ."

"What did you know?"

"That I loved you. And you sensed it."

"No."

"I'm certain you did. Don't you remember . . . When you tried to seduce me . . ."

"I just thought that you . . . that you needed a man. I thought you were ready to . . . I made a mistake."

She bent down and kissed my lips. Her cheek was on mine. "You were not wrong, Peter. You did not make a mistake. I was ready . . ." She clung to me, her kiss passionate. My arms closed around her. There was a knock. Natasha rose and straightened her glasses. "Avanti!"

A hotel porter bowed politely. "Scusi, signora, il treno a Roma arriverà alle sette."

"Grazie, Benito. Facciamo le valigie."

Benito disappeared.

486

"We must pack," said Natasha. "The train arrives in an hour."

5

I remember very little of the trip to Rome and my arrival at the clinic. Natasha had given me a potent sedative before two men carried me on a stretcher from the hotel to the train. From time to time I awakened and always found Natasha by my side.

When I regained consciousness I was in a pleasant large room. Natasha looking wan and exhausted and a slight rosy-cheeked man in a white coat were standing near my bed. "Good morning, Mr. Jordan. I'm happy to make your acquaintance. Dr. Petrovna has already told me about you."

"Good morning, Professor."

"You're quite safe here. Whatever you've done, no one will take you to account until you are able to defend yourself. Now you must think only of regaining your health, Mr. Jordan."

He stepped to the window and filled a syringe with the contents of an ampoule. I looked at Natasha. Her black eyes were moist.

"I must return to Misha. But I'll be back."

"Please,"-I said. "Please, come back."

"I promise."

I wanted to say: I love you. But I said, "I need you so."

She took my hand and held it to her cheek.

Professor Pontevivo, the injection ready, came to my bed. "If you would say good-by, Mr. Jordan. You'll be asleep in just a moment."

"For a long time?"

"Oh, yes," he answered. "For quite a long time."

"Take care, Natasha," I said. "Kiss Misha for me." She nodded and rose.

I turned over; the professor threw back the cover. I was still looking at Natasha's beautiful face. The needle jabbed my back. I think then I said, "I love—" Perhaps I only thought I said it. Natasha's face, the room melted into a gossamer nothingness and I fell into a long deep sleep.

6

Rome, June twenty-sixth, 1960.

Since I began to record this intimate account of my life more than three and a half months have passed. Almost six months since I came to Professor Pontevivo's clinic.

Winter gave way to summer, my illness to health, my fear to hope.

Bianca, the little white cat, completely recovered, purrs on my lap as I stroke her.

I think I have only a few events left to report.

I remember nothing of the first six weeks in Pontevivo's clinic. Deep narcosis induced an artificial hibernation, while in Germany swastikas were defacing synagogues, the French general Massu was removed from his position after bloody riots in Algeria, the Soviets had experimented with rockets in the Pacific, and Moscow presented an ultimatum to the West concerning Berlin.

While under narcosis I had lost thirty pounds. Very weak, I continued to be given infusions. Slowly my health returned under constant care.

Up to April eighth I did not leave my room. I received no mail, no newspapers. There was no radio in my room. I knew nothing of the bloody racial unrest in South Africa, nothing of Khrushchev's tumultuous visit to Paris, of the second atom bomb detonated in the Sahara, of the assassination of Prime Minister Verwoerd in Johannesburg.

From April fifteenth on I was allowed German and English newspapers and received my first mail. Natasha wrote every second day. Since her letters were censored by an interpreter of the Italian court at the request of the Hamburg public prosecutor she wrote of her daily work, of Misha and other such inconsequential matters. Sometimes, Misha would enclose a drawing for me which Suora Maria Magdalena would hang in my room.

Other letters also censored arrived from Seaton, the Wilson Brothers and Herbert Kostasch. They expressed incredulity over what I had done but were obviously consoled by the turn of events. They offered financial and legal assistance and wanted to visit. I accepted the money. Visitors were not allowed. A lawyer I would not need until later.

A forwarded picture postcard from Rio de Janiero arrived. It said, "If Sugarloaf Mountain could think, it would imagine God to look like Sugarloaf Mountain." A detective brought the card and inquired about the sender of this strange greeting. Now that I knew Schauberg and Käthe had arrived in Brazil I could have told the truth. Brazil did not extradite people such as Schauberg.

The card had a postscript. "Going on to another country." I wanted to give Schauberg more time to find a safe haven so I told the detective that I had no knowledge of the sender. Months have passed and I have not heard from Schauberg again. I wonder if he is still alive, if he and Käthe are happy together?

I wrote to Natasha, and my letters too were general and innocent. My mail would certainly be censored.

In April South Korea was in revolt and President Syngman Rhee was overthrown; Southern Iran suffered an earthquake worse than that at Agadir. In Istanbul students revolted; Prime Minister Menderes resigned. I also read an obituary of a spinster who had worked forty of her seventy-one years in a bookstore. It sharply reminded me that I was but one of millions, merely a single life; a selfish, miserable life in a world that also held people who were kindly, decent and conscientious.

7

On April twenty-seventh I received a notification from a Los Angeles lawyer. Joan had instituted divorce proceedings. She had also begun an action against me for the seduction of a minor and the instigation of an illegal abortion.

Two days later a bundle of newspaper clippings arrived from my friend Gregory Bates. Screaming headlines reported my crime. Joan had told reporters all she knew.

Under a hypocritical pretense of righteous indignation the tabloids and magazines were digging into the most intimate details of Shirley's and my relationship. Thanks to syndicated columnists the scandal developed its fullest impact exactly at the time my movie was premiered at one of Hollywood's best-known cinemas.

Two days later, May second, a telegram arrived from Kostasch who had been at the première.

SENSATIONAL SUCCESS. CRITICS ACCLAIM MOVIE BEST OF LAST FIVE YEARS. PETER JORDAN NEW AMERICAN STAR. MILLION-DOLLAR BUSINESS CERTAIN. GOD BLESS YOUR WIFE. SHE HELPED ENORMOUSLY. CONGRATULATIONS AND SPEEDY RECOVERY, KOSTASCH.

8

Poor Joan, she had really helped us. The critics were praising the movie and called me a truly great actor! The notices and the scandal provided publicity beyond the wildest expectations of any agency men.

By May the film was playing in three thousand movie theaters in the USA. Synchronizations into fourteen languages were feverishly prepared.

It was also a certainty that *Come Back* would be nominated for an Oscar and was estimated to net at least thirty million dollars. I was a rich man.

In June the movie was shown in London, Paris and Vienna to quivering, eager audiences. The fact that I, at the time of my comeback, my artistic triumph, was ill in an Italian clinic, guarded by police, added a tragic touch—at least for the readers of tabloids and magazines. And it was they who went to see my movie—in spite of the heat of that summer!

In June too, the advertising campaign began in Italy. My eczema had now completely healed. The papers were full of stories of the scandal I had already read in English and German papers.

The carabiniers guarding me and the staff at the clinic brought postcard photographs of me and asked for my autograph.

Daily, film fans stood outside the high gates of the clinic. They too asked for autographs. I was told that gigantic placards were announcing *Come Back* all over Rome.

The June heat was excessive. Natasha and Kostasch had been trying for weeks to obtain permission to visit me but were always refused by the Hamburg public prosecutor's office. I was still not allowed visitors and we continued to write vague innocent letters knowing that strangers read them first.

I continued to tell my story to the silently circling spools of the tape recorder. Lately I have been dictating in the park. I am tanned and look years younger. I still dreamt frequently of Shirley and often held her little golden cross in my hand while I taped my story. As deeply as I had loved Shirley, as constantly as the thought

491

of her still stirred me, with the passing of time the conclusion grew strongly that this was really Natasha's and my story I was telling and that Shirley had been but an interlude in my long restless search for the vibrant womanly love that meant Natasha.

In mid-May Pontevivo had hypnotized me for the first time. Thirteen more sessions followed until in June I was thoroughly examined. That examination took two days.

The professor asked me to his apartment on the upper floor of the clinic. It was an evening in mid-June.

I took the elevator for the first time without fear.

Pontevivo received me in his library, its walls lined with books to the ceiling. A well-stocked bar. The professor was smoking a large cigar, a drink in his hand. He was in an expansive mood as he looked at the report of my examination.

"You are in perfect health! Heart, liver, everything normal. You can live to be ninety, my dear Jordan. Naturally you can also indulge in a drink—within reason. May I prepare one for you?"

I felt a strange misgiving.

"No, thank you."

"Just one whisky!"

"No, really. Thank you."

"Well, now. Today is a happy day—for all of us. A day to celebrate! As I told you, you can have a drink if you observe moderation. And during our fourteen sessions I have made sure that you will. One or two drinks a night won't hurt you. And I know you won't drink any more than that!"

"I really don't want a drink."

"Just one."

"No."

"Don't be childish. Just smell that aroma. Isn't it delicious? Really, you can believe me: it is not at all dangerous if you have one or two drinks!"

492

My uneasiness grew. The smoky aroma of the whisky I had once loved so much revolted me now.

"It makes me shudder," I said.

"Mr. Jordan, you're ridiculous."

"I'm sorry."

"You're not going to drink with me?"

"I can't."

"What do you mean, you can't?"

"There's something in me . . . I'm not putting on an act . . . Something in me resists . . . I told you, I cannot drink!" I yelled.

A door opened as soon as I had yelled and the two most powerful attendants in the clinic entered. They looked at Pontevivo who nodded.

Very quickly one attendant behind me held me in an unbreakable grip.

"Hold his nose," said the professor, quickly filling a glass with whisky. The second attendant held my nose. I was forced to open my mouth to breathe.

"And now a little drink," said Pontevivo.

"No . . . no . . ." I tried to step back but the attendant held me. I kicked at Pontevivo. He evaded me. The glass came closer, closer.

Suddenly I felt that fist.

I had not felt it stir in months.

There it was again.

"Don't . . . don't . . ."

The glass came still closer. Closer.

"Please, Professor . . . I can't . . . I . . ."

"Yes?"

"I'm dying . . ."

The fist stirred. It rose. Toward my heart. Paradoxical. It was all wrong. Whisky used to save my life. Now it was going to kill me? My breathing was a rasp. The attendant held me powerfully.

"Professor . . . please . . . please . . . the fist . . ."

The fist rose higher. Had I become insane? Was the professor mad?

"Hold him. Hold his nose."

"Don't .. don't . . ."

I squirmed. I whimpered. I kicked. Whisky flowed down my throat. I spluttered, gasped. Whisky splashed into me.

Fear, terrifying fear choked me while I fought for breath yet swallowed still more whisky.

The fist reached my heart, closed around it. I collapsed, falling into red flaming fog and I knew: This is death. Finally.

He killed me, this slight Professor Pontevivo, this figment of my still sick mind, this person that never really existed, this madman has killed me.

Finally.

9

He was sitting by the window, laughing. Only the little bedside lamp gave light. Behind him I saw the brightly lit façade of the Colosseum. I was in my room, in my bed. I said, "Thanks."

"You're welcome."

"When I passed out, did you give me one . . . one of those injections?"

"The first and the last. How do you feel?"

"Wonderful."

"You made a fine mess of my carpet."

"You ought not to conduct experiments of that kind in your library."

"Ah, but yes. Once you leave here alcohol will not be offered to you in hospital rooms or laboratories but in hotels, bars, restaurants, on carpets, in luxurious surroundings. What's a carpet? It can be cleaned." He laughed again. "You have no idea how often that carpet has already been cleaned!"

"Now I understand what you meant when some time ago you said that you were going to remove one complex under hypnosis and substitute another."

"I hope that I have been successful, Mr. Jordan. I hoped to remove the complex that you are guilty of Wanda Norden's death. The new complex is that you feel you will die when you drink alcohol!" He rose. "If you remember I once said that a psychiatrist can change people. I have tried to do just that. Now you really can drink within reason. But since your past has proved that there are no reasonable limits for you as far as alcohol is concerned it is better you do not drink at all. Quite apart from the fact that for some time to come you won't have any opportunity to drink."

"I see. So that I would not drink you substituted a fear of drink."

"Fear of that fear. In the past you thought that you would die if you didn't drink. From now on you'll think you'll die if you do. Fear of the unknown is a basic and most powerful emotion of humanity."

"With me it is chiefly fear of death. I really did believe I was dying when you had that whisky poured into me."

"What do you imagine death to be—and whatever follows?"

"I don't know."

"That's what I said: fear of the unknown." He cleared his throat. "And now I must confess something to you. I'm not infallible. Even my method is not perfect. Nothing is. You could have a relapse even now."

"I could? How? Why should I?"

"Mr. Jordan, I know what happened that night in 1938 in Berlin. We both know that your guilt was not entirely unjustified. You left Wanda Norden to her fate when you took that walk for an hour. That was the simple thing to do. You could have made another choice."

"To protect Wanda."

"Or at least tried to protect her." His voice was very low. "In everyone's life situations occur where one must choose between an expedient or more difficult solution. Sometime in the future you too will again have to make such decisions."

"I'm sure I will."

"If you really want to remain healthy and not again become what you once were you must in all future decisions find the strength, the will and the moral integrity to choose the right one—which in all probability will always be the more difficult one. If you do not . . ."

"Then everything will start all over again. I understand."

"That's correct. You are too intelligent not to develop another new guilt complex which will torment you. Because you are tormented you will want to escape. How? The way you know so well."

"I will drink again."

"Yes. Despite my post-hypnotic suggestions. Mr. Jordan, you are thirty-seven years old. It was still possible to cure you. Ten years later it would not be possible. I abhor pathos—but you must change your life. From now on you must always choose the more difficult way. Only then will the success of my treatment endure."

The little white cat jumped on my bed. I stroked her.

"I have already made such a difficult choice."

"You have?"

"I would like you to send my tapes to the German court in Hamburg—as a confession."

His eyes lit up. Impetuously, he shook my hand. "I'm very happy, Mr. Jordan, very happy indeed! And I'd like you to accept the tape recorder as a present from me. Perhaps there will be something you will want to add, something which might be of interest to the court."

"Thank you very much, Professor."

"You're most welcome. I'm sorry but now I must notify the police that I consider you cured. You will not be able to stay here much longer."

"I'm sorry too, Professor," I said while Bianca purred on my lap. "I really am."

10

Come Back was premiered in Rome on June twenty-fourth. The critics were as enthusiastic as was the public.

Since the première the number of autograph hunters had risen sharply. As I could hardly sign autographs all day a notice had been placed on the tall gates:

SIGNORE PETER JORDAN DA AUTOGRAMMI SOLTANTO DALLE 16 ALLE 18

On the twenty-sixth two German police inspectors presented their credentials and a warrant for my arrest. The warrant had been countersigned by the public prosecutor in Rome.

Both men were most polite and pleasant. They assured me that since they were certain their trust in me was not misplaced they would gladly dispense with handcuffs to avoid any unpleasant attention. We were to leave by plane for Hamburg at eleven-thirty on the twenty-seventh.

I wound up my affairs, paying my bills, handing out tips until in the late afternoon my fans were beginning to call for me.

"Signore Jordan! Signore Jordan, per favore . . ."

"Venite qui! Venite qui, prego!"

"Pietro Jordan! Pietro Jordan! Maledetto Pietro!"

"Vicino da noi!"

Despite the incredible heat of that summer's day at least a hundred people were crowded outside the gates holding out photographs and autograph books damp with perspiration for me to sign.

The carabinier sitting in the shadow of a tree laughed at me as I walked to the gate. At first they had always escorted me. What could happen? The gate was closed and tall; the guard stood outside his guardhouse.

I wore linen trousers and a blue short-sleeved shirt and as soon as I arrived applause greeted me. Acclaim today, tomorrow I would be in a Hamburg prison. How strange life could be.

They passed photographs and books through the iron gate, and I wrote and wrote and wrote: "Cordialmente, Peter Jordan. Coi miei complimenti, Peter Jordan."

"Grazie, Signore, grazie!"

They kept coming, more and more people, more and more arms stretched through the iron bars of the gate. And I wrote and wrote.

They stood close to the gate but at the edge of the crowd. At first I saw Misha, who laughed at me silently. Then I saw Natasha.

11

Natasha in a white low-cut dress emblazoned with bright glowing colors, a red scarf over her black hair. The lenses of her glasses were dark. She held a book in her hand; Misha, a photograph.

I continued to sign autographs and slowly made my way toward her. She spoke English. No one paid any attention to her. The people were all looking at me, wanting my signature.

"I've been here a week. They let me go with the child—I said I was going to Austria."

"They are taking me back to Hamburg tomorrow. At eleven-thirty."

"I'm going to give you your photograph now. Underneath it is Bruno's passport. It has a valid visa for the Congo."

."A visa?"

"In Bruno's name. It was quite easy. They know me at the consulate in Hamburg. I'm going to follow you with the boy in the fall."

"That's crazy. We can't do that."

"You must not go to prison. I don't want to lose you. Before you reach the airport tomorrow morning a man will act as though he had been hit by the car taking you there. I've found an old artist ... You'll be able to escape ... There is a plane for Leopoldville at ten-thirty. They will hold the plane until you get there. The ticket is inside the passport. The Congo does not extradite ..."

Now Misha gave me his photograph. He was still laughing at me. He seemed very happy to see me again.

Then I held the photograph and the passport which Natasha handed me. Her face was pale, but behind the dark lenses of her glasses her vivid black eyes were aflame with a mad passion.

"I'll be there to help you, should it become necessary ..."

I passed just the photo back to her. A new one was pushed into my hand right away. Natasha stood close, very close to me. Her beautiful lips formed words that I readily understood. She pulled Misha along with her and in a moment had disappeared into the crowd of people who continued to hold out photographs to me through the bars of the fence.

"Per favore, Signore ..."

"Grazie, Signore!"

The passport which had belonged to Misha's dead father was now in my trouser pocket.

12

That night I took a closer look at it.

The visa was valid for a year and renewable. There was also an international vaccination certificate signed by the doctor who had vaccinated me as was required by the Congo. The doctor's name was Dr. Natasha Petrovna.

On the ticket, flight 413 from Rome on June twenty-seventh, 1960, was noted that Herr Bruno Kerst was coming by train from Hamburg. The plane would wait as long as was reasonably possible since the train arrived rather late from Germany.

While I heard the steps of the carabinier on the gravel below my room and the chirping of the crickets I looked at those three documents which, with a bit of luck, meant freedom for me.

It was probably an easy country into which to disappear or where false passports were readily obtainable. Or one could simply stay there. I was rich now. Kostasch would surely be able to make payments to me through an account under some fictitious name.

And I would be free! I would remain free! Now that I was healthy I must be free. Otherwise I would surely go to prison, if not in Germany first, and in the States later.

The ticket. The vaccination certificate. Valid visa. Valid passport. I had everything I needed. And Natasha would follow in the fall.

Fall was only a few months away.

Rome was a busy airport. It was simply impossible to check all passengers for a man who had escaped when someone appeared to be hit by his car; nor could anyone be sure that such a man, probably with a newly assumed name, had even taken a plane out of Rome.

How long did a flight to Leopoldville take? Two hours? Three? Four?

What could two German detectives do in a city strange to them in three or four hours? They could alert the police of Europe, Africa and America. To look for whom? Where? What could they really do? Very little. Nothing.

When I had been asked by the two German inspectors how at Christmas I had crossed into Italy, I declared: "With my own American passport."

"Incredible thing to happen. You were already on the wanted list!"

"Well, it was Christmas! The officials were simply inattentive."

"Where is your passport now, Mr. Jordan?"

"I threw it from the train once I'd crossed into Italy. You can search me too. The Italian police already have. I don't have any travel documents at all now."

One of the men had telephoned his Italian colleagues, who had verified my statement. No, I no longer possessed my American passport.

I wondered where it really was?

I was certain that the hotel had turned over my things to the German police. Apparently they had not found the passport or the detectives would not still be so interested in it. There could be only one explanation: Schauberg, sensing trouble after that drunken phone call I made the night of the twenty-second, must have somehow gained entrance to my suite and taken it. Brave, smart, resourceful Schauberg!

I hoped he and Käthe were well, wherever they were: in Bolivia or Peru. He made it using false passports. Why shouldn't I?

He had wanted a new start. With Käthe to help him.

I wanted a new start too. I could not do it alone either.

I looked around the room where I had spent six months of my life, hovering between life and death, reason and insanity; this room with its bright wallpaper and modern furnishings, the small radio, the tape recorder.

The tape recorder! I would have to take it with me tomorrow morning, only to leave it behind in the car when the artist Natasha had hired would feign an accident. I would have to run fast tomorrow morning at eleven, very fast!

Tomorrow would be a day which would lead me to the good, to the bad; me, one life among millions.

13

The morning of June twenty-seventh, 1960, was already inhumanly hot. I carried my jacket over my arm while my baggage and the tape recorder were loaded into the car. The false passport was in my trouser pocket.

Nurses, doctors and attendants, in their midst Pontevivo, had come to bid me farewell. I thanked them all and said good-by to the professor last. He said, "I must thank you too. You have taught me many things."

"I have?"

"You have given me new understanding."

"Understanding?"

"Of the artist's soul. Farewell, Mr. Jordan. Stay well. Someone said, 'A difficult time may be likened to a dark portal. Go through it and you will be invigorated. Then all will become light.'"

The moment he offered me his hand, Bianca, the little cat, rubbed along my leg, mewing sadly. I petted her for the last time and she ran under a eucalyptus bush.

I stepped into the waiting car. An Italian detective was at the wheel. I sat in the back seat between the two Germans. The car rolled across the gravel toward the gate.

The nurses, doctors and attendants waved to me and I returned their farewell gesture. The white villa, surrounded by palms, olive trees, stone pines and many, many flowers disappeared from sight.

The sun was a white-hot disc. The windows of the car were open but still it was sticky and hot.

As we drove past the Colosseum I saw on its walls for the first time dozens of those brightly colored posters I was to see presently all over the city. Posters showing my face. Huge letters proclaimed:

PETER JORDAN
NEL SUO SUCCESSO MONDIALE
COME BACK

Everywhere in the suburbs my face looked from houses and walls.

I looked at my watch. It was ten-forty. The German inspectors had taken off their jackets. Their shirts were soaked with perspiration, especially where they carried their shoulder holsters. One mumbled longingly, "I'll be glad to get back to Hamburg!"

"A kingdom for a beer," said the other.

In the distance on our left the studios of Cinecittà became visible. The oppressive heat of that summer's day seemed to vibrate the horizon where the Albani Mountains rose.

We drove approximately fifteen kilometers to the Ciampino airport very quickly. Frequently a plane would roar above us, about to land or beginning its climb. The earth here was brown, scorched, the few trees dusty, leafless and withered. The tires hummed on the hot surface of the Via Appia Nuova.

A few minutes before eleven the car swung into a wide curve toward the glittering Aeroporto Ciampino. Bustling traffic there. The Italian detective had just passed the parking area and entered the one-way road leading to the entrance of the airport. At that spot a seemingly drunk man stepped off the sidewalk and staggered directly into the path of our car.

The driver cursed, braked, and pulled at the wheel. The car skidded. The old man fell and began to yell piercingly. People converged on the scene immediately.

The force of the car skidding had thrown me against one of the inspectors and I hit him hard in his stomach.

He pulled back. I tore the door open and kicked his legs outside the car. I jumped out and ran, my jacket in my hand. Behind me I heard the inspectors yell. Glancing over my shoulder I noticed many excited people shouting, milling about, and thereby preventing the detectives from pursuing me. The small crowd showed a menacing attitude to the occupants of the car since it appeared that they were trying to evade responsibility for the accident. The old man was still lying on the ground, writhing as if in pain, still yelling.

I reached the entrance to the airport. Inside it was cool. A heavy-accented voice reverberated through the building. I heard the end of a message for "Herr Bruno Kerst for Leopoldville. Last call!"

I slithered on the slippery floor but did not fall. I raced to the passport control.

"Signore Kerst?"

"Sì . . ."

While I had been running I had put on the glasses Natasha had given me. The Italian official examined the passport, the ticket, the vaccination certificate while I stuttered, "Il treno . . . ritardo . . . capito?"

"Sì, capisco." He was still turning the pages of the passport. He looked at me. I looked at him. I could hear the commotion of the people arguing with the detectives outside.

"Che è successo?"

"Incidente . . . auto . . ."

Then I saw Natasha. Wearing dark glasses, she was standing near a large window from where she could see the plane waiting to take off. Misha was by her side.

The official returned the passport to me.

"Grazie, signore. Adesso vista doganale."

To the customs!

The voices outside grew louder. A whistle shrilled. Breathless, I said, "Baule già aeroplano . . ."

"Ah, bene! Buon viaggio, signore!"

I raced through the barrier. Once more I saw Natasha. She raised her hand. I stepped through the exit. My plane, the ramp still in place, a stewardess standing in its open door. A steward hurried toward me.

"Are you Mr. Bruno Kerst on flight to Leopoldville? We have been waiting for you. Come on, hurry, please!"

Both of us hurried toward the plane; the smiling stewardess in the door urged me with gestures to even greater speed.

Ten more meters. Five. One more. The last one. My hand touched the hot handrail of the ramp steps. I turned around. No one pursued me. Now all I had to do was to climb quickly up those steps, the cabin door would be secured, the plane would start.

I did not hurry up those steps. I let go of the hot handrail.

"What's the matter, sir?"

"I'm sorry. I won't take this plane."

"You don't want to fly to Leopoldville?"

"No."

No, I did not. I could not. I must not. I had suddenly realized that as I put that last meter behind me and reached for the rail of the steps. I had realized that in a second's illuminating impulse.

Many thoughts can flash through a man's mind in a second.

14

". . . you must in all your future decisions find the strength, the will and the moral integrity to choose the right one——which in all probability will always be the more difficult one . . ."

Professor Pontevivo's words.

The more difficult way. Hamburg. The easy way. Leopoldville.

I had chosen the easier way once before. On November ninth, 1938. In Berlin. For one hour. That little stroll twenty-two years ago had destroyed two lives and almost my life too. Only mine? Not Shirley's too? Not Joan's life?

I had been cowardly and weak twenty-two years ago. I had wanted to escape; escape my responsibility.

Now I had been about to do it again.

My experiences had shown me that one cannot escape. Not from one's self, only to nowhere. No one can escape his memories. Wanda. Shirley. Joan. And now Natasha. A sequential chain. An inexplicable web in which all are tightly woven.

Last night I had decided to begin a new life. Was this the way? A new deceit, another crime?

I embody evil. I corrupt people as decent as Natasha to violate their moral code: to cheat, to break the law.

No. Natasha must not become so evil as I.

Never!

And that's why I must not go to Leopoldville. That's why I must not try to escape.

I should have understood before.

A new life——yes.

But not this way. "Are you listening?" The steward was red-faced with anger.

"I'm very sorry, really, but I cannot fly to Leopoldville."

I walked slowly back to the airport building to the accompaniment of his irritable complaints. "But this is preposterous! We have been waiting for you! You've fouled up our time schedule!"

Behind the large window I could see Natasha's solemn

506

face and Misha's surprised one. I threw away Bruno Kerst's glasses. As I entered the cool hall Natasha came to me and took my hand.

"It won't work," I said. "That way it wouldn't have worked, Natasha."

She nodded.

Voices in back of us. The German detectives, Italian policemen came running. They were out of breath but were all talking at the same time in Italian, English, German.

"Es tut mir leid," I said. "Scusi. I'm sorry."

A handcuff was snapped on one of my wrists.

"I'm sorry too," my captor said. "But you don't want it any differently."

"No."

"What do you mean, no?"

"I don't want it any different." A crowd increasingly growing was collecting around us. The other inspector said to Natasha: "I know you. From Hamburg. You are Dr. Petrovna, aren't you?"

"Yes."

"Did you help Mr. Jordan in his attempt to escape?"

"Yes."

"You will have to answer for that in court."

"Yes."

"Will you return to Hamburg with us on your own volition or will we have to ask the Italian police for help?"

"I'll come voluntarily," said Natasha. We were standing side by side, still holding hands. One inspector held my handcuffed wrist.

He asked, "Why didn't you take that plane? We couldn't have caught up with you."

"I'm sure of that."

"Why did you come back here?"

"Do I have to answer that?"

"Naturally not," he said, embarrassed.

"Then I'd rather not answer."

Some people meanwhile had recognized me. Even at the airport were posters showing my face. Reporters appeared, camera flashbulbs blazed. One more scandalous story. A few more dozen pictures in a few thousand newspapers and magazines all over the world! Another hundred thousand people who will stream into the cinemas! More money into my bank account! An Italian policeman said something to one of the Germans.

"If you don't mind we'll go to the plane now. They are not quite ready but we have permission to go aboard ahead of time," the detective said to me.

Misha was shocked and touched my handcuffs; the hoarse sounds he made sounded distressed. Questioning, he looked at me, at Natasha, at the detectives.

"Let's go then," I said.

The Italian police cleared a path through the crowd for us. I walked between Natasha and the officer to whom I was handcuffed. The other German held little Misha's hand, who did not take his eyes off his mother and stumbled often. Natasha looked straight ahead but did not let go of my hand. Near the exit to the planes I saw for the last time one of those huge advertisements.

PETER JORDAN
NEL SUO SUCCESSO MONDIALE
COME BACK

15

The plane was half-filled.

Misha sat at the window, his mother by his side and one inspector next to her at the center aisle. His partner sat on the other side of the aisle and I at the window. Natasha and I could not talk to each other that way. She and Misha had a long conversation as usual using their sign language. She seemed to be patiently explaining something to him. Finally he appeared to understand; he waved to me, apparently reassured.

I was still attached to the detective by handcuffs. He was no longer angry, only taciturn. He released the handcuffs only during lunch.

The sun shone until we reached Milan.

Then the clouds appeared. Frequently rain pelted the windows; dark, dirty patches of clouds raced past. But we climbed, higher and higher . . .

I am recording this last part of my report in my prison cell in Hamburg, using that same tape recorder Professor Pontevivo had given me—as if he had known that I would have something to add.

My cell is large and quite comfortable. My examining justice is very understanding. Natasha was not arrested. So far it is uncertain what her punishment, if any, will be. Her attorney thinks that she will receive a suspended sentence. She will also be tried by a medical panel. Her attorney hopes that that can be avoided.

Today is July fourth. A Monday. I have been here one week. The first few days were busy with formalities and hearings. It is raining in Hamburg and quite cool. From my barred window I looked out on a yard enclosed by the other three walls and their barred windows. My trial is to begin soon. On Tuesday my attorney is coming for another conference. With him will be the man from the First Civil Court of Los Angeles representing the "People of the State of California v. Peter Jordan." It is his intention to have his court's charge separated from the German indictment, to be tried under American statutes.

Since I shall be quite busy starting tomorrow I shall try to finish my story today. The ninth tape is almost completed. The other eight have been sent at my request to the examining judge by Professor Pontevivo. The finished report will have fully recorded my former life; a new one is about to begin.

A new one: Yet in my hand I hold something intimately tied to the past: the little golden cross Shirley once gave me. The little cross, warm in my hand, had been my constant companion.

I shall keep it. A new part of my life does not mean a new life. This cross is part of my life, my expiation. I cannot abandon Shirley's precious gift. Just as I cannot relinquish my past. That tiny symbol will always remind me . . .

16

We climbed higher and higher through the hurrying, dirty-gray clouds.

After lunch the steward served drinks. Natasha ordered cognac, the two detectives whisky. My seat companion was now friendlier. "Shall we drink to the fright you gave us?" he asked.

"No, thanks."

He gave me a suspicious glance, then he remembered. "Ah yes, naturally. Please forgive me." He raised his glass to Natasha, who returned the gesture. I turned my head to the window. The smell of the drink made me feel nauseous.

The voice of a stewardess announced that we were flying above the Simplon and would soon be able to see the Rhône valley. The plane was still climbing. Suddenly blinding sunlight streamed through the cabin.

The light seemed super-terrestrial. We had to close our eyes. Then I looked at Natasha. She nodded and smiled. The moment she had told me about, had longed for, in a sense had come. Natasha was flying above the Alps again with a man she loved.

A part of her hope had been realized. We were together—but forcefully separated. Yet Natasha's smile gave a sense of fulfillment. She straightened her glasses and in her look I read the strength of confidence.

Misha quickly motioned to his mother. She rose and from a blue flight bag she took a sketch pad and the crayons I had once given him. He waved to me and began to draw, his tongue moving from side to side with excitement.

The announcer, repeating it in English and French, told us that we were flying above the summit of the Jungfrau. Soon we would see the massif of the St. Gotthard. Passengers were crowding the windows, many taking photographs.

Dark, almost black clouds blanketed the Rhône valley. They became lighter, almost white. From the valley, as though bursting from a mass of white cottonwood, rose the snow-covered Silverhorn of the Jungfrau. The peak glowed and glittered in all colors of the spectrum, a gigantic diamond, transcendental; indescribable.

"Did you ever see anything that beautiful?" asked my detective companion, his voice a little hoarse. He ordered more drinks.

I looked out on the sea of clouds and the Jungfrau that thrust through them. Natasha and I smiled at each other. Misha was busily drawing and glancing through the window.

The St. Gotthard too was as magnificent as the Jungfrau, resplendent, a rainbow view.

Natasha's eyes and mine met again. From that moment on I knew that nothing would separate us: neither prison bars, nor people, nor events; that each would wait for the other until both were free to begin that "little while" of happiness.

Speaking with his hands, Misha gave his drawing to his mother. Natasha spoke to her detective, who spoke to mine.

He told me, "His mother is explaining to him that it is the peak of a mountain but he insists that it is an island.

He says it is a wondrous, beautiful island. His mother told him that then it is an inaccessible island. He said, I think one can get there if one tries very hard and does not become dizzy. Naturally, it is an island in the sky."

Natasha passed the drawing to her seat companion who admired it before handing it to his partner. We looked at it together. A movement made my handcuff clank.

Misha had indeed drawn an island in a blue-white sea, glowing and glistening in all the colors of the Jungfrau. On the island stood three people: a little boy between a woman and a man. The woman wore horn-rimmed glasses. The man held a glass in one hand.

I was still looking at the drawing when my man said, "He would like the drawing back. He made a mistake."

The sketch was passed back to Misha who erased something, corrected a part and returned it to his mother. He looked at me, his mouth smiling broadly, his eyes sparkling.

Natasha looked solemn when she studied the drawing. So did both detectives when they saw it. There had been one change. The man's hand was now empty.

My detective was moved. "He erased the glass because he knows that you don't drink any more."

The plane changed course. We were flying directly toward the St. Gotthard. The sun suddenly shone through my window and its rays were too strong for my eyes. I had to close them.

I leaned back into my seat. Fresh ozone-laden air from the small ventilators hit my face. I heard the detective's voice. "What a lovely boy he is!"

"Yes," I said.

"So polite. So intelligent. So talented."

"Yes," I said.

"Will he always be deaf and dumb?"

"Yes."

"How sad."

"Yes," I said. "Isn't it sad?"